TOMORROW IS
ANOTHER DAY

Mary Jane Staples

CORGI BOOKS

TOMORROW IS ANOTHER DAY
A CORGI BOOK : 0 552 14744 3

First publication in Great Britain

PRINTING HISTORY
Corgi edition published 2000

1 3 5 7 9 10 8 6 4 2

Copyright © Mary Jane Staples 2000

The right of Mary Jane Staples to be identified as the author
of this work has been asserted in accordance with sections 77
and 78 of the Copyright Designs and Patents Act 1988.

Set in 11/12pt New Baskerville by
Phoenix Typesetting, Ilkley, West Yorkshire

Corgi Books are published by Transworld Publishers,
61–63 Uxbridge Road, London W5 5SA,
a division of The Random House Group Ltd,
in Australia by Random House Australia (Pty) Ltd,
20 Alfred Street, Milsons Point, Sydney, NSW 2061, Australia,
in New Zealand by Random House New Zealand Ltd,
18 Poland Road, Glenfield, Auckland 10, New Zealand
and in South Africa by Random House (Pty) Ltd,
Endulini, 5a Jubilee Road, Parktown 2193, South Africa.

Reproduced, printed and bound in Great Britain by
Mackays of Chatham plc, Chatham, Kent.

To
Pat, David, Helen and Diana.

THE ADAMS FAMILY

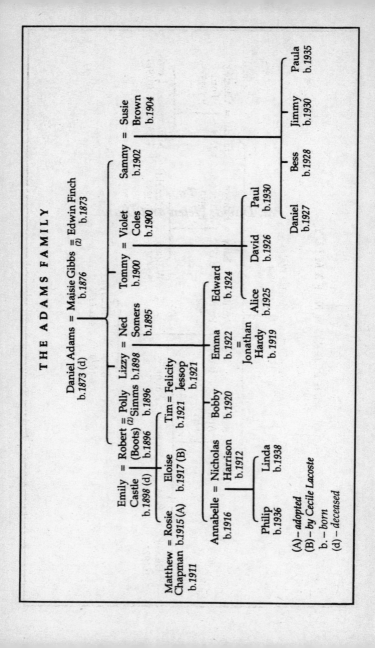

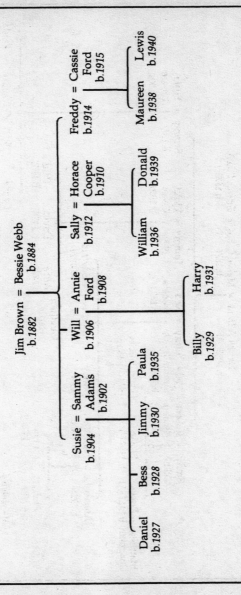

THE BROWN FAMILY

Jim Brown = Bessie Webb
b.1882   b.1884

Susie = Sammy Adams
b.1904   b.1902

Daniel b.1927
Bess b.1928
Jimmy b.1930
Paula b.1935

Will = Annie Ford
b.1906   b.1908

Billy b.1929
Harry b.1931

Sally = Horace Cooper
b.1912   b.1910

William b.1936
Donald b.1939

Freddy = Cassie Ford
b.1914   b.1915

Maureen b.1938
Lewis b.1940

Chapter One

October 1941

Miss Leah Goodman, younger daughter of Mrs
Rachel Goodman, received a letter from Edward
Somers, younger son of Lizzy and Ned Somers.
Leah, now fifteen, was a boarder with her sister
Rebecca at a high-class establishment for young
ladies in Wiltshire, well out of the way of bombs,
strains and stresses. Their mother had been
widowed a few months ago, their father having
suffered a fatal heart attack, and the girls were only
just coming to terms with their loss.

Leah was pleased to receive the letter from
Edward, who was living the life of an evacuee with
his elder sister Annabelle and her children in
the village of West Grimstead, Wilts, and read it
happily.

Dear Leah,
　　*Well, this must be about the sixth time I've written
to you since my cousin Rosie's wedding day, when
you brought a present from your family and we
enjoyed a long talk, although you were very sad about*

losing your dad. I've been enjoying your replies to my letters since then. I did mention a while ago that I'd come and see you once you were really over your sadness, and I'm thinking in a positive way about that now.

It would have to be on a Sunday because as I told you in one letter, I'm working as an assistant in a public library in Salisbury, the one near the cathedral, and I'm kept busy all day on Saturdays. I'm sticking with this work until I'm eighteen next September, when I'll volunteer for the RAF and hope to meet up with my sister Annabelle's husband Nick, who's a pilot and serving overseas, and a great bloke. Annabelle misses him a lot, and doesn't like it that he's missing out himself on watching their children grow. Of course, if the war ends before I'm eighteen, I'll do some thinking about a permanent career and I expect you will too.

Anyway, would you like me to come over one Sunday afternoon and take you for a walk? That's if you're really feeling better about losing your dad. Well, I'd like to see you instead of just writing to you, I don't think we should stay just pen friends. Looking forward to hearing from you.

Yours sincerely,
Edward.

Oh, gosh, thought Leah, we've only met once, but I think he must really like me.

She replied in her free time that evening.

Dear Edward,

I was very pleased to hear from you again and your mention of your cousin Rosie's wedding reminded me of how beautiful she looked in her bridal gown. I'd heard a lot about all your family from Mama, who always says your parents and uncles and aunts are lovely people. Rebecca and I look on your Uncle Sammy as our uncle too, he never forgets our birthdays.

Yes, I'd like us to meet if I can get our headmistress to approve, it's a blessed liberty that us girls here aren't allowed to mix with boys, and I think our headmistress must have mixed with the wrong kind when she was young herself, but that wasn't our fault, was it?

I think working as a library assistant until you volunteer for the war must be very interesting for you, I know it would be for me with all those thrilling history books in the reference and study sections. I'm utterly gone on history, especially as I think our country's history is just about the most enthralling in the world, don't you? I mean, I can't think of any other country with as many world-famous people as Great Britain, can you? I know France had Napoleon, but we had Marlborough and Wellington and Drake and Nelson, didn't we? And Florence Nightingale and Queen Elizabeth and Mary Queen of Scots, wasn't it a shame she had her head cut off, I'm sure she didn't deserve that. And now there's Mr Churchill, who's just the greatest, and if the war does go on and on I'd want to join one of the Services myself, or be an ambulance driver like your Aunt Polly was in the Great War, according to Mama. Mama said she braved gunfire and bursting shells.

Well, that's all for now, Edward, I expect you think it's a mouthful, but please write again and let me know which Sunday you'll call for me at the

school, which our headmistress always reminds us is
an academy – how posh.
   Sincerely, Leah.

Edward thought it a lively happy letter, that it spoke of a girl he could get to like very much. He didn't for one moment think there was any obstacle because she was Jewish. As far as that kind of thing was concerned, he'd have pointed to the fact that the family's longest-standing friends were Leah's mother, Mrs Rachel Goodman, and Mr Eli Greenberg, the well-known rag-and-bone merchant of South London, and both belonged to the people of Moses.

What he did think about was how much like her attractive mum she was in her vivid looks and her warm personality.

He wrote saying he'd call at her school this coming Sunday afternoon.

The pulled bell jangled loudly, but Edward had to wait quite a while before one of the large double doors opened and the sharp enquiring eyes of a tall woman in a square-shouldered jacket, pleated skirt and pale grey blouse took note of his presence.

'Good afternoon,' said Edward, lean, lanky, seventeen and personable, 'I've called to—'

'Boy, go away.'

'Excuse me,' said Edward, 'but I—'

'You're a boy. Go away, boy.'

'Who's that?' The voice of another woman boomed through the vaulted hall of the Winterbourne Academy for Young Ladies, a boarding school set in the Wiltshire countryside a few miles south of Salisbury.

'A boy,' said the woman at the door.

'A boy? Boy?' The booming voice contained a shudder. 'Doesn't he know boys aren't allowed, that they should be neither seen nor heard? Send the rascal away.'

'Boy,' commanded the sharp-eyed, square-shouldered woman, 'be off with you.'

'But I've called for Miss Leah Goodman,' said Edward, bravely standing his ground. 'I wrote to say I was coming today.'

'What impertinence. Boys are forbidden. Be off with you, do you hear?'

'Could I just see Leah for a moment?' asked Edward.

'What's that, what did he say?' boomed the unseen woman.

'That he wants to see Leah Goodman.'

'Inform the wretch that if he doesn't go away, we'll send for the police,' called the female boomer.

'Boy,' said the woman at the door, 'take yourself off this instant, or you'll be locked up.'

'I only want to take Leah for a walk,' said Edward, not given to crumpling under attack. The sons and daughters of Lizzy and Ned Somers all owned a large amount of resolution in the face of intimidatory factors. 'I mean, I'm not going to run off with her. Well, her mother's a close friend of my family.'

'More impertinence. Boys are forbidden, didn't I say so? Go away, you rascal.'

The door slammed on Edward.

'Mind my nose,' he said to the deeply grained oak, then turned and left.

'Sissssst!' The little hiss came from somewhere.

He turned again, facing the handsome building. Its many windows, caught by autumn sunlight, winked at him. One was open, Leah's dark glossy head leaned out of it.

'Oh, hello, Leah—'

'Shush. Catch.'

Something white was tossed down to him. He caught it. It was a page from an exercise book wrapped around a blob of plasticine. He unwrapped it, Leah watching him from a first floor window. It was a scribbled note.

Headmistress is out, only some stuffy teachers here. I saw you coming up the drive. Next Saturday afternoon I'll visit your library. Today we're all gated because a girl was caught with a boy. Sorry about the dragons.

Edward looked up at her. He smiled and nodded. Leah returned his smile. Crikey, what a flower of summer, he thought. The door to the academy opened again, and the square-shouldered woman shouted at him.

'Boy, stop that loitering, or I'll set the dog on you!'

'What sort of a dog is it?' called Edward, and Leah, listening at the open window, wanted to laugh because his question had a bit of bland sauce to it.

'A dog with teeth, boy!'

'I don't think I'll stay to meet him,' said Edward,

and resumed his walk down the drive. He looked back in a little while. He caught the flutter of a waving hand at the open window. He smiled and went on.

The following Saturday Edward picked up a novel by D.H. Lawrence from his trolley-load of returned books, and made a study of the indexed fiction shelves, looking for the section under 'L'.

'Sisssst.' The little whisper of caution reminded him of Leah at the window last Sunday. He turned his head casually. Two girls in round dark blue school hats, warm maroon blazers, white blouses, school ties and navy blue skirts, materialized to eye him critically. Neither he nor they, standing between shelf stacks, could be seen from the counter, where two middle-aged lady assistants were dealing with borrowers. Library users were borrowing books regularly to enjoy the escapism of adventurous or romantic fiction during the evening blackouts, as rigorously observed in this cathedral city of Salisbury as in cities under periodical attack from the air.

'Hello, girls,' he whispered, quietness being compulsory in public libraries, 'what can I do for you?'

They studied his face, his legs, his brown hair and his suit.

'Yes, that's him,' whispered one girl to the other.

'Yes, Leah did say he was ugly, didn't she?' whispered the other.

'Well, not ugly exactly, more that he was a bit unfortunate in his looks.'

'Awful unfortunate, I'd say. And what did she say

about his legs?'

'That they were short and fat.'

'You sure?'

'Course I am. This is him, you can see that. Except he's grinning.'

'Leah didn't say anything about him grinning.'

'He shouldn't be, not with a war on. Ask his name.'

The whispers were travelling only a short distance.

'What's your name?'

'Edward.'

'Did Leah say Edward?' asked the first girl of the second.

'Wasn't it Rudyard?'

'That's Kipling, silly.'

What a couple of young female perishers, thought Edward, good as Elsie and Doris Walters on the wireless.

'I think she did say Edward,' whispered the first girl.

'Yes, this is him, I bet.' The second girl addressed Edward. 'Were you expecting Leah Goodman?'

'She did say she'd be here,' whispered Edward. Library users were moving about, inspecting what was on offer on crowded shelves amid a murmur of talk from the busy counter. 'Isn't she coming?'

'She can't, she's got tonsillitis.'

'That's a shame,' said Edward, 'and I'm sorry.'

'She wrote you a note.' A shoulder bag was opened and an envelope extracted, the girl holding a corner of it very gingerly between fingertips.

'Does it bite?' asked Edward.

'No, but I don't want to catch tonsillitis, do I?'

Edward took the envelope with a grin, opened it and read the enclosed note.

Dear Edward,

I've got tonsillitis, so I'm not allowed out, what rotten luck. I'm able to swallow my disappointment as I'm better than I was, when I could hardly swallow anything, but I'm still sorry about not seeing you. I'll be all right by next Saturday, I'll come to the library then and make sure I can stay for an hour or so by doing some history study at one of the tables. Ever so sorry about today, Leah.

PS. If Pauline and Cecily say silly things, don't take any notice, they're both a bit cuckoo, poor dears.

Edward moved forward and glanced at the counter. The two assistants were still busy.

'Thanks for bringing the note,' he whispered to the girls. 'Tell Leah I hope she'll soon be up and dancing.'

'Did she send kisses with the note?' asked the girl Pauline.

'She shouldn't have,' said Cecily, 'they're forbidden.'

'All these rules,' said Edward, and put the D.H. Lawrence novel back in place.

'Are you after Leah?' whispered Cecily.

'After her?'

'Well, you could be,' whispered Pauline, 'boys are always after something, and we know what, don't we, Cecily?'

'Shame on you,' said Edward, 'you've been reading naughty books.'

One of the counter assistants, stamping a

borrowed novel, turned her head as the small but distinct sound of giggles reached her ears.

The library user, a pleasant lady, smiled and said, 'That sounds like me in my school days.'

'We were all gigglers once, Mrs Piper, even in a library,' said the assistant, Miss Williams.

'Well, it's nice to hear young people not letting the war get them down,' said Mrs Piper, gathering up her book, 'especially a war that's likely to make them grow up far too quickly. Good afternoon, Miss Williams, and thank you.' She departed. She was followed out almost immediately by two schoolgirls muffling more giggles.

Edward showed himself in a while, pushing his now unburdened trolley.

'There you are, Master Somers,' said Miss Williams. 'Good. There's another pile of returned books to see to. Would you sort them out and replace them?'

'I'm here to serve, Miss Williams,' said Edward.

Miss Williams smiled. She had a very good idea who was responsible for the giggles.

Chapter Two

Another Saturday in the cathedral city of Salisbury, existing in tenuous fashion with its apparent air of untroubled quiet. In such a war as this, no city in Britain or Germany knew where or when enemy bombers might strike.

Edward, busy collecting loads of returned books and replacing them on their relevant shelves, heard a voice behind him, a clear voice with a little sing-song tone to it.

'Excuse me, please, but could you possibly find Thomas Carlyle's *History of the French Revolution* for me?'

He glanced over his shoulder. A girl, with a round school hat of blue perched on the back of her glossy black hair and large eyes of velvet brown, smiled at him. Crikey, thought Edward, what a vision, even better than I remembered.

'What was that, miss?' he asked, just for the pleasure of hearing the note of music again.

'I've been trying to find the *History of the French Revolution* by Thomas Carlyle,' said Leah. 'I've got to do some studying for my term exams.'

People in the library didn't seem to mind that

she wasn't whispering. Leah, of course, was giving the impression of a student earnest about tracking down Thomas Carlyle's classic work. Miss Williams glanced across from the counter, and gave Edward a smile and a nod, which meant help the young lady, Master Somers.

'It's in the history section,' he said. 'This way, miss.' His lanky frame took off for the correct shelving. Leah, catching him up well after he'd arrived, delivered a whisper.

'Crikey, what d'you mean, this way? I'm only five feet four and your legs are about two feet longer than mine.'

'Here we are, miss, history section,' said Edward, then dropped his voice to a whisper. 'You told your friends I had short fat legs.'

'Is Thomas Carlyle's *History of the French Revolution* here?' asked Leah. Then, whispering, 'No, I didn't, I never mentioned your legs. Edward, it's ever so nice to see you.'

'My pleasure, glad you're better, you look like a duchess's daughter,' whispered Edward. 'Let's see,' he said, 'Thomas Carlyle. Carlyle. Here we are, miss, *History of the French Revolution.* It's a bit heavy. I'll carry it to a table for you.'

'Thank you, how kind,' said Leah. Another whisper. 'My life, you do sound important.'

'Well, my Uncle Boots told me and my brother Bobby years ago that it doesn't do for anybody to sound like a nobody, and my Uncle Sammy practises that,' he whispered. 'Um, there's a table, miss,' he said. 'Follow me.' He carried the thick volume to a reading table, a vacant one that was shielded from the counter. Leah hitched her pleated school skirt and sat down. Edward placed the book on the table. She looked up at him. He looked down at her. Eyes met. Leah had the rich colouring of her kind, and it deepened a little because he seemed very taken with her. Her dark lashes visibly quivered. Edward was thinking crikey, what a gorgeous girl. He knew his cousin David was a bit gone on a girl called Kate, now living with Uncle Boots, and he also knew his mum and dad had fallen for each other when his mum was only fourteen and his dad seventeen. And Uncle Boots had married Aunt Emily when he was only twenty, while his sisters, Annabelle and Emma, had had stars in their eyes at seventeen. Ringing bells, he thought, do most of us in our family take an early jump into deep water?

As for Leah, she was thinking oh, my life, who wants to be just his pen friend?

Coming to, she said, 'Thanks ever so, I can do my studying now, I've brought a pencil and exercise book.'

'Very good, miss,' said Edward.

That made her whisper, 'What d'you mean, very good? That's what a butler would say.'

'Call me if you need any more help, miss,' said Edward. In a whisper, 'Have you got a boyfriend?'

'Dozens,' whispered Leah, 'but they're all forbidden.'

'Well, I'm going to try to be unforbidden,' whispered Edward and went back to his work, leaving Leah wondering if he meant he'd like her to be his best girl. She thought in terms like that.

She opened Thomas Carlyle's classical work. Edward finished replacing returned books, then went back for others. The library had its usual influx of Saturday borrowers, but Miss Williams was unoccupied at the moment. She smiled at the young assistant.

'What a lovely girl, Edward,' she murmured.

'Pardon?' said Edward.

'Yes, the one hidden from me at the moment,' said Miss Williams quietly, but still smiling. 'But she came in looking like Elizabeth Taylor.' Elizabeth Taylor was a young and beautiful film star who had made a name for herself in a very popular film featuring a horse.

'D'you think so?' said Edward.

'Yes. Is she your girlfriend? I think you've been having a chat with her.'

'Well, I helped her to find a history book. She's studying at one of the tables.'

'One that I can't see from here.'

'Oh, can't you?' said Edward. 'Still, I'm sure she won't start a riot.'

'Good luck,' murmured Miss Williams, who had lost her fiancé in 1915, when he was killed at Ypres. It had made her sympathetic towards young lovers, and that gave Edward encouragement to indulge in some whispered conversations with Leah.

'When's your birthday, Leah?'

'Next August, on the twenty-fifth. I'll be sixteen.'

'Crikey, don't the years run away? You were only one fourteen years ago. We'll both be old in another fifty.'

'Aren't you quick-thinking, Edward? You worked that out in a flash.'

'It wasn't too difficult. You're like your mum in your looks, Leah, did you know that?'

'Well, yes, everyone says so.'

'She's a beautiful woman.'

'Yes, isn't she?'

'You're laughing.'

'Yes, but not out loud. It's forbidden in here.'

'Can't get away from rules, can we, Leah?'

Interval.

Then, 'Here I am again.'

'I don't mind being interrupted.'

'What d'you think of the war, Leah?'

'Rotten, Edward.'

'We're lucky, I suppose, being out of the way of bombs.'

'We've got to bless God we're lucky enough not to be among those poor people who get taken away by those awful Nazis.'

'Yes, there's all kinds of rumours.'

'They're not rumours. Mama gets to know they're not.'

'Churchill talks about war criminals.'

'Yes, and they are.'

'Your mum works for Uncle Sammy now, Leah.'

'Yes, and she simply loves her job.'

Interval, and a beckoning finger from Leah. Up sidled Edward.

'D'you want something, Leah?'

'The library's ever so busy.'

'It always is on Saturdays.'

'I'll have to go in a minute, I've got to catch a bus and be back at the school by four.'

'That's a blow. I was thinking of taking you to the pictures this evening.'

'Well, that's a nice thought, Edward, but I wouldn't be allowed to go with a boy.'

'Couldn't you tell your headmistress I'm an old aunt of yours?'

'One of the prefects might spot us and tell her my old aunt wears a suit and tie.'

'You've got some sneaky prefects, then.'

'Edward, are you going to come to the school again tomorrow afternoon?'

'Yes, I'll give it a go.'

'I'll try my best to get permission to go for a walk with you.'

'Suppose they set the dog on me?'

'There isn't a dog.'

'Good-oh, I won't lose my trousers, then.'

'No, don't do that, Edward, some of the teachers would faint. Mind, some of the forward girls wouldn't. Let's hope we can meet tomorrow, then.'

Edward and his sister Annabelle, with her two children, five-year-old Philip and three-year-old Linda, lived as evacuees in a rented cottage in West Grimstead, five miles south-east of Salisbury. Annabelle, nearly twenty-five, was much like her mother, Lizzy Somers, with her chestnut hair, brown eyes and admirable figure. It was for the safety of her children that she'd chosen to move to Wiltshire, her RAF husband all in favour. And it had seemed sensible for Edward to join her, especially as the children liked him. When he matriculated from his grammar school in Salisbury at the end of last term, he'd talked about going home, but their mum and dad wouldn't hear of it because of continuing air raids, so he'd talked of Rachel Goodman's young daughter Leah instead, having met her at cousin Rosie's wedding.

He began to exchange letters with her.

Now, on this Sunday morning, Annabelle said, 'You're really going to challenge the dragons again, the teachers who saw you off double-quick last Sunday?'

'Leah said she had hopes of being allowed out.'

'I can imagine that,' said Annabelle. 'Girls at a boarding school are all chained up whenever boys are around. Edward, are you a bit gone on Leah?'

'Frankly, yes,' said Edward, 'she's a dreamboat.'

'I've never met Rachel Goodman's daughters,' said Annabelle.

'But you've met Rachel,' said Edward, 'and Leah's as much like her as you're like mum.'

'Excuse me,' said Annabelle, 'but mum's over forty.'

'I meant you're as much like her when she was your age,' said Edward. 'We've seen old family snapshots.'

'Does Mum know you've got this crush?' smiled Annabelle.

'I shall inform her when my relationship with said Rachel's younger daughter is on a promising footing,' advised Edward.

'Bless us all,' said Annabelle, 'you sound like a solicitor's clerk.'

'Kindly note I don't intend to be a solicitor's clerk,' said Edward. 'I'm thinking of going into business with cousin David after the war, like Uncle Sammy did with Uncle Boots and Uncle Tommy after the last war.'

'Let's hope both of you have got some of Uncle Sammy's business flair, then,' said Annabelle.

'I've been writing to David recently about it,' said

Edward, 'and he's in favour, with quite a bit of savings. Have I got any savings?'

'Well, have you?' asked Annabelle.

'A few quid,' said Edward, who earned thirty shillings a week for his job at the library. 'Listen, sis, how much have you got? I'll need to put an equal share with David into the business.'

'Don't look at me,' said Annabelle. She received an allowance from the RAF as the wife of a sergeant-pilot, and her Great-Uncle John, a commanding figure in the insurance world, was insisting on paying the rent of the cottage, but she was by no means well off.

'I'll have to row my own boat, then,' said Edward.

'Which means don't buy Leah fancy presents,' said Annabelle.

Leah was talking to her sister Rebecca, a studious girl with ambitions to be a lawyer.

'Leah, are you saying you'd like Edward Somers as a boyfriend?' enquired Rebecca.

'Yes,' said Leah, 'so if Miss Murchison wants to talk to you about him, you will tell her he's famous for his respectability and good behaviour, won't you?'

'Famous?' said Rebecca.

'Yes, isn't that an impressive word?' said Leah. 'It's bound to impress our headmistress, and you can also say our family's known his family for years.'

'I should say what isn't true?' said Rebecca.

'Well, Mama's known all of them for years,' said Leah, 'which makes it nearly true.'

'Leah, have you got a crush?' asked Rebecca.

'I should have a silly crush just because I like him?' said Leah.

'Leah, he's a Gentile,' said Rebecca.

'What's that got to do with it?' asked Leah.

'Enough to make it awkward,' said Rebecca. 'Pa would have discouraged it for your own sake. It can't come to anything, and Mama would tell you so.'

'Becky, Mama told me she'd never stand in the way of whatever friendships I made,' said Leah. Neither girl knew that when their mother was fifteen she was in love with Sammy Adams, and that in his younger days she was his one and only girlfriend.

'Mama didn't mean friendships with Gentile boys,' said Leah.

'Yes, she did,' said Leah, 'because I told her then that I liked Edward. It was the day I met him at his cousin Rosie's wedding. I took Mama's wedding present to the house.'

'Well, all right, Leah, if Mama really doesn't mind, I'll speak up for Edward if Miss Murchison asks about him.'

'Thank you, Becky,' said Leah.

'But it mustn't come to anything,' said Rebecca.

'My life, d'you think we're going to elope to Gretna Green?' said Leah.

'I hope you haven't already got silly things like that on your mind,' said Rebecca.

'Becky, I've only seen him three times,' said Leah, 'and I only want him for a friend, don't I?'

'Watch out for some of the bilious girls if they get to know you've got a Gentile boyfriend,' warned Rebecca. 'They're not known for being too kind to us and the other Jewish girls here.'

'Miss Murchison doesn't like that,' said Leah. 'She expelled one girl, telling her she was no better than the worst kind of Nazi, and she lets Rabbi Morris come once a month to instruct us in our faith. And all the other girls are as nice to us as anything. Pauline and Cecily are my best friends here.'

'They're a couple of sauceboxes,' said Rebecca, a prefect.

There were girls about in the extensive grounds to the rear of the academy when Edward arrived that afternoon. He pulled on the ancient bell knob. He heard its echoing jangle and waited. One of the double doors opened in a while, and the same sharp-eyed, square-shouldered teacher as before regarded him critically.

'Hello again,' said Edward, 'is it all right for me to see Leah Goodman this time?'

'It's Master Impertinence, I see,' said the teacher. 'Very well, come in, young man. Follow me.'

She led him through the hall and up the wide stone staircase of the imposing building. She turned on the landing and entered a corridor, her stride brisk, her no-nonsense air visible. The corridor, like the stairs, was not carpeted. That seemed a no-nonsense factor too, thought Edward. She stopped outside a door and knocked.

'Come in,' called a pleasant voice.

'In you go,' said the teacher to Edward, and in he went. The door was pulled to behind him. He found himself in a handsome study, its walls lined with books, the furniture oak and the desk large. Behind it sat Miss Murchison, the headmistress, a slim lady in her forties, her dark hair smooth, with a centre parting and buns. Her eyes were gently inquisitive, as if her disposition was mild. Seated in front of her desk were Leah and another girl, both looking prim in their school uniforms. Leah had her round blue hat on.

'Good afternoon,' said Miss Murchison.

'Good afternoon, ma'am,' said Edward politely. There was no spare chair.

Miss Murchison looked him up and down. Leah kept her face straight and her eyes demurely lowered. Her sister Rebecca regarded Edward with interest.

'You are——?' said Miss Murchison, pleasant of voice.

'Edward Somers, ma'am, matriculated and an assistant in a Salisbury public library.'

Blessed angels, thought Leah, he's sounding important again.

'Public library, yes, I see,' said Miss Murchison, looking as if that reminded her of something. 'I understand, Master Somers, that you wish permission to go walking with Leah Goodman.'

'Yes, I'd like that,' said Edward.

'I further understand you and your family are entirely respectable, and have known Mrs Goodman as a friend for many years.'

'My parents and my aunts and uncles have known her since before I was born, ma'am.'

'You are an evacuee from South London?'

'Yes, living with my sister and her children in West Grimstead,' said Edward.

'Only if we are absolutely sure of the relevant credentials do we allow any of our students to be in the company of young men for a stated period of

29

no more than an hour, as long as they stay within our grounds,' said Miss Murchison.

'That's fine with me, ma'am,' said Edward, thinking he was probably being interrogated to make sure he bore no signs of a desire to muck about with Leah's girlish purity.

'Providing, of course, such students have a chaperone,' said Miss Murchison.

'A teacher, you mean?' said Edward, who suddenly had a feeling Leah was fighting an urge to giggle. Well, she had a hankie to her mouth.

'In this case, Master Somers,' said Miss Murchison, 'Leah will be accompanied by her closest friends, Pauline Gates and Cecily Roberts. So you may go walking with her, for an hour.' She consulted a watch pinned to her light grey blouse. 'From now, at three-ten, until four-ten precisely. The afternoon is quite pleasant. You may go with him, Leah.'

'Thank you, Miss Murchison,' said Leah, and she and Rebecca both came to their feet. With Edward, they left the study.

'You passed with a push,' said Rebecca. 'I'm Leah's sister. Rebecca.'

'Happy to meet you,' said Edward. 'Was that your headmistress?'

'Yes, Miss Agnes Murchison,' said Rebecca.

'Shouldn't she be in the Army interviewing recruits who might have criminal records?' asked Edward.

Leah spluttered giggles.

'You're speaking of the headmistress we all love,' said Rebecca, her interest in Leah's potential boyfriend deepening. She'd expected a young male of adenoidal appearance, with perhaps a pimple or two, but although he was gangly and youthful, he wasn't adenoidal or gauche. He'd held his own with Miss Murchison in quite an adult way. 'Leah, would you like me to come with you instead of Pauline and Cecily?'

Leah saw through that at once. Rebecca had taken a fancy to Edward herself.

'No, you go and study your law books,' she said, and departed in haste with Edward. Studious Rebecca might be, but she had her wiles and whims. Down the stone stairs Leah went with the younger son of Lizzy and Ned Somers, a couple regarded by Mama as among her most treasured friends. Mama was like that about all the people related to Sammy Adams.

As soon as Leah and Edward reached the hall, Pauline and Cecily materialized.

'Hello,' said Pauline to Edward, putting herself on his left.

'Hello,' said Cecily, putting herself on his right.

'Excuse me,' said Leah, 'you two have to walk behind.'

'She's going to be a spoilsport,' said Pauline.

'She can't have him all to herself,' said Cecily, 'it's forbidden.'

'Would you both like kicks?' asked Leah, by no means meek and mild.

The tall sharp-eyed teacher appeared. She saw a boy surrounded by three girls. She shuddered.

'Scandalous! Boy, be off with you,' she said.

'Excuse me, Miss Wheeler,' said Leah, 'but Miss Murchison has just given me permission to show my friend round the grounds, and Pauline and Cecily are to come with us.'

'Oh, it's Master Impertinence, I see,' said Miss Wheeler. 'He shouldn't be standing in the middle of you three. Close contact is forbidden, you know that. Separate at once.' The three girls peeled away, Edward battling not to yell with laughter. 'That is correct, a seemly distance. Now you can go.'

They left the academy and emerged into the autumn sunshine, Leah with Edward, Cecily and Pauline behind them.

They began their walk, Leah and Edward with a seemly distance between them. Say about four inches.

Chapter Three

'I expect you feel you've had a Holy Inquisition,' said Leah.

'Not exactly,' said Edward, as they took a path that led them around the building to grounds that had the appearance of a parkland. Autumn had laid its artistic hand on the massed boundary of trees, and October's yellow and red and gold blazed in the sunshine. Girls were strolling along various paths. 'It was more laughs than scars,' said Edward.

'Did you think it was all a bit comical, then?' asked Leah.

'Yes, except does it get serious if a girl is caught being kissed by a feller?' asked Edward.

'Serious?' said Leah. 'My life, it's deathly. You can choose either to be expelled or burned alive at the stake. No-one's ever chosen the stake, as we all know being burned alive isn't half excruciating. Excuse me, Edward, but were you thinking of kissing me?'

'Like my Uncle Sammy says, I can't tell a porkie,' said Edward, 'I think of it each time I see you.'

'Oh, my soul,' said Leah, 'that's as many as four times.'

'But I want you to know, of course, that I wouldn't risk you getting burned at the stake,' said Edward.

Leah laughed softly and glanced at him. He returned the glance. She, he thought, looked a peach in her blazer, blouse and skirt. He, she thought, looked as if he could give a girl bliss, which was exactly what her mother, years ago, had thought about Sammy Adams every time she looked into his blue eyes.

They heard Cecily and Pauline exchange comments that were meant to be heard.

'Leah's gone all soppy.'

'Yes, poor thing.'

'And him with short fat legs and all.'

'What do we do if he puts his arm around her?'

'Scream.'

'Out loud?'

'No, not out loud, you silly, we don't want to be spoilsports. Thunderboom's about.'

'Take no notice, Edward,' murmured Leah. Strolling girls were glancing at them from a distance, and in the middle of the parkland a portly woman was briskly walking up and down. She too was directing glances at Edward and Leah.

'Who's that?' asked Edward.

'That's Miss Purbright,' said Leah. 'Thunderboom.'

'Thunderboom?' said Edward. 'Is she a Red Indian, then?'

'No, a thunderboomer,' said Leah, 'and she's where she is to make sure no boys climb over the walls and entice any of us into the trees.'

'I think I heard her booming when I called last

34

Sunday,' said Edward. 'D'you get many blokes climbing over the walls and enticing girls into the trees?'

'Only those who are madly in love with some of the girls,' said Leah. 'That's why Miss Murchison has to train her staff to be bloodhounds. Well, it just wouldn't do, would it, if a desperate boy and his girlfriend eluded capture. Parents don't like their daughters getting lost in the woods with desperate boys.'

'Well, if I got lost in the woods with a desperate girl,' said Edward, 'I think my mum would have fits. She's a bit old-fashioned.'

Leah's involuntary giggles bubbled, at which Pauline and Cecily made themselves heard again.

'Is he tickling her?'

'He's not supposed to.'

'What's she giggling for, then?'

'P'raps he's being funny.'

'My Aunt Alice told me you've got to watch funny boys.'

'My Aunt Edith told me you've got to watch all boys.'

'Well, we'd better keep watching this one, in case he runs off with Leah when Thunderboom isn't looking.'

Leah smiled at Edward as they walked on.

'I told you they were a couple of cuckoos,' she said, 'but they're nice friends. Edward, d'you have relatives in the war?'

'Any amount,' said Edward. 'My brother Bobby, my brother-in-law Nick, my Uncle Boots—'

'I've heard about your Uncle Boots,' said Leah. 'Mama says he's a delight.'

35

'Well, he's very easy-going and hardly ever been known to lose his temper,' said Edward. 'He's in the Army, then there's his son Tim and his daughters Rosie and Eloise, they're all serving – hold on, I think a party's coming to meet us.'

A group of five girls were advancing on them. Arriving, they planted themselves in front of Leah and Edward. The foremost girl, thin and aggressive, spoke.

'Who are you?' she asked Edward.

'D'you mean am I friend or foe?' smiled Edward. 'Friend.'

'A friend of hers?' The girl cast a disdainful look at Leah.

'Leah, you mean?' said Edward. 'Yes, our families know each other.'

'That's disgusting, mixing with her kind, all Jews are sickening,' said the girl, 'and you're sickening too for going with one of them.'

'Steady on,' said Edward, aware that Leah was stiffening beside him.

'She's Jewish and so's her family,' said the aggressive girl. 'You ought to be ashamed, going with a fat Yiddish tart like her. You must be Jewish yourself, you must like greasy fat—' She stopped, and a yell came from her. Edward, who didn't have the self-control of his Uncle Boots, had smacked her face. It was actually no more than a light slap, but it brought a yell from the girl, who then let go a series of hysterical screams.

'Serve her right,' said Pauline.

'Give her another one,' said Cecily.

All the other girls looked uncomfortable. The patrolling teacher, Miss Purbright, broke into a scamper, her portly figure bobbing. Up she came, followed by pupils mesmerized by the screams.

'Silence! Silence!' The command boomed from Miss Purbright. 'Be quiet, girl! Explain!'

'He hit me, he hit me!' screamed the thin girl.

Miss Purbright glared at Edward.

'Miss Purbright,' said Pauline, 'Mavis asked for it, she—'

'Silence! Boy, did you hit this young lady?'

'I smacked her face,' said Edward.

'Rascal! Blackguard!' Boom, boom. 'How dare you, you young villain!'

'But Mavis was saying horrible things about Leah,' protested Cecily.

'What, what?'

'Horrible,' said Pauline.

Miss Purbright looked at Leah. Leah, flushed and upset, said nothing. The thin girl's hysteria died away.

'What things?' asked Miss Purbright, and this time she didn't boom.

'I'd like it, Miss Purbright, if you'd ask Mavis,' said Pauline, and the portly teacher eyed the accused girl as if she'd prefer not to hear the answer. There was none, in any case. The girl, looking flushed and hot, simply stared in dislike at Leah. I think I know what's eating her, thought Edward. Leah's a peach and she's a piece of string. She's jealous of Leah's looks, and she's a little bitch. All the same, he wished he hadn't landed that smack. It would have been better for Leah if he and she had simply walked away.

'I must ask you, young man,' said Miss Purbright, 'I must ask you why you committed this assault.'

'Sorry, a rush of blood,' said Edward.

'The reason?' demanded Miss Purbright.

'Lost my temper for a second,' said Edward.

'The reason, boy?'

'There were words flying about,' said Edward.

'I see,' said Miss Purbright. 'Come with me, boy, and you, Mavis. You too, Pauline, Cecily and Leah. Your headmistress will deal with the matter.'

They all ended up in Miss Murchison's study. The lady looked sadly aggrieved as she listened to Miss Purbright.

'I'm to understand Master Somers struck Mavis?' she said.

'Yes, he did,' said Mavis Watkins, 'and it nearly knocked me over. If my dad—'

'Be quiet,' said Miss Murchison. 'Answer only when I speak to you. To begin with, Master Somers, boys should not hit girls under any circumstances. Haven't your parents taught you that?'

'Not specifically,' said Edward, 'it's something that's always been understood. I apologize for forgetting myself, ma'am.'

'So you should,' said Miss Murchison. 'You've heard Miss Purbright tell me you refused to give a reason. I insist you give one now.'

'If it's all the same to you, ma'am,' said Edward, 'I'd like to keep quiet and let the girl do the talking.' He nodded at Mavis, who looked as if she'd dearly like to kick him where it would most hurt.

'I shall come to Mavis later,' said Miss Murchison. 'Which of you other girls would like to offer an explanation?'

'Me, ma'am,' said Cecily.

'I,' said Miss Murchison correctively.

'Yes, I would,' said Cecily.

'Proceed,' said Miss Murchison, and Cecily, incensed enough to tell tales, did her very best to describe how Mavis had addressed Leah, word for word. In the handsome study, her description sounded almost lurid. Miss Murchison's firm mouth compressed. She glanced at Leah. Leah had recovered, and she acknowledged the glance with a little sigh and a wry smile. Miss Murchison looked at Mavis. 'How much of this is true?' she asked.

'None of it,' said Mavis. 'That rotten beast just came up and hit me because of something she said about me.'

'Something Leah said?' enquired the head-mistress, her pleasant voice now edged with distaste.

'Yes.'

'What was it?'

'I mean it was something she must have said.'

'In other words, you assumed she did,' observed the headmistress. 'You said nothing to Master Somers about Leah's religion?'

'No, nothing,' said Mavis. 'Her religion's her own fault, not mine.'

'Go to your dormitory and wait there,' said Miss Murchison.

'What for?' asked Mavis, still very flushed.

'I shall be speaking to you there and telephoning your parents this evening,' said Miss Murchison, and nodded at Miss Purbright, who opened the door, watched as Mavis walked out in a rage, and followed her to her dormitory. 'Cecily and Pauline, you may go,' said Miss Murchison.

'Miss Murchison,' said Pauline, 'it's true what Cecily told you about—'

'Yes, I understand,' said Miss Murchison. With a slight softening of her stern front, she added, 'Thank you. You may both go.'

Cecily and Pauline left. Leah and Edward remained. Miss Murchison looked thoughtful.

'I'm sorry it happened, Miss Murchison,' said Leah.

'No, no, Leah, I'm the one who must apologize for such a dreadful attitude on the part of one of our pupils,' said the headmistress. 'And I do apologize. Unfortunately, blind prejudice does exist throughout the world. Fortunately, in some cases, champions of the victims arise. All the same, young man, I will never countenance any kind of physical assault on a girl. There are more civilized ways of dealing with culprits. Are you often inclined to lose your temper and commit assault and battery?'

'I hope that's not a serious question, ma'am,' said Edward, who had only ever engaged once in physical violence, and that was when at the age of twelve he had a fight with a school bully. It cost him a black eye, a bloody nose and a split lip, and his mum, naturally, had a fit. His dad, having got the full details, gave him half a crown for his trouble. 'I don't have what's called a short fuse.'

'You had that only a little while ago,' chided Miss Murchison.

'Well, I can't tell a porkie—'

'A what?' said the headmistress.

'Oh, he means a lie,' said Leah. 'Pork pie is cockney for lie, Miss Murchison, and it's always shortened to porkie.'

'Extraordinary,' said Miss Murchison, 'extraordinary.'

'I admit I did lose my temper for once, ma'am,' said Edward.

'Alas that in allowing you into the grounds the incident happened,' said Miss Murchison.

'Oh, I'm sure Edward wouldn't do anything like that again,' said Leah.

'The intrusion of boys into the precincts of an academy for young ladies inevitably causes upsets, Leah,' said Miss Murchison. 'But far worse, of course, is the wicked prejudice to which you were subjected, and I earnestly hope it will never happen again. However, in future I think it would be wise not to allow Sunday visits, Master Somers, but you may continue, Leah, to go to Salisbury on Saturday afternoons for an hour's study in the reference section of a certain library. It may, of course, be the branch where Master Somers works, in which case you will observe the standard library rules of conducting yourself quietly. You will be accompanied on the bus journey by one or two school friends, in accordance with our own rules.'

'Yes, Miss Murchison,' said Leah.

'Again I apologize for the behaviour of one of our students,' said the headmistress, 'and you may go now, Leah. Master Somers, thank you for attending this interview, and Leah will show you out.'

'Goodbye, ma'am,' said Edward.

'Goodbye,' said Miss Murchison.

'Blessed angels,' breathed Leah on the way to the stairs, 'that was another Holy Inquisition, for Mavis this time. I should be sorry for her? I think I am, because I believe Miss Murchison is going to expel her.'

'I'm sorry for her too,' said Edward, 'not because she might be expelled, but for having what my Uncle Sammy would call mucked-up mental equipment.'

'What's mucked-up mental equipment?'

'A twisted mind,' said Edward.

They reached the hall, where he supposed that its sharp-eyed and square-shouldered guardian lurked close by.

'I'm sorry the afternoon got spoiled, Edward,' said Leah.

'Yes, rotten hard luck,' said Edward. 'I hope there aren't too many other people like Mavis around.'

'Oh, they come up out of their dark holes sometimes,' said Leah, 'like that man Himmler does. Edward, it looks like we'll only be able to meet on Saturdays, and only at your library.'

'It's better than not meeting at all,' said Edward, 'and it'll put some enjoyment into my Saturdays. I don't mind settling for that for the time being, Leah.'

'I will too,' said Leah.

'And we'll be out of the way of Thunderboom,' said Edward.

'Yes, isn't she a giggle?' said Leah. 'Goodbye till next Saturday, then?' They were close to the double doors. There were sounds somewhere, somewhere. Up above and out in the school's parkland mostly. But it was quiet down here, so Leah lifted her face, closed her eyes and pursed her lips, just as her mother had done when inviting a kiss from Sammy years ago.

'Hold tight,' said Edward, and kissed Rachel's younger daughter with feeling.

'Oh, my life,' breathed Leah when it was over. One of the doors was open and Edward was walking down the drive. She came out and showed herself. He turned. She waved. He responded. 'Oh, my life,' she breathed again to the open door, 'are we going to be able to do that in the library?'

Rebecca had said nothing could come of the relationship.

Well, a kiss had arrived.

Leah smiled, and decided not to think in negative terms.

Miss Purbright, suspecting Mavis was unwell, persuaded Miss Murchison to call the doctor in. He diagnosed gastric flu, and Mavis was given a bed in the school clinic and looked after by the matron. Miss Murchison forgave her for all she had said to Leah, and when Leah visited her, Mavis apologized profusely. Her illness and her apology saved her from being expelled.

Not that Miss Murchison fully trusted her.

Nor did Leah.

You could cure gastric flu. You couldn't always cure prejudice.

Chapter Four

The Western Desert, November 1941

'Achtung! Achtung!'

The sudden ferocious night attack on a German redoubt outside the besieged British-held port of Tobruk in Cyrenaica raised a frantic alarm call.

A British Commando force of some seventy men and officers, trained to strike at night, had been landed by submarine east of the harbour. The Commandos, faces blacked out, flitted like moving shadows around the right flank of the German and Italian positions to smash straight into the rear of the planned objective. Lobbed grenades blew up manned outposts and inside the perimeter of the redoubt, bursts of machine-gun fire raked awakening Germans rushing from sandbagged dugouts.

For ten minutes the Commandos dealt death and destruction before the Germans were able to organize any effective counterfire. Three rushing Commandos ran into a volley of bullets, and were killed outright. Elsewhere, other men of the assault force were wounded. It was not enough, however, to save the redoubt from being overrun by men whose training for hit-and-run raids in the desert at night had turned them into a pack of wolves, and the German casualties were fearsome. Well before reinforcements could arrive, the Commandos melted away, their work done at the cost of three dead and three wounded.

Two of the wounded were able to join the exodus, one of them being Colonel Lucas, the fiancé of ATS Lieutenant Eloise Adams, presently serving at Army HQ in Cairo. Colonel Lucas had bullets in his right arm.

The third man, severely wounded, could not be moved and had to be left, much to the bitter self-torture of Colonel Lucas, for he was Eloise's half-brother, Lieutenant Tim Adams. He had bullets in his ribs and chest. He was treated at a German casualty station, where the consensus of medical opinion was that he hadn't much hope. Nevertheless, he was conveyed to the nearest German-controlled hospital. This was in Benghazi.

'Mister?' A hand tugged at the tail of the jacket of Mr Sammy Adams, businessman, entrepreneur and live wire. Sammy, tall and personable, with blue eyes sometimes electric with mental activity, turned and found himself looking down at a small girl about four or five years old. She was dark-haired, with mournful hazel eyes, and wore a navy blue dress with a sailor collar, a bit old-fashioned in this day and age, thought Sammy, and hardly enough to keep out the November cold. He noted tear stains on her cheeks, and a quiver to her mouth. 'Please, I'm lost,' she said.

'Lost?' said Sammy. 'Well, we'll have to do something about that, won't we? Where's your mummy?'

He looked around, hoping to locate a woman visibly agitated about her missing offspring. He was on the corner of the New Kent Road, at the Elephant and Castle, a junction on which converged several roads, including Walworth Road, an old and familiar thoroughfare of his. Tramlines criss-crossed the junction. On all sides, however, was the evidence of war from the air. Buildings, shops, flats and pubs were grey jagged ruins, and there was an air of desolation starkly removed from what Sammy remembered as a thriving, bustling place of constant movement and surging life.

'I don't 'ave a mummy or daddy, they've gone,' said the small girl tearfully. 'Please, I'm lost. Auntie went and left me.'

'Auntie?' said Sammy, and passers-by glanced as he went down on one knee to give the small girl a kind smile. 'Your aunt, you mean?'

'Yes, Auntie Lily,' she said, her voice catching on a sob.

'D'you know her other name, me pet?'

'Yes, I fink so,' said the tearful child. 'Mrs Follers.'

'Follers?' said Sammy.

'Yes, I fink so.' The little girl thought. 'She's a widow lady.'

'Well, me infant,' said Sammy, 'd'you know where she lives?'

'Please, it was somewhere but I don't know where.'

'What's your name?'

'Phoebe.'

'Well,' said Sammy, gently cheerful, 'you're the first Phoebe I've ever met in the New Kent Road. I've met many a Maggie and Ethel, but never a Phoebe. Um, Phoebe what, Phoebe Smith?'

'Phoebe Willis.' The little girl, gazing into Sammy's sympathetic blue eyes, said with a gulp, 'Please, could you look after me, mister?'

Jesus pray for me, thought Sammy. Shades of long ago, shades of Rosie as a five-year-old infant, deserted by her mother and appealing heartbreakingly to his brother Boots to look after her.

'Well, little Phoebe Willis,' he said, 'first of all we'll go and see a friend of mine, shall we?' He could always find time for kids, as long as the moment didn't relate to a crisis concerning profit or loss. He was where he was to look at a large bomb site next to the Post Office a little way down the road, with a view to purchase and post-war development. People were always going to a post office, and an adjacent store would accordingly receive a handsome percentage of their custom. A store, not a shop, that was what Sammy had in mind as a money-spinner close to a rebuilt post-war Elephant and Castle. 'Come on, let's go and talk to him, eh? How old are you, Phoebe?'

'Please, I'm four.'

Four. Sammy sighed for her, then straightened up, took her hand and walked with her. He felt her fingers clinging tightly and hopefully. Poor young mite. But what did she mean, her aunt had left her? And was Follers the right name? It didn't sound right to him.

She trotted beside him, casting frequent upward

glances, and he gave her reassuring smiles. Sammy was like his brothers, Boots and Tommy, in that he was fond of kids. He began to wonder if little Phoebe's parents had been air raid victims, if she'd been taken in by her aunt, and simply got lost this morning by wandering away when her aunt had gone into a shop. Kids did do that, they did wander off instead of staying still. Mind, when he'd been a kid himself, he'd never ever stood still. Standing still was the most unprofitable activity ever, if you could call it an activity.

Approaching the local police station, Phoebe gulped again and said, 'Mister, I 'member now, that's where Auntie went and left me and told me to wait.'

Christ, thought Sammy, that could only mean one thing. The young mite had been dumped in the hope that the police would find a home for her. Why would any human being want to dump little Phoebe?

'But you didn't wait, me infant, you went to look for her, did you?'

'Yes, I was frightened. I got lost.' Hesitantly, she asked, 'You're – you're not my daddy, are you?'

A little taken aback, Sammy said, 'I don't think so, Phoebe. Come on, let's see what my old friend can do, shall we?'

The middle-aged desk sergeant looked up as a well-dressed gent entered hand-in-hand with a small girl.

'Good morning, sir, what can – oh, it's you, Mr Adams. Haven't seen you nor any of your brothers for a year or so. Is that your little girl?'

'Morning, Sergeant Burrows,' said Sammy, 'how's yourself and Mrs Burrows?'

'In the pink you could say if it wasn't for still having to spend some nights in our air raid shelter, or me being called out while me plates of meat are still in chronic need of a rest.'

'Know how you feel,' said Sammy. 'Phoebe, this is a friend of mine, Jack Burrows, a kind policeman who was born to be a help to little girls.'

Phoebe clung tighter to Sammy's hand and pressed close to his leg.

''Ello, please,' she said timidly.

'Pleased to meet yer, young 'un,' said Sergeant Burrows, and Sammy put him in the picture.

'Well, there's been some sad things come out of the war and the bombings,' said Sergeant Burrows, 'and this is one of them. She's been living with her aunt, a Mrs Lily Follers, a widow?' He scratched his grizzled hair with a pencil. 'Can't say I know any lady of that name.' He smiled down at Phoebe. 'She left you outside of here, did she, and told you to wait?'

'Yes, and I went and got lost,' said Phoebe.

'Let's see, it's Phoebe Willis, is it?'

'Yes.'

'Willis? Willis?' Sergeant Burrows thought. 'Well, there's a Willis family in Brandon Street which I've known personal for years on account of their sons breaking a few windows and the like, but they don't have a little girl. Would they be an aunt and uncle, maybe?'

'Please, I don't know,' whispered Phoebe, not letting go of Sammy's hand.

'And you can't remember where you were living?'

'I don't know,' said Phoebe.

'Was it Walworth, say, or Bermondsey, or Kennington?'

'Where's them?' she asked. Then, 'Oh, I 'member a park.'

'Well, that could be helpful,' smiled Sergeant Burrows, although to his knowledge not a single London district was without its park. 'Your Auntie Lily now, was she fond of you?'

Phoebe swallowed.

'Yes, she was nice,' she said, and gazed up at the sympathetic policeman. 'You're not my daddy, are you?' she said, and that touched the sergeant and made Sammy sigh for her.

'Well,' said the sergeant, 'I do have two grand-daughters just like you. Little angels, they are.'

'Wiv a mummy and daddy?' said Phoebe.

'Bless you, yes, me little one,' said Sergeant Burrows. 'Mr Adams, that's a funny name, Follers.'

'Is it Follers, Phoebe?' asked Sammy.

'Yes, she's me auntie,' said Phoebe, mouth quivering again.

'Can you remember how you came to be living with her?' asked Sammy.

'I don't fink so,' said Phoebe, looking unhappy.

Sammy thought she was perhaps too young to remember what might have happened a while ago. And if she had lost her parents in an air raid, perhaps shock and trauma had blanked out her memory. Her little tremors were again putting him very much in mind of five-year-old Rosie at the time she realized she was all alone in the world.

50

'Well, I'll see that enquiries are made, Mr Adams,' said Sergeant Burrows, 'I'll see if we can trace a family called Willis and a woman by name of Follers.'

'Or Follows?' said Sammy.

'Ah, that's a point,' said Sergeant Burrows, and smiled down at Phoebe again. 'Mrs Follows?' he suggested.

'Yes, I fink so,' said Phoebe.

Sergeant Burrows looked at Sammy.

'Follows,' he said, 'Follows. H'm, still a bit of an uncommon name.'

'Well, do what you can,' said Sammy.

'Of course, you'll understand all the orphanages have been evacuated?' said Sergeant Burrows.

'I wouldn't believe it if they hadn't,' said Sammy, 'it's a lousy war for kids.'

'Now, where can we place this little angel for the time being, with the Salvation Army?' mused the sergeant.

'I'll take her home,' said Sammy. 'We'll give her board and lodging while you make your enquiries.'

'Well, that's very Christian of you, Mr Adams.'

'Here's my office phone number, and my home number.' Sammy wrote them down on a slip of paper provided by the sergeant. 'And my address?'

'If you would, Mr Adams,' said Sergeant Burrows, and Sammy wrote that down too.

'Keep in touch,' he said.

'I will, Mr Adams, and me kind regards to Mrs Adams.' Sergeant Burrows smiled. 'Who was once Miss Susie Brown of Brandon Street, as I remember when a copper on the beat.'

'As we both remember,' smiled Sammy. 'So long

for now. Come on, then, Phoebe, off we go.'

The clinging fingers clung even tighter as they left the station. A little later Sammy helped her into the passenger seat of his car parked in Deacon Street, and she sat awestruck as he drove through the wartime traffic of South London to the house of his mother and stepfather in Red Post Hill. His own house on Denmark Hill had been bombed into a ruin, and he, his wife Susie and his youngest child, Paula, were presently living with his mother and stepfather.

'Sammy?' Susie, having listened with incredulity, stared at him, then at nervous little Phoebe. 'Oh, Lord, you poor child, but there, don't worry now, we'll look after you. Sammy, doesn't she have anything, anything at all?'

'Only what she's wearing,' said Sammy. A small hand touched his, crept into it, and fingers curled again. He applied a gentle squeeze and smiled down at her. 'Listen, me pet, when your aunt took you out this morning, did she give you anything to carry, like a bag with clothes in it? Or did she give you a note?'

'No, she just took me on a bus and then we walked,' said Phoebe.

'Well, never mind,' said Susie. She was thirty-seven, Sammy thirty-nine, and there was little they didn't know about children, having four of their own, three of them presently existing as country evacuees. Their youngest, little Paula, was attending school at the moment, a nursery school. 'Phoebe, would you like a nice hot Bovril?' The child needed something warm inside her. Susie couldn't think why her aunt hadn't dressed her in a coat.

'Yes, please,' said Phoebe. She thought. 'I don't fink I 'ad any breakfast.'

Something was very wrong, thought Susie. No breakfast and no coat? Her heart went out to the child.

Sammy, sharing Susie's thoughts, said with forced cheer, 'Well, blow that, eh, cherub? We'll do you a sandwich as well as a hot Bovril, shall we?'

Someone entered the house then.

'Sammy, that's your mum, back from shopping,' said Susie.

'Well, if she's not an answer to a prayer, who is?' said Sammy.

His mother, Mrs Maisie Finch, known to her family as Chinese Lady for reasons that went back a long way, was sixty-five and still upright. She wore good corsets that kept her back straight and her bosom firm. She was a great believer in firm bosoms, and had more than once been heard to comment disparagingly or sorrowfully on women who let themselves go. Her eldest son Boots had once said, 'Let themselves go where, old lady?' She didn't answer, she simply gave him a look. She was renowned for sometimes using a look in place of words.

When put in the picture concerning Phoebe she was at once sympathetic, motherly and practical.

'She must stay here, of course, till something's found out about her and if she's got any other relatives. Her Aunt Lily sounds like she's gone peculiar. We can find clothes for her, Susie, or buy some. And she can have Eloise's room. Eloise won't be needing it, not now she's gone soldiering overseas, which shouldn't have been allowed, nor wouldn't, I'm sure, if Queen Victoria was still alive.'

'She'd be a hundred and fifty, Ma,' said Sammy, glancing at Phoebe, now sitting at the kitchen table.

'Is that a joke?' said Chinese Lady. 'How could anyone be a hundred and fifty and still be alive? And don't call me Ma. Now, child, what can we do first for you?'

'Please, I'm firsty,' said Phoebe, nervousness peeping again.

'She's hungry as well, Mum,' said Susie, 'and we're going to give her hot Bovril and a sandwich to be going on with.'

'I'll see to it,' said Chinese Lady, 'and I'll give her a glass of water first.'

Inside five minutes, Phoebe, having gratefully swallowed a glass of water, was hungrily eating a Marmite sandwich and sipping hot Bovril.

'Susie, can I leave you and Mum to keep a kind eye on her?' asked Sammy, knowing he was lingering when he should have been applying himself to business. 'I need to get back to the offices. You all right now, me pet?' he said to Phoebe.

Phoebe glanced up and said quickly and hopefully, 'Could I come wiv you, please?'

Lord, thought Chinese Lady, we've got another case like we had with Rosie and Boots. That girl already can't take her eyes off Sammy.

'He's got his work to do, love,' she said, 'but he'll be back later in the day. You'll be all right with me and Susie, so don't worry.'

'Are you goin' to look after me?' asked Phoebe.

'It'll be a pleasure, child,' said Chinese Lady.

'And you'll meet my own little girl Paula this afternoon,' said Susie.

'So long now, Phoebe me cherub,' said Sammy, and gave her a gentle, reassuring pat. 'I'll be back, you bet.' He smiled. Phoebe gulped.

'Yes, a'right,' she said.

Sammy was back just before six. Chinese Lady was giving Phoebe a bath, and Paula, having made friends with the unfortunate young girl after being given a slightly censored version of the story, was sitting on the bathroom stool, chatting away to her like a little old lady intent on spreading cheer.

Susie came down the stairs as Sammy entered the hall.

'Sammy, I need to—' Susie checked as Sammy kissed her hello.

'How's Little Miss Lost?' he asked.

'Mum's giving her a bath,' said Susie. 'Sammy, look at this. I found it just a few minutes ago when I was undressing her for the bath. It was pinned to the underside of her frock, just above the hem. I think her aunt must have done that before she put the girl into the frock.' She handed Sammy a small sheet of notepaper. 'Sammy, I hate what it says, and I think you'll have to ring Sergeant Burrows.'

Sammy read the note, the handwriting a scrawl.

I can't cope with her any more. I can't cope with anything. You'll find me in the river. Lily Fellowes.

'Jesus Christ,' said Sammy, 'what's going on, Susie? This is a suicide note, and I've got an

55

horrendous feeling we've found it far too late.'

'Perhaps that's what she wanted,' said Susie, 'why she put it where it wasn't going to be found until someone undressed Phoebe. And her name's Fellowes, you notice, not Follows.'

The phone rang.

Chapter Five

'Mr Adams? Sergeant Burrows here.'

'Just the bloke I need to talk to,' said Sammy.

'It's like this,' said Sergeant Burrows. 'I put WPC Rivers in charge of the said enquiries concerning a family called Willis. Consequent on the little girl saying her parents had gone, WPC Rivers spent hours trying to find out if a married couple of that name had died in an air raid in some part of London. Councils and ARP organizations have got registers of air raid casualties in their particular districts, as you might know.'

'Right,' said Sammy, with Susie standing beside him.

'WPC Rivers spent the whole afternoon making enquiries,' said Sergeant Burrows, 'but drew blanks every time. Then she took a needed break and had a cup of tea. It freshened her up smart, like, and she began to feel there was something at the back of her mind that was nothing to do with air raid casualties, something that made the name of Willis feel a bit familiar. It set her thinking, and she made some different enquiries that led to her getting in touch with Scotland Yard.'

'Bloody hell,' breathed Sammy, 'are you going to tell me Phoebe's parents have got a police record?'

'I'm going to tell you, Mr Adams – I'm having to tell you – that a Mr and Mrs Frank Willis of Bow were murdered in their own house just before the war by a man called Wilfred Peters.'

'Christ,' breathed Sammy, 'I remember that case, the headlines and the name. Peters. The newspapers referred to him as "the Butcher" after he was found guilty but insane.'

'A lunatic, Mr Adams, a psychopath, now locked up in Broadmoor for the rest of his natural,' said Sergeant Burrows. 'There was no motive, just a crazy need to kill somebody. He broke in and murdered Mr and Mrs Willis in their bed with a long knife. It grieves me to also tell you they had a daughter called Phoebe, not yet three at the time, who was in the next room, in her bed, when the murder was being committed. She was found under her bedclothes, where she'd obviously buried herself to shut out the noises of her mother's screams. God help us, Mr Adams, if those screams hadn't brought neighbours to the house, it's possible little Phoebe would've been murdered herself.'

'The headlines are all coming back to me,' said Sammy heavily. 'Peters, yes, who couldn't remember that maniac, but I'd forgotten the names of the victims.'

'Mrs Lily Fellowes, sister of Mrs Willis, who lived nearby, took Phoebe into the care of herself and her husband, and – here's a turn of the screw, Mr Adams – it was her husband who was killed by a bomb while on duty with the AFS during the initial blitz on London.'

'Holy Moses,' said Sammy, 'did that coming on top of the murder of her sister and brother-in-law gradually send her off her head? There was a note pinned inside Phoebe's dress, Jack, and Susie's only just found it. I was about to phone you when you rang. Listen.' He read the note over the phone.

'I don't like any of that,' said Sergeant Burrows, 'especially the bit about looking for her in the river. Action's needed, Mr Adams. I'll ring you back.' Down went the phone, and Sammy put his own receiver back.

'Sammy,' said Susie, 'he's told you something that's shaken you. What was it?'

Sammy took her into the front room, which Chinese Lady still insisted on calling her parlour, and delivered an accurate account of all that the Walworth police enquiries had uncovered, including the fact that the murdered parents had lived in Bow.

'Oh, my God, that poor little darling,' breathed Susie. 'Do her mother's screams still live in her mind, I wonder, or do we hope that because she was only two at the time, she remembers nothing? Do you remember anything that happened before you were three, Sammy?'

'No, Susie love, I don't,' said Sammy, 'I can only go back to when I was about six.'

'I can't remember my infant years, either,' said Susie, 'but there's a kind of sadness about Phoebe, don't you think?'

'I'm going to put that down to the natural sadness of a little girl who at least knows that unlike other kids she doesn't have a mum and dad,' said Sammy. 'Susie, Boots and the rest of us had to live without our dad from the time when we were only kids, and we missed him, I can tell you, but we still had a mother who was a woman and a half. Every kid needs parents, Susie, every kid likes to come home to a mum and dad. There's no real substitutes.'

'There were for Rosie,' said Susie. 'Boots and Emily.'

'What's happening?' asked Sammy. 'Boots has got another parentless girl under his roof. That girl Kate Trimble. And we've got Phoebe.'

'But Kate's not four years old,' said Susie. 'Polly's assured us that at sixteen she's priceless. Well, Sammy love, let's hope further police enquiries will lead Phoebe to other relatives who'll care for her if—' She checked.

'If her Aunt Lily is floating in the river somewhere?' said Sammy.

'Yes,' said Susie.

Mr Edwin Finch, Chinese Lady's second husband, arrived home then. Sixty-eight, he was well beyond retirement age, but in his work for British Intelligence he was invaluable and, accordingly to his chief, too necessary to the department to be allowed to retire. As a brilliant cypher expert, he was presently resisting a suggestion to transfer his talents to a place called Bletchley Park in Buckinghamshire, the centre of British infiltration of German Intelligence. He was too old for such concentrated work, he said, and further he wished to spend his remaining years at home with his wife.

On hearing about Phoebe from Sammy and Susie, he did not express himself dramatically, he simply said the girl had at least enjoyed one

60

moment of good fortune, which was when she made her plight known to Sammy. She must stay, he said, until an alternative offered itself, an alternative that gave her a chance of happiness. He played his own predictable part when Phoebe, dressed by favour of Paula's wardrobe, came down from her bath accompanied by Chinese Lady and Paula. He gave her the kindest of smiling welcomes, and Phoebe looked up at his distinguished figure, then at Sammy.

'Is he your daddy?' she asked.

'Yes, he's my dad,' said Sammy, smiling at his stepfather. He nodded at Chinese Lady. 'And that lady's my mum. And the pickle is my daughter. You've met the pickle.'

'My mummy and daddy went away and didn't come back,' said Phoebe. 'Auntie Lily told me so. Can I be wiv you, please?'

'Well, I'm going upstairs to have a wash and brush-up after me day's hard labours,' said Sammy. 'If you and Paula want to come up and see me wash my face and brush my hair, you're welcome.'

'Crikey, what a thrill,' said Paula, in her seventh year.

'Come on,' said Sammy, and took both girls by the hand and went upstairs with them.

'Boots was like that with Rosie,' said Chinese Lady, and looked at Susie. 'Best not to make too much of a fuss of her, Susie.'

'I know,' said Susie, 'but she's such a forlorn little thing.'

The phone rang again, this time when Sammy was on his way downstairs with giggling Paula and a happier Phoebe. He answered it, leaving Paula to take Phoebe into the kitchen.

'Mr Adams?' It was a woman's voice.

'Yes, that's me,' said Sammy.

'This is WPC Rivers, Mr Adams. You read a note over the phone to Sergeant Burrows, a note written by a Lily Fellowes.'

'I did, yes,' said Sammy. 'Has anything happened?'

'Mr Adams, a woman jumped from Waterloo Bridge into the river this afternoon. A Polish soldier made an attempt to prevent her, but was too late, and she drowned before anyone could reach her. The Polish soldier found her handbag on the parapet, and handed it to the police as soon as they arrived. The unfortunate woman, Mr Adams, was a Mrs Lily Fellowes, a widow, and the aunt of Phoebe Willis.'

'And the sister of Phoebe's murdered mother,' said Sammy grimly.

'Yes, frightful, Mr Adams,' said WPC Rivers. 'Mrs Fellowes lived near her murdered sister in Bow. She had no children, but our colleagues in the area are trying to find out if Phoebe has any relatives who might be willing to take care of the child. In the meantime, Mr Adams, will you and your wife keep her, or do you wish us to make arrangements?'

'We'll look after her,' said Sammy.

'Thank you, Mr Adams. Sergeant Burrows, not here at the moment, asked me to give you his compliments, and we shall keep in touch with you, of course. How is the little girl?'

'Better than she was this morning,' said Sammy, 'but she's a sad infant.'

'It's a sad story, Mr Adams.'

'You can say that again,' said Sammy, 'and it's not the first of its kind to hit my family. Anyway, thanks for letting me know about Mrs Fellowes. I didn't expect anything different.'

'No. Oh, by the way, Mr Adams, could you let us have that note at your early convenience? It'll be wanted at the inquest.'

'I'll drop it in as soon as I can,' said Sammy.

'Thank you, sir.'

'It's a lousy war,' said Sammy, and hung up. He couldn't remember when he had last felt so depressed about events or so sad for a child.

He and Susie tucked the little girl up in Eloise's bed at eight o'clock, Susie praying no air raid would happen, since she had a conviction that air raids had contributed not only to the mental breakdown of Mrs Fellowes, but to Phoebe's nervous timidity.

'There, is that comfy?' she said softly.

'Yes, it feels nice,' said Phoebe, wearing one of Paula's nightdresses. Her expression was of a child at last relaxing, her dark hair spilling softly over the pillow.

'Hold on a tick,' said Sammy, and out he went, Phoebe's eyes following him. Back he came, with one of Paula's new teddy bears. 'Like to cuddle Rupert?' he said, and Phoebe took it.

'Oh, I like 'im,' she said.

'Well, now you're really comfy, eh?' said Sammy.

'Yes.' A little sigh. She looked at Susie and said hesitantly, 'You're not my mummy, are you?'

Susie felt pain. Sammy felt wrenched.

'Perhaps we'll find her for you one day, Phoebe,' said Susie.

'Yes.' Another little sigh. 'I fink I'm a bit tired now.'

They said good night to her. Her lids drooped and her eyes closed. Susie and Sammy left, Sammy putting the light out but leaving the door ajar.

'Susie, I've had headaches in my time,' he said on the landing, 'but I've never had one like this. Should we have put her in with Paula, d'you think?'

'Sammy, we mustn't put her too close to any of us,' said Susie, and Sammy thought of the year 1920, when the family had let little Rosie become so close to them that when a parting happened, everyone was shattered.

'I'd just like to see her not so sad, Susie.'

'Yes, Sammy,' said Susie softly, 'so would I.'

Phoebe's lament was still on her mind.

'You're not my mummy, are you?'

Sammy woke early, at six-forty to be precise. He knew why. He slipped silently from the bed, leaving Susie sleeping, and went to look in on Phoebe, putting the landing light on. It enabled him to see her as he entered the room and crossed to the bed.

She was awake and looking up at him, the teddy bear beside her in the bed. Her lashes quivered and unhappiness made itself known.

'Please, I'm – I'm wet.'

Oh, my God, thought Sammy, does she have to suffer that as well, poor little mite?

'Oh, well, never mind, cherub,' he said, 'we'll soon put that right. Let's get you out, shall we?'

He turned back sheet, blanket and eiderdown, uncovering her. He lifted her out. The back of her nightie was damp rather than wet. He saw the stain of dampness on the bottom sheet, and he wondered if she had woken when it happened and had been lying there waiting for someone to come. If it had been only a few minutes ago, the nightie and sheet would have been wet.

'I'm sorry,' she whispered, her arms around his neck.

'Don't you worry, me pet, lots of little girls and boys have accidents,' he said, 'especially when they get lost.' He carried her to the bathroom, set her down and switched the light on. She stood looking at him, a child unhappy, uncertain, and shivering a little. He filled the handbasin with hot water. 'Come on, let's get you warm and then dry,' he said.

She lifted her arms and he drew the nightie off, placing it over the side of the bath. Then he sponged her down with hot water, front and back, and the rivulets ran from her onto the bath mat.

'It's nice,' she said.

'You're steaming,' said Sammy, his smile encouraging.

'It wasn't my fault, was it?' she said, expression visibly asking for reassurance.

'Of course not,' said Sammy, 'you had a bit of a worried time yesterday, didn't you? There, you're all right now, infant, washed all over. Hold on a tick.' He fetched a warm bath towel from the airing cupboard on the landing, and he used it to rub her down briskly and vigorously. Her delicate skin glowed. 'How's that? Bless me, you're a pink little lady now.'

The uncertain eyes peeped, the anxiety retreated a little.

'Am I going to stay wiv you again today?' she

asked as he gave her a final rub-down.

'You bet,' he said. He was down on one knee in front of her, and her eyes flickered as she glanced upwards.

'Sammy?'

He turned his head. Susie, in a dressing-gown, was at the open bathroom door, staring.

'Oh, hello, love,' he said casually, 'would you have a look at Phoebe's bed and make it comfy again before she gets back in?'

'Sammy?' Susie was still staring. He gave her a little nod. It impelled her into Eloise's bedroom to take a look at the bed. She was quickly active then, stripping it down to the bare mattress, the centre of which was damp. She returned to the bathroom. Phoebe was wrapped in the bath towel and up in Sammy's arms. 'Put her into our bed, Sammy, it's still warm. Hers is cold. Wrap her in one of your pyjama jackets.'

'Please, I'm sorry,' whispered Phoebe.

'Oh, there's nothing to be sorry about, lovey,' said Susie.

'Nothing at all, me pet,' said Sammy.

Phoebe was snug in their bed, cuddling the teddy bear, her eyes closing again. Hers was the tiredness of a child who had been awake well before Sammy had looked in on her.

He and Susie were in Eloise's bedroom, and Sammy had the mattress off.

'Poor little angel,' he said, 'what she must have felt like when she woke up and realized she'd wet the bed.'

'We're not surprised it happened, are we?' said Susie.

'I'm not,' said Sammy.

'Sammy, will it happen again, I wonder?' said Susie, bundling up sheets to put into the wash.

'It might if today is as upsetting for her as yesterday was,' said Sammy. 'Which it would be if she got to know her aunt had committed suicide.'

'Well, she mustn't get to know,' said Susie, 'but on my way back from taking Paula to school, I'll buy some waterproof sheeting, just in case she isn't over yesterday's upset.'

'What I can't get out of my mind,' said Sammy, 'is the night when her parents were murdered in their bed and she was in the next room listening to her mother's screams.'

'Well, I'm praying, Sammy, that she really was too young to remember,' said Susie. 'I'll let her sleep on a bit this morning, and I know Mum will look after her when I take Paula to school.'

Phoebe, however, was awake again when Sammy took a peep at her just before he left for work. But her eyes were dreamy.

'Hello,' he said quietly.

''Ello, mister, I'm ever so comfy,' she murmured.

'Stay that way, Phoebe, stay that way,' said Sammy, and as her eyes closed again he slipped out.

Chapter Six

Libya

The cloudy condition of the wounded soldier's mind thinned a little as he slowly came awake. Vaguely he was aware of two faces, a man's and a woman's. He tried to say something, to ask what had happened. The attempt did not achieve more than a mumble, but it at least suggested he was no longer in crisis.

'He's coming to,' said the man.

'You can be proud, Herr Doctor,' said the woman.

'Well, he's no longer laden with bullets, Fraulein Lieutenant. Touch and go, the one so close to the heart, necessitating very delicate surgery, but one does what one can, for friend or foe.'

'Will this one fully recover?'

'He'll recover enough to be transported to a prisoner of war camp. Beyond that, I reserve my opinion for the time being. I leave him with you now, Fraulein Lieutenant. Keep a careful eye on him today, and call me if there should be a relapse.'

'Very good, Herr Doctor.'

The patient did not understand a word of this dialogue in German. Existing in a remote kind of way, he could not summon up interest, in any case. However, an hour later, when his eyes opened again, he was immediately conscious of his surroundings. White-painted walls, the smell of antiseptics, a large fan whirring high above his head, and beds. His chest felt tender, very tender, but nightmarish dreams had gone and his head was cool instead of hot and fuzzy.

'Anyone at home?'

A head turned his way from a bed on the other side of the ward. From somewhere else, a figure in immaculate drill appeared.

'Good morning, Herr Lieutenant,' said Lieutenant Anneliese Bruck, German Army nurse.

'Pardon?' said Lieutenant Tim Adams.

Clinical in her regard of a wounded enemy, her blue eyes and blond hair admirably Aryan, she said in English, 'You do not speak German?'

'Where am I, then?' asked Tim, voice weak.

'You are in the German hospital of Benghazi.' It was actually Italian-built but German-controlled.

'Bloody hell,' breathed Tim.

'Excuse me?' She was not without an excellent understanding of his language. Her paternal grandmother was English, but fully Germanized and a devotee of the Fuehrer.

'Are you a German nurse?' asked Tim.

'I am Lieutenant Bruck, a German Army nurse.'

'Well, if it's all the same to you, I'd like to go home,' said Tim, vocal chords under strain.

'Unfortunately, you will have to wait until the war is over,' said the clinical figure of Aryan perfection.

'I'm not—' His voice cracked. He dragged moisture into his throat. 'I'm not in favour of that.'

'You are not to talk. You were badly wounded during your attack on a German unit. Bullets have been taken out of your chest. You are lucky to be alive and can thank our surgical team for that. If you wish to recover, rest quietly for the sake of your wounded chest and damaged ribs. You are still under sedation, but there will be some pain in a while.' Her English was as correct as she was, but Tim was mentally wandering again, her words coming through a curtain of cotton wool. 'If the pain is severe, I will give you tablets.'

'A German angel?' His voice seemed to float now. 'I didn't know there were any.'

'You have been listening to BBC propaganda.'

'I've got to—' He wanted to say he'd got to get out of here, but he lapsed back into the enveloping clouds.

Anneliese Bruck regarded him with professional neutrality. He needed a shave, his stubble adding to the darkness of his desert tan, although beneath the tan he had the drawn look of a man suffering the debilitating effect of his wounds. Some time today she would have to get an orderly to shave him. It was the correct thing to do, and the ward sister did not, in any case, approve of patients looking as if their personal appearance was suffering neglect. Anneliese knew the British night attack on a German position outside Tobruk had been daring and savage. Many German soldiers had been killed or wounded. But there it was, the rules of war were that wounded enemies should be hospitalized and cared for in the same way as German wounded.

Automatically, she took the pulse of this British officer, Lieutenant Adams, and satisfied herself he was at rest and not in crisis before leaving him.

Tim lay in sedated sleep. He did not know it, but he had been in this German-controlled hospital in Libya for a week, and undergone more than one operation.

Tim's wife Felicity, formerly an ATS officer, was still a patient in a convalescent and rehabilitation centre for disabled Servicemen and Servicewomen near Farnham in Surrey. She was hoping to receive a letter from Tim. She knew he was operating with a Commando unit in the Western Desert, and that he could not write to a regular timetable. But it was now quite a while since she had heard from him, and she was sure she would not have to wait much longer.

Felicity, blinded during an air raid on London while she was on leave, had been undergoing rehabilitation in this hospital for many months, and her progress was of a kind that now delighted the staff, especially her most caring nurse, Clara Dickens.

Clara had just collected a telegram from reception. It was addressed to Felicity.

'Oh, hell,' she said.

'Look on the bright side,' said the reception clerk.

'If there's a bright side to wartime telegrams, I've never heard of it,' said Clara. Gritting her teeth, she went out into the extensive grounds at the rear of

the hospital. She knew Felicity was out here somewhere. She always was unless the weather was too
discouraging, or she was taking instruction in
respect of indoor activities, activities that came
naturally to most people except those suffering a
sudden loss of sight. Clara saw her, coated on this
cold day, but walking in her steady determined way,
and using her white stick to fend off any malicious-
minded obstacles.

Clara, catching up with her, said, 'I'll join you for
five minutes.'

'Help yourself,' said Felicity. The cold day was
grey with clouds, but she was wearing her dark
glasses. She always kept her scarred and sightless
eyes hidden.

'I'll help you practise writing again this afternoon,' said Clara. 'I'll have time.'

'I'll write down the alphabet,' said Felicity. 'I'm
told I'm still all over the place with joined-up
letters.'

'Sloping a little, that's all,' said Clara. 'By the way,
there's a telegram for you.'

Felicity stopped in her walk, and her mouth
compressed.

'Telegram?' she said.

'Shall I open it?' asked Clara.

'No, burn it,' said Felicity.

'You don't mean that,' said Clara.

'Well, open it and read it, then,' said Felicity, 'but
if it's the usual kind of wartime telegram, I'll love
it, won't I?'

'Fingers crossed,' said Clara. She opened the
telegram. It was from the War Office, and the words
leapt to her eyes. They were to the effect that

Lieutenant Tim Adams had been wounded in action and taken prisoner. Clara, who knew Tim well and had attended his wedding to Felicity, was not sure if she was more relieved than distressed. Anything was better than a message of death.

'I don't like your silence,' said Felicity, keeping her feelings in check, although her right hand was gripping her stick in a way that turned her knuckles white.

'Felicity dear,' said Clara, 'Tim's been taken prisoner.'

'Oh, my God,' said Felicity.

'It could be—'

'Worse? Is that what you're going to say? Well, you're right, aren't you?' Felicity couldn't help bitterness raising its voice. 'I'm thrilled, aren't I, that he's only a prisoner of war and not a corpse? I only have to wait now until the war ends before we meet again. Bloody marvellous, I don't think.'

'Even so,' said Clara gently, 'let's both agree that that's more acceptable than a funeral.' She had to complete the message. 'As it is, Tim was wounded in the action.'

Felicity sighed.

'That's it, give me all of it,' she said, suffering for Tim as well as for herself.

'I'm so sorry, my dear,' said Clara.

'I know,' said Felicity. She reached, found Clara, and patted her arm. 'It won't be the wound that'll bother Tim, it'll be the prisoner of war camp. He'll hate that. I'm already hating the thought of it for him. I wonder how he expects me to take the news? I think I know. Will you do something for me, Clara?'

'Of course,' said Clara.

'There's a half-bottle of brandy in my locker. Will you fetch it? Bring two glasses, one for you, one for me.'

'I'm on duty—'

'Don't be a drip, Clara, be a friend. Let's do what I know Tim would favour, make a hole in the brandy bottle to celebrate he's still alive instead of having to get our hankies out.'

'Wait there,' said Clara, and off she went to get the bottle. Never mind the rules, she thought. Well, a good many rules were broken for patients in a place like this, and I'm willing to break a hundred for Felicity.

She would have to write letters for her. To Tim's relatives.

The following morning, Sammy woke early again. Well, blow this for a lark, he thought, it's bad enough air raids cutting short my beauty sleep, without losing some of it on quiet nights. Have I still got little Phoebe on my mind? Yes, so I have, but considering what's happened to her, it's only natural. Shall I take a look at her? No, she'll be enjoying a sound sleep this time, there were no upsets during the day, according to Susie and Chinese Lady, and she seems to like Paula.

All the same.

He moved. Susie woke up.

'Sammy?'

'Don't wake up, Susie, it's only half-six.'

'I am awake. What're you up to?'

'Never touched you, Susie, I swear.'

'I don't mean that, Sammy Adams, I mean why're you half out of bed?'

'It's not my best position, I grant you, Susie, one leg in, one leg out.'

'Have you got Phoebe on your mind?'

'Well, I woke up, Susie, and thought I'd just take a look at her.'

'You're a nice old fusspot, Sammy. All right, do that.'

Sammy entered Eloise's bedroom quietly. Dawn in November was late, but again the landing light enabled him to make out the sleeping figure of Phoebe when he reached the bedside. She was on her side, huddled up on the far edge of the bed, sleeping. Far edge? He slipped a hand under the bedclothes. The middle of the bottom sheet was wet. He experienced a sudden surge of anger at what life had done to her, and that was followed by a sense of overwhelming pity.

He moved quietly to look down at her from the other side of the bed. She was asleep, yes, but he'd swear she'd been crying, that her face was marked by tear stains. God, the poor kid. She'd had her moment of weakness, had woken up, found herself wet, moved to a dry side of the sheet and cried herself back to sleep. He worried then about exactly what to do. If he woke her up she'd give him that desperately unhappy look of a child in shame of herself.

'Sammy?' It was a whisper from Susie as she entered the room in her nightdress.

'It's happened again, Susie,' he whispered, 'and not long ago. The sheet's still wet.'

'Oh, Lord, the poor lamb.' Susie felt stricken for the girl.

'But there's a waterproof under the sheet?'

'Yes, it'll protect the mattress. Sammy, I wonder, is it a regular weakness of hers?'

Sammy thought about the aunt's suicide note.

I can't cope with her any more.

He worried.

'If it is, what's the reason, Susie?'

'A disturbed mind?'

Their whispering was fraught with a shared and intense pity.

'Susie, I'd like us to have her for at least three months. I'm sure we could make life a bit happier for her.'

'Yes, perhaps any kind of happiness would be a cure.'

'I can't make up my mind if we should wake her or not.'

'Let's leave her, Sammy. It's going to be unhappy for her either way. I'll come back when the alarm goes, and take it from there, don't you think so?'

'At half-seven? Seems best, Susie.'

They went back to their bed, but neither could sleep, and at seven-twenty the door opened and little Phoebe, pale-faced and dark-eyed, showed herself.

'Please, my bed's wet,' she gulped.

Sammy was out at once, swift in his movements. He picked her up and cuddled her against his chest.

'Well, bless you, pet,' he said, 'aren't you a good girl for coming to tell us?'

'I'm sorry,' she whispered, her face against his shoulder.

He had a thought.

'Did you sometimes have to tell your Aunt Lily?' he asked.

'Yes.'

'And what did she say?' he asked, with Susie listening.

'She – she'd say, "Oh dear not again, oh dear."' Phoebe did her familiar gulp.

A sigh escaped Susie. Sammy felt distressed, and he cuddled the child closer.

'But she was a kind aunt, Phoebe?' he said.

'Yes. She didn't get cross, she just said, "Oh dear oh dear." Like that.'

'How old did you say you were, lovey?' asked Susie.

'Four,' whispered Phoebe. 'Auntie told me I'll be five next Jan'ry, on the sixth, she said. I 'member that.'

Sammy thought, Jesus, she really was under three when the murder of her parents happened.

'Right, we won't forget January the sixth, me pet,' he said.

'Please, can I 'ave a hot sponge wash like yesterday?' she asked.

'Just the ticket,' said Sammy. 'Off we go, then.'

He took her to the bathroom, while Susie stripped the drying sheet from the unlucky bed.

During the process of being sponged down with lovely hot water, Phoebe lifted flickering eyes to Sammy and said hesitantly, 'You're not my daddy, are you?'

That again? Oh, hell, thought Sammy, I'm going to fall to pieces in a minute.

'How about seeing me as an uncle, eh, me cherub?'

'Yes, a'right,' said Phoebe in a quiet little voice.

Susie wondered later if she should take the girl to the local doctor and consult with him. Sammy was against that, reckoning it would prove another upset. He was convinced the cure would only come with a change in the girl, a change from sadness to a natural childish enjoyment of life. It was possible, he said, that her aunt had taken her to see a doctor more than once. Susie was inclined to agree, to hope that the child's new environment would eventually do the trick.

She intended to take Phoebe for a trip to the shops to be equipped with new clothes, and Sammy provided her with a generous amount of clothing coupons before he left for his offices.

'Just a minute, Sammy,' said Susie, standing at the front door with him. Phoebe and Paula were in the kitchen, finishing breakfast in company with Chinese Lady. 'Where did all these coupons come from?'

'From my wallet,' said Sammy.

'And how did they get into your wallet, my lad?' asked Susie.

'By hand, Susie.'

'If they're black market—'

'Now, Susie, you know you don't like black market operations.'

'Sammy, can you truthfully say—'

'Of course I can, Susie. Got to fly now.' Away he went, and Susie, deciding not to go after him, decided also, with her fingers crossed, that the clothing coupons came primarily from the goodness of his heart, and accordingly anything dubious about them could be discounted for the sake of little Phoebe.

When she returned from taking Paula to school,

she found Phoebe interesting herself in watching Chinese Lady polishing the brass fender in the parlour.

'Has she been all right, Mum?' asked Susie.

'She's been a nice quiet girl,' said Chinese Lady, remembering that little Rosie had been a chatterbox.

'Well, that's good,' said Susie. 'Phoebe, would you like to come out with us in ten minutes? We'll go to the shops and buy you some new clothes. Would you like that?'

'Oh, yes,' said Phoebe, presently wearing one of Paula's frocks. 'Fanks,' she said, and then, 'I like being wiv you.'

'We'll all have a nice time,' said Chinese Lady with a smile. Having been told of Phoebe's second unhappy accident in bed, she had taken that in the way of an understanding woman. It was nothing, she said, that you couldn't expect of a child suffering her kind of upset, and that as soon as she realized she was being cared for, misfortunate accidents would stop. Mind you, she said, if someone who's a stranger to her turns up to take her away, well, goodness knows what it might do to her. She seems a very sensitive child.

'I think, Mum,' said Susie, 'she can't understand why she doesn't have parents, why they went away and never came back.'

'She had to be told they went away,' said Chinese Lady, 'she couldn't be told what actu'lly happened to them. And I suppose no-one had the heart to tell her they were dead.'

'I feel tragically sad for her,' said Susie.

Chapter Seven

Midway through the morning, Sammy advised his general manager, Mrs Rachel Goodman, that he was going to visit the Elephant and Castle again.

'I see,' said Rachel who, as a thirty-nine-year-old full-bodied widow of well-preserved symmetry, was highly eligible in the eyes of certain mature gentlemen of her race. Rachel, however, was not thinking of marrying again. She was happily attached to her job with Adams Enterprises and its associated companies. 'You're really interested in that area for post-war development, are you, Sammy?'

'I can't tell a porkie, I'm considerably interested,' said Sammy, 'and I can depart confident you'll see the business won't collapse while I'm out.'

'I should let that happen, Sammy?' smiled Rachel, deep brown eyes as velvety as her voice. 'Never. Oh, how's the little girl?' She had been given the story of luckless Phoebe, although Sammy hadn't mentioned the girl's weakness.

'A bit brighter,' said Sammy, shrugging himself into his overcoat.

'By the way, I must tell you,' said Rachel. 'Leah and Lizzy's son Edward are getting very thick, Sammy.'

'You mentioned a while ago they were pen friends,' said Sammy. 'Now they're rubbing noses, are they? Well, good luck to 'em, Rachel, hope they have happy days together. The war's cheating them of a home life.'

'I should encourage their relationship, Sammy?' said Rachel wryly.

'Good idea,' said Sammy. 'Yes, do that, Rachel, let 'em have their time together while the war's on. By the time it's over – a couple of years yet, I reckon – they'll be old enough to make serious decisions, y'know.'

'But, Sammy, suppose—'

'I'd hope that you and Lizzy and Ned would let 'em make up their own minds,' said Sammy. 'Mind, I'm not God, so I can't say me wisdom's perfect, but if we're learning anything about the bleeders running Germany, it's that we shouldn't let religious differences make life a gorblimey misery for some people. There you are, Rachel, spoken from me heart.' And Sammy, smiled, clapped on his titfer and left.

Rachel silently thanked life for people like Sammy, like Boots, Tommy, Vi and Susie. And Lizzy and Ned. They all seemed to reflect the sense and outlook of Chinese Lady, in that they would always take other people as they found them, never mind if they worshipped their own God or someone else's. As for Polly, she'd pour ridicule and contempt over anyone who thought the practice of religious prejudice could be justified.

Rachel felt glad she had told Leah she would never seek to influence her in respect of the friendships she formed.

Sammy's first stop was at the Walworth police station, where Sergeant Burrows greeted him with a smile.

'Well, hello again, Mr Adams,' he said.

'How'd'y'do, Jack,' said Sammy, 'still a lousy war.'

'Not as lousy for old Joe Stalin as it was,' said Sergeant Burrows, 'his armies are standing up to Hitler a bit firmer outside Moscow, and it's my belief the ruddy Nazis won't get one jackboot inside the city. The Russian winter's come nice and early.'

It was sleeting heavily in central Russia, and Germany's armoured divisions were struggling through rivers of icy mud, their soldiers close to freezing in the same lightweight uniforms they'd worn during the summer campaigns.

'Well, when the snow arrives, Corporal Hitler's not going to like that any more than Napoleon did,' said Sammy, and wondered why the war, colossal though it was, had taken second place to his concern for little Phoebe. 'I've brought that suicide note, Jack.' He produced it and handed it to Sergeant Burrows, who scanned it.

'It's a promise, that it is, a promise from Mrs Fellowes that she wasn't going to see the day out,' he said. 'I was going to ring you today to let you know the police in Bow have been looking into her suicide with the help of people who were friends or neighbours of Phoebe's parents and aunt. There's one thing you might like to know, Mr Adams.

There's an aunt, an uncle and grandparents.'

'Tell me more,' said Sammy.

'She's got a paternal grandad, a widower, who lives in Canada,' said Sergeant Burrows. 'Seems he went there in 1937 to join his other son and his wife, who'd emigrated earlier. They might be willing to take Phoebe. Then there's her maternal grandmother, a widow, living in Leigh-on-Sea. These grandparents and the Canadian aunt and uncle, Mr Adams, seem to be Phoebe's only relatives now that Mrs Fellowes has gone.'

'Are the Bow police getting in touch with them?' asked Sammy.

'They're trying to find addresses, Mr Adams,' said Sergeant Burrows. 'They'll do their best. What d'you think now you've had Phoebe for a couple of days, would a new life in Canada suit her? That's if her aunt and uncle there would have her, of course, and they sound the best bet, to my way of thinking.'

Sammy saw the sense of that, but had an odd feeling of not being too enthusiastic.

'Better, I suppose, than living with just her grandma in Leigh-on-Sea,' he said. 'Are there any official objections to her living with us until something's sorted out?'

'Phoebe got lost in this parish, Mr Adams. That little incident's ours, and you and Mrs Adams have got our official approval as temp'ry guardians.'

'Well, we'd like to have her until she's recovered from her upsets, Jack,' said Sammy.

'How is she?' asked Sergeant Burrows.

'A pet,' said Sammy.

'Well, bless her.'

'I concur,' said Sammy, then went to look at the

bombed ruins next to the Post Office in New Kent Road. His new venture, Adams Properties Ltd, was in the market for acquiring sites suitable for post-war development. He made an estimate of the size of this particular site, but his natural enthusiasm was a bit limp, and he walked to the Elephant and Castle junction. There, the damage was wide-spread. Dormant interest resurfaced. This was it, sites around the junction itself. He dismissed the New Kent Road site, and thought about calling on estate agents. No, first of all he'd contact his old friend Eli Greenberg, the well-known rag-and-bone man. Eli knew everything about local property owners. He knew everything about everybody of note. Besides, a chat with him might be just what the doctor ordered for a bloke a bit off colour at the moment.

He drove to Mr Greenberg's yard in Camberwell, the yard his old friend had acquired after his Blackfriars place took a direct hit from a bomb. Arriving some time after noon, Sammy parked in the yard, and immediately observed that what Eli had lost he'd replaced. The large covered area of the yard was stacked high with secondhand house-hold goods of every description. He'd probably bought a lot of stuff at knock-down prices from the owners or tenants of bombed houses.

As Sammy emerged from his car, Mr Greenberg himself came out of the shed he used as an office.

'Vhy, Sammy, it's you, ain't it? Vhat a pleasure.'

There he was in his long overcoat and old round black hat. The hat, rusty with age, crowned his heap of iron-grey hair, and his grey-flecked beard curled with happiness.

'How's yerself, Eli old cock?' smiled Sammy.

'All the better for seeing you, Sammy, ain't it?' said Mr Greenberg who, on the last occasion he'd spoken with Sammy, had plunged into grief at hearing he and Susie had lost their house and all their belongings during an air raid. 'Tell me, is Susie bearing up?'

'Like a champion, Eli.'

'Ah, vhat a sveet vife, Sammy, and a brave one,' sighed Mr Greenberg. 'Ain't I a privileged man, don't I have friends I love, don't I have freedom to do business? Ah, Sammy, vorse and vorse are all the stories coming out of Germany, and here I am in my yard vith no-one knocking on my door in the middle of the night to take me avay vith my good lady and my stepsons, never to be heard of again.'

'It's as bad as that, Eli?' said Sammy.

'Bad, Sammy, is a vord for the devil himself. Himmler. A fortunate man I am that I vas born here in the time of good Queen Victoria, ain't I?'

'Born here, Eli?' said Sammy, who knew he'd emigrated from Russia with his Latvian father and Russian mother before the Great War of '14-18.

'Vell, nearly, Sammy, nearly, you might say, and don't I have papers that say I belong?'

'You belong, Eli. Listen, how about a beer and a sandwich and some business talk?'

Mr Greenberg beamed.

'Ain't you a man after my own heart, Sammy?' he said. 'Don't ve both know the blessings of friendship are painted vith sunshine vhen there's business talk? But might I ask, Sammy, if it vill make me a poorer man this time?'

'No, not this time,' said Sammy.

Over beers and sandwiches in a pub, they talked of the devastated Elephant and Castle, and of Sammy's need to contact the owners of certain sites. After a while, Mr Greenberg offered a suggestion.

'Vell, there's two vays of making a profit, Sammy,' he said, tapping his nose. 'Buying the sites, then building shops and offices for rent on the vun hand, or selling the sites on the other.'

'Selling?' said Sammy.

'Buying now and selling later, eh, my friend?' chuckled Mr Greenberg. 'Prices now? Low, Sammy, low. Later, vhen the var is over and developers vant to build? High, Sammy, and higher than high, ain't it? Five hundred per cent higher, even a thousand.'

'Eli old cock,' said Sammy, 'you're making me think. All that profit without having to even clear the sites. True, it'll be capital tied up for a bit, but so it would be, anyway. Now, about owners who'll sell. Ancient coves, Eli. Old blokes, too old to be thinking of post-war development, and preferring, according, to part with their ruins and their free-hold deeds for a bit of oof in their banks that'll make them feel they've got no financial worries from now until they peg out, bless 'em. Plus other owners that won't object to being tempted.'

'Vhy, ain't that profitable thinking, Sammy, ain't it?' enthused Mr Greenberg. 'But don't forget all owners of bombed properties are entitled to Government compensation.'

'Which they won't get until well after the war,' said Sammy. 'My offer to each will be the estimated compensation, which'll be the estimated cost of rebuilding what Fatty Goering knocked down, which is what Adams Properties will get as the new owners. But of course developers are going to rebuild with a lot more ambition, precisely what I had in mind.'

'Sammy, my friend, leave it to me to examine prospects,' said Mr Greenberg. 'I know vun or two owners, vun or two. Some might sell, old or not old. Vell, vhat are they sitting on, Sammy? Bricks and valls that ain't standing up and not earning them a penny. Might I ask about capital?'

'No problems, Eli. Make your enquiries.'

'A pleasure, Sammy. Say at ten per cent of asking prices?'

Mr Greenberg would deserve a decent commission for doing the work that Sammy hadn't the time to do himself, and he knew it. But ten per cent gave him pain.

'That's ruination, Eli, and you know it. Say two per cent of the eventual purchase prices, old cock?'

'Sammy, Sammy, don't make jokes, not vhen ve're talking business.'

'A whole two per cent is no joke, Eli.'

The pleasure of bargaining began. It took Sammy's mind off images of little forlorn Phoebe for a while.

'Take this,' said the immaculate German Army nurse. Tim, head and shoulders propped on pillows, took a tablet from her and popped it into his mouth. 'Drink this and swallow,' she said, and gave him a glass of water. The tablet went down amid gulped water.

'Thanks,' he said, his chest and ribs painfully sore.

'We do our best for everyone,' said Lieutenant

Anneliese Bruck. 'That includes shaving you.'

'I'd still like to go home,' said Tim.

'You are absurd.'

'I dispute that,' said Tim, thinking of Felicity and if she'd been officially advised of what had happened to him. It was something he hadn't bargained for, falling into the hands of the Hun. Hell's bells, though, would he have been written off as dead? It was obvious he'd been so badly wounded that he'd had to be left. Even now, he felt drained, as if he'd lost most of his blood and none of it had been put back. He eyed this very correct German nurse contrarily. 'I'll wager most of the men and women involved far from their lands in this war would like to go home,' he said.

'We who fight or strive in other ways for our Fuehrer do not think like that,' she said.

'Well, you must like war,' said Tim.

'Don't be impertinent,' she said, 'be grateful that you have been saved from dying. The tablet will ease your pain in a few moments. Be grateful for that too.'

She's a bloody Nazi, thought Tim.

'Thanks, anyway,' he said, and handed back the glass. She took it, gave him a severe look and disappeared.

The ward was comparatively quiet. The German officers sharing it with him all had serious chest or stomach wounds. One spoke, the only one who seemed able to.

'*Wie geht es Ihnen, Herr Lieutenant?*' How are you?

In French, Tim said, 'I've got only a few words in German, how about French?'

In French, the German said, 'I asked how you were.'

'Lousy,' said Tim in English.

'Ah, so? I know lousy.' The German officer, lying flat on his back, was nevertheless not too ill to talk. 'The war, *Anglais*, why don't you give up?'

'We will,' said Tim, 'just as soon as we've handed you a beating.'

The German officer laughed. Well, he made a brave attempt that sounded like a painful gurgle.

'I like good jokes, not bad ones,' he said.

'Same here,' said Tim in English.

'Excuse?'

'I share your liking for good jokes,' said Tim in French.

'I am here because of you, Lieutenant.'

'Is that a joke?' asked Tim.

'Not so. Your attack surprised us. Ah, you swine, your dirty comrades put bullets into me in places I didn't know I had. Now I am full of holes plugged with medical gauze. Where did we hit you?'

'Chest and ribs,' said Tim.

'Are you hurting?'

'All over,' said Tim.

'Good.' The German wheezed into another laugh. 'So am I. In my damned belly. What do you think of the nurse who is turning her nose up at you?'

'What do you think of her?' countered Tim.

'I would like to make love to her, of course.'

'If you could manage that flat on your back and full of plugged holes,' said Tim, the cutting edge of his pain easing, 'I'd be surprised and so would she.'

'Ha-ha, and so would I myself. What did you say to her that made her look sorry for you?'

'That I'd like to go home,' said Tim.

'Ah, a good joke this time.'

'She obviously thought it a bad one,' said Tim. 'I was serious, of course.'

'Of course, but it is still a good joke. Good luck, *Anglais,* and if when we meet again I have to kill you, it won't be because I dislike you.'

'Same here.'

'Excuse?'

'Fortunes of war,' said Tim.

'Silence!' It was a growling command, uttered by the ward sister, Captain Hearst, as she entered. She was a large beefy woman. 'Silence. It is not permitted to talk, but to rest. Silence.' She glared and departed.

'That woman,' said the German officer, 'is the only woman I know who has a bottom like an elephant and sings bass.'

'What's her cooking like?' murmured Tim and drifted pleasurably off into a nap.

'Herr Lieutenant, sit up.'

He came to at the sound of the cool, professional voice. She was standing just beyond the foot of the bed. Beside the bed was an orderly holding a tray that contained his tiffin. Out here in the Western Desert, that was the word for lunch. Tim sat up, slowly. She tut-tutted, came around the bed, embraced his shoulders with one arm and helped him into a sitting position. She exuded an anti-septic aroma.

'Thanks, Mother,' he said.

'That is not amusing. Eat your lunch.'

'What is it?' asked Tim as the orderly placed the tray on his lap.

'Sauerkraut and sausage.'

'Didn't I have that yesterday?' asked Tim.

'Eat it.'

'If I said I'd prefer a salad—'

'Herr Lieutenant, you are a fool.'

'Better than being an iceberg,' muttered Tim.

'What? What?'

'Thanks,' said Tim, 'I'll eat it.'

He was the only patient with a tray on his lap. The German casualties were either forbidden food because of stomach wounds, or, like the talkative one, feeding from the spouts of what looked like teapots and contained liquid food.

The ward seemed hot, despite the whirring ceiling fans and the fact that the outside temperature was moderate at this time of the year. Heat slowed up the knitting of broken bones, and didn't make the sauerkraut and sausage the best kind of lunch as far as Tim was concerned. He thought again of Felicity, his prime reason for regarding a prisoner of war camp as the worst place on earth. To live behind barbed wire out of all personal contact with her for the duration of the conflict was a prospect that made him grind his teeth.

He was in Benghazi, he knew that. The coastal road would take him straight back to Tobruk. How far? Two hundred miles? A hell of a long walk.

'And not in my present state of health,' he muttered.

'What?' She was there again, enquiring and suspicious. 'What is that you say?'

'I might get to like this sausage,' he said.

'It is good German sausage shipped at great risk for the men of our Afrika Korps,' she said.

'Lucky old Afrika Korps,' said Tim.

Anneliese, the twenty-two-year-old daughter of a colonel, a surgeon serving with the German army in Russia, took on a look of impatience. This wounded English officer had an irritatingly misplaced sense of humour.

'You would do well to remember you are a prisoner of the Korps,' she said.

'I'm not in a position to forget it,' said Tim. 'By the way, Nurse Bruck—'

'I am Fraulein Lieutenant Bruck.'

'Well, Fraulein Lieutenant, would you know what happened to my wallet?'

She moved to his bedside locker, opened it, took out his wallet and placed it on his lunch tray. Tim put down his fork and picked up the leather wallet, soft from use. Its spine was damaged.

'Yes, a bullet did that,' she said, 'a bullet that lodged itself close to your heart and which our team of surgeons extracted with great care and skill.'

'I'm truly grateful,' said Tim.

'Good,' she said, and left him alone.

He opened the wallet and knew at once that his captors had poked their noses into it. There wasn't much, some Egyptian dinar notes, Felicity's last letter, and two snapshots, but the items were out of place. He took out the snapshots, both of Felicity, and taken when they were stationed with 4 Commando in Troon. He had used the camera one Sunday when they had ventured out into the countryside, she wearing a civvy skirt and jumper. The jumper looked a treat in the way it defined her figure. She was laughing. Laughter always came easily to her in those days. He felt the pangs of nostalgia. Felicity, so breezy, so outgoing, an ex-captain of her school hockey team, and set perhaps on becoming a games mistress when the war was over. He had felt he ought to save her from that by marrying her. She had laughed at the idea, and told him they were breaking the rules by being out together. Well, he was only a corporal then, she an ATS second lieutenant. But he'd persevered and she had weakened. Then came the frightful moment when, enjoying an evening in the West End while on leave, she was caught in an air raid with her companions. It cost her her sight.

The pangs were acute.

God, somehow he had to effect a change of circumstances, to give himself a chance to avoid ending up in a prisoner of war camp.

His chest felt raw and his stomach was quarrelling with the sausage and sauerkraut.

When Sammy arrived home, Chinese Lady brought Phoebe to him for inspection, Paula trailing behind them. Phoebe was arrayed in a new dress of oyster pink, new white socks and new shoes. Her dark hair shone from brushing.

'Here's our little guest, Sammy,' said Chinese Lady, and Phoebe's dark-lashed eyes glanced up at him in an enquiring way, as if she wasn't sure how he related to her circumstances. Sammy's response was a smile and some encouraging words.

'Well, well,' he said, 'what a pet. I don't know I've ever seen a better-dressed young cherub, or a prettier one.'

'Crikey, don't mind me,' said Paula, but with a giggle.

'No offence, Plum Pudding the Second,' said Sammy. That was his favourite way of addressing his youngest daughter and her lingering traces of puppy fat. 'Phoebe, have you had a nice day?'

'We went to the shops and bought fings for me,' she said.

'So I see,' said Sammy.

'I was very fankful,' she said solemnly. 'Auntie Lily didn't bring any of me clothes when—' She stopped. 'Has she gone away?'

'Well, yes, she has,' said Sammy.

'Mummy and Daddy went away. Has Auntie Lily gone to look for them?'

'Oh, I expect so, lovey,' said Chinese Lady.

'Come and look at my doll's house, come on,' said Paula, sorry for any child who didn't have a mum and dad, and she took Phoebe by the hand.

'Yes, a'right,' said Phoebe, and the little girls disappeared.

'Poor young mite,' said Chinese Lady, not for the first time.

'I suppose she asked her aunt questions about her parents,' said Sammy. 'I wonder what answers she got?'

'I suppose the sort of answers that tried to tell her that her parents wouldn't ever be coming back,' said Chinese Lady. 'Sammy, there's a grave somewhere.'

'Yes, there has to be, somewhere,' said Sammy, 'and I daresay one day Phoebe will find it. Where's Susie?'

'Listening to the wireless and ironing bedsheets that had to be washed,' said Chinese Lady. 'I wish you could do something about that wireless while you're here, Sammy, it spends all its time talking about the Germans and Russians. A nice bit of music would be a change.'

The cantankerous wireless, however, wasn't as unhappy a problem as Phoebe's weakness, which was the kind of thing Chinese Lady, thankfully, had never had to face up to with any of her own children.

Sammy advised Susie of his conversation with Sergeant Burrows, and of the fact that Phoebe had a grandmother in Leigh-on-Sea, and an aunt, uncle and grandfather in Canada. Susie agreed that Canada looked like the best bet for the child, and she hoped something satisfactory could be sorted out fairly soon.

Worryingly for her temporary guardians, little Phoebe wandered forlornly into their bedroom early the next morning to tearfully tell them her bed was wet again. Sammy thought it was hopeful, at least, that she was coming to tell them about her accidents. He and Susie attended to everything again, and by the time breakfast was ready, Phoebe was engaged in little girls' talk with Paula, her worries forgotten for the moment.

Later, Chinese Lady made a tentative suggestion to Susie that perhaps there was something Phoebe could wear at night, like uncontinental people did. She meant incontinent.

'Oh, lor', I don't think she'd accept something like a nappy, Mum, not when she's nearly five,' said Susie. 'It seems to me that she's got an odd little sense of dignity, which makes her weakness all the more unhappy for her.'

'You sure you mean dignity, Susie?' Chinese Lady

was doubtful. 'You don't get dignity till you come of age, till you're adultified, that's my belief. Of course, for young women, it's when their wedding day comes and they've got to enter the church proud and reverent, which can be very dignified. Still, I think you're right, love, best not to try putting a nappy on Phoebe at bedtimes. We'll just have to hope she'll come to be happy while she's here, and not go to bed all worried.'

'Yes, that's what Sammy and me think,' said Susie, 'that if we can make her forget her upsets, she'll be fine by the time relatives offer to have her.'

'Well, we all hope so,' said Chinese Lady.

Chapter Eight

'I don't know that Sammy and Susie ought to be looking after someone else's child,' said Aunt Victoria, mother and mother-in-law respectively of Vi and Tommy Adams. Sixty-three, and with silver an unwelcome intruder in her hair, Aunt Victoria's favourite pastime was finding fault. 'No-one knows nothing – anything – about her parents and if they were respectable or not.'

'Mum, they're dead, and the poor child's an orphan that's just lost the aunt who was looking after her,' said Vi, forty-one and rated by husband Tommy as the best and most equable of the Adams' wives. 'Sammy found her lost and wandering.' That was as much as Vi knew, for Sammy and Susie had told only Chinese Lady and Mr Finch the full story relating to Phoebe, her parents and her aunt.

'Well, I hope she doesn't have headlice, which she could have picked up all too easy wandering the streets down there in Walworth,' said Aunt Victoria.

'Mum, she's a clean little girl,' said Vi. She and Tommy had both called at the house in Red Post Hill to meet the child, and had come away feeling she really did look like a little girl lost. 'I think it's lovely of Susie and Sammy to take her in and look after her until other relatives have been found. Susie said the police are doing their best about that.'

Aunt Victoria shuddered a little at the mention of police. Her governing star was respectability, which meant being able to look her neighbours in the face and be on close terms with the vicar and his wife.

'Well, I will say your dad is admiring of Susie and Sammy's goodwill,' she said. 'Mind, I'm more sensitive myself about fam'ly things, especially about Boots's wife Polly having a baby soon and Rosie letting the fam'ly know she's expecting too. I never heard nothing more embarrassing, a stepmother of Polly's age and her stepdaughter both expecting, and I can't hardly work out what it's going to mean. Well, all I can think of is that Rosie's baby will be Boots's grandchild, and Polly's baby will be – well, I just don't know what.'

Vi smiled.

'A sister or brother to Rosie, and the aunt or uncle of her own baby,' she said.

'I don't know how I'm going to explain that to my neighbours,' said Aunt Victoria, shaking her head.

'Mum, just tell them the fam'ly will be celebrating some new additions,' said Vi.

'It doesn't seem right, celebrating in a war like this,' said Aunt Victoria, 'especially about one baby being the aunt or uncle of the other. Goodness knows what the vicar's wife will say.'

Down in Dorset existed the training ground of an Army corps put together by General Sir Henry

Simms. There, his son-in-law, Colonel Robert Adams, known as Boots, received a letter addressed to himself and his wife Polly.

Dear In-Laws,

I'm sorry to have to tell you I've received one of those wretched telegrams hated by wives and mothers in wartime. Tim's been wounded and taken prisoner. Clara, who's writing this for me, is trying to cheer me up by pointing out the telegram could have had a black border round it. I kick against being cheered up, as I'm entitled to a week or two of feeling rotten ratty about losing my darling Tim for the duration of the war. Perhaps you know more about these things than I do, so I'm asking if you can confirm my belief that Tim will be allowed to write to me from his prison camp, and to receive letters from me.

And perhaps you'd like to know that my rehabilitation has reached the stage that will enable me to be discharged in a month or so, but that's hardly a consolation at this particular moment.

Love from Felicity.

Boots and Polly, shaken by the news, nevertheless concocted and sent an immediate reply.

Dear Felicity,

Your news didn't make us very happy ourselves, but Clara's right in effect, the family might have lost Tim completely in the action. As it is, the regular German Army abides by the Geneva Convention and will keep him hospitalized until he's recovered from his wound. We realize news of his capture will be a blow to everyone concerned, but yours is the greater upset, and we send you our sympathy and offer you all the support you may need.

Yes, Tim will be able to write to you, although only a few words on a postcard, and you can write to him through the War Office. Such letters from home will be handled by the International Red Cross although liable to censorship by the German authorities, but we're sure you'll want to write. On a postcard, Tim will be able to let you know of his recovery.

We imagine that on your discharge you'll go home to your parents. Should you feel in need of a change from time to time, we have four bedrooms here, and one will always be waiting to welcome you for a short or long stay, just as you like. We don't have to emphasize how delighted we'd be to have you. I can drive up to collect you, preferably on a Sunday, and preferably, of course, after Polly has had her baby. As we mentioned when we last wrote to you, we have a girl, Kate Trimble, resident, and she'll be on hand to give you the kind of help you'll obviously need if you're not to bump into the furniture.

Our love and very best wishes to you, we're thinking of both you and Tim.

Sincerely, Robert and Polly Adams.

Clara read this reply to Felicity in a cosy corner of the recreation room, the weather outside being close to a howling gale, the sky a fury of dark heaving clouds.

'There, does that letter help a little, Felicity?'

'Yes, and thanks for reading it in your motherly voice, which prompts me to ask if you're thinking of embracing marriage and motherhood some time?'

'I've been thinking of it for a fortnight, ever since Dr Railton began to give me come-on signs.'

'Dr Railton? Our psychology professor? What's he like to look at?'

'Dark and satanic, but then I like devilish men.'

'Has he been devilish to you, Clara?'

'Believe me, dear one, like all men of his kind, he's got six pairs of hands and no respect for my uniform.'

'He doesn't sound like a man who'll propose marriage.'

'He's not going to get me into bed unless he does,' said Clara. 'What d'you think of your in-laws' offer to have you as a guest?'

'Love it,' said Felicity, 'but yes, I'll naturally wait until Polly's had her baby and is into a routine. I don't want to be around during the very first nappy stages. Listen, when you kneel at your bedside tonight to recite the Lord's Prayer, say one for Tim.'

'That's how you picture me at night, do you, kneeling at my bedside?' said Clara.

'What else, you angel?' said Felicity, who was doing her best to hide just how badly she felt about Tim being in the hands of the Germans.

She had given the news not only to Polly and Boots, but to Tim's grandparents, Chinese Lady and Mr Finch. She'd received a very sympathetic reply, written by Mr Finch in just the right kind of words. That and the reply from Polly and Boots brought forth a feeling that she had acquired a very supportive family, although she was not inclined to favour the kind of close family relationships that could be smothering.

Polly could have told her that the Adams family would take her to their bosom irrespective of her inclinations.

Boots transmitted to Rosie, his adopted daughter, the news that Tim was now a prisoner of war. It was on a day when Rosie, an ATS captain, had had to convey to her commanding officer, Major Henrietta Robbins, the fact that she was having to apply for her discharge on the grounds that she was pregnant. Major Robbins, hearty, horsy and blunt, was hardly overjoyed.

'Damn it, Rosie, damned bad show. What was that husband of yours thinking about, the idiot?'

'I suppose he was thinking he'd like to be a father,' said Rosie.

'Not the time to be thinking like that,' said Major Robbins. 'Couldn't he have waited until the war was over?'

'I have to confess, ma'am,' said Rosie tongue-in-cheek, 'our thinking coincided.'

'Don't like the sound of that,' said Major Robbins. 'Good mind to put you on a charge for behaviour detrimental to the ATS war effort. I mean, where the hell am I going to get a replacement I can rely on as much as I rely on you? Look here, tell you what, if you'll keep quiet about this for the time being, so will I. Leave your application for a discharge for a month or so until I can fasten on to a suitable replacement. What d'you say, eh?'

'Very well, ma'am,' said Rosie.

'Good man,' said Major Robbins with hearty relief.

It was during the evening of that day when Rosie,

relaxing at home in the cottage near Bere Regis, received a phone call from Boots, her adoptive father, that told her Tim was a prisoner of war. It upset her very much. She and Tim, as brother and sister, had always been close, always supportive of each other, and her deep affection for him increased when he married Felicity, a tragically blinded young woman. She could understand all too well how traumatic captivity would be to him, and to Felicity too. Tim would suffer prolonged frustration and Felicity would endure the bitterness of a young wife already cruelly savaged by fate.

She wrote to her.

Dear Felicity,

As Tim's elder sister, I wrote to you after your wedding to him to welcome you into the family. I haven't so far had the pleasure of meeting you, but have heard a great deal about you from Tim and my father, and also from my sister Eloise when she was stationed in Troon.

I want you to know how very sorry I am that Tim is now a prisoner of war, and I'm certain everyone in the family sympathizes with you. I feel for you, believe me. I understand from my father that your convalescence may come to an end in a month or so. I hope the family will then have a chance to get to know you. I myself would very much like to meet the wife of my brother.

Love and sincerest sympathy from your sister-in-law, Rosie.

When Clara read this letter to her, Felicity felt touched. Polly could have told her it was one more sign of the Adams family taking her to its bosom. She would, however, have added a rider to the effect that friendship with Rosie could be a treasured thing.

Felicity, through her incomparable medium, Clara, wrote an immediate reply to Rosie.

> *Dear Rosie,*
>
> *Thank you so much for your letter, it lifted my spirits, although you'll understand I've still got gritted teeth about Tim. Your brother has been my lifeline ever since that lousy German bomb cut my eyes to pieces, and it's frankly painful thinking of him in a prisoner of war camp. I'm counting the days until I hear from him, even if it's only a few words on a prisoner's postcard. And I'm hoping he'll do what I think you and I and all his family know he's capable of, escaping from German barbed wire.*
>
> *One day I'm sure I'll have the pleasure of meeting you. Tim has only ever spoken of you in most loving terms. I'm beginning to think that all of his family are worth meeting.*
>
> *Very sincerely, Felicity.*

Felicity was being drawn into the Adams' net.

Polly had not long to go now, just a matter of a few weeks according to the doctor in Corfe Castle village. She was resigned to the astonishing news, confirmed by a Dulwich gynaecologist, that she was going to have twins. What she objected to, was looking as if she'd managed to swallow a barrage balloon. Do you realize, she said to Boots, that before the day of happening arrives, I'll be too big for this cottage, that I won't be able to get in or out of its doors? Tricky, said Boots, now adjutant to her father, General Sir Henry Simms. Tricky, said Polly, tricky? That, she said, is the kind of masterly understatement of which only you are capable of uttering. Considering that you alone did this to me, you should ask to be shot full of burning arrows. But oh no, not you, you old smoothie, you go about looking as if you've earned a halo. If I get one, said Boots, I'll keep it under my hat. Oh, very funny, said Polly, but do you like me looking like a baby elephant? I've got a very soft spot for baby elephants, said Boots. Polly laughed.

'Next thing I know, you'll be giving me a bun,' she said.

'A bun?' said Boots. 'But I've already given you two. Or d'you want to rephrase that?'

'I want to kick myself for giving you the chance to make the most frightful joke of your life,' said Polly.

Their daily dialogues were a little more sober now, and had been since receiving the depressing news about Tim. However, much better news, uplifting to the whole country, followed when, during the third week in November, General Auchinleck forestalled Rommel's intended attack by launching the British Eighth Army at the Afrika Korps in an attempt to retake Libya. The Germans fell back under the weight and impetus of the assault. That, together with growing Russian resistance to Hitler's armies of the East, gave the country reason to feel more optimistic about the outcome of the war.

Polly still liked to be active, but found that in carrying so much weight about she needed a little rest in the afternoons. Their resident guest, Kate Trimble, was always happy to keep her company. Polly and Boots had taken the sixteen-year-old girl in after a call for help from Tommy and Vi's elder son David. David, an evacuee, had befriended Kate in a positive way while she was living in a Devonshire village with her aunt, having lost her parents in a bombing raid. Unfortunately, like little Phoebe, she too suddenly lost her aunt, although not by reason of suicide. In fact, by reason of being arrested for an act of sabotage, and proving to be working for Germany. Boots and Polly did not hesitate to give Kate a home and care, as well as protecting her from any officious busybody who might suggest an orphanage was the best place for her. The lively girl did not need any persuasion from Boots to become a helpful companion to Polly during the long hours he put in on his staff work. There was one slightly disturbing note: Kate had the same kind of dark auburn hair and green eyes as Emily, Boots's late first wife.

However, engaging and perky, hailing from Camberwell, Kate proved a treasure in her willingness to be useful and in her gratitude for being given a home by two people she found fascinating. She wondered what her late dad, a good old cockney and a trade unionist, would have said about her landing up under the roof of a woman obviously upper class and a man who was all of educated and distinguished. She hoped her dad was resting in peace alongside her mum, and not having a fit. She wanted him to know she was happy, and she wanted her late mum to know that too. But supposing later on Colonel Adams's nephew David, her best friend, fell in love with her? He was already very middle class. Oh, well, her dad, if he was resting in peace, might only turn once or twice in his grave.

Meanwhile, she excelled in the kitchen of her new guardians, having taken that over from the batman, Lance-Corporal Higgins, presently hobbling around on crutches consequent on breaking a leg. Yes, if it wasn't for this blessed war, she'd be even happier. There was some awful fighting going on in Russia and the Middle East, and the German bombers still kept mounting air raids over Britain. Everything just went on and on, and before she and David knew it they'd be old enough to go into uniform for King and country. If David went into the RAF, she'd join the WAAF.

Sammy and Susie, living with Chinese Lady and Mr Finch, felt they should look for a new home and avoid outstaying their welcome. Chinese Lady wouldn't hear of it, insisting she liked having them, that the big house was for a family, that it didn't like itself when only she and Edwin were there. Houses that become family homes, she said, have got their own kind of souls, and when they're empty or nearly empty they make grumbling noises that echo. Don't go looking for somewhere else, she said, wait till a furnished house comes on the market, a place in Denmark Hill, or wait till after the war. Mind, if you're not comfy here, well, she said, that's different.

Sammy and Susie, who knew she did indeed like having them around, assured her they couldn't be more comfy. They had made good some of their losses, having bought new clothes and replacements of all other personal items, and Paula had been fully fitted up with everything she needed, including dolls and teddies that were a must to her. They had lost every stick of furniture, but didn't need any new stuff until they'd acquired a new home. Susie said there was no point in buying anything until that happened. You bought a house first, and then the kind of furniture that suited it. Susie love, said Sammy, I do happen to know that. Oh, good, said Susie, it's nice you're not just a pretty face, Sammy dear.

'It's news to me that I've got that kind of a face,' said Sammy, 'and I don't know that I want one like it, either.'

'Oh, well,' said Susie, 'grin and bear it, Sammy love.'

In Eloise's bedroom, little Phoebe slept and dreamed.

Sammy and Susie had their ongoing problem with the young girl. She continued to wet her bed. Not every night, no, but all too regularly, and each time it made a tearful and forlorn child of her, a child who, in her sadness, would suddenly ask, 'Why did my mummy and daddy go away?'

Sammy and Susie could only tell her that one day they'd try to find out.

'Yes, a'right,' Phoebe would say.

However, Mr Finch thought she was at least coming to feel secure, due to having faces now familiar close by, and to living in the homely atmosphere created naturally by his resilient, old-fashioned wife, and often marked by amusing little flurries of fussiness. Also, Paula made a friend of the orphan girl, so much so that occasionally a little laugh or a giggle was heard from Phoebe. But there it was, she still had regular accidents in bed. Sammy thought it encouraging that it wasn't every night. Susie said she was beginning to think it was all to do with the child having no parents and wondering why they had gone away and left her.

'You could be right, Susie,' said Sammy, 'except at her age I'd have thought she wouldn't keep things like that in her memory. Little kids just don't have much of a memory, do they?'

'I think Phoebe has,' said Susie. 'We do have a problem, Sammy, and we've simply got to do our best to solve it.'

'On top of which,' said Sammy soberly, 'there's this family worry about what's actu'lly happening to Tim, and do we do anything about Felicity or for her?'

'Apart from her parents,' said Susie, 'Boots and Polly are now her closest relatives, and if I know Boots he'll ask if he wants any of us to go and visit her.'

'D'you realize we've never met her?' said Sammy. 'She's our niece by marriage, and we haven't set eyes on her yet.'

'We will one day, Sammy,' said Susie, 'she's one of the family.'

Chapter Nine

Sammy received a personal phone call at his office one morning. Sergeant Burrows was on the line.

'Morning, Mr Adams, how's yourself?'

'Well, I like what's happening in the Middle East,' said Sammy. The Eighth Army had driven deep into Libya and reached besieged Tobruk to link up with its defenders and raise the siege. German and Italian forces were still falling back, the British advance continuing despite heavy fighting.

'And have you noticed the Russians have retaken some of their captured towns?' said Sergeant Burrows.

'I like that too,' said Sammy, 'but I don't think you've phoned me to talk about what's coming out of my dear old Ma's wireless set.'

'No, just to let you know our colleagues in Bow traced Phoebe's widowed grandmother, the one living in Leigh-on-Sea. Unfortunate, like, she's got chronic arthritis, Mr Adams, and can't have the little girl. But she'd always be pleased to hear about her, and to have her visit occasional.'

'I see,' said Sammy. 'Poor old lady. Could

someone tell her damp sea air can't be doing her arthritis much good?'

'It can't, and that's a fact,' said Sergeant Burrows.

'If you'll give me her address,' said Sammy, 'I'll write to her about how Phoebe's doing.'

'I'll get it and let you have it,' said Sergeant Burrows. 'Regarding her other relatives, them that's in Canada, they've been traced as well, from letters found in Mrs Fellowes' house, and they've been notified about Phoebe's circumstances. I'll let you know what their answer is when it reaches Bow. It won't be tomorrow, of course, not from Canada.'

'No hurry,' said Sammy, 'we're happy to look after the infant for the time being.'

'It still seems her one chance is a new life in Canada,' said Sergeant Burrows.

'Well, if it comes off,' said Sammy, 'I hope to God she doesn't get torpedoed on the way there.'

'Is that a serious remark, Mr Adams?'

'Yes, Jack, it is,' said Sammy. 'That little girl has had all the bad luck going, and whoever dishes it out could just have a final body blow lined up for her.'

'See what you mean,' said Sergeant Burrows. 'By the way, the inquest on Mrs Fellowes is tomorrow, ten in the morning. I believe the coroner would like you and Mrs Adams to be there, seeing you're the temp'ry guardians of the unfortunate lady's little niece.'

'Yes, we've been officially informed,' said Sammy.

'Right. Good luck, Mr Adams.'

'We all need some,' said Sammy. 'It's a lousy war.'

*   *   *

The German officer, still flat on his back, along with others badly wounded, stirred and looked up at a whirring fan before turning his head to eye the British officer, who lay in the bed closest to the door and was accordingly usually the first to be surveyed by the nurse or the sister entering the ward.

'How are you today, *Anglais*?' he asked in French.

Tim, propped on heaped pillows and looking drawn but not critical, said, also in French, 'Fine, and how are you, Hansel?'

'Rolfe. Rolfe Schaeffer. Captain.'

'I'm Tim Adams. First Lieutenant.'

'Happy to know you, you swine,' said Captain Schaeffer. 'I hope to have the opportunity of blowing your head off.'

'Who needs enemies with friends like you?' said Tim.

'Bad jokes, good jokes, old jokes, you speak them all,' said the German, dark-haired, and gaunt from the draining severity of his wounds.

'I like to be popular,' said Tim.

'With jokes like that?' Captain Schaeffer issued a wheezing laugh. 'What do you think of your warmonger, Churchill?'

'Makes good speeches without shouting,' said Tim.

'A fat man, I think.'

'Chubby,' said Tim.

'Now you'd like to ask me about Hitler?'

'No, I know about Hitler,' said Tim. 'Everybody knows about Hitler. Will it offend you if I say God was good to me in making sure I wasn't born next door to him?'

'Ah, a good joke this time.' Captain Schaeffer attempted another laugh, but winced instead. 'Damn my plugged wounds. I was lucky they weren't lower or I'd have spilled my guts. You see what I owe you, Lieutenant?'

'I'm under the doctor too,' said Tim.

'Silence!' Captain Hearst, the beefy sister, bawled her way into the ward, accompanied by two doctors, Lieutenant Anneliese Bruck following on. They walked straight past Tim to reach the stomach cases. Screens went up around one bed. Tim heard the murmur of voices. He knew stomach cases were critical, and that Captain Schaeffer, although undaunted in spirit, had to be included among the critical. In turn, the screens went up around each of the relevant beds, and the examinations of the wounds and diagnoses of condition were all conducted in murmurs. Captain Schaeffer was the last to be examined and the first to arouse more than a murmur. In fact, he aroused a laugh in the doctors, and that earned him what Tim thought was an obvious scolding from the ward sister.

The screens having been put away, the medical team headed for the door, passing Tim again without a word or a glance.

'What about me, don't I even get a goodbye kiss?' he said, as the doctors and nurses exited. A whisk of cotton drill brought Lieutenant Bruck back. She regarded him in her clinically neutral way.

'You are saying?' she said.

'I'm in trouble,' said Tim.

'If you are going to speak something stupid, I advise you not to.'

'I'd like a bottle,' said Tim. 'Could you be an angel?'

113

She gave him a searching look. Tim tried a smile. She frowned, left the ward and called an orderly. Only the orderlies supplied and emptied bottles and bedpans.

In the bloke came with a bottle. He had a cropped head and wore a hospital apron. He handed Tim the bottle with a quite friendly word, then disappeared. Tim made just as friendly use of the bottle, while Captain Schaeffer lay as if exhausted by the examination. The other cases all seemed sedated.

After thirty minutes, Anneliese Bruck returned, shaking a thermometer.

'Temperature,' she said, and stuck the thermometer under Tim's tongue, which kept him quiet. She waited while she took his pulse. Out came the thermometer and she read it. 'Why is it up?' she said. 'It should not be. Have you been attempting to get out of bed?'

'No,' said Tim, 'I've been attempting to remove this bottle without spilling it, and it's still between my legs. As to my condition, when do I get a new chest and a new set of ribs?'

For a moment he thought the ice maiden was going to crack, he thought he detected a twitch. But she didn't crack. Her expression became severe.

'You are ridiculous,' she said, and took herself and the thermometer away. A minute later, the orderly reappeared. With a grin on his face, he relieved Tim of the bottle.

'*Gut*,' he said, still grinning, and went away. Back came the Aryan nurse with a glass of water and some tablets.

'Take these,' she said.

'I recognize them, they're salt tablets,' said Tim.

'Swallow them with this water,' she said, 'they will lower your temperature.'

Tim popped them into his mouth and washed them down with all the water in the glass.

'Thanks,' he said. 'Any news?' he asked.

'News?' she said, taking back the glass.

'Yes, d'you know what's happening?' he asked. He was aware that up to the time of his capture the men of the Eighth Army were wondering who was going to be ready to attack first, Auchinleck or Rommel. Tim felt that by now one or the other would have made his move, and that, irrespective of which, the British Long Range Desert Group would be attempting to destroy some of Rommel's fuel supply dumps. He himself had been scheduled to take part in that.

'There is no news I have to give you,' said Lieutenant Bruck, and turned to leave.

'Fraulein Lieutenant?' Supine Captain Schaeffer was quietly requesting her attention. She advanced to his bedside, and he spoke in a murmur to her. She responded with murmurous words of her own, leaning a little. Then she left the ward, giving Tim a glance on the way.

'Hope to see more of you,' he said.

'You will,' she said, disappearing.

'I have little English,' said Captain Schaeffer. 'What is it you say to Lieutenant Bruck that makes her so stiff?'

'Just a few friendly words,' said Tim.

'She's cross with the British for being foolish enough to go to war with us. Yes, it was foolish, for Hitler would have made a pact of friendship with you to put Greater Germany and the British Empire together. Who could have stood against such a combination?'

'I don't think Churchill likes Hitler enough to have him for an ally,' said Tim.

'Ah, well, it's too late now,' said Captain Schaeffer, sounding tired. 'However, I will tell you something, since I think you asked the goddess for news. I understood that word. So I asked her myself, and she has informed me that your army has attacked General Rommel and he's falling back. But it will be only to re-group, you will see.'

'All the same, we beat him to the punch,' said Tim.

'It will do you no good, *Anglais*,' murmured Captain Schaeffer and drifted into sleep. In other beds, the badly wounded Germans lay like logs, and from some issued little dribbling sighs.

Tim wondered when his own condition would improve and rid him of a feeling of debilitating damage. He had his mind fixed on the walk of escape to Tobruk. Once there, he would have to slip through the lines of besieging Germans. He fancied his chances at night because of the protracted night manoeuvres he had engaged in with Commandos and the SAS. If he had known Tobruk had been relieved, he would have fancied his chances even more.

In the desert, the British and Imperial forces of the Eighth Army were driving on.

There had been three air raids on London since Susie and Sammy had taken Phoebe to live with them, and on each occasion she had shown no great fright when lifted out of bed and carried to the garden shelter, warmly wrapped up. And there, like Paula, she had lapsed back into sleep despite the noise of the night bombers. Strangely, she did not have accidents on those nights.

She was beginning to have childish trust in Susie and Sammy, and careful though they were not to show too much affection, there had been times when they gave her compulsive little hugs of re-assurance.

The inquest into the death of Mrs Lily Fellowes took place before an understanding coroner. Friends and neighbours of the unfortunate woman testified to the fact that during the past twelve months she had shown signs of mounting worry and moments of vagueness, although never at any time had she mentioned suicide, and nor had she shown any neglect of her little niece. She had cared for her day in, day out. Everyone knew, of course, said one witness, what a dreadful blow it had been to her, the murder of her sister and brother-in-law in 1939, and how that had been followed only fifteen months later by the death of her husband in an air raid, which was not only another dreadful blow but left her in very reduced circumstances.

Supplementary testimony was offered by witnesses who had known the sister and brother-in-law. They spoke of them as a couple devoted to each other and their child Phoebe. No parents could have been more loving. And so on. Everything pointed to the possibility that the murder of such an admirable couple, followed by the death of her husband, could have affected the mental stability of Mrs Fellowes even more than was evident. The coroner touched on that aspect, suggesting that to have left her young niece outside a police station on the day of her suicide implied only that the state of Mrs Fellowes' mind was questionable, not the affection and care she gave the orphaned child.

Eventually, all statements taken, he referred to certain notes, then lifted his head and spoke.

'I believe the child, Phoebe Willis, is at present in the care of a Mr and Mrs Adams. Are they in court?'

Sammy and Susie both stood up.

'We're here, sir,' said Sammy.

The coroner regarded them. He saw a tall and exceedingly pleasant-looking man of visible self-confidence, and a well-dressed woman of quite charming appearance.

'Thank you, Mr Adams,' said the coroner. 'I understand that you and Mrs Adams are willing to care for the child until relatives in Canada offer to take her.'

'We're very happy to have her,' said Susie.

The coroner glanced again at notes that contained a glowing reference from the Walworth police station in respect of the suitability of Mr and Mrs S. Adams as temporary guardians.

'If that is so, Mrs Adams, then I need make no recommendations regarding the present welfare of the child,' he said. 'I feel that is in excellent hands, and I hope this will be the case with her long-term welfare. Thank you both.'

He closed by announcing his verdict. Suicide while of unsound mind.

*   *   *

On their way home, Sammy and Susie called in at the Walworth police station in Rodney Road. Sergeant Burrows, an enduring stalwart of law and order, expressed profuse pleasure at seeing Susie, whose family he had known during the years when they lived in Brandon Street, close to the East Street market.

'And if I might say so, Mrs Adams, you look like you've been growing younger, which I'm not meself, what with old age just round the corner.'

'I don't believe that,' smiled Susie, 'not in a man still as vigorous as you, Sergeant. We've called, by the way, to let you know we're back from the inquest.'

'Verdict, might I ask?'

'Unsound of mind, poor woman,' said Sammy with feeling.

Out to the desk came WPC Elizabeth Rivers, a sturdy female arm of the law with a deceptively jolly smile when in confrontation with a crook.

'Gotcher, Fred me lad,' she'd say cheerfully.

'Fair cop,' the apprehended one would say, 'but I ain't feeling as 'appy about it as you are.'

'Sorry about that, Fred,' she'd say, 'and Mrs Fred won't be too pleased, either. Oh, well, can't be helped. Would you like to come along with me and Constable Johnson?'

'No, I bleedin' wouldn't, but I'll 'ave to, I suppose.'

'It's what comes of being naughty,' she'd say.

She was happy to meet Sammy and Susie, Sammy particularly. She took one look into his electric blue eyes and her uniform rippled as she quivered.

She and Sergeant Burrows listened as Sammy and Susie, in sober vein, gave their account of the inquest.

'Finally,' said Sammy, very sober, 'just before the coroner gave his verdict, he asked if we were present.'

'So we stood up and heard him thanking us for looking after Phoebe,' said Susie quietly, as if that amounted to very little against the tragic nature of the inquest.

'And he agreed we should keep her until her Canadian relatives ask to have her,' said Sammy. 'We're only too willing, so we thought we'd drop in and let you know that.'

'That's all right, isn't it, Sergeant?' said Susie, very fetching in a winter coat with a fur collar, and a matching hat.

'It certainly is, Mrs Adams, and I'm frankly pleasured you'll continue to have the little girl,' said Sergeant Burrows.

'You need to know that, don't you?' said Sammy.

'So we do, Mr Adams, the incident of one orphaned child found lost in this parish being recorded,' said Sergeant Burrows.

'Our official interest remains,' said WPC Rivers, dreaming of being an orphan herself and in the care of Sammy Adams while his wife went off to join a five-year expedition to the North Pole. It was the kind of dream she'd never thought to have as a conscientious policewoman and a law-abiding woman. 'Sergeant,' she said, 'I suppose we have a certain responsibility here, which I'll be happy to take on by making periodical calls on Mr and Mrs Adams and the child. Without, of course,' she added, 'implying for one moment that super-vision is necessary. It would be just a formality, and I'd be willing to make the calls during my off-duty hours.'

'Oh, I know Mr and Mrs Adams too well to rec-ommend them kind of formalities,' said Sergeant Burrows. 'I'd say that if one or two hiccups cropped up, they'd let us know.'

'Of course,' smiled Susie.

'That goes without saying,' said Sammy.

WPC Rivers sighed.

'What's up with you?' asked Sergeant Burrows after Sammy and Susie had left.

'Well, I'll be frank,' said the lady constable, 'if Mr Adams calls again and lets you know in advance, tip me the wink and I'll wear something like the last of the seven veils instead of my uniform. What a lovely bloke, I could eat him.'

'Constable Rivers, have you got unlawful adultery on your mind?' asked Sergeant Burrows.

'Not half,' said the lady copper. 'Well, no-one's perfect, and there's a war on.'

'Sammy,' said Susie, as they motored home, 'I think that policewoman took a fancy to you.'

'A fancy to me?' said Sammy, driving through a wintry drizzle that was dampening newspaper plac-ards boldly proclaiming the continuing advance of the Eighth Army in Libya. 'What gave you that idea?'

'She sagged when you said hello to her.'

'Sagged?' said Sammy.

'Yes. It meant your smile turned her all weak.'

'Never heard of a female policeman sagging,'

said Sammy. 'Don't they all wear reinforced corsets and chain-mail knickers?'

'Sammy, your imagination's gone all feverish,' said Susie, smile hovering.

'Well, I ask you, Susie, a sagging female policeman?' said Sammy. 'It ain't allowed in the Force.'

Susie laughed.

'Sammy, it's a filthy day, the war's going to go on and on, Tim's a prisoner of war, and our little Phoebe still suffers tearful moments in her bed, poor darling, but I'll tell you something.'

'What's that, Susie?'

'That I still like being married to you, Sammy, and I'll chop that policewoman's head off before she can get even one foot inside our front door.'

'Got you, Susie,' said Sammy. He dropped her off at home. He didn't go in, he drove to his offices. Susie thought it was because he wanted to avoid coming into contact with Phoebe while he was still reflecting on what it meant to him to have her around indefinitely. He knew and Susie knew that if her Canadian relatives did decide to have her, a sea passage to Canada would take time to arrange. Only the most urgent cases were taken aboard ships as passengers. The delay could last several months.

That could be fatal to my own emotions, thought Susie. I wonder what Boots would advise? According to everything I've heard, he went through this kind of thing with Rosie. No, I won't talk to him. Sammy and me have got to work it all out ourselves.

She entered the house, and out into the hall came Phoebe and Chinese Lady.

'Oh, there you are, Susie,' said Chinese Lady. 'Phoebe's been asking when you'd be back.'

'Well, here I am, lovey,' said Susie.

'Please,' said Phoebe, gazing hopefully up at her, ''ave you been looking for my mummy and daddy?'

Oh, Lord, thought Susie, what answer can I give to that?

'I will one day, Phoebe, one day,' she said.

'A'right,' said Phoebe, and a little sigh followed.

Chapter Ten

Two weeks now, Dr Coburn had said. He was the
GP in Corfe Castle village, and keeping a practised
eye on Polly.

Thank God, thought Polly, I can just about last
out for two weeks. I ought to be decorated and
wrapped in my country's flag for lasting this long.
No, two flags, one wouldn't be enough for my size.
I've always enjoyed being slim, but nicely figured
where I should be, and look at me now. This is what
has come from being potty about Boots and letting
him prove what a precocious bandit he is in bed,
the adorable pillager.

It was afternoon, with rain lashing the county of
Dorset, and she was relaxing on the living-room
sofa, with Kate offering to read a story she had
recently put together. Kate had a fertile imagination which she used to produce melodramatic
fiction relating to the war.

'Is the story of the kind I believe you used to read
to David when you were living with your aunt in
Devon?' smiled Polly, happy to get her weight off
her feet.

'Yes, and they always made his eyes pop out,' said

Kate. 'This one's about me being in the Secret Service and trackin' down a dangerous German spy. Would you like me to read it?'

'Go ahead, dear girl, let's have the works,' said Polly.

Kate began reading from an exercise book.

'"How I Captured the Dangerous German Spy, Baron von Heinkel, by Kate Trimble of the Secret Service. It was dark midnight when our famous war leader said goodbye to me on the steps of 'is country castle with a shake of his hand and a low bow and I departed on me mission to unmask Baron von Heinkel that had been sent to England by Hitler in order to blow up the Houses of Parliament, the Tower of London and Buckingham Palace and our beloved King and Queen as well. I'd found out that the Baron was going to attend a ball in a famous country mansion tomorrow evening although no-one would know who he was or what name he was using and no-one knew either what he looked like as he was what's call anonymous, but I 'ad a plan that I hoped would expose—"'

Polly interrupted with a gasp and a cry.

'Oh, my God!'

'Mrs Adams – Aunt Polly – oh, what's up?' Kate was startled.

'Kate – phone the doctor, the district nurse – Kate, quickly!'

Polly was in labour, two weeks early.

Kate proved a godsend, which subsequently made Polly think shades of Emily had been hovering. Emily, she knew, had been the family's godsend in the old days.

Summoned by Kate's urgent phone calls, the village doctor and district nurse together dealt with the crisis in a fashion expressive of rural experience, the kind that seemed to indicate there was no crisis at all, even though by the time an ambulance arrived from Wareham Hospital, Polly was too far into labour to be moved.

Kate also phoned Corps headquarters in an attempt to summon Boots, but he was out with Sir Henry, observing manoeuvres. However, a despatch rider was sent to contact him, and Sir Henry at once gave him permission to make a dash for home.

He arrived an hour before Polly was eventually delivered of her twins, a boy and a girl. If it had felt a strenuous and protracted labour for her, there was nothing wrong with the birth or with the infants.

'Ye gods,' she breathed faintly, when given sight of the babes, washed and swaddled, 'how did I manage little Red Indians? Where's Geronimo, my husband?'

Boots, allowed into the bedroom then, took a long look at the red crinkly faces and bubbly mouths of the newly born infants in the cradling arms of the district nurse. He smiled, tickled their swaddling clothes, then gazed down at Polly, weak but triumphant beneath the bedclothes.

'Hello, wonder woman,' he said, and bent low. He kissed her flushed brow. 'Proud of you, you darling.'

Polly smiled faintly.

'I think I've lost weight,' she murmured. The babes began to bawl. 'Saints and martyrs, I know what that means,' she said.

Boots had a word with Kate later, after a proud and happy grandfather in the shape of Sir Henry Simms had come and gone.

'Kate, many many thanks, I'm delighted you were here, and I'm delighted you kept your head. You were splendid.'

'Oh, I was only too pleased to help,' said Kate, and again her dark auburn hair and green eyes reminded him of Emily. Polly sometimes felt Emily had found a way to come back and haunt her. Only the fact that there was a perky openness about Kate kept that feeling from taking a permanent hold. 'Twins, would you believe, Uncle Boots, twins.' Kate had fallen easily into the habit of calling him uncle. She thought him a very attractive man with his air of whimsical good humour and his distinguished looks, and her feelings for him sometimes bordered on infatuation, although images of his extrovert nephew David were nearly always hovering in the back of her mind. 'I expect you 'ardly know what's hit you,' she said.

'Oh, I know, Kate,' smiled Boots. 'A little in advance, but let's say, shall we, that the infants decided to arrive early to save my wife carrying all that weight any longer. I call that considerate of them.'

'Oh, I couldn't not agree, especially the way you put it,' said Kate. 'Uncle Boots, has it made up a bit for your son being a prisoner of war?'

'Well, at least we know from the International Red Cross that the regular German Army treats prisoners of war correctly,' said Boots. He knew the War Office had its suspicions about the attitude of Himmler's indoctrinated troops of the Waffen-ss towards prisoners. He also knew the War Office was following up rumours that a company of the Waffen-ss had massacred a number of captured British soldiers subsequent to one of the battles that marked the fighting retreat to Dunkirk. 'And if I know Tim, he'll do his best to engineer an escape from his camp along with other officers who won't resign themselves to a long captivity.'

'Oh, let's hope so,' said Kate. 'What names you goin' to give the twins?'

'I'm letting Polly have that privilege,' said Boots. 'Incidentally, because you've been such a help and an asset since you've been here, she'd like to know if you'd care to be a godmother. Would you?'

'Not half, I'd love that,' said Kate. 'It'll be an honour that I'd carry with me all me life.'

'What's the time?' asked Boots.

'It's gone eleven,' said Kate, 'and no-one's 'ad any real supper, just some sandwiches. Still, who cares now there's twins?'

'Well, I'm going to have a whisky, and you can have a sherry,' said Boots, 'and perhaps you'd ask my wife and the district nurse if they'd like some – yes, some what, under the circumstances?'

'Uncle Boots, I don't think you could give Mrs Adams ruinous drink,' said Kate, 'and I expect she's asleep, anyway. But if the district nurse is awake, I'll ask 'er if she'd like a nice pot of hot tea.'

'Spoken like my mother,' smiled Boots.

'Well, it's nice the district nurse is staying the night,' said Kate.

'All women are invaluable,' said Boots. 'And so are you, Kate, you're a godsend.'

Kate went warm with pleasure.

*   *   *

The following morning the news of the birth travelled to the family by way of the established medium, Chinese Lady. Boots had a long chat with her on the phone, and spoke to Susie too. Although it took Chinese Lady's mind off worrying about Tim, she wasn't sure if the event wasn't another kind of shock.

'Susie, it's a wonder I'm not all of a tremble,' she said after the phone conversations. 'Polly at her age having twins and two weeks early, I can't hardly believe it. No-one told me she was expecting twins, but I suppose I'm glad they didn't, as I'd of done a lot of worrying for her if they had. I must say I've always been admiring of Polly, even if she does talk upper class, but that son of mine, you'd of thought from his talk that women over forty have twins every day.'

'Every day, Mum?' said Susie.

'You know what I mean, Susie. What was I saying? Yes, about Boots. He talked like a circus had come to town, which made me think that's where he'll end up one day, in a circus. And when I asked him how Polly was, he said she was still in bed but eating a good breakfast, and that the twins had had theirs and were burping like one-year-olds. Imagine him being that airy-fairy when Polly didn't even get to hospital. It was all so sudden she couldn't be moved except up to her bed. Thank goodness the district nurse is coming in every day to see to her and to help with the babies.'

'I'm sure Boots will see Polly's well looked after,' said Susie. 'I thought he sounded over the moon about her and the twins, not airy-fairy, and that it's lifted him a lot after the news about Tim. I think he's really tickled at being a father again.'

'Well, I'll admit he sounded proud of Polly,' said Chinese Lady. 'He spoke some very compliment'ry things about her, and about the girl who's living with them. Of course, he's always liked being a father.'

'He's always liked children,' said Susie, and turned as Phoebe, who had been watching and listening, plucked at her sleeve. 'Phoebe?'

'Please,' said Phoebe, 'the man's not my daddy, is he?'

Susie winced. Such moments, demonstrating as they did Phoebe's longing for her lost parents, affected her deeply.

'No, lovey, he's this lady's eldest son,' she said, and lightly touched the child's hair in a consoling gesture. Noting it, Chinese Lady sighed. It was all too remindful of the time when the family had taken little Rosie in to care for her.

She coughed and said, 'I'd better phone Lizzy and then Vi about Polly's twins. It wouldn't surprise me if it gave both of them a turn.'

It didn't. It astonished Lizzy, but didn't make her grope for a supportive chair. She said her brother Boots had always looked as if butter wouldn't melt in his mouth when he was a growing boy, but he'd turned into the dark horse of the family. Fathering twins, well, I never, she said. Still, he and Polly needed something special to console them after hearing Tim was a prisoner of war. It was worrying, very worrying, Tim in the hands of Hitler's Germans, and what could be done about letting him know he now had a little brother and a new sister? I'm sure Boots will see to it, said Chinese Lady.

Vi, on being told, was breathless for a few moments and then said what a lovely surprise, twins in the family, I'll send the happy parents a congratulations card. Are mother and babies doing well, Mum? According to what Boots told me over the phone, said Chinese Lady, everyone's doing a knees-up.

'Oh, that's Boots all over,' said Vi.

'And don't we all know it,' said Chinese Lady.

The Germans bombed Glasgow and Liverpool that night. London was left alone. Sammy and Tommy were on standby ARP duty, and so was Lizzy's husband Ned, but no call came and they were all allowed a night's undisturbed sleep.

Happily, Phoebe also slept right through, and without having any little accident. Sammy and Susie were living in the hope that the child's extended time with them would effect a cure.

Sammy, thinking about the Willis family in Canada, Phoebe's uncle, aunt and grandad, felt he and Susie simply had to allow for an outcome that would mean the child joining them. He knew that his own attachment to her, and Susie's too, had to be reined back a bit. It was difficult to believe that so much of what was happening was following the same course as the events which had brought five-year-old Rosie into the old Walworth home of the family twenty-one years ago.

Perishing Amy, he thought, it's taking my mind off business, and only Susie's ever been able to do that to me up to now.

Over breakfast, Chinese Lady didn't know what was most on her own mind, Polly's twins, Tim a prisoner of war, or the problems concerning little Phoebe. Perhaps it would be just as well if someone in authority came knocking at the door fairly soon to say the child's uncle and aunt in Canada were going to give her a home and that she could go there immediately. The longer she was here, the more upset everyone would be in having to let her leave. They all felt pleasure whenever anything brought a smile to her face, Edwin as much as anybody. Look at him now, smiling because Paula's made Phoebe giggle. And I'm getting as soft as he is.

Perhaps Mr Finch read her thoughts then, because he got up and switched the wireless on, as if he needed something to take his attention off Phoebe.

That wireless, there it was, talking about the war again, and about Hitler's armies again, just as if it was determined to aggravate her.

As far as Mr Finch was concerned, it was broadcasting encouraging news about the war on the Eastern Front, where in some sectors the Russians, counterattacking, had retaken towns from the German hordes and shaken their sense of invincibility.

It was the fifth of December, and in the Western Desert the Eighth Army was beyond Tobruk in the north, and in the south a Long Range Desert Group had foraged far forward to cut the coastal road between Benghazi and El Agheila. Farther south, a British armoured column was heading for the Gulf of Sirte. Rommel was having to concentrate on the necessity of repeatedly regrouping his retreating forces.

Tim, propped up on pillows, felt raw in the chest as a German surgeon's questing fingers travelled over it.

'*Gut,*' muttered the surgeon from time to time, '*gut.*'

'Does he mean I'm improving?' asked Tim.

'Silence!' rasped the ward sister, burly Captain Hearst, in German.

'What's she saying?' asked Tim of the crisp and immaculate Lieutenant Bruck.

'Silence,' said the clinical young lady.

Tim grimaced. Fingers drummed an investigative tattoo on his chest, his hospital pyjama jacket, open, showing teak-brown flesh scarred by the operational scalpel. All dressings had been removed two days ago. Captain Hearst, who would, Tim thought, strike terror as a female sergeant-major, eyed him aggressively. The surgeon said something to him.

'Can you say it in French or English?' he asked.

'You are requested to take a deep breath and hold it,' said Lieutenant Bruck.

Tim did so. It made him aware of his tender ribcage. The surgeon said something else.

'Breathe out,' translated Anneliese, 'and repeat the exercise.'

Tim spent a minute or so breathing in and out, the surgeon almost with an ear touching his chest.

'*Gut, gut.*'

'I'm definitely improving?' said Tim.

The surgeon, straightening up, spoke to Captain Hearst, who in turn spoke to Anneliese. The surgeon and Captain Hearst then departed, and Anneliese spoke to Tim.

'You are to do that as a regular exercise.'

'Right,' said Tim, feeling he needed her as a friend, the kind who would let him know in advance his date for discharge into the hands of a German escort. He could then plan to go walking one night, say a day or so before the escort arrived, providing he could slip the hospital guards. 'Would you like to tell me your first name?' he asked, buttoning his pyjama jacket.

'No.'

'Is it Helga?' he asked, with Captain Schaeffer looking on from across the ward.

'No.' She came round to the side of his bed and readjusted his pillows, finishing by giving them a thump.

'Is it Hilda?'

'What?'

'Is it Hilda? Or Bertha?'

'No, and it is not for you to know,' she said in her well-formed English. 'Or to ask.'

'I think you're cross with me for not being a German,' said Tim.

'I have a responsibility to help you recover,' she said. 'Apart from that, I have no other feelings about you, except that I think you talk too much.'

'I thought it was supposed to be good therapy for struggling chests,' said Tim. 'Where did you learn to speak such good English?'

'From my grandmother, who was born sixty-eight years ago in your city of Bath.' She eyed his pillows as if she thought they needed another thump.

'Your grandmother's English?' said Tim.

'She was. She is now German by naturalization, and proud to be so.'

'Oh, well, we've all got our funny side,' said Tim. 'Tell me, how badly wounded is Captain Schaeffer?'

The question seemed to surprise her.

'Why do you ask that, Herr Lieutenant?'

'He seems a very decent bloke,' said Tim.

'You are saying you like him?'

'I don't dislike him, and we're in the same boat at the moment,' said Tim.

She glanced across at the supine captain, then stooped and whispered, 'He was very bad, soon he will be very good. Our German Army surgeons are brilliant.'

'Thanks,' said Tim. 'By the way, could you get me one of those postcards prisoners of war are allowed?'

'No.'

'Why?' asked Tim.

'It is not permitted,' she said. 'Also, we do not stock them.' And she departed with a rustle.

Captain Schaeffer lifted his head, a faint smile on his gaunt face.

'What was it you were asking her, *Anglais*?'

'Her first name,' said Tim, 'but she refuses to tell me.'

'It is Anneliese. Are you now yourself wanting to make love to her?'

'No, I'm not wanting to at all,' said Tim, 'I've a lovely wife back home.'

'Ah, I congratulate you.'

'In any case,' said Tim, 'how do you get past a barrier of ice?'

'There are ways of melting the barrier.'

'I'll leave that to you, Rolfe,' said Tim. 'How are you feeling today?'

'Better,' said Captain Schaeffer, 'much better than these other poor devils, who are full of morphine to kill their pain. By the way, did you know your army is still advancing and has relieved Tobruk?'

'Thanks for telling me,' said Tim, uplifted.

'It will still make no difference,' said Captain Schaeffer with a smile of confidence. 'General Rommel will know when to counter-attack, and then – ah, for you, *kaput*. So sorry, *Anglais*.'

'Well, I suppose we all have good days and bad days,' said Tim, and began a deep breathing exercise. His chest endured it quite well.

Tobruk, he thought, my lot have passed Tobruk. They're nearer to me. Just the job. Keep coming, you squaddies, I'm getting better every day.

Later that day, an orderly brought him an official postcard and a pencil, and waited while he wrote a few words to Felicity, and addressed it care of the International Red Cross.

Handing the card back, he asked, 'Where did you get it?'

The orderly said, '*Ja, gut,*' and left.

Which told Tim nothing. But I've got a feeling, he said to himself, that my proud Aryan nurse has a kind heart. However, when she was changing his dressing just before she went off duty, and he was trying to thank her, she refused to concede she had

had anything to do with a gesture that was against the regulations.

'Well, will the card get posted?' he asked, noting the raw look of his chest.

'I don't know and nor will I ask,' she said, but her application of the new dressing was made in caring fashion.

'Anyway, thanks for having a kind heart,' said Tim.

'Herr Lieutenant, be so good as to keep quiet,' she said.

'Understood,' said Tim.

'That is the last dressing you will need,' she said.

'Thanks,' said Tim.

Chinese Lady alighted from the bus at Manor Place, Walworth, and was at once conscious of being in surroundings old and familiar. At the dignified age of sixty-five, and carrying herself as well as she always had, she crossed the road and entered Browning Street, named after Robert Browning the poet, born in the locality.

A little sigh escaped her as she saw the bomb damage on the righthand side of the street, Browning Hall in ruins. It had contained a clinic to which she had taken Tommy for treatment when at the age of nine he had been suffering from conjunctivitis.

King and Queen Street, that too showed ugly scars. It was the street she had always used when going from home to the East Street market, the market where housewives could always make a shilling do the work of two. What years they had been, years of struggle and striving, when she always hoped that an old Fry's cocoa tin held spare pennies for the gas meter. German zeppelins had prowled the skies during the Great War, but had never been the chronic menace that German bombers were in this war.

The damage was heartbreaking, but the people out and about didn't seem frightened or cowed. They seemed brisk and lively. Well, she knew as well as anybody did, just how enduring Walworth people were. No-one was carrying a gas mask. Everybody did during the first year of the war, but no-one bothered now. Gas attacks from the air had never happened.

She walked on, looking and observing, familiar scenes creating a sense of nostalgia, bomb damage causing a tightening of her firm mouth. Brandon Street, where Susie had lived with her family during and after the Great War, looked sadly battered. She turned left and went on to Wansey Street, and there she observed no damage. The terraced houses seemed as neat and well-kept as ever. Wansey Street had always looked very tidy and respectable, and just a bit superior to its immediate neighbours.

She knocked on the door of a very well-kept house. Mrs Rebecca Cooper answered her knock. Mrs Cooper was a handsome, church-going woman with striking blue eyes and a charitable disposition. She was the adoptive mother of Horace, who was married to Susie's sister Sally. Mrs Cooper and her husband Jim were accordingly regarded by Chinese Lady as relatives.

'Hello, Mrs Finch, I'm happy to see you,' said Mrs Cooper. 'Mrs Hardy has just arrived, so do come in and I'll put the kettle on.'

Mrs Jemima Hardy, Sussex-born, was the mother of Jonathan, married to Emma, the younger daughter of Lizzy and Ned, so Chinese Lady saw her as a relative too.

The three ladies were to share a pot of tea together, and to have a cosy chat about their families in Mrs Cooper's parlour. Which they would have done had it not been for the fact that the *Luftwaffe*, in revenge for constant daylight raids by the RAF, launched one of their own. The sirens screamed the alert just as Mrs Cooper was filling the pot, and the people of London scattered for public shelters or their own. The three sociable ladies finished up in the Coopers' garden shelter, although not before Mrs Cooper had calmly finished making the tea and bringing it on a tray to the shelter. The bedlam of the raid kept them there for an hour, while the bombs were unleashed indiscriminately.

'It be a filthy old war,' said Jemima.

'Was there ever one more deliberately aimed at civilians, at women and children, than this?' said Mrs Cooper.

'Hitler and his heathens are at work,' said Chinese Lady. 'I always thought that man was up to no good from the day I first heard about him on our wireless. That wireless of ours has always been aggravating, but it was never more aggravating than when it first mentioned Hitler.'

'Ours be just the same,' said Jemima.

'I'm sure I don't know why they were ever invented,' said Chinese Lady, 'they never were as nice to listen to as a piano.'

'We should all cherish our pianos,' smiled Mrs Cooper.

'And our fam'lies,' said Chinese Lady, to whom the reason for God's world was the family factor.

Somewhere not far away a heavy bomb crashed down and the resultant explosion sent shudders through the shelter.

The ladies endured. Walworth endured. London endured. Fire engines raced, ambulances rushed, and in Whitehall the Prime Minister and his Cabinet were confined deep underground.

Chapter Eleven

Saturday, 6th of December

In the modern city of cosmopolitan Alexandria, the imposing Grand Square was bounded by magnificent buildings of Italian-style architecture, including the law courts, a theatre, the exchange and an English church. The altogether handsome area, redolent of welcome sea breezes, offered the attractions of culture, entertainment and spaciousness.

A wedding was taking place in the English church. Lieutenant Eloise Adams, recently promoted from second lieutenant, was marrying Colonel Lucas of the LRDG. They were both in uniform, he with his wounded arm in a sling. The atmosphere had a touch of exultation to it because of the Eighth Army's advances in Libya.

Colonel Lucas's wound had kept him out of the action. He and Tim should both have been with the Long Range Desert Group that had cut the coastal road between Benghazi and El Agheila. However, convalescence had given the Colonel the opportunity to keep his promise to marry Eloise, although not in Cairo as originally suggested. They both decided Alexandria was preferable, not only for the ceremony but for their honeymoon of five days, after which Colonel Lucas would have to return to his desert base.

He was now beside her in the church, a tall, rugged-looking officer with a purposeful air, his eyes a clear blue in his darkly tanned face. No-one would have said he was the handsomest of men, but Eloise, delightful to the eye herself, thought him utterly exciting in his uncompromising masculinity and his qualities as a fighting soldier. She identified completely with that, and it was her earnest wish that in the end he would be the man to first lay hands on Hitler the monster and hang him.

The service proceeded. Colonel Lucas, who was known to her and his friends as Luke, made his responses with characteristic firmness. Eloise made hers like a young lady whose Anglo-French parentage lent her English composure and Gallic charm. That is, with poise and grace.

On being advised by the smiling English rector that they were now man and wife, they kissed, and the moment they were out of the church and in possession of the marriage certificate they were surrounded by Army and ATS friends. The congratulatory pressures became very celebratory.

'No, no,' exclaimed Eloise at one point, 'only the best man should kiss me, not all of you.'

'I'm happy with my lot,' said Colonel Lucas, the recipient of kisses from ATS personnel.

Cameras clicked in the cool sunshine of December.

Eloise called for help. A warm firm hand took hers. She glanced up. There he was, her husband.

'Shall we run, Mrs Lucas?' he asked, smiling.

'Yes, to the taxi and the hotel,' said Eloise.

There was no reception because pressure of work demanded the immediate return of most guests to Army Headquarters in Cairo. Away the newly-weds went, ducking rice thrown by their friends as they made for the waiting taxi, their valises secure in the locked boot. Like Cairo, Alexandria was noted for its cliftie wallahs, the term given by the British to the light-fingered element of the population.

Passing Egyptians showed gleaming teeth in benevolent smiles at the picture of two British officers, one a lady, hurrying hand in hand to a parked taxi. Either the British or the Germans would win the desert war, and one or the other would make no difference to Egyptians. Or so they thought. They were blissfully ignorant of Himmler's purification programme that was carried out on any 'racially inferior' inhabitants of conquered countries. Himmler, together with Hitler, saw all peoples, except the British and Scandinavians, as inferior to the Germanic.

The taxi moved off, and Eloise, hugging Luke's arm, said, 'I'm only sorry Tim couldn't be here.'

Tim was to have been best man.

Colonel Lucas sobered up, and a little grimace showed.

'We had to leave him, Eloise, he couldn't be moved. But at least it wasn't in the desert's nowhere land. He was in the middle of a German redoubt and we knew they'd look after him. The Wehrmacht, the German regular Army, don't apply the barbaric rules of the ss.'

'But a prisoner for the rest of the war, Tim will hate that,' said Eloise.

'I'll be surprised if he accepts it,' said Luke. 'I've got faith in Tim, a damn fine soldier. One of the best. He'll find a way out of any prison camp. That being said, how's your beautiful body today?'

'I'm being asked a question like that in this taxi?' said Eloise.

'Fair point,' said Luke. 'I'll ask again tonight, in our hotel room.'

Eloise, not noted for modest denials of her virtues and assets, said, 'Oh, you won't be disappointed. Alexandria is going to be exciting for you and happy for me, and we have nothing to worry about except Tim.'

Neither of them knew, any more than the American people did, that at this moment a fleet of Japanese aircraft carriers and battleships was steaming full pelt for the American naval base in Pearl Harbor.

Eloise did not disappoint Luke in the least that night, and if his virility caused her to bite his shoulder and issue little yelps, well, she didn't actually complain. No, not at all, for he came up to her own hopes and expectations, and his wounded arm didn't limit him in the least. It was obviously very much on the mend.

'What happened?' she asked afterwards. It was actually an invitation for him to tell her how much he had enjoyed making love to her. 'What happened, Luke?'

'The usual thing expected of a bride and groom,'

murmured Luke, 'or were you expecting something else?'

'Something else?'

'A game of cards?'

'A game of cards on a wedding night?' said Eloise, making little movements in the bed as she tried to do something about her tangled-up nightdress.

'Didn't Henry the Eighth play cards on the night of his wedding to Anne of Cleves?'

'How humiliating for her. Why did he do that?'

'Because, my lovely lady, Anne of Cleves didn't have your kind of looks or your kind of body. Far from it, apparently. She was lumpy. Will you do me a favour?'

'Oh, I'm in the mood to do you a hundred favours, darling.'

'Good. Oblige me, then, by staying just as you are for the next twenty years.'

Which request made Eloise happy enough not to bother any more with her nightie.

In a little while, however, she was saying, 'Luke, my blushes.' There weren't any, of course, not in a young woman half-French.

All the same, her virile bridegroom said, 'Don't worry about your blushes, Mrs Lucas, they're natural in a bride.'

She awoke late the following morning, and for a little while eyed the ornate frieze of the bedroom in dreamy fashion. Coming to, she realized she was wearing nothing, nothing, and that the night had been amazing. She turned to see if Luke was awake, but found he was missing.

He entered the bedroom at that point. He was in his pyjamas, his scarred right arm covered by the sleeve of his pyjama jacket. Eloise pulled the sheet tightly over her naked body.

'Good morning, young lady,' he said, looking dangerously vigorous. 'I heard raised voices and went to investigate. Would you like to know the latest news first?'

'What do you mean, first? And where is my nightie?'

'God knows. Somewhere in the bed, I fancy. Don't worry about it. Well, I'll give you the news first. The Japanese have bombed the American Pacific Fleet anchored in Pearl Harbor. They've since declared war on America and the British Empire.'

'No, I can't believe such news,' gasped Eloise.

'It's true,' said Luke, 'but as there's nothing much you and I can do about it, let's go down for a leisurely breakfast and talk about how we can spend the days in front of us.'

'Oh, there are many ways we can enjoy ourselves in Alexandria,' said Eloise.

'Yes, I meant the nights as well,' said Luke.

Later that week, something happened that turned the war into a truly global conflict. Hitler had another attack of megalomania. He backed his other Axis partner, Japan, by declaring war on the United States, the most powerful industrial nation in the world. At home in Britain, Churchill smiled. He could not see how an alliance of the Empire, Russia and America, together with China, which had long been at war with Japan, could possibly lose out against the Axis. Victory would take time, but it would come. He made plans to head for the United States and to meet President Roosevelt.

Across the border from Egypt, the British and Empire troops were driving on in Libya. Armoured detachments that were using the coastal road from Derna to Benghazi were pressing forward despite German and Italian resistance.

Rommel was losing ground but not his head. His withdrawals were of a controlled kind in the main, and he was prepared to make a stand to save Benghazi.

Tim was prepared himself to get out of bed at the right moment, to slip the night watch and make an attempt to reach the coastal road, even if his legs went wonky on him from time to time. He couldn't take the risk of waiting until the Eighth Army reached Benghazi, since if it did, the Germans would have evacuated the hospital in advance, taking him with them. He could only wait until he felt fit enough, and he knew he was still well under par.

Through information whispered to him by Lieutenant Bruck, Captain Schaeffer came to know that Germany was now at war with America, and Japan at war with America and Britain. He passed the news to Tim, who said he couldn't believe it.

'I agree,' said Captain Schaeffer. 'Well, who can believe the unbelievable?'

'If it does happen to be true,' said Tim, 'someone's made a big mistake.'

'The Japanese Emperor?' suggested Captain Schaeffer.

'No, your Fuehrer,' said Tim.

'Wishful thinking will do you no good, you swine,' said Captain Schaeffer amiably. 'However, when the war is over and Germany is master of the western world, I will come and visit you in your home and show you the scars you and your friends left me with.'

'I'll look forward to it,' said Tim. 'Bring your wife and kids.'

Captain Schaeffer smiled, like a man who, in his belief in the superiority of the Germanic race, was certain that victory lay with his Fuehrer. After a little while, however, he lapsed into frowning thought, as if certainty was under attack from doubts.

At their home in Dorset, Rosie and her husband, Lieutenant Matthew Chapman, were discussing the dramatic turn of events over Sunday dinner. Matt was staggered by Hitler's declaration of war on the United States at a time when his armies were beginning to find the Russian winter a fearful hazard. Rosie felt that with some mighty help from the Americans, Britain could think positively about mounting an invasion of Europe to force Germany to fight a two-front war. An invasion would lift the whole country, she said, and every available unit in the Army at home would want to be part of it.

'Yes, I daresay,' said Matt, 'but take that gleam out of your eye. You won't be going. You've got a prior engagement, with the maternity ward.'

'Oh, I promise to keep the engagement,' said Rosie, fair hair the colour of ripe corn, eyes a deep and striking blue. 'Did I tell you Major Robbins was vexed with you for exercising your conjugal rights?'

'Did I exercise them on her?' said Matt, tucking

into the meal of roast chicken, the chicken a gift from a local farmer. 'I don't remember. Is she positive about it?'

'No, you feeble comic,' said Rosie, 'she's only positive you ought to be court-martialled for conduct detrimental to the ATS. "Damn the man," she said, "doesn't he know there's a war on?" She asked me what on earth I was doing to let it happen. I said my resistance level took the night off.'

'And what did Boadicea say to that?' asked Matt, mesmerized as he often was by Rosie's exceptional looks and engaging tongue.

'She said, "Bloody bad show, Rosie."'

Matt laughed.

'She sounds like the female backbone of the Empire,' he said. 'When is she going to accept your resignation?'

'She's dodging it,' said Rosie, 'but as I feel fine, I'm not pushing her. I will, of course, when it's a must. By the way, much as I love our home here, I'd still like us to rent a suitable place near Bovington, something close enough to REME for you to use as a billet. We could let our cottage to an Army officer and his wife, perhaps. You'd be able to get approval for billeting, wouldn't you?'

'So far,' said Matt, 'I haven't trodden on the CO's corns, and as he's as much interested in old bangers as I am, which gives us something in common, I daresay he'll listen to a request for a favour with both ears instead of a deaf one.'

'That's promising,' smiled Rosie. 'I really would like us to be together as much as possible when little Oomph is born.'

'Little Oomph?' said Matt.

'Yes, I call it that because I think that was what I mouthed – oomph – at the moment when it happened,' said Rosie.

'But you didn't know you were conceiving, did you?' said Matt.

'Well, no, one doesn't actually know at the time, old thing,' said Rosie, 'but one can experience a kind of informative intuition.'

'Say that again, Rosie.'

'Informative intuition,' said Rosie.

'Which made you yell oomph?' said Matt.

'Well, it's not the kind of moment when you make conversation,' said Rosie. 'Everything's a giddy, incoherent blur, and you're simply not capable of saying something like, "Did we leave a note for the milkman?" Of course, darling, if the little one's a girl she'll be Oomphie, I suppose.'

Matt laughed out loud. Rosie regarded him with a smile, liking him because he was as easy-going and good-natured as Boots, her adoptive father. Liking one's husband was as important as being in love with him. Polly had told her once not to make the mistake of looking for a husband with Boots's characteristics. Rosie did not think she had ever consciously looked. Simply, not long after getting to know Matthew, she had experienced her first real interest in a man, and if he was like Boots in some ways, well, all to the good as far as she was concerned.

'Well, Oomph or Oomphie,' said Matt, 'a place for us near Bovington is what we'll go for, Rosie. I'll make enquiries. If a billet with you is a lot to ask for when so many men are overseas and out of any real contact with their families, I'm still going to ask, blow my boots off if I won't.'

'Lovely,' said Rosie. 'Oh, I'm going to phone Polly and Boots again this evening, and find out how my infant sister and brother are.'

'Give them my regards,' said Matt, thinking that although Rosie was not the natural daughter of Boots, she considered herself the natural sister of the twins. Nothing would ever shake her ingrained belief that she was born to belong to the Adams family.

If the world was astounded by Japan's act of war, Chinese Lady was fretful. She declared herself fed-up with all these aggravating goings-on that would cost a lot more lives and bring misery to a lot more people. She asked her husband what the Government was going to do about it. Mr Finch said that for a start Mr Churchill was arranging to meet Mr Roosevelt. Well, said Chinese Lady tartly, let's hope that means our wireless is going to talk more about Mr Churchill and Mr Roosevelt than Hitler and Stalin. I never did like Stalin's Bolsheviks any more than I like Hitler's Nazis, she said, they're all heathens that ought to have been done away with by drowning. You're quite right, Maisie, said Mr Finch. Look at the misery that our old friends and neighbours in Walworth have had to put up with, said Chinese Lady, and what about poor Emily dead from a bomb, our grandaughter-in-law Felicity blinded by one, Tim now a prisoner of war in the hands of them Nazi hooligans, and little Phoebe a war orphan? Um, not a war orphan, Maisie, said Mr Finch. You know what I mean, Edwin, said Chinese Lady, and it's all going to get worse now them Japanese have started bombing people on the other side of the world. Yes, things will get worse before they're better, Maisie, said Mr Finch.

'Nor won't my temper improve,' said Chinese Lady.

'However,' said Mr Finch, 'the fact is that with the United States now our ally, things will get better in time. In time, Maisie.'

'I'm glad to hear you say so, Edwin. Would you like a nice cup of tea?'

'I would, Maisie.' Mr Finch smiled.

'That's good,' said Chinese Lady, 'I'll make a pot for both of us.'

It was Sunday afternoon, and Susie and Sammy had taken Paula and Phoebe to tea with Lizzy and Ned. Vi and Tommy were also there. The grown-ups talked about the serious consequences of Japan's declaration of war. The little girls had their own kind of conversation, and Japan didn't rate a single mention.

Sammy tucked Paula up in bed that evening. His youngest daughter was a delight to him.

'Excuse me, Daddy,' she said, as she snuggled down, 'but is Phoebe always going to be with us?'

'Paula me pet,' said Sammy carefully, 'she's just staying with us until we hear from her aunt and uncle in Canada.'

'Well, blow them, Daddy,' murmured Paula, already slumbrous, 'why can't they let us keep her?'

'We're only her friends, not her relatives,' said Sammy.

Susie was tucking Phoebe up.

'There, comfy?' she said.

'Yes fanks,' sighed Phoebe in sleepy content, 'it's been nice today.'

Bless her, thought Susie, I hope she'll like Canada, because I think that's where she's going to end up, and Sammy and me have got to face that.

Sammy came in.

'She's asleep?' he said.

'Yes, already,' said Susie.

Sammy looked down at the sleeping infant.

'Susie, will it be another dry night for her, I wonder?' he mused. 'It was last night.'

'Fingers crossed, Sammy,' said Susie, as they left the bedroom.

When the alarm sounded the following morning, Sammy went, as usual, to take a look at Phoebe. She was awake and looking tearful.

The bed was wet.

Since the child herself had said yesterday had been nice, the news distressed Susie. It convinced her that the weakness had definitely been caused by the loss of her parents, that deep in her young mind was a memory of a loving mother and a loving dad. Friends and neighbours had emphasized at the inquest that her parents did give her love, a love that had suddenly been taken away from her. Susie thought the girl didn't remember the night of the murder, that kind nature had blanked it out for her, but she did in some way remember a happy and precious existence with her parents. Sammy didn't disagree with any of that. He wondered, he

said, if her aunt and uncle in Canada would give
that kind of existence back to her.

Susie prayed that they would.

'I'm not proud, Susie,' said Sammy, 'I'll pray as
well.'

Chapter Twelve

The Japanese began landing troops in Malaya. A British naval force steaming to intercept a fleet of escorted Japanese transports, was attacked by a large flight of bombers. The pride of the British squadron, the battleships *Prince of Wales* and *Repulse*, were sunk.

The loss horrified the people of Britain, while the people of America began to realize what they were up against in the Far East as the Japanese made landings in the Philippines to threaten United States bases there.

Saturday, the 13th of December

In the office of General Sir Henry Simms at Corps headquarters, Dorset, his desk had been swept clear of everything except a large atlas of the world. With Sir Henry was his adjutant, Boots, and his deputy, Lieutenant-General Montrose, earmarked for command of the Corps in the event of it being sent overseas. Sir Henry's age, sixty-seven, made him ineligible for an overseas command.

He was in serious vein this morning as he

commented on the situation in the Far East.

'I doubt if we're prepared for what Japan can throw at us,' he said. 'We're going to prove vulnerable everywhere, Hong Kong, Malaya, Singapore, our Pacific islands.' He touched the map at the relevant points. 'They've a huge navy equipped with a multitude of aircraft carriers, and can carry out landings by sea wherever they choose. And, by God, they can invade Burma from the territory they've won over the years from China.'

'I think you're wondering, Sir Henry, why we're stuck here in the south of rural England,' said Montrose.

'I'm wondering how the Army is going to cope with demands that will mean despatching a large number of units to the Far East,' said Sir Henry. 'What we're building up and down the country is an army that can provide reinforcements for the Middle East, and form the larger part of the striking force that must eventually cross the Channel to take on Germany by an invasion of France. The term for that, as you know, is the Second Front, for which Stalin is clamouring. There's no hope of that now or in the immediate future, and it's something, in any event, that we'd find difficult to achieve without American manpower which, thank God, we're now going to get. But I'm frankly depressed, gentlemen, about what I think is going to be the Army's inability to have any real effect on the situation in the Far East. The Far East is, in fact, too damned far.'

'It's the Navy's battleground, isn't it?' said Boots. 'Sea power is needed if the Japanese landings are to be stopped.'

'The heart of our Far East sea power went down

156

with the *Repulse* and the *Prince of Wales*,' said Sir Henry, 'and to make matters worse I believe the Navy's short of aircraft carriers. The *Repulse* and the *Prince of Wales* had no air cover, and their loss has taught us a bitter lesson.'

'What's on your mind, Sir Henry?' asked Boots.

'London's asking corps commanders to recommend what infantry divisions are sufficiently up to scratch to be sent to the Far East,' said Sir Henry, 'but I don't believe any of them could reach there in time, and I've said so. I think the Japanese have been planning their moves for years.'

'The buggers have jumped us,' said Montrose.

'I think Churchill's going to have to settle for a long-term plan,' said Sir Henry, 'for a future campaign aimed at taking back enemy gains. Any comments of a helpful kind, gentlemen?'

'Yes, a multiple increase of armoured divisions as a long-term policy, and a stiff Scotch the moment we get to the mess,' said Montrose.

'I'm slightly relieved by knowing America is with us now,' said Boots, 'and by hoping that Churchill and Roosevelt might get to be buddies.'

A public library in Salisbury that afternoon.

'Edward, listen,' whispered Leah, a history of the English Civil War on the table in front of her. Her weekly get-together with Edward in the library was of a very patchy kind. 'We can't keep meeting like this.'

'Here behind the shelves, you mean?' whispered Edward.

'Yes, and with lots of people about and us always having to talk in whispers.'

157

'It's true I've heard girls prefer to make themselves heard, Leah.'

'My life, what a sauce. I should believe it's girls who've got loud voices and not boys? Not much. Whispering must be a lot harder for you than me.'

'I'll have a think about our situation,' murmured Edward, and returned to his work, putting himself in sight of the counter in a busy way. He effected a casual disappearance again after five minutes. 'Leah?'

'Edward?'

'Look, I get an hour's break for lunch from one to two,' whispered Edward. 'If you could be in Salisbury by one, we could have lunch together in a restaurant. Could you wangle it, Leah?'

'Oh, I could tell Miss Murchison I'd like to come earlier and bring sandwiches,' whispered Leah. 'We're studying the English Civil War next term and I could say I'd like more time here, where there are so many books of reference.'

'Smashing,' whispered Edward. 'Let's go for that if you can manage it, shall we?'

'I'll speak to Miss Murchison,' whispered Leah.

'Ah, there you are, Master Somers.' Miss Williams appeared. Edward, caught leaning over the table, straightened up.

'Yes, Miss Williams?' said Edward, while Leah bent her head over her exercise book. Miss Williams smiled.

'One of the books you took away last time was *The Four Just Men* by Edgar Wallace,' she murmured. 'I've a borrower asking for it. He hasn't been able to find it.'

158

'It must still be on the trolley,' said Edward, and took a look. He found the novel and gave it to Miss Williams, who departed with another smile. All the same, Edward, not wanting to take liberties with the latitude she allowed him, forbore to indulge in any more whispering interludes with Leah until it was time for her to go, when he then said he'd wait for her outside the library at one next Saturday.

'What about the sandwiches I'll be bringing?' whispered Leah.

'Oh, we'll polish them off together on our way to the restaurant,' whispered Edward.

'If Miss Murchison won't give me permission, Edward, I'll write and let you know.'

'D'you have to get her permission to share sandwiches?'

'I didn't mean that, you silly, I meant about spending my lunchtime here.'

'Well, I'll hope for the best, Leah.'

Leah left then. Outside, Pauline and Cecily were waiting for her.

'Listen, what do you and Edward get to do in there?' asked Pauline.

'Oh, I study and he puts returned books away,' said Leah, as they began their walk to the bus stop in the murk of the afternoon.

'And that's a thrill?' said Cecily.

'Who said I go there for a thrill?' asked Leah.

'What a soppy question,' said Pauline to Cecily. 'Whoever heard of anyone getting a thrill in a public library, you potty thing?'

'Well, Edward could manage some kisses with Leah behind shelves, couldn't he?' said Cecily.

'Does he manage that, Leah?' asked Pauline.

'All the time,' said Leah.

'Crikey, some girls have all the luck,' said Pauline.

Sunday, the 14th of December

The infant twins had lost their red, crinkly look, and much to Polly's relief they now had the appearance of babes related to the indigenous natives of Britain, not to Geronimo's Apaches, although she assured Boots they were as ferocious as Apaches in the demands they made on her.

'What demands?' asked Boots.

'What demands?' said Polly, up and about and going a bit daffy at times in suspecting her waistline might be ruined. 'What d'you think?'

'Ah, yes,' said Boots, 'I understand.' He paid her the compliment of making a favourable study of the button-up bodice of her dress.

'I don't want to hear any screamingly funny remarks about my boz,' said Polly.

'Perish the thought,' said Boots, 'I've never had more respect for it than I do now, and my admiration is total. Take a bow, Polly, for being such a popular mother with the twins. But regarding their demands, I assure you, my precious, that if I could help you out, I would. Unfortunately, I'm not endowed with a boz myself.'

'You'll be endowed with a broken leg and two black eyes if you come out with any more funnies like that,' said Polly.

'Aunt Polly? Uncle Boots?' Kate called from the kitchen. 'Lunch in ten minutes, put your bibs on.'

'Heard you, Kate,' called Boots. 'The twins have had theirs?' he said to Polly.

'And their afters as well,' said Polly. 'What a life for an old lady like me.'

'D'you feel old?' asked Boots.

'Blissfully, no, I don't,' said Polly, 'I feel transformed from a heavyweight to a sylph, even if my waistline isn't back to normal yet. Listen, old sport, about their names.'

'Your say-so,' said Boots.

'I thought Bert and Gladys,' said Polly.

'You thought what?' said Boots.

'Just testing you,' smiled Polly. 'How about Clementine and Winston?'

'Could they live with that?' said Boots. 'At school, it's bound to be Clemmie and Winnie.'

'Still testing you,' said Polly. 'Seriously, I'd like Gemma and James. How do those names grab you, old love?'

'I'm in favour, Polly,' said Boots, not inclined to deny her any of her whims and wishes in view of her breathtaking achievement in becoming the mother of twins at the age of forty-five.

'You're a chummy old darling,' said Polly, 'and if those Japanese stinkers have given us an extra headache, well, we'll survive along with Tim, won't we?'

'So we will, Polly, along with our Gemma and James as well,' said Boots.

'I'm confidently placing bets on Tim jumping German barbed wire and making a successful dash for home,' said Polly.

'Easier said than done, Polly.' Boots was sober. He was wondering if the extent of Tim's wounds had been the reason why he fell into German hands.

'Buck up, old sport, let's have faith,' said Polly.

'Come on, wakey-wakey,' called Kate, 'I'm just about to serve dried egg omelette topped with crisp-fried streaky bacon, and it looks 'eavenly. Well, it should, being all me own work.'

Chapter Thirteen

'Herr Lieutenant, what are you doing?' Anneliese Bruck, who practised a strict observance of the book of rules, put the question in correct English.

'I'm getting out of bed,' said Tim. His bedclothes were turned back, his pyjama-clad legs hanging over the side of the bed.

'You do not have permission,' said Anneliese.

'Well, you give me the OK.'

'I mean you do not have permission from the doctor.'

'No, but I want to leave the room,' said Tim.

'Leave the room?'

'Yes. I want to do a wee,' said Tim, whose chest was healing slowly.

Anneliese eyed him in unamused fashion, and spoke clearly.

'You are not allowed out of bed until the doctor says so. I'll get an orderly to bring a bottle.'

'Look, I don't want any more bottles,' said Tim, 'I'm getting a complex about them. I want to go to the loo. It's down the corridor, isn't it?' He came to his feet and experienced pleasure at being able to remain upright. 'If you'd like to give me your arm, Anneliese, I'll manage the walk easily and enjoy the exercise.'

'It is not permitted to address me by my given name,' she said sharply. 'I am Fraulein Lieutenant.'

'Slip of my tongue,' said Tim. 'Be a sport now, lend me your arm. Come on, *jaldi, jaldi.*' That was desert lingo for get a move on.

She looked for a moment as if she would like to give him a thick ear, then just the suspicion of a smile appeared for a fleeting second.

'Very well,' she said, 'but if we meet Dr Gruhn he will ask who has given you permission to be out of bed.'

'Let's tell him General Rommel,' said Tim.

'You are an idiot, Herr Lieutenant,' she said, but she linked arms with him and they proceeded out of the ward and down the corridor. She might look a very cool young lady, thought Tim, but she had a warm body. Felicity returned to his mind. Felicity had a very warm body and a lovely frame, with superb legs and thighs. I'm on my way, Felicity. Well, I'd like to think I am, but I'm only going to the loo.

Anneliese opened a door.

'Thanks,' said Tim, 'we may be on different sides, but you're a very understanding nurse.'

She asked a meaningful question with a straight face.

'Can you manage now without my help?'

'With your help, I wouldn't know where to look,' said Tim. An orderly approached. Tim entered the toilet and shut the door quickly. The last thing he wanted was help from any orderly.

The orderly, in fact, was not interested in him,

but in giving Lieutenant Bruck the latest news picked up from Cairo radio broadcasts. The British Eighth Army was pressing the Afrika Korps defending Derna, and their forward tanks were well on their way to Benghazi. South of Benghazi, Rommel was attempting to regain control of the coastal road cut days ago by the British Long Range Desert Group. Rommel needed to clear the way for retreating German armoured divisions. And, said the orderly, for patients and staff if the hospital had to be evacuated.

When Tim reappeared, Anneliese accompanied him back to the ward without a word. She saw him into his bed, tidied the blanket and straightened his pillows. Tim thanked her.

'I need no thanks,' she said, and went to see to one of the critical cases. The man had begun to issue bubbling groans. She took a long look at him, felt his pulse, and left the ward in a hurry. She re-appeared, Captain Hearst and a doctor with her. The screens went up around the suffering man. Tim caught the eye of Captain Schaeffer, now making good progress towards recovery.

'He's bad?' asked Tim.

'Dying,' said Captain Schaeffer.

'More fortunes of war,' said Tim.

Captain Hearst, the large woman, poked her head out from around a screen.

'Silence!' she hissed, and back went her head.

'A cow,' murmured Captain Schaeffer.

'But perhaps her heart's in the right place,' whispered Tim.

'Ah, so? In her fat bottom, you mean?'

The dying casualty of war could not be saved. He

was dead an hour later, and it was obvious to Tim that Lieutenant Bruck was upset. He managed to have a word with her when she brought him salt tablets and water.

'War's a lousy way of settling things,' he said, 'and I'm sorry that officer died on you.'

'Sorry?' she said.

'Yes,' said Tim. 'It's a fact, isn't it, that you don't like to lose a patient?'

'You and your British troops were responsible for killing him,' she said stiffly.

'Yes, that's what happens in a lousy war,' said Tim, 'but most of us have still got feelings.'

'I am glad to hear it,' said Anneliese, departing.

'D'you know the latest news, Rolfe?' asked Tim of Captain Schaeffer in French.

'I know my company has just lost Lieutenant Richart,' said Captain Schaeffer.

'That's bad news for his family,' said Tim.

'The news you want is that General Rommel is still falling back,' said Captain Schaeffer. 'But what are your thoughts now concerning Japan making war on you and America?'

'They're mad.'

'The Japanese?' said Captain Schaeffer.

'To go to war with America? They're crazy,' said Tim.

'But Hitler and Mussolini have declared their support,' said Captain Schaeffer, whom Tim thought about thirty and a veteran of war.

'I don't want to offend you, Rolfe,' he said, 'so I'll keep any further opinion of Hitler's mental condition to myself.'

'The Fuehrer wisely disregards the opinions of

foreigners,' said Captain Schaeffer. 'It will be the end result that will count.'

'What end result do you have in mind?' asked Tim.

'Total German victory everywhere, *Anglais*.'

'Is that a hope or a prayer?' asked Tim.

'A prediction.' Captain Schaeffer might have said a confident prediction, but didn't.

'You'll understand why I can't wish you luck,' said Tim.

'Ah, you're not a bad fellow,' said Captain Schaeffer, 'and I hope the Commandant of your prisoner of war camp will allow you a few privileges.'

'Would he allow me the privilege of going on a long walk?' asked Tim.

'Perhaps. Try convincing him you are actually an admirer of the Fuehrer.'

'Would he give me a railway warrant then and save me walking?' asked Tim.

Captain Schaeffer smiled.

'Another good joke,' he said.

Tim wondered if the Eighth Army advance was bringing the Desert Rats closer to Benghazi.

Sammy was in his office when Sergeant Burrows came through again on the phone.

'I've some news for you, Mr Adams,' he said.

'Didn't you know me as far back as when I ran a stall in the East Street market, Jack?' asked Sammy.

'That I did,' said Sergeant Burrows. 'My beat included doing duty as market bobby some days.'

'Then you don't have to call me Mr Adams,' said Sammy. 'What's the news, good or bad?'

'Well, is it good to tell you that the Bow police

have heard from Canada, and that the brother of Phoebe's unfortunate father, a certain Herbert Willis, landed in England about a month ago with a new detachment of Canadian troops? He volunteered, he's now Private Willis. His father, Phoebe's grandfather, cabled Bow with the information, and asked for his son to be contacted. That's being done.'

'Then what's going to happen?' asked Sammy.

'I suppose you could expect a letter or a call from Phoebe's Uncle Herbert,' said Sergeant Burrows.

Well, thought Sammy, that'll start the ball rolling for Phoebe and a new life, I suppose.

'Right, Jack, understood,' he said. 'We'll wait, Susie and me, for Uncle Herbert to turn up.'

'Phoebe doing all right?' enquired Sergeant Burrows.

'We're getting a few smiles out of her,' said Sammy.

Sergeant Burrows was silent for a moment, then said, 'Might I advise caution? Lonely kids can get attached a bit quick to people giving 'em a lot of kindness and attention.'

'Meaning Phoebe might kick at being taken away from us and carted off to Canada?' said Sammy.

'That wouldn't please her relatives,' said Sergeant Burrows. 'Willing relatives in cases like this here one don't like them kind of developments. Everything starts getting messy, Mr Adams, very messy, take it from me.'

'Anything that helps Phoebe's well-being won't get messy as far as Susie and me are concerned,' said Sammy.

'I'm sure,' said Sergeant Burrows.

*   *   *

When Rachel entered Sammy's office five minutes later, he was sitting at his desk, wrapped in frowning thought and doing nothing, simply nothing. Since coming to work for him and the firm, Rachel had never known him to be doing nothing.

'Sammy?'

'Eh? Oh, it's you, Rachel.'

'Are you expecting someone else?' asked Rachel.

'Only a bloke called Uncle Herbert,' said Sammy.

'I should know an Uncle Herbert? I don't,' said Rachel.

Sammy explained the position, and Rachel said she supposed he and Susie would be pleased if Phoebe's Canadian relatives proved willing to have her.

'Up to a point,' said Sammy.

'What d'you mean?' asked Rachel.

'Well, I don't think Susie and me would like it if Phoebe wasn't in favour,' said Sammy.

'Sammy, a child of her age wouldn't really understand what was best for her,' said Rachel.

'That's a fact, Rachel, and Susie and me know it,' said Sammy. 'The Willises are Phoebe's Canadian family, and when her Uncle Herbert comes to collect her, we'll hand her over. We've got to, even if she cries her eyes out. As I said previous, we might not like it, but family's family, and it's what Phoebe needs.'

'Very wise, Sammy,' said Rachel.

There was a light knock on the door then, and in came Susie and Phoebe herself, the little girl wrapped in a warm winter coat and wearing a woollen pull-on hat.

'Oh, hello, Rachel,' said Susie, smiling. 'Would you like to meet Phoebe? I've brought her to see what Sammy looks like as an important business-man. Phoebe, this is Mrs Rachel Goodman, a friend of ours.'

''Ello, please,' said Phoebe shyly.

'My life, there's a pretty girl,' said Rachel.

'Isn't she just?' said Susie.

Phoebe gazed up at Rachel, a warm-looking velvety woman, who smiled down at her. Susie had a sudden feeling the child was going to ask if Rachel was her mummy. She had that wistful look on her face. Sammy spoke.

'Have you been to the shops, Phoebe?' he asked, and the girl at once turned her attention on the man who had found her on the day her aunt left her outside a police station.

'Yes, it was nice, and now we've come to see you,' she said, and Rachel thought there existed a shy eagerness for Sammy to take notice of her. My life, Sammy, be careful or there'll be no stopping her tears when her uncle from Canada arrives to claim her.

'Well, here I am, Phoebe,' said Sammy, 'up to me ears in work, which is me daily headache.'

'Oh, blessed fing,' said Phoebe.

'Well, we mustn't take up his valuable time, Phoebe,' said Susie, 'or his headache will crack. Let's go back home now, shall we?'

'Yes, a'right,' said Phoebe.

'Such a sweet child, Susie,' said Rachel. 'I've heard all about her from Sammy, and I do hope there's a happy ending for everyone concerned. I must get back to my work now. Goodbye, Phoebe.'

'Goo'bye,' said Phoebe, and Rachel went back to her office.

'See you this evening, Sammy,' said Susie.

'Yes, we'll have a chat when I get home,' said Sammy. He wasn't going to talk about an Uncle Herbert now, not with Phoebe there.

He had a word with Susie when he arrived home that evening. Phoebe was at play with Paula in the parlour, Paula exercising a little bossiness that Phoebe didn't seem to mind at all, and Chinese Lady was in the kitchen doing what came naturally to her, preparing supper for everyone. Sammy spoke to Susie in their bedroom, letting her know the details given to him by Sergeant Burrows.

'This man, Herbert Willis, is in England with the Canadians?' said Susie.

'Yes, Phoebe's uncle,' said Sammy, 'and we can expect him to get in touch with us.'

'Well,' said Susie, 'I suppose the sooner the better. I suppose he'll be able to make arrangements for Phoebe to get a passage aboard a ship so that she can join his wife, her aunt, although I can't think the child should go by herself.'

'I'm pretty certain the arrangements would include someone who'd look after her,' said Sammy.

Susie, inevitably, had a worrying thought.

'Sammy, what if she suffers her weakness on the ship, what if she wakes up wet every morning?'

'Don't make me think about that, Susie, I'll get heartburning.'

'Sammy, I think we'll have to tell her uncle about it.'

'Oh, hell,' said Sammy, 'I'm going right off the idea of Phoebe on a ship, especially one that's going to cross the Atlantic. There's always something on the news about ships being sunk in the Atlantic. Believe me, I've thought of German torpedoes flying about and dealing Phoebe that kind of final blow.'

'No, don't think like that, Sammy,' said Susie. 'She deserves the chance of a new and better life. The best thing is to wait for her uncle to contact us and to find out exactly what he's got in mind for her.'

'I hope it's something that'll make her happy in the long run,' said Sammy.

'We share that hope, Sammy love,' said Susie. She smiled wryly. 'It's silly, I know, but I like her name. I like having a Phoebe around.'

'That's two of us,' said Sammy, 'but let's make sure we go along with what's bound to be best for her, which is to give her to the people closest to her, the Willis family. That family includes her father's brother and her grandfather. Agreed, Susie?'

'Agreed, Sammy,' said Susie.

But she made a little face.

They'd had that kind of dialogue before. It was as if repetition was a way of trying to convince themselves they really would be happy to see Phoebe depart for Canada.

Chapter Fourteen

The British and Empire forces pounded on in Libya, the Afrika Korps under attack from tanks, guns and the RAF, the latter giving air cover and making low-flying attacks on German positions and supply columns. The combined German and Italian army of one hundred thousand men was suffering defeat and losing planes by the score.

In the Far East, however, the well-organized Japanese were beginning to gobble up American and British bases.

In Russia, Hitler's all-conquering armies were locked in desperate battles with the Russians in the harsh icy conditions of winter. Casualties on both sides were appalling.

'Watch the Russians,' said General Sir Henry Simms to Boots, 'they've the advantage of inexhaustible manpower.'

'And Stalin has the advantage of owning no qualms about pouring millions into the mincing machine,' said Boots.

'Has Hitler?' asked Sir Henry.

'No,' said Boots, 'except that he'll run out of

men long before Stalin will. If he doesn't take Moscow by Christmas, he's in trouble.'

'The man's a genius in some ways, Boots, but first and foremost a blackguard,' said Sir Henry. 'Any news of Tim?'

'None,' said Boots, 'but I'm not expecting any yet.'

'True, it's early days yet. How's his wife?'

'Biting the bullet,' said Boots, 'and writing optimistic letters in her nurse's hand about the prospects of the Americans polishing off Germany in time for Tim to be home by next August Bank Holiday, when she says she'll get him to take her to Happy Hampstead funfair.'

'Eh?' said Sir Henry.

'That's what she says.' Boots smiled. 'It's where Emily and I used to take Tim and Rosie when they were young, and I daresay Tim's mentioned it to Felicity.'

'Went there myself once,' said Sir Henry. He and Boots were in the mess, enjoying some post-lunch brandy. 'Nearly fifty years ago, I'd say. I was a young cadet. Took a cab there with other cadets. Let's see, yes, Queen Victoria was still reigning, God rest her for being the last monarch to put Prime Ministers in their place. Well, damned if we didn't see at the funfair something we rarely saw in those days.'

'And what was that?' asked Boots.

'Legs, Boots, legs,' said Sir Henry, and chuckled at the memory. 'Damned fine legs some of those cockney girls had, damned if they didn't. We offered to take a grand bunch of 'em back to town with us and wine and dine 'em. Well, they looked us up and down, and would you like to know what one of them said?'

'Try me.'

Sir Henry chuckled again and brought forth some passable cockney.

''Ere, listen, sonnies, do yer muvvers know yer out playing tin soldiers?'

Boots laughed.

'Cockney girls, Sir Henry, are a race apart,' he said, 'and I should know, I'm the son of a prime example.'

'Damned fine woman, your mother, Boots,' said Sir Henry.

Something out of the ordinary was going on, thought Tim. It was December the nineteenth, and the hospital seemed alive with unusual vibrations. Through the open door of the ward he glimpsed the orderlies scurrying about in their plimsolls. He wondered about the desert war. Captain Schaeffer hadn't conveyed much news to him over the last few days, except to say Rommel was re-grouping in preparation for a counter-attack that would shatter the British.

Anneliese Bruck came in.

'Salt tablets,' she said, and handed the tablets and a glass of water to Tim, who was sitting up and relaxing against heaped pillows. He'd been doing deep-breathing exercises, and convincing himself they were performing wonders for his chest.

'Is something happening?' he asked.

'Why do you ask?'

'There's a lot of hurrying about,' said Tim, 'and you look flushed.'

'I do not,' said Anneliese.

'Have you been hurrying about yourself?' asked Tim.

'No, and I am not flushed.'

'Did you hear that two-line poem?' Tim offered it. '"Sometimes ladies in a rush, take on a very pretty flush."'

The cool facade yielded to amusement and she showed a smile.

'Take your tablets, Herr Lieutenant.'

Tim took them and washed them down.

'Are you sure nothing's happening?' he asked.

'I am only sure your sense of humour is absurd,' said Anneliese.

'Tell me,' said Tim, 'are the rumours of unpleasant incidents in your concentration camps true?'

Anneliese stiffened.

'Ah, more propaganda from your BBC,' she said. 'There are no concentration camps, only camps for criminals and Communists, where they are put to healthy open-air work. That, Herr Lieutenant, is an improvement on your grey prisons.'

'It isn't true that you put Jews into concentration camps?' said Tim.

'Jews are the enemies of the Third Reich and they are sent for resettlement elsewhere,' said Anneliese coldly, and left.

'Now what have you been saying to her?' asked Captain Schaeffer.

'I was asking her about your concentration camps,' said Tim.

'Ah, so?' Captain Schaeffer looked only mildly

176

interested. 'And she told you they were labour camps?'

'Yes, good for the health,' said Tim. 'Are they?'

'Of course,' said Captain Schaeffer.

'Were you in the Polish campaign?' asked Tim.

'Yes.'

'I met some Polish soldiers when I was based in Scotland,' said Tim.

'So?'

'I don't think they'd believe these camps are good for the health,' said Tim.

'Don't swallow lies, *Anglais*, or I shall think you a simpleton,' said Captain Schaeffer. 'By the way, I was also in the army commanded by General Rommel that sent the British running for their ships at Dunkirk.'

'Well, it's a small world, Rolfe,' said Tim, 'I was among the runners.'

'Then you ran fast and well,' said Captain Schaeffer, smiling, 'or you would not be here.'

In came hefty Captain Hearst and two doctors. She did not bawl for silence. She gave Tim a brief glance and went on. The screens began to go up around the German officers whose severe wounds required constant observation and treatment, and who were kept in a sedated condition to offset pain. The murmured words accompanying each examination seemed to Tim to be of an urgent kind. He had to give the nurses and doctors their due. They had been unsparing in their efforts to keep these men alive. One couldn't fault their care, their skill and their German thoroughness.

He thought of Felicity, as he so often did.

Nostalgia arrived as he remembered their time together in Troon, Felicity a picture of vitality and in love with her work for 4 Commando.

He thought too of his late mother. Emily. She wouldn't expect him to settle for a prisoner of war camp. She'd say, 'Come on, Tim lovey, don't forget your legs are made for walking.'

So they are, he thought, and I'll use them as soon as the right time arrives, you bet I will.

He didn't know it, but the forward units of the Eighth Army were nearer to Benghazi by the hour. If Rommel couldn't stop their steady rate of progress, the hospital would have to be evacuated in a few days.

Not knowing this, either, Tim would have to make a guess at the right time and chance his condition.

Saturday, the 20th of December

'Here I am,' said Leah.

Edward, outside the entrance to the library, with the cathedral soaring in consecrated majesty against the pale blue of the wintry sky, turned to find her beside him, a smile on her face. Because of her rich colouring, she always seemed to have a warm look, like her mother. Perhaps, also like her mother, it was a reflection of a warm nature. Her round school hat, worn on the back of her head, was a dark blue halo, her winter coat a royal blue.

What a gorgeous girl, thought Edward.

Heading towards the adult age of eighteen, he had an altogether pleasant feeling that he was in love. It wasn't confusing or alarming, it was a kind of enjoyable discovery, and the fact that she was Jewish was an irrelevance.

'Leah?'

'Edward?' A faint flush touched her at the way he was looking at her.

'It occurs to me,' said Edward, 'that in this library—'

'We're not in the library, we're outside,' said Leah.

'Well, good,' said Edward, and kissed her lips.

'Oh, my goodness, in public?' breathed Leah, delighted.

Hovering at a distance were Pauline and Cecily.

'Did you see that?' said Pauline.

'He kissed her,' said Cecily, and giggled. 'D'you think he's Jewish himself?'

'How do I know?' said Pauline.

'But she's not supposed to be kissed except by Jewish boys, is she?' said Cecily.

'She's not supposed to be kissed by any boy, according to Miss Murchison,' said Pauline.

'Well, we'd better follow them,' said Cecily. Edward and Leah were on the move. 'In case of the worst,' she added.

'What d'you mean, the worst?' asked Pauline. She and Cecily were both fifteen, both not quite sure about the facts of life. Parents kept the facts of life to themselves, but knowledgeable girls passed titbits of information, which induced in Pauline and Cecily the feeling that ultimately they could expect something that was swoony, blushmaking and unbelievable all at once and at the same time. 'What worst?'

'Oh, you know,' said Cecily.

'Crikey, you're talking about a fate worse than death,' breathed Pauline.

'What's a fate worse than death actually?' asked Cecily, as they began to follow Leah and Edward through streets in which shop windows were decorated for Christmas.

'Well, all I know is that in novels it's rows of dots,' said Pauline. 'Except that Chrissie Beamish knows a girl whose sister suffered it on holiday in Devon.'

'Oh, gosh, did it ruin her?' asked Cecily.

'No, Chrissie said she shut her eyes all the time it was happening and thought about Devon cream teas.'

'What a spoof,' said Cecily. 'I bet she didn't.'

'Well, her sister told Chrissie that she loved Devon cream teas. There, look now, Cecily.'

Edward and Leah were entering a restaurant.

'Now what do we do?' asked Cecily.

'Find somewhere where we can sit and eat our sandwiches,' said Pauline.

'I've got Leah's as well as mine,' said Cecily. 'What do we do with them.'

'Eat them as well, of course, soppy,' said Pauline. 'Then we've got to meet Leah outside the library at three o'clock and catch the bus back to school with her.'

'Will she be all right till then?' asked Cecily.

'Of course she will,' said Pauline. 'Well, I'm pretty certain you don't suffer a fate worse than death in a restaurant.'

'Still, if they get a corner table Leah might suffer something,' said Cecily.

'Well, I said the other day that some girls have all the luck, didn't I?' remarked Pauline.

Leah and Edward were sitting at a table for two in the modest restaurant. They had ordered a simple lunch from the wartime restricted menu, grilled soya sausages, tinned tomatoes and baked beans.

Leah said Miss Murchison had been surprisingly amenable, only insisting that she should be accompanied by her friends Cecily and Pauline, and that they could all take sandwiches. The sandwiches, however, must not be consumed surreptitiously in the library. The park would be suitable, and the wrappings placed in one of the park's waste baskets. Leah could then spend the rest of the time studying in the library. Leah's response was a respectful yes, Miss Murchison, thank you.

'So here you are,' said Edward.

'Yes, and Cecily's got my sandwiches,' said Leah.

'Well, we won't need them now,' said Edward. 'Listen, how did your school take the news of Japan declaring war?'

'Oh, nobody could believe it at first,' said Leah, 'especially the girls whose parents or other relatives are in places like Singapore and Malaya. Everyone agreed it was utterly rotten of the Japanese, and they were voted proper stinkers. Miss Murchison addressed us all at assembly the next morning. Oh, my life, Edward, she made a very stirring speech about us and our Empire, and how we must all gird ourselves up for new battles and contribute part of our pocket money to funds for building new warships. At the end we all sang "Land of Hope and

Glory", although Miss Wheeler at the piano was a bit overcome and played one or two wrong notes. Well, her brother's in Singapore. He's a Civil Servant and working there, and his family's with him. Edward, you don't think Singapore's in danger, do you?'

'I shouldn't think so,' said Edward, 'we've got a lot of troops there.'

Up came a middle-aged waitress with their hot lunches.

'There we are,' she said, 'enjoy yourselves, Christmas is coming.' A number of people in the restaurant had parcels of obvious Christmas content beside their chairs.

Christmas, thought Edward, wasn't a festive occasion for Leah, but she said, 'Oh, yes, time for mistletoe.'

'And kisses,' said the homely waitress. 'Me, I'll be giving my feet a rest.'

Off she went, slightly flatfooted.

'I'll come round, Leah,' said Edward, as they began their meal.

'Come round where?' asked Leah.

'To your school,' said Edward. 'Well, I suppose all you girls who won't be going home for Christmas will be hanging your mistletoe there.'

'Bless me, I should let you come to the school?' said Leah. She popped a piece of sausage into her mouth, her white teeth overcame any resistance it might have put up, and down it went. 'Edward, you'd get dragged in and mobbed by the prefects, including my sister. There'll be a lot of us who won't be going home, those who live in or near

London or whose parents are overseas. You'd meet an awful fate.'

'I'll give it a miss, then,' said Edward. He demolished a mouthful of succulent baked beans. 'After all, I don't want to be the victim of an awful fate at my time of life.'

'I should hope not,' said Leah, and thought of how he had kissed her right there outside the library. In public. 'Edward?'

'Is there something, Leah?'

'Are we close friends?'

'I'd say so, wouldn't you?' said Edward, thinking she was a very natural girl. There was nothing repressed or awkward about her.

'I'd really like us to be,' said Leah.

'Well, we like each other, don't we?' said Edward.

'And we get on well together, don't we?' she said.

'A girl like you,' said Edward, musing a bit. 'You must know other fellers.'

'Oh, not in that way,' said Leah. She thought of Michael Morrish, the son of Solly Morrish. Mr Morrish was a family friend and had been a business colleague of her late dad. His son Michael, eighteen, insisted on writing to her, and so they corresponded. But she was not in the least attracted to him, and did her best to discourage him from thinking that later on there could be an arrangement. She only ever thought of him when one of his letters arrived, whereas Edward was on her mind an awful lot. 'Edward, we can be friends for as long as you want,' she said, trying to let him know that if he met and fell in love with a Christian girl later on, she'd understand, even if deep in her subconscious she hoped he wouldn't.

'I'll tell you something,' whispered Edward.

'What?' asked Leah, swallowing tinned tomato but forgetting to taste it.

'You're lovely,' said Edward.

'Oh, my life,' breathed Leah, and thought that sausages, tinned tomatoes and baked beans simply didn't go with such a romantic pronouncement. It ought to have been something like poached salmon, with strawberries and cream to follow.

'I know you're young,' said Edward.

'But you're not old,' said Leah.

'We've lots of time in front of us,' said Edward.

'Yes, it'll be years before we're fifty,' said Leah.

'The war should be over by then,' said Edward.

'Blessed angels,' said Leah, 'if it's not, there'll hardly be anyone left.'

'The last war went on for four years, did you know that, Leah?'

'Well, not half I don't,' said Leah, 'it's history and I'm really keen on history. But I hope history won't repeat itself. I mean, we don't want this war to last for four years, do we?'

'Not now we've got our friendship going,' said Edward, 'and can look forward to making our own bit of history. That's if Miss Murchison will let us.'

'Edward, what bit of history?' asked Leah.

'Confidentially,' said Edward, 'confidentially—'

'Yes?' said Leah.

'Only time will tell,' said Edward.

'Oh, my life,' breathed Leah again.

Edward remembered something that was common knowledge to the Adams and Somers families, that Leah's mother Rachel Goodman had been Uncle Sammy's one and only girlfriend in his young days. What else was part of that little bit of family history? Oh, yes, that it hadn't come to anything because Rachel was Jewish and had to marry a man of her own kind. What a lot of old cobblers, thought Edward. On the other hand, everyone thought that Uncle Sammy's wife, Aunt Susie, was God's gift to him. Well, Grandma Finch had actually said so out loud.

Leah. A girl like her, so warm and outgoing, was already a gift to the world.

Edward, who had that which was present in the family generally, a sense of humour, also had a serious approach to life, and it was in serious vein that he regarded his relationship with Rachel Goodman's younger daughter.

Rebecca spoke to her sister that evening.

'Look here, Leah, exactly what's going on between you and Edward Somers?'

'Pardon me, I'm sure,' said Leah, 'but nothing is going on. What a sneaky question. I'm simply his girlfriend.'

'You're what?' said Rebecca.

'His girlfriend,' said Leah.

'Don't be silly,' said Rebecca.

'Becky, you've got green in your eyes,' said Leah.

Rebecca laughed.

'Well, all right, he's quite dishy, I'll admit,' she said, 'but you know neither of us could have him as a serious boyfriend.'

'He's only serious in a nice way, he says things with a twinkle in his eye,' said Leah. 'Really serious boys have got the world on their shoulders, and it bows them down with gloom.'

'I didn't mean that, and you know it,' said Rebecca. 'And you also know Michael Morrish will speak for you to Mama one day.'

'I should be thrilled?' said Leah. 'Not likely. He'll read me the Mosaic Law from the Torah every evening, and all day every Sabbath. Becky, he's Orthodox, and Mama isn't. Nor was Papa. Nor are we. And our school rabbi doesn't ask us to shun Gentiles, nor any of the other Jewish girls, only to conform.'

'Which means you can't possibly be thinking your future can include a serious relationship with Edward,' said Rebecca.

'I'm simply thinking I like being his girlfriend,' said Leah, 'and I'm sure that with a little help from me, my future will look after itself.'

'Leah, at fifteen you're just too smart for your own good,' said Rebecca.

'Becky, you're the clever one of the two of us,' said Leah.

'I may be the better scholar,' said Rebecca, 'but that doesn't mean I'm smart.'

'Oh, I am sorry,' said Leah. 'Never mind, there's still time.'

'You cheeky monkey, clear off,' said Rebecca.

Chapter Fifteen

Monday, the 22nd of December

In the South of France, part of Vichy France, the
December weather was mild. In the Department of
Haute-Garonne, the river reflected the mild blue
of the sky, and the area around the ancient little
town of Lys seemed as peaceful as always. There
were undercurrents, however. Not in the good
earth, but in people who could not shut their eyes
to the fact that Vichy France existed on sufferance.
It was permitted by Hitler as a gesture of goodwill
for Marshal Petain's surrender of the French Army
to the German Army in 1940. France had simply
had no stomach for a new war with Germany after
the 1914-18 conflict had cost the nation over a
million men and years of economic depression.
Not every man and woman had favoured capitu-
lation, however, and nor did some citizens of Vichy
France like their Government's collaboration with
Nazi Germany. It destroyed any illusion that Vichy
was an independent State.

In the attic of a house on the outskirts of Lys,
a broad-shouldered, rugged young man and a

splendid-looking young woman were at its tiny window, a window dusty and spotted. They had made no attempt to clean it. Nevertheless, it did not hamper the view in any serious way. The young man, standing back from it, had his binoculars trained on a series of barrack-like huts close to a railway siding. From the attic, he could see them inside the high surrounding walls. There were over a hundred such huts, and visible were figures of men, women and children apparently moving freely about until one noticed the presence of watchful uniformed Vichy policemen and guards.

'Take a look,' said the young man, Captain Bobby Somers, RA.

'It's the same as always?' said the young woman, Lieutenant Helene Aarlberg of FANY. She was French herself.

'The same,' said Bobby, and made way for her as he handed her the binoculars and she took her own look at the Lys concentration camp.

'How angry I am that nothing can be done for those poor wretched people,' she said. Her mouth compressed, her hands tightened around the binoculars, and Bobby thought her tense body was visibly vibrating with disgust. He knew how appalled she was that her countrymen could be guilty of herding Jewish people into an assembly centre, a concentration camp, from which they were to be transported to Germany. She found it incredible that France, renowned for its devotion to freedom and liberty, should be going along with Nazi Germany in the latter's persecution of Jews. She was never the soul of meekness and placidity, and made no bones about her primitive

188

desire to boil Hitler and his Nazis in oil.

Bobby, the elder son of Lizzy and Ned Somers, had known her since the days of the Dunkirk evacuation when, cut off from the beaches by German reconnaissance units, he had been offered shelter by Jacob Aarlberg and his wife who owned a farm. Helene, their nineteen-year-old daughter, disgusted with the men of the British Expeditionary Force for scuttling back to their island, had not been in the least welcoming. She gave Bobby the kind of hard time that made him think that if he bumped into her on a dark night she'd take only a few seconds to do him a serious injury. All the same, he came to admire her in no uncertain way for her healthy looks and her unquenchable spirit. Eventually, he decided his presence in the farmhouse was putting the family at too much risk, and that he simply had to make an attempt to cross the Channel in whatever craft he could find in Dunkirk. Surprisingly, Helene announced she would take him herself in her sailing dinghy. She did warn him, however, that in such a small boat the Channel crossing would be an act of madness. Bobby demurred. He would sail the boat himself, he said. You're an idiot, she had replied, if you think you could succeed on your own. He could not dissuade her from joining him, and so they went together. She skippered the boat with skill, Bobby helping manfully, but her small craft, midway across the Channel, capsized in a squall. By favour of miraculous fortune, however, they were picked up by a British MTB, which landed them at Portsmouth the following morning. There, they were interviewed by the Press and a BBC reporter, all fascinated by their heroic endeavours, which Helene insisted weren't heroic but crazy. After which, they travelled to Bobby's home, where his mum received the French girl with open arms.

By that time, Helene Aarlberg had come to regard Bobby as an adventurous madman, an English imbecile who made terrible jokes, and the man she would most like as her husband. When, she asked, could they marry? When the war is over, said Bobby, who thought wartime marriages brought far more tears and upsets than joys. Bobby had a practical approach to many things, which helped to temper Helene's flights of Latin fancy.

She had always regarded the English as unimaginative and somewhat boring, although she had never known any until she met Bobby. The Somers and the Adams families, extrovert lovers of life, changed her opinion, and so did her contact with all kinds of other people. I have discovered, she said once to Bobby, that all the English are crazy.

'What about the Welsh and Scots?' asked Bobby.

'They're all crazy too,' said Helene, 'all still making jokes about Hitler, the German god of war, who will destroy the whole world if he can. Is that something to make jokes about?'

'D'you feel, then, that you're living in a madhouse?' asked Bobby.

'Yes,' said Helene, 'but I am very happy about it.'

'Are you?' said Bobby.

'But yes, of course,' said Helene. 'I am now mad myself.'

'Welcome to the club,' said Bobby.

'What does welcome to the club mean?' asked Helene.

'Come in and enjoy yourself,' said Bobby.

'Ah, you will make love to me, Bobby?'

Having said marriage should wait until the war was over, they had become lovers while they were undergoing training for work with the French Resistance.

They had now been in Lys for several weeks, their special assignment that of keeping the concentration camp under regular observation and passing details to their French contact, a man they knew only as Paul and whom they met in Carbonne from time to time. Bobby's papers, supplied by London, identified him as Henri Beaumonte of Marseilles, a freelance French journalist with American outlets. Arranged by London, the outlets looked convincing on paper, but were phoney, and all Bobby's cabled commentaries on the situation in Europe landed in the lap of an agent in New York, and from there into a box file marked 'Matters in Abeyance'. However, to Paul and any other Resistance people, Bobby was known only by his code name, Maurice.

Helene's papers showed her to be Claudette Dubois of Lyons, owner of a millinery shop in Lys, and her code name was Lynette.

'The truck's about due,' said Bobby. From the window they had a view of the road that led to the camp. Every Monday, at about three in the afternoon, a closed truck arrived with a new complement of rounded-up French Jews. The truck collected them from the railway station four kilometres from Lys.

'Yes, and when it delivers its cargo,' said Helene, 'the camp will be nearly full and then, in another week or so, it will be empty. All of the inmates will be on a train to Germany.' During their first week in Lys, they had seen such a happening, since when the camp had been slowly filling up again. 'Ah, here it is.' She had spotted a large covered truck approaching from a bend, travelling slowly down the road to the camp. When it was close enough she was able to make out two guards sitting in the cabin with the driver. 'What swines,' she hissed, 'and the worse for being French.'

'Stay cool,' said Bobby.

'Cool? How can I, you idiot? I'm on fire. People who persecute others for being of a different religion are all swines, and my blood boils because we are sure this is a persecution leading to death.'

The truck was crawling and uniformed policemen on duty at the camp gates were watching. In the camp, guards were harrying inmates, getting them off the tarmac to make way for the truck and its human load. That routine was the same too. The camp's entry compound was always cleared for the arrival of every batch of new inmates.

'The gates are opening?' said Bobby.

'Yes,' breathed Helene through clenched teeth, 'and the truck is turning in from the road. Now it's driving in.'

'Same as always,' said Bobby.

'Yes, we are sure about that now,' she said.

'Well, we'll be relying on the punctuality of the truck next Monday,' said Bobby.

'It's stopping,' said Helene. 'Now they'll unload their wretched cargo of human beings.'

Guards were opening up the large truck and

dropping the tailboard. Then came gestures accompanied, Helene was sure, by requests to come down. Requests, yes, to deceive them into thinking they were among friends. Men, women and children began to pour from the truck, slipping, sliding or jumping. Every person seemed to be carrying some kind of luggage, even if only in the shape of a tied parcel. The armed guards began to form them into a queue, but without pushing or harrying them, established inmates watching from a distance.

'How many this time?' asked Bobby.

'I'm expected to count them one by one?' said Helene testily. 'The old, the young and the middle-aged? Look at the old ones, look.' She handed the glasses back to Bobby, who took her place as she moved aside. He made a studied observation of a scene that was becoming all too familiar. Old people, some in obvious distress, were being helped down from the truck by young men, while the guards and the police seemed to be appealing to them to hurry. What, thought Bobby, was hurry all about when the forming queue would only move very slowly towards the interrogation point at the administration block? It was a demented attitude fostered, perhaps, by the guilty consciences of the camp's personnel. Get it over with, get them processed, documented and get them into their allocated huts. Smile, yes, but get them out of the way. The meaning of it all confirmed Bobby's established belief that if any war at all could be said to be justified, it was this war against Hitler and his Nazis, who had turned even civilized Frenchmen into thugs.

He fully understood Helene's angry vibrations. She was sick with shame at what was happening in her own country. It was their contact, the man called Paul, who had convinced them that when the assembled inmates of this camp were transported by train to Germany they would be put to death in one way or another. Resettlement was an illusion, but they were made to believe it, and so, when the time came for them to take another train journey, they boarded the trucks that took them back to the station without inconveniencing the camp staff by becoming hysterical.

'I wonder why the International Red Cross isn't taking a hand?' he murmured. 'All kinds of rumours must be reaching them.'

'The Nazi Boche must practise methods of covering up murder,' said Helene.

Bobby turned, put the binoculars away under a floorboard, and said, 'Time to go, Lynette.'

'Yes,' said Helene, smoothing her dress and putting her hat on. Bobby picked up his trilby, dusted it against his knee and put it on. Helene took up a hatbox and down they went. In the hall of the old, well-built house, Helene called.

'Madame Petrie?'

The owner of the house, a thirty-year-old widow of plump affability, appeared. Her husband had been killed while serving as an officer during the German advance into France. She was carrying a small wicker basket shaped like a trug. In it were little decorative accessories for hats. She made them herself of silk, taffeta and coloured ribbon.

'You will take these with you, Ma'amoiselle Dubois?' she smiled.

'With pleasure,' said Helene, and the dainty accessories were transferred to the hatbox. 'Settlement for everything at the end of the month?'

'Yes, just as usual, ma'amoiselle, thank you,' said Madame Petrie. She smiled at Bobby. 'Your health is good, M'sieur Beaumonte?'

'I can't complain,' said Bobby, and the affable widow sighed as his smile showed strong white teeth that seemed to confirm he was virile with health.

'But what is going to happen to the world now that Japan and America are at war with each other?' she asked.

'One could say a lot more fireworks,' said Bobby, who had welcomed a particular aspect of the news, Germany's declaration of war on America. It brought the hugely formidable United States into the war as allies of Britain and Russia. 'Fortunately, Madame Petrie, France has opted for a peaceful existence.'

'Ah, Marshal Pétain, our wise old one, commands us all to be peaceful citizens, m'sieur,' said the equable lady.

'Which seems good for my fiancée's millinery shop,' said Bobby. 'Au 'voir, madame, until next time.'

'Au 'voir, m'sieur, ma'amoiselle,' smiled Madame Petrie, and saw them out. She was not a Resistance worker, she was a sympathizer, like certain other people in Lys. She never asked why Helene and Bobby went up to her attic each time they came to give her new orders for accessories or to collect finished items. If she were asked, she would undoubtedly say it was to make love.

In an attic? For the fun of it, she would say.

On their way back to the shop, which was off Lys's attractive square, Helene said, 'I hate hats.'

'I know,' said Bobby. Helene, a farmer's daughter, preferred a beret. 'But as the owner of a hat shop, it wouldn't do, I suppose, for you to appear in public without something fashionable on your head. And I must say I like the creation you're wearing today. It looks like a lark about to ascend, its wings already spread.'

'Yes, it's ridiculous,' said Helene, yet a little smile flickered, enough to dispel the worst part of her dark mood. 'But I don't design them myself. Simone does.' Simone was Madame Simone Clair, manageress of the shop.

'The lady has a flair for the ridiculous,' said Bobby.

They were walking in the easy and natural way of people who had nothing to be furtive about, and in truth there was never anything going on in Lys that suggested the police or agents of the Gestapo had its small population under surveillance. The existence of the concentration camp on the outskirts of the town might have caused some citizens to deliver a protest, but no-one had ever spoken a single word about it in the hearing of Helene and Bobby, who both thought the people chose to ignore it and thus avoid being a nuisance to the authorities. Certainly, it did not change their unhurried way of life. They were pleasant people not given to frowns. All the same, and despite their seeming indifference to the meaning of the concentration camp, they produced sympathizers.

Helene was seen out from time to time, carrying

her hatbox. Madame Simone Clair, always in the shop, was a sympathizer. Helene had a list of other women of this kind, women who would always let her into their houses for the ostensible purpose of trying on an ordered hat.

Bobby's regular outings with a notebook and pencil took him into the path of citizens, to interview them about the situation in Europe and write down their polite but usually guarded answers, while encouraging them to say something complimentary about Pétain and Vichy France . . . He and Helene had an abundance of time on their hands, which they used to establish themselves as part of the day-to-day scenes in Lys, a little town of four thousand inhabitants. So far, they had never been stopped and questioned. Now and again they travelled on an ancient bus to Carbonne to meet Paul and to talk to him about the concentration camp. He never appeared in Lys himself. A Jew, he was known there. In Carbonne, he practised as a lawyer, with papers identifying him as a Catholic. Currently, he was concerned with the possibility of arranging the escape from the camp of a brilliant Jewish scientist, his intention being to deliver him into the hands of Allied agents waiting across the nearby Spanish border. He needed the help of Helene and Bobby, and they had promised it.

Arriving back at the shop, they found Madame Clair busy attending to a customer. Casually, the manageress advised them they had a visitor, a friend.

Up in the apartment above the shop, a brisk and cheerful young woman greeted them.

'Ah, my friends, hello,' she said and exchanged

pecks in the Continental manner. She was the area radio operator for the Haute-Garonne Resistance, a slowly growing faction of anti-Vichy elements, their purpose being to hinder collaboration with Germany and to build up files on leading collaboraters.

'You haven't called just for a coffee, have you, Marcelle?' said Bobby. He and Helene knew the radio operator only by her code name of Marcelle. She was actually a Scot from Edinburgh, with a degree in French. Bobby caught her Scottish accent whenever she spoke in English, although that language was rarely used by any of them.

'Coffee?' said Marcelle, and laughed. 'Ah, you are the practical one, Maurice. But no, I've called to tell you that in that hatbox there, brought by me from Paul, are the items you will need next Monday. Paul wants to know if you're still happy about what you have to do.'

'Happy and determined,' said Helene.

'And praying to some extent,' said Bobby. 'Have a cup of coffee.'

'Is there no champagne?' asked Marcelle.

'Is there a reason for it?' countered Helene, hat off and the deep auburn tints of her dark brown hair visible in the light.

'My very good friends, the RAF bombers yesterday attacked and badly damaged the three German battle cruisers anchored in Brest,' said Marcelle. 'A bold and magnificent daylight raid, covered by squadrons of Hurricanes and Spitfires. I picked up the BBC broadcast. That's worth champagne, isn't it?'

'Marcelle, that is very happy news,' said Helene, 'but I regret we have no champagne.'

'How sad,' said Marcelle, but laughed.

'Put yourself in the best chair and have a cup of coffee,' said Bobby.

'Oh, very well, Maurice,' said Marcelle, 'I'll make do with coffee.'

'With cognac,' said Bobby.

'What a nice man you are,' said Marcelle, which made Helene give her a look. Helene liked to keep other women at a distance from Bobby.

Marcelle returned the look with a cheerful smile, then warned them in sober vein not to take for granted the benign atmosphere of Lys. There were eyes and ears always taking note, she said, as there were bound to be in view of the existence of the assembly centre for Jews. It might not look so, but it is so, she said. Therefore, be very careful when you come to what you are going to do on behalf of Paul and his Resistance friends.

'Of course we shall be careful,' said Helene, 'we aren't headless chickens.'

'Personally,' said Bobby, 'I'm investing in the future, which means I'm not going to let caution take second place to mad heroics. Lynette is more heroic than I am—'

'No, no, we are the same,' said Helene.

'But I'll make sure she shares caution with me,' said Bobby.

'Ah, you are going to give me orders,' said Helene, very much a believer in her own worth.

'Just a friendly talk,' said Bobby, a bit of a chauvinist. Well, he believed men were men, and that women should be good sports and play the game to the men's rules. That way, everything went to plan. Most of the time.

His grandma, Chinese Lady, would have told him it was a man's duty to protect and provide, not to lord it.

Chapter Sixteen

Christmas was in sight, and despite the war the people of Britain prepared to celebrate the birth of Christ in the traditional way. It would be a limited celebration, especially among families whose nearest and dearest were away doing their bit for King and country, or whose children were evacuees. But the effort would be made.

Chinese Lady, about to write a letter to her granddaughter Annabelle, who was in Wiltshire with her children and her younger brother Edward, reflected on the sorrowful fact that with so many of her family scattered far and wide, Christmas wouldn't be what it ought to be.

Annabelle's husband Nick, an RAF pilot, was in hospital in Malta following a crash-landing in his plane. Everyone knew Malta was under constant attack from German and Italian bombers and fighters, and that the RAF fighters were suffering regular casualties. Annabelle was receiving air mail letters from Nick, who had broken legs and fractured ribs, but considered himself highly fortunate that his plane hadn't exploded. Chinese Lady considered the war in the air criminal in the way it inflicted dreadful deaths on fighter pilots and bomber crews. Can't someone stop it? That was the question she asked her husband Edwin. It can't be stopped until it's over, Maisie, he replied in his quiet way. I can't think why the Japanese had to come into the war, she said, I always thought they were a polite people and a bit short-sighted. They fooled us, Maisie, said Mr Finch.

However, Annabelle's sister Emma was happy. Her Sussex-born husband Jonathan had a lame knee due to a wound and was now a sergeant-instructor at an artillery training camp in Somerset. Emma herself was living not far away from his camp, boarding with a farmer and his wife, and doing useful work for them. She remarked in a letter to Chinese Lady that she was getting to be as strong as a horse, but was fighting it. Well, she said, Jonathan is against his wife, me, acquiring beefy biceps like some Land Army girls here. She saw him some Saturdays and most Sundays, and the farmer's wife had set aside a nice room for them to use, which they appreciated during these months of winter, because a log fire made it warm and cosy. And, wrote Emma, there was a lovely large sofa ideal for two. Chinese Lady, not as prudish as she often seemed, let her mouth twitch as she guessed what lay behind that remark. Well, Emma and Jonathan were a healthy young married couple very much in love. Jonathan's parents, Job and Jemima Hardy, were among Chinese Lady's favourite people and, accordingly, were often invited to Sunday tea, although one couldn't get the traditional shrimps and winkles as easily as before the war. Still, the Camberwell Green fishmonger did put some aside for her now and again, and when she called for them he'd hand them to her already wrapped up and say, for the benefit of other customers, ''Ere we are, missus, 'ere's the fishtails for yer cats.' Obliging fishmongers were a welcome breed of men to Chinese Lady. They helped her to put on the kind of Sunday tea that was the only proper one, in her opinion.

One very depressing thing was the fact that her very dear grandson Tim was now a prisoner of war. She could only hope that much as the Germans liked making war, they at least treated prisoners in a civilized way. Edwin assured her that the regular German Army practised an honourable respect for captured enemies, but he kept quiet about the Waffen-ss, rumoured to be taking no prisoners on the Russian Front.

Tim's capture meant unhappiness for his wife Felicity, that poor blinded young woman. She was having to do without him until the war was over. She was leaving the convalescent hospital in the New Year to stay with her parents in Streatham, and later was going to spend some time down in Dorset with Polly and Boots. Boots had said that although there were the twins as well as the girl Kate, their permanent guest, there would always be room for Felicity. Boots seemed to have got very fond of his daughter-in-law. Well, she was a brave young lady, fighting the loss of her sight the way she was, and of all people Boots would understand what she was having to put up with, and be the most admiring. But it was still going to be hard for Felicity. She might not see Tim – well, meet with him – for perhaps as much as two years, if this war lasted as long as the Great War.

Chinese Lady was not a vindictive woman, but if, when the war did come to an end, Hitler was beheaded with an axe, she would be totally in favour, although she wouldn't want to be present at the execution, which she thought would be best done in private in the Tower of London. She expected he'd still be bawling and shouting right up to the last. She was sure he'd never had his mouth shut from the time he was born. And even when his head was off his shoulders, it wouldn't surprise her if he still had something to say.

As for Tim's cousin Bobby, Lizzy and Ned's eldest son, well, Lord knows where he and Helene, his young French lady, were. Somewhere overseas. Chinese Lady had found Helene very likeable, and not a bit fast, considering she was French. Helene and Eloise, Boots's French daughter, had both been nice surprises. Eloise could be very elegant and ladylike, and Helene acted like a nice healthy-minded girl, probably because she was a farmer's daughter and not one of them Paris croquettes. (Chinese Lady meant coquettes.) But what was she doing overseas? No-one had had any letters from her yet, nor from Bobby. But Bobby would be doing his duty, of course. He was like his grandfather Daniel, a born soldier, who followed the country's flag wherever the Army went when it had orders to keep the peace.

The family knew what Eloise was doing. She was working at a desk in Cairo. Chinese Lady hoped Helene was doing much the same, and not soldiering with Bobby. Soldiering was a very unfemale thing and young ladies didn't ought to be allowed anywhere near it.

And what about Freddy Brown, family-related as Sammy's young brother-in-law? He was now overseas too, and Cassie, his wife, had written to say she was sure he was in the Western Desert, fighting against the Germans and Italians there, like Tim had been. Cassie was living in Wiltshire with her children, not far from Susie's sister Sally, who was married to Horace Cooper. Horace, at least, was still in the country. He was a physical training soldier, a sergeant, who put the muscles of recruits in proper order. He'd told Sally that the muscles of some recruits were in all the wrong places. Chinese Lady tried to imagine what men looked like with their muscles not where they should be, but the images she conjured up put a chronic strain on her peace of mind. Her peace of mind came from everything being in its rightful place, not just men's muscles. The events of the war and what they were doing to all the families of Britain meant nothing was as it should be. Well, she thought, someone's going to have to pay for it in the end, and I hope it's them German Nazis. It's their fault that a lot of my grandchildren have to live in the country and won't be home for Christmas. Nor would Rosie and her husband. Rosie had written suggesting she and Matthew were thinking about it, but Chinese Lady had replied to say they'd better not because of Rosie's intimate condition and no-one being able to rely on them aggravating German bombers staying away.

Still, she thought, as she began her letter to

Annabelle, Lizzy and Ned, Tommy and Vi, and Vi's parents, will be with us, and they're all family.

Captain Rosie Chapman was delivering an unwanted Christmas present to her commanding officer, Major Robbins, in the form of an official application for discharge. Rosie was now three months pregnant.

'Curse it, Rosie,' said Major Robbins, 'do you have to put this piece of bumph on my desk?'

'Afraid so, ma'am,' said Rosie, 'it's really time I did, particularly as my husband has found a cottage for us close to Bovington REME.'

'It's a first-class shambles,' said Major Robbins. 'If he'd had any respect for your commission and the war effort, he wouldn't have put you in the family way or found you a place far from here. It means I'm losing my best officer. It grieves me that the fellow has no sense of what's right or proper at this time in the affairs of the country. Damned bad show, Rosie. Hope you don't mind my saying so.'

'I quite understand your feelings, ma'am,' said Rosie.

'Husbands are all right in their way,' said Major Robbins, 'but get odd ideas about their place in a woman's life. Now, if you could have got yours to run a sweet shop, that might have kept him behind his counter and taken his mind off you and your bed. I get mine to poke about in the garden and the garden shed, well out of my way. That's the place for husbands, Rosie, the garden shed. It's given mine a happy feeling that he's not important, and he's comfortable with that.'

'Mine's important to me,' said Rosie, 'and to REME.'

'Well, he's mucked up things here,' said Major Robbins. 'I'll have to knock Lieutenant Johnson into shape and get her to take your place before the Yanks arrive. They'll be here some time in the New Year, bringing American bumph in triplicate with 'em.'

'They'll keep it to themselves,' said Rosie.

'No, they're generous buggers,' said Major Robbins, 'they'll spread it around. And that won't be all they'll spread. I'll have to get my girls to sew lead weights in their skirts. I was in Washington once with my old man. Damned if one of their senators didn't try to ravish me. I gave him a clout that sent him cockeyed.'

'Well, I sincerely hope he won't arrive with the American forces and come looking for you,' said Rosie, who always had to struggle to keep her face straight when in conversation with her hearty no-nonsense commanding officer.

'I'll break his neck if he does,' said handsome, full-bosomed Major Robbins. 'Well, it looks as if your discharge will have to be accepted, early in the New Year, I daresay.'

'You can rely on my continued help until then, ma'am,' said Rosie.

'Good man,' said Major Robbins.

'What's going on?' asked Tim of a German orderly who spoke a little English.

'War,' said the orderly, but there was no grin and no cockiness. Most often, a German air of superiority was visible, but it had been missing lately.

'Yes, I know about the war,' said Tim, resting against heaped pillows, 'but who's winning?'

'Eh?'

'Who's winning?'

'Ah, who is best, *ja?*'

'Yes, at the moment, who's on top?' asked Tim.

'On top?'

'Bloody hell, yes, who's winning?' asked Tim.

'Rommel,' said the orderly.

Well, he didn't say that with a smile, either, thought Tim.

'Understood,' he said, and he smiled himself.

Lieutenant Bruck came in, eyed the orderly, spoke sharply to him and gestured. He shrugged, picked up Tim's lunch tray and left.

'You are not to speak to orderlies or ask questions of them,' she said to Tim.

'Why?' enquired Tim mildly.

'It is forbidden.'

'Can I ask a question of you, Fraulein Lieutenant?'

'No,' she said, and went across to Captain Schaeffer to hand him a pill and a glass of water. Captain Schaeffer raised himself, took the pill and swallowed it with a draught of water. He thanked her and asked a question.

Tim heard her say, '*Ja, Herr Hauptmann.*'

On her way out, she glanced at Tim.

'You're looking good today,' he said. She looked good every day, of course, in her cool, immaculate way.

She stopped to say, 'In this ward, Herr Lieutenant, there are men who are not good at all.'

A second stomach-wounded case had died, and

the others were still critical, if stable.

Tim wanted to say well, when you all happily followed Hitler into war, what did you expect, just a few toothache cases?

Instead, he said, 'It's happening everywhere. I think the whole world has got a very nasty headache. It needs a pill.'

'The whole world needs a pill?' she said.

'It'll have to be an outsize one, say as big as a football,' said Tim. 'Well, I suppose the world has got an outsize mouth.'

There was a suspicion of a smile before she said, 'You are still suffering from an absurd sense of humour.' And she left.

'Were you asking her about the fighting?' Captain Schaeffer spoke in French as usual.

'No, I never get answers to those questions,' said Tim.

'Ah, so?' Captain Schaeffer smiled. 'I can tell you she has just told me that our Afrika Korps is making a magnificent stand.'

'Is that a fact?' said Tim. 'So why is everyone looking gloomy?'

'You are deceived, *Anglais.*'

Tim didn't think so. In the bed he did some leg exercises, stretching them. His chest only felt sore now, his breathing much improved. I've got a feeling my mates are getting closer, he thought, and I've got another feeling it'll be time in a day or so for me to try going walkies at night. Is there a guarded perimeter around this hospital? If so, could I climb it? Probably not without falling to pieces, but I'd have to give it a go. Wish me luck, Felicity. Keep the home fires burning.

*   *   *

Little Phoebe was still experiencing forlorn moments on waking up, Sammy and Susie still persevering with the problem by giving her as much comfort as they could. They tried always to make her feel it wasn't a big worry to them, and that she wasn't to worry about it herself. They kept the problem from Paula. Their ebullient and talkative daughter was coming to delight in having a playmate who was responsive to her chatter and liked all the games she devised. Phoebe never spoke about her unhappy moments in bed. Despite her responsiveness to Paula, Sammy felt she never quite lost her little air of loneliness. He was constantly put in mind of Rosie during the days when, having been deserted by her mother, she lived in hope of belonging to Boots and Emily.

A letter arrived by Monday's midday post. It was addressed to Mr and Mrs S Adams. The news that morning had been about the continuing advance of the Eighth Army, the ferocious battles on the Russian front, which were denying the Germans any further advance on Moscow, and the invasions being mounted by the Japanese in the Far East. Susie, opening the letter, hoped its news would be cheerful. She read it in the kitchen, with Chinese Lady and Phoebe hovering.

> *Dear Mr and Mrs Adams,*
>   *Might I introduce myself, I'm Herbert Willis, Private Herbert Willis just now, being a volunteer with the Canadian Army and over here with my regiment. I've been informed by your police all about my*

*niece Phoebe that happens to be the only child of my
unlucky brother and his wife and I don't need to tell
you what happened to them at the hands of a mad
lunatic. That was horrible bad luck for Phoebe, and
it's turned me sick knowing she's had more bad luck,
losing her Aunt Lily like she did, in the Thames. Well
I'm going to have to come and see you to talk about
Phoebe and what can be done for her, which I'll do
as soon as I get my first leave in this old country
though it won't be tomorrow or next week, we've got
some hard training coming up. Right now, I've got
to thank you for taking care of my brother's little girl,
which I appreciate a lot. I won't let you down, I'll
come and visit you as soon as I can, so if you could
kindly hang on to Phoebe till then I'll be grateful.
Yours truly, Herbert Willis, Private.*

Susie passed the letter to Chinese Lady, who read
it and said, 'Well, that's something to think about,
Susie.'

'Phoebe, you've got an uncle, an Uncle Herbert,
did you know?' smiled Susie.

'I don't remember,' said Phoebe. Hesitantly, she
asked, 'Does 'e know where my daddy is, please?'

'Well, one day soon he'll be coming to see us,'
said Susie, 'and we'll ask him then, shall we?'

'Yes, a'right,' said Phoebe, who always seemed to
want to please the people who were looking after
her.

Later that day, when Paula was home from
school and playing with Phoebe, Chinese Lady,
speaking to Susie, said she supposed that although
Herbert Willis was with the Canadians in England,
his wife would be happy to have Phoebe.

'Yes, I suppose so too,' said Susie.

'And I suppose he'll be able to make arrangements to send Phoebe on a ship,' said Chinese Lady. 'Would it be expensive?'

'Oh, I'm sure me and Sammy would help if he's only getting a soldier's pay,' said Susie.

'Susie, you won't mind letting the little girl go?' said Chinese Lady gently. Like Sammy, she too had memories of Rosie, particularly the memory of the day when the girl's grandfather took her away, causing actual grief to Boots and Emily, especially Boots.

'Mum, Sammy and me have got to think first about what's best for Phoebe, not our own feelings,' said Susie. 'And what's best for her just now is making her happy enough to cure her of her weakness, which is still happening a lot. That's what we're mostly trying to do until her uncle and aunt agree to have her.'

'Yes, Susie,' said Chinese Lady, 'you're a blessing to the child.'

Chapter Seventeen

Tuesday, 23rd of December

Lieutenant Anneliese Bruck hurried into the ward, her expression stiff, her firm lips compressed. She's having a crisis, thought Tim, and so is everyone else on the staff. Since this morning, the sounds had all been of a noisy kind, of rushing feet, shouting voices and the arrival of vehicles. No breakfast had been served, only some pretty foul coffee. And midday had seen nothing of any lunch, apart from a dry bread roll for patients not suffering from stomach wounds. The time was now four in the afternoon, and there was no doubt about it, the hospital was being evacuated.

'You are to get up,' said Anneliese to Tim. 'An orderly will be here soon to help you dress.'

'Something serious is going on?' said Tim.

'With so much happening all day, I don't think you need an answer to that,' she said. 'I am quite sure you know we are having to evacuate the hospital. Please get out of bed.'

'Right, will do,' said Tim, swearing to himself for not having made his move during the night. He had meant to, he had planned to stay awake for that purpose and choose a quiet moment for slipping out of the ward. There were always quiet moments if the severe cases required only a minimum of attention, but the night staff were far more active than usual, and he was given no chance at all to make any kind of move. In the end he fell asleep. He did not wake up until ten. Nobody had roused him, and the coffee that had been placed on top of his locker was cold. He noted the ward had been invaded by orderlies. They were stripping the patients' lockers, filling valises with each man's uniform and all personal items. But they did not touch Tim's locker.

Later, during the afternoon, the severely wounded Germans had been stretchered out one by one, and Tim realized then that the activity during the night had been a prelude to the urgent activity of the day. Now there were orderlies at Captain Schaeffer's bedside. It was his turn to be prepared for a stretcher. Tim, sitting up, said, 'Everyone's leaving, Anneliese?'

Watching the orderlies, she overlooked the use of her Christian name and said, 'Everyone. I shall accompany ambulance casualties myself.' She turned and looked down at Tim. She hesitated before saying, 'Possibly, I may not see you again. You are close to recovery.'

'Let me thank you, then,' said Tim, 'not just for your caring attention, but for putting up with me. We're not on the same team, but I shan't forget you. May I kiss you?'

'What?'

'I'd like to, as a compliment to my nurse.'

'That is not a compliment, but an impertinence,' she said, yet she did not look particularly offended, and her proud blue eyes were not all that cool. 'Your escort—'

She was interrupted by the booming sounds of gunfire. She stiffened. Captain Schaeffer, a wry smile on his face as the orderlies carefully and skilfully slid him onto a stretcher, said in French, 'Your friends seem to be closing in, *Anglais*.'

'So I hear,' said Tim.

'Goodbye,' said Anneliese abruptly, and swept out, beckoning to the orderlies to follow.

Captain Schaeffer, stretchered, was carried to the door. He was the last of the German casualties in this ward.

'*Auf Wiedersehn*, you swine,' he said to Tim, but with a smile.

'Good luck, Rolfe, your turn to make a run for home,' said Tim, and heard Schaeffer's response to that as he disappeared.

'We'll be back. *Heil Hitler*.'

The sounds of the British guns were now incessant, Benghazi and its defences under heavy fire, but the Italian and German troops were making a stand in an effort to give Rommel time to effect further regrouping.

Tim eased himself slowly out of bed. A thought struck him, and he slipped back between the sheets. Why make it easy for the Germans to hand him over to the escort? The ward, empty except for himself, seemed to provide a sounding-board not only for the gunfire, but for the thumps, bangs and shouts accompanying the evacuation. He waited for the arrival of the expected orderly, wondering if he could bribe the bloke by flashing the dinar notes that were in his wallet.

It was some time before the man hurried into the ward. He looked angry at finding the British officer still in bed.

'Up, up,' he said in English.

'You can leave me, if you like,' said Tim, and offered the dinar notes. Whether or not the orderly understood the words, he understood what the proffered dinars meant. He knocked Tim's extended hand aside with a sharp blow, then opened his locker, took out his Commando uniform, his underwear and boots, and flung everything on the bed. He followed that by flinging words.

'Up. Dress. Quick. I will come back.'

Out he went, almost at a run, as if a sudden barrage of new shouts contained demands for his presence.

Tim still did not hurry. He came out of the bed in leisurely fashion. He had been up on several occasions during the last few days, sometimes to go to the bathroom, sometimes to exercise his limbs. On each occasion, since he was a prisoner, he'd been escorted by an orderly. Standing, he tested his legs. They felt fairly willing to go to work. Even if he wasn't at his physical best, they'd take him for a walk given the chance. Telling himself to breathe evenly, he took his hospital pyjamas off and examined his scarred chest. Not very pretty. Felicity would comment. No, she wouldn't, you idiot, she's blind.

The Eighth Army's guns had stopped shelling. That could mean tanks and infantry were moving forward. If they kept coming, their advance units could be in sight of Benghazi by nightfall, and in the port not long after daybreak. So, keep coming, you squaddies, I'll be relying on you if I can duck my way out of this evacuation.

Felicity, she'll be relying on you too.

He had another thought. It concerned doing something quick instead of taking his time. The noises of the evacuation were at a minimum within the building, and he could hear motor engines firing outside, together with the crunching sounds of vehicles moving off. He dressed himself. His stuff had been laundered, bloodstains eliminated. A bloke couldn't fault the German sense of hygiene, although their liking for being correct hadn't encompassed making repairs to his shirt, jersey and sheepskin-lined jacket. He pulled on his boots, breathing deeply the while. His chest and ribs were sore but not actually complaining.

He took up his beret, went to the open door and glanced up and down the corridor. It was empty. He dropped his beret a little way down. It fell softly to the floor. He walked past it and entered the next ward, which positively reeked of sick men, antiseptic medicine and disinfectant. But it was clear of all casualties. He put himself behind the door.

Someone came up the corridor at a run. Through the crack below the top hinge of the door, Tim spotted the orderly. The run was checked, an exclamation followed, and Tim suspected the beret had been seen. Would it fool the orderly into thinking the bird had flown, dropping the beret in his hurried flight, or would he see it as an obvious trick?

Tim heard the man issue imprecations. He heard him rush into the vacated ward. He heard him shout.

'*Schweinhund!* Out, out!'

But the bird really had flown, if only to the next ward.

Tim's every limb tensed.

There was a series of guttural imprecations as the orderly came out of the ward. Tim glimpsed him again, the beret in his hand, before he disappeared, running fast. Outside, vehicles were still moving off, but the hospital itself was now completely quiet.

Tim stayed where he was for two minutes. Then he came out from behind the door, and took another look down the corridor. At which moment, a figure appeared, walking briskly. For a split second, Tim had Lieutenant Bruck in his sights. He withdrew in a flash, but he knew she'd seen him. Bloody hell, he should have stayed where he was for at least five minutes.

He waited, hidden behind the door again, but without much hope.

She passed this ward and entered her own ward. He heard her, her voice delivering words in her clear, correct English.

'Come out, Lieutenant Adams. Show yourself, you fool. Do you hear me? Show yourself. Your escort has arrived. Lieutenant Adams?'

She was addressing an empty ward. He knew it and she must know it too. He would swear she had seen him, just as he had seen her, if only for that split second.

She came out of her own ward and Tim anticipated a stop at this ward and another demand for him to show himself. But she did not check in her return walk down the corridor. Through the crack, he glimpsed her as she passed by, and she said nothing as she went. He waited. What was she going to do now, send the escort in after him?

Outside, the sun was sinking fast, as it did over the Western Desert. Two German military policemen advanced hurriedly on the Army nurse as she emerged from the hospital.

'Well, Fraulein Lieutenant? We've no time to hang about. Where is this prisoner?'

'Gone, as I told you,' said Anneliese.

'You've checked?'

'Yes,' she said. 'So did the orderly. It seems he must be in one of the forward ambulances.'

'But we understood he's not an ambulance case, he's a British prisoner of war sufficiently recovered to be handed over to us.'

'He's still an ambulance case,' said Anneliese. 'I'm not concerned with his nationality, only with his condition, which is still in need of attention. Speak to Captain Hearst if you aren't satisfied and can catch her up, but look out for her blowing your heads off. I must go now, in this ambulance.'

'Well, the British won't be far from the town by nightfall, and will probably send in night patrols to probe about, so get going, Fraulein Lieutenant, while we try to catch up with your forward vehicles.'

The military policemen ran for their own vehicle, and Anneliese took her place in the last ambulance, up with the driver. Her valise was at her feet. In it was the beret of a British Commando of the desert, handed to her by an orderly who was full of furious words concerning the Commando's disappearance. Duty-bound to investigate the matter herself, she had done so. As the ambulance moved off, she heard the fiery sounds of an aerial dogfight in the purple-red sky above Benghazi. She turned her head, looked at the Italian-built hospital and delivered a silent message, a faint smile on her face.

'Goodbye, Lieutenant Adams, take care not to show yourself again until all of us are gone.'

After all, what did one man matter when millions were now involved worldwide, and the Fuehrer had made a mad decision to go to war against America while still in savage conflict with Stalin's hordes and had the British Empire at his throat here in Libya?

The ambulance raced to catch up with the convoy and the retreating German fighting units.

The advance armoured columns of the Eighth Army entered Benghazi during the morning of Christmas Eve, and Tim, emerging from the deserted hospital, took his delayed walk and, subsequently, his first ride in the sweaty, claustrophobic hellhole of a tank's interior. The tank commander delivered him into the embrace of an accompanying RAMC unit.

He was sure by then that Anneliese Bruck, the epitome of the ideal Aryan woman in the eyes of Himmler, had given him his freedom.

Some days later, when German Army units had helped the convoy break through the British Army's road block, and her patients were in hospital in Tripoli, Anneliese was asked by Captain Schaeffer what had happened to Lieutenant

Adams, the British Commando officer with the chest wounds.

'I believe he avoided his escort and escaped,' she said.

'Did he?' Captain Schaeffer was sceptical.

'Yes.'

'Did you have something to do with that, Fraulein Lieutenant?'

'Why do you ask such a question?'

'Curiosity. What did you think of him?'

'He was like you, Herr Hauptmann, a man, a soldier.'

'But an enemy.'

'He was still a man, a soldier.'

'So, were you in love with him, Fraulein Lieutenant?'

'That is an impertinent question which I shan't answer,' said Anneliese.

Chapter Eighteen

'It's Christmas Eve, Clara, and I haven't had a Christmas card from Tim,' said Felicity. 'Have I?'

'Well, no,' said Clara Dickens, her fast friend and caring nurse, 'but under the circumstances—'

'Curse the circumstances,' said Felicity.

'All right, curse them, and I hope that will improve them in your favour,' said Clara. They were in the kitchen that was for use by rehabilitating patients, and Felicity, aproned, was blindly stirring a Christmas pudding mixture.

'Prisoners of war are allowed to send Christmas cards, aren't they?' asked Felicity, dark glasses perched on the bridge of her fine nose.

'I suppose so,' said Clara, 'although I'm not sure.'

'Well, you should be,' said Felicity, 'I'm not in sympathy with uncertain minds. I need a plain yes or no.'

'Can I offer a plain yes, they are allowed, and a plain no, they aren't?' suggested Clara.

'Is that a funny?' asked Felicity.

'It's the best I can do,' said Clara. 'Hold on while I pour a little old ale into the mixture.' She poured some from a bottle. It turned the mixture sticky and aroused a Christmas aroma. The military convalescent hospital was allowed the privilege of receiving a generous ration of ingredients.

'Well, that smells as if it's helping the pudding,' said Felicity, resuming her stirring with a wooden spoon. 'How am I doing, dearie?'

'Just the job,' said Clara.

'Tomorrow,' said Felicity, 'wrap a slice of the pudding in greaseproof, put it in a container and send it to Tim via the Red Cross.'

'I'll make enquiries about the possibility of him getting it,' said Clara.

'What a bloody awful Christmas he'll have, poor darling,' said Felicity.

'He'll survive, Felicity,' said Clara.

'He better had,' said Felicity. 'Believe me, I've got the kind of feelings for that man that I never thought to have for any of 'em.'

'I know,' said Clara.

'How the hell does it happen to an intelligent woman?' asked Felicity, giving the mixture a blind bashing.

'I believe it's the initial eye-to-eye contact,' said Clara.

Felicity did not wince. Such comments could not be avoided during the course of the many conversations she enjoyed with Clara, and neither attempted avoidance.

'Eye-to-eye? Yes, I see,' she said, and smiled. 'Merry Christmas, Clara.'

'Same to you, lovey,' said Clara. Felicity was to spend Christmas with her parents. An ambulance would be taking her home this evening, and bringing her back on Boxing Day. And early in the

New Year, she was to leave the hospital for good. With a disabled officer's pension.

It wasn't a pension she needed, thought Clara. It was Tim, the husband whom she often referred to as her lifeline.

Earlier that morning, Paula was saying goodbye to her father at the front door before he went to his offices. She wanted to ask him something, and did.

'Daddy, why can't we keep Phoebe?'

'Keep her, Plum Pudding?' said Sammy guardedly.

'Well, you must know she doesn't have a mummy or daddy. They went away and left her, didn't they? So can't she stay with us? She's ever so nice really, she doesn't get cross with me like Bess used to.' Bess, her sister, was an evacuee in Devon, along with her brothers, Daniel and Jimmy.

'Bless me,' said Sammy, 'I can't see why anyone should get cross with you, me pet.'

'No, nor me, I'm ever so good,' said Paula with the right amount of self-belief.

'So you are,' smiled Sammy, giving her hair a little ruffle. 'Anyway, I'm off now, I don't want to be late or me workers might forget to wish me a merry Christmas.'

'But, Daddy, you haven't said about Phoebe,' protested Paula.

Sammy could have said Phoebe had enjoyed a dry night for once, but didn't.

'Phoebe's got close relatives, me sausage, and we can't keep her if they want to have her.'

'Crickey, what a blessed nuisance,' said Paula. 'Phoebe just doesn't know about any relatives, except her Aunt Lily, and she went away too. Phoebe told me so. No wonder she's been awful sad some mornings.'

Sammy knew which mornings they were.

'Well, I like you, Paula me precious, for cheering her up the way you do,' he said, 'and we'll give her a nice Christmas, eh?'

'Yes, she and me's going to finish making paper chains today,' said Paula.

'That's the stuff,' said Sammy. 'So long till this evening, pet.' Off he went.

'Daddy, come back!' yelled Paula.

He stopped and turned.

'What's up?' he asked.

'You forgot to kiss me,' said Paula. Sammy rectified his omission, and his young daughter said, 'Daddy, Phoebe likes you and Mummy ever so much.'

It's getting at me all the time, thought Sammy as he went on his way, and I'm losing me sense of proportion, which won't do me business brains much good. Well, there's those Oriental Japs knocking hell out of us and the Yanks in places I've hardly ever heard of, there's bloody Hitler and old Bolshevik Joe murdering each other in Russia, there's our blokes out there in the desert trying to roll up Rommel, there's Fatty Goering, the German balloon, still sending us bombs, and there's our fighting nephew Tim a prisoner of war, which is hurting Chinese Lady considerable, never mind what it's doing to his blind wife, name of Felicity.

And here am I with me upset mind fixed on little Phoebe.

That's got to be a daft sense of proportion all

right. I'll get mentally retarded, and Susie'll have to put me in a home with a box of coloured bricks to play with.

Did Boots get like this over five-year-old Rosie?

As far as Chinese Lady was concerned, the sooner the little girl's Uncle Herbert arrived and made arrangements for her future in Canada, the better. Lonely little girls of sweet appeal could curl their fingers around one's heart. Phoebe was greatly in need of love and security, just as Rosie had been years ago, and it was up to her Canadian aunt and uncle to provide that by adopting her. Chinese Lady was sure they would, but it was taking time for Herbert Willis to call, and Sammy and Susie had to be very careful about not letting their feelings get the better of them. A quick settlement of the problem could be happy for everyone, especially for Phoebe, and make up a bit for the chronic miseries of the war.

It was a wonder people still had some spirit left. All those towns and cities being bombed, as well as London, and it was still going on, driving people into their shelters a lot too often. But no-one seemed downright downhearted. Edwin had said a few days ago that that kind of spirit would carry the country and its people through every setback until Hitler's evil empire collapsed. Yes, but how's our family going to come out of it, that's what I'd like to know, said Chinese Lady. Edwin smiled and thanked her for saying 'our family'.

'Edwin, of course it's your family as well,' she said.

'I'm a fortunate man, Maisie,' he said.

'Edwin, we've all been fortunate in lots of ways,'

she said, 'and no-one can say the Lord hasn't been good to us.'

'The Lord, Maisie, has been very good to me,' he said, 'and I'm sure the family will survive and flourish. And multiply,' he added, with a smile.

'Lor,' said Chinese Lady, thinking of Polly's twins and Rosie expecting her first, 'I hope multiplying won't mean I won't be able to count them. Which reminds me, Edwin, we haven't seen the twins yet.'

'Then perhaps in the New Year we could take a train to Dorset, stay at a hotel for the weekend, and visit Boots and Polly while we're there,' said Mr Finch. 'Would you like that, Maisie?'

'Edwin, you're a good man.'

'You, Maisie, are an exceptionally good woman.'

At her housework on Christmas Eve, Chinese Lady was dusting and tidying her husband's study. Putting the cork back into a bottle of Stephens ink, she noticed a long brown envelope to one side of his blotter. On top of it was a folded foolscap document. She picked it up to place it in the envelope, and in doing so saw that it was Edwin's will. She made a little face. She wasn't fond of wills, especially family wills. They related to passing on. Only the Lord knew how much grief Emily's passing on had given the family. The thought of anything fatal happening to Edwin brought a sharp little pain to her being.

She did not consider reading the will. It was something very private, but somehow she found herself scanning it. There were little pencil corrections here and there, and she realized Edwin had been going over it.

She sat down in his desk chair. It was wrong to read his very private words, she knew that, but reading became compulsive. The introduction to his bequests was devoted to the happiness and pleasure he had been given by the Adams and Somers families. It wasn't set down in that legal jargon solicitors used so that only they knew what it meant. It was like a very nice composition about the affection he had for all the family members he had been privileged to know and observe during his many years among them. He mentioned only Boots by name.

'Of all the friendships I have enjoyed, Boots will know why I have especially cherished his.'

He was leaving something to all his step-grandchildren. Chinese Lady, struggling with emotion, felt he had rightly decided Boots, Polly, Lizzy, Ned and all the others of that generation, did not need anything except his assurance that he cared for them. He had given them that.

To my dear wife Maisie, whose loving care for my well-being, devoted attention to my needs, and exceptional tolerance of my imperfections, have been steadfast and unfailing, I give devise and bequeath the residue of my estate absolutely. In her I have found a companionship and understanding that have made my life with her wholly privileged. I give to her my love and my gratitude for all she has meant to me.

Chinese Lady put the will back as she had found it, on top of the envelope. She sat unmoving for long minutes, her emotions disturbed, her eyes wet.

Why had Edwin been going over his will?

'Edwin?' It was close to midnight, and she and Edwin were about to retire. One was always late to bed on Christmas Eve.

'Maisie?'

'Did you have a headache when you got home from the office this evening?'

'A headache?'

'I thought – well, I thought you looked a bit tired, like.'

'No headache, Maisie, no, none at all, and I don't recall feeling tired.'

'You're all right gen'rally, are you, Edwin?'

'Never felt better, Maisie, apart from age preventing me from performing high jumps. Why do you ask?'

'Oh, I just thought – well, we're both getting on a bit, but of course I don't want to fuss.' She was sixty-five, he was sixty-eight. 'You'd tell me, wouldn't you, if you had to see the doctor about anything?'

'My dear, if I had to see him at all, you'd be the first to know. Maisie, it's now past midnight.'

'Oh, yes. A merry Christmas, Edwin.'

'And a very happy one to you, Maisie.'

Leah had received a Christmas card from Edward. Inside, he'd written a greeting.

Leah, if you'd like to share Christmas with me in your thoughts, I'll celebrate Passover with you when the time comes. Here's a kiss.
    Edward

She didn't show the card to Rebecca. She kept it to herself and slept with it under her pillow that night. Leah was a romantic.

Chapter Nineteen

Little Phoebe woke up on Christmas morning and was tearful again. Sammy, first into her bedroom, comforted her, attended to her, gave her the hot sponging that she liked so much, and helped her to dress. When Susie came in, he was watching the child in her exploration of her Christmas stocking.

'Oh, look, I've got presents,' she said to Susie. Susie saw the stripped bed and Sammy's wry expression.

'Well, I never,' she said, 'I think Father Christmas has been, Phoebe.'

'Did he come down to Paula too?' asked Phoebe, clutching a bright new penny in one hand and a little rag book in the other. There should have been a shiny red orange, but all fruit that had to be imported was scarce. Phoebe had other little gifts to make up for the absence of a Christmas orange. 'Did Paula 'ave presents too?' Phoebe was earnest to know.

'Yes, he never forgets all little boys and girls,' said Susie, smiling.

In came Paula in her nightdress to show the

presents she'd found in her own stocking, and the two girls were soon chattering excitedly.

They were bonding like sisters, and Susie wondered if Paula would miss Phoebe as much as she and Sammy would when the inevitable parting came about.

Emma and Jonathan woke up in his parents' house in Kennington. Jonathan had obtained three days Christmas leave and brought Emma home with him.

'Merry Christmas, Emma.'

'Merry Christmas, Jonathan.'

'Love you, Emma, that I do.'

'Jonathan, I like that.'

'Durned if I thought when I first met you that I'd be in bed with you one day.'

'Oh, I think you had that in mind after a day or so.'

'That I never did, nor after a week or so.'

'When then?'

'Well, Emma, two minutes after marrying you, it did occur to me that you'd expect me to do the honours that night. It fair gave me the shakes.'

'The shakes?'

'Well, it wasn't going to be like peeling an apple, Emma. I can peel an apple without thinking about it. A wedding night's different, and as you were the first girl I'd ever married—'

'Oh really?'

'Fact. So I thought when we get to bed, what do I do that I'm expected to do? I'd never had a problem like that before, Emma.'

'A problem? A problem?'

'Well, you be a lovely girl to go to bed with, Emma.'

'Thank you, Jonathan, I like to think you're right.'

'And if you remember, you had a fancy for Rhett Butler and his wicked ways.'

'I never did.'

'And me being only a simple country chap—'

'Simple? Don't make me die, Jonathan, it's Christmas.'

'I thought, as a simple chap, I'd get tied up in knots.'

'I can't remember you doing that.'

'No more can I, Emma. It all went blank, and I didn't come to until the morning after. Can you tell me if – I mean, did I – did you – did we?'

'Oh, I think so, Jonathan.'

'You be certain sure, Emma?'

'Fairly sure, Jonathan.'

'Lovely girl, you are, Emma.'

'Yes, don't I be, Jonathan.'

Someone knocked on the bedroom door.

'If that's Father Christmas,' said Jonathan, 'he's a bit late. Come in, Father Christmas.'

In came Job, still a fine figure of a man at nearly fifty. He carried two cups of tea.

'It's a fine morning, so a happy Christmas, you young people,' he smiled. Emma and Jonathan returned the greeting, sat up and took the tea.

'Thanks, Pa,' said Jonathan.

'You're welcome,' said Job. 'Your mother and me have been praying a tidy bit for Emma's cousin Tim, that he won't be too downhearted, wherever they Germans have got him.'

'He won't be downhearted, Dad,' said Emma, glowing with the health of a young wife of nineteen whose daily work was in the open air, and whose fulfilment as a wife was well looked after by Sussex-born Jonathan, a terrible saucy husband. 'Tim's like my brother Bobby, he's always looking for a way through the brickwork when his back's to the wall.'

Tim at this moment was back in the hospital at Benghazi, now under British control and staffed by RAMC personnel. He was undergoing a prolonged mid-morning examination by a Major Dalby, a surgeon.

'Hurt?' said Major Dalby, giving Tim's chest a very exploratory going-over as a final test of his condition.

'I can't tell a lie, it does hurt,' said Tim, wincing even though the pressure of the examining hand was gentle. 'Bloody hell, yes.'

'Know what you've got, do you, Lieutenant?'

'Yes, some bullet holes and damaged ribs,' said Tim, 'but I've been breathing nearly as good as the next man. Is there something else, then?'

'Cracked sternum.'

'Sternum?' said Tim.

'Breastbone,' said Major Dalby.

'I knew about my ribs,' said Tim, 'not about my sternum. If anyone mentioned sternum, it was in German, and it probably sounded like a dhobi wallah swallowing his wet washing.'

'You were hit first in your right side, which probably spun you round and helped you collect the next bullets in your chest,' said Major Dalby, lean, balding and chatty. 'What were you wearing?'

233

'Sheepskin-lined jacket over my jersey and shirt,' said Tim.

'The jacket took some of the impact, or your sternum might have been shattered, and you'd probably be dead by now,' said Major Dalby. 'Well, you need an X-ray before your condition can be fully diagnosed. Still, the rest of you is up to scratch, and as it's Christmas Day, there's an issue of rum.'

'That's for sailors,' said Tim.

'The whisky rations took a pounding, and we waylaid a Navy supply truck,' said Major Dalby. 'We'll give you a jar of Christmas rum and then arrange to put you on a flight tomorrow, probably to Alexandria.'

'How about Southend?' asked Tim.

'A bit off the map at the moment, Lieutenant,' said Major Dalby.

'Merry Christmas,' said Tim.

David, Lizzy and Ned's younger son, spent Christmas with Boots, Polly and Kate. He met the twins, fat, gurgling and bubble-blowing, and then joined Kate under the mistletoe in the kitchen. He did the obvious.

''Ere, wait a minute, I wasn't ready,' said Kate, sixteen and perky. 'I'm doing bread sauce for the chicken I found wandering about all plucked and ready for the oven.'

'Wandering about?' said David.

'Oh, all right, on the doorstep, then,' said Kate. 'Present from Father Christmas, I suppose. There I'm ready now.'

So David kissed her again, amid the aroma of a Christmas dinner cooking.

'I liked that,' he said, 'hope you did too.'

Kate looked at him, her best friend. After her Aunt Hilary had been arrested for an act of sabotage, leaving her to fend for herself, David had been a tower of strength in getting his Uncle Boots and Aunt Polly to take her in. A lover of the open air of Devon, even in winter he looked as if he'd just come in from mowing summer hay. Mind, he had a very aggravating way of not taking her seriously.

'Listen,' she said, 'was that just a Christmas kiss or what?'

'Both,' said David.

'A Christmas kiss and a what?' said Kate.

'Well, what did what feel like?' asked David, thinking her green eyes dewy with kitchen steam.

'A kind of passin' thought?' said Kate, a Camberwell cockney.

'Pardon?' said David. He had the same kind of dark brown hair and grey eyes of his Uncle Boots and his long-dead grandfather, the first husband of Grandma Finch. 'What's a passing thought?'

'Nothing very much,' said Kate.

So David kissed her again, and Kate, going weak at the knees, wondered what her late dad, a good old Labour Party man, would think of her relationship with this boy who, although he had cockney parents, talked middle class. Fancy wanting to be middle class. She'd told him off about that lots of times, but it all bounced off him. Oh, crikey, he was helping himself to a lot more than he should under the kitchen mistletoe.

'Get off,' she gasped, and declared herself scandalized.

'Why?' asked David.

'Why? Why? You know why all right. Talk about wandering hands, and on Christmas Day as well, which is supposed to be holy.'

'I only tried to improve a bit on a passing thought,' grinned David.

'Well, look what it did to me apron,' said Kate, 'it's all crumpled and crooked, and me dress feels like it's been in a fight.'

'Suits you,' said David.

'Suits me?' said Kate, prettily flushed. Prettily flushed was always a good condition to be in on occasions like this. It made the opposition pause for thought. 'What d'you mean, it suits me?'

'Well, a crumpled apron on a girl makes her look sexy,' said David.

'Oh, yer saucy 'a'porth,' said Kate. Then, 'You sure it does?'

'Fact,' said David.

'All right, kiss me again like that,' said Kate.

'Anything happening in the kitchen?' called Boots a moment later.

'Yes, Kate's mixing bread sauce,' called David.

'Is it in trouble, David?'

'The bread sauce, Uncle Boots?' said David. 'Not from where I'm standing.'

'Well, something called for help,' said Boots. 'Have a look at the chicken.'

'Oh, she's OK, Uncle Boots, her apron's just a bit crumpled, that's all.'

That brought forth a little yell from Kate. Boots smiled. The young lady cook was entitled to her own kind of Christmas fare.

'Is there something between those two?' murmured Polly, her twins asleep in their cots.

'Only Kate's apron, I imagine,' said Boots.

'What a delightful thing it is to be young,' said Polly.

'For some,' said Boots. 'I'm enjoying being the ancient father of twins myself.'

'I'm still having giddy moments when I'm wondering how I came to be their mother,' said Polly.

'D'you need an explanation?' asked Boots.

'Not the kind I'll get from you,' said Polly.

Rosie and husband Matthew arrived an hour before dinner was served. David was all of delighted to seen cousin Rosie, a gorgeous example of fascinating femininity in his opinion, and he gave her a very affectionate greeting before meeting Matthew.

Kate pulled him back into the kitchen after that.

'Listen,' she said, 'Rosie's your cousin, ain't she?'

'Yes,' said David.

'So what d'you mean by kissin' her like that?'

'I like kissing her like that,' said David.

'Well, it's not decent if she's your cousin,' said Kate, 'especially as she's goin' to have a baby.'

'She's actually an adopted cousin,' said David.

'I don't want any feeble excuses, so take that,' said Kate, and hit him over the head with a wooden spoon.

'Kate, did you do that?' he asked.

'Yes, me, I did it,' said Kate. 'Merry Christmas, David.'

Little Phoebe and Paula had an exciting Christmas Day amid a crowd of adult well-wishers. Chinese Lady and Mr Finch entertained Tommy and Vi, Aunt Victoria and Uncle Tom, and Lizzy and Ned, as well as Sammy and Susie. They all talked at once and, for that matter, so did Phoebe and Paula. Sammy noted, however, that from time to time Phoebe cast shyly hopeful eyes at Tommy and Vi, and Lizzy and Ned. It made him think she was going to ask if either couple were her mummy and daddy.

Come on, Herbert Willis, he thought, let's hear from you.

Hermann Goering allowed Britain a day of peace by keeping his *Luftwaffe* bomber squadrons grounded in Northern France. His inactive airmen were able to enjoy their festivities, and he partook of a huge dinner himself. But he promised Britain a hail of bombs in the New Year.

The Japanese took no notice of Christmas Day at all. They made the day hell for the Americans and British in various parts of the Far East.

Stalin's Soviet hordes pounded the freezing Germans in the Russian snow. The fighting was savage and barbaric, symbolizing the hatred the opposing forces had for each other. Many prisoners on both sides were slaughtered out of hand. The German sense of invincibility, promoted by Hitler as something godlike, was being questioned by the Germans themselves as their casualties became enormous. Russian casualties were no less.

Stalin, however, was counting not his losses, but his huge reserves of manpower.

Hitler was screaming at some of his generals. His ambition to take Moscow well before Christmas had been frustrated by ice, snow, constant Russian counter-attacks and, in his opinion, by the cowardice and timidity of certain generals.

He himself stood by his omnipotent infallibility. Well, all the people around him, Goebbels in particular, never failed to give him the impression he was second only to God. And sometimes, not even second.

27th of December

Felicity received a postcard that bore the markings of the International Red Cross. Clara read to her the words written in pencil.

Darling Girl. In hospital recovering from wounds, then to POW camp. Thinking of you always. Love, Tim.

That had reached Felicity with the help of a sympathetic German orderly backed up by a German Army nurse and the efficiency of the Red Cross.

'Read it again, Clara,' said Felicity.

Clara did so.

'Now we know,' she said.

'Yes, that by now Tim's probably in a bloody prisoner of war camp,' said Felicity.

'And isn't going to forget you,' said Clara.

'That's my consolation, is it?' said Felicity.

'It would be for me,' said Clara, 'I'd hang on to that tooth and nail.'

Felicity wasn't sure whether the card was a relief or a blow. It's both, she decided. It's a relief to know he's recovering, and a blow to realize he's definitely lost to me until this hell of a war is over. One day,

I'll let it all out, I'll bloody well cry for a week.

'Look here, Clara you chump,' she said grittily, 'am I supposed to feel happy about taking consolation to bed with me instead of Tim, and for God knows how long?'

'Let's have some hot Bovril and then go for a walk,' said Clara.

'That's it, be my lifelong friend,' said Felicity.

'I hope I will be,' said Clara.

'Bless you, ducky,' said Felicity, 'and I'll make the Bovril.'

'Don't try anything too ambitious with the hot water,' said Clara.

'Fusspot,' said Felicity.

Rachel received a letter from Leah.

Dearest Lovely Mama . . .
Rachel, noting that, braced herself for an impossible request.

I want you to know Edward and I are seeing each other every week, and last Saturday I actually had lunch with him in a little restaurant in Salisbury. This coming Saturday we're repeating it. Miss Murchison is giving me permission to miss school lunch on Saturdays, but of course she insists on Pauline and Cecily chaperoning me. I go to the reference section of the library afterwards to study, where Edward and I can only whisper to each other.

Mama, I'm getting to like Edward very much, do you mind? You did say you would never dictate to me about friendships, but I have to tell you it's getting to be a special friendship with Edward. Of course, I know it won't necessarily be more than that,

I'm only saying it's a very happy one for me at the moment. Please could I have your approval? Your loving and well-behaved daughter,

 Leah.

 PS . . . Aren't the Japanese sickening rotters? Poor Mr Churchill must be wondering how many more headaches he's going to suffer.

Rachel, of course, was reminded of her time with Sammy when they were in their teens. If Leah's feelings for Edward developed in the same way as her own had for Sammy, there might be heartache ahead. Rachel's father, Leah's grandfather, would expect both his granddaughters to marry men of their own kind. Although not strictly orthodox, he would ask for observance of religious principles as far as marriage was concerned. He was in Palestine at the moment, and had been there for months, one of a deputation of Jews seeking an audition with a representative of the Pope, to petition for his Holiness's intervention on behalf of the persecuted Jews of Germany and Poland. The Pope, so far, had been unresponsive.

Rachel decided to reply as sensibly as she could to her younger daughter. She told her she understood her liking for Edward, and to enjoy her friendship with him while she was young. Yes, while she was young. She emphasized that. It represented a necessary note of caution. She refrained, however, from pointing out that if the two of them fell in love later on, then difficulties would arise. On the other hand, the Somers and Adams families were so broadminded and tolerant about most things that Lizzy and Ned might not object to Leah as a daughter-in-law.

No, I'm running ahead, thought Rachel, I'm taking on board something that goes back to my feelings for Sammy and how much I'd have liked him to marry me. I'm putting Leah in my place of all those years ago, giving her my feelings.

But she knew that if there was ever a possibility of Leah marrying into the Gentile family she herself had so much affection for, she would raise no objections. She would be immensely happy for Leah. The decision would probably rest with Leah's grandfather.

I'm still running ahead, she thought.

Chapter Twenty

The long-distance flying-boat took off from the waters off Alexandria at dawn and rose into the sky. Aboard were fourteen passengers, including two Very Important Persons, one of ministerial status, the other an adviser to Lord Beaverbrook, Churchill's live-wire Minister of Production. Each was accompanied by assistants. There were also wounded Army and RAF officers due for convalescent leave or special medical treatment, although none was a stretcher case.

The plane headed west to fly off the north coast of Algeria, under the administration of the Vichy Government, and on to the Bay of Biscay for a stop at Gibraltar, from where it would fly due north on a route west of Portugal to the British Isles.

Above Algiers, two patrolling *Messerschmitts*, radios buzzing with information, turned to intercept and destroy the British flying-boat. Ten minutes later, the pilot and navigator of the latter saw them coming, bright hurtling flashes in the sky at a short distance below. The *Messerschmitts* screamed under the flying-boat, made a lightning ascent, wheeled in the sky, and came back at the seaplane from above.

The pilot took swift avoiding action, dropping low and fast. The passengers, despite restraining straps, were vaulted upwards.

'Bloody hell,' gasped Lieutenant Tim Adams, 'who's driving this thing?'

'Must be my girlfriend,' gasped an RAF pilot, 'she's better at walking her dog.'

The *Messerschmitts* dived in pursuit. Their guns opened up and tracer bullets chased a course for the tail of the seaplane. At an acute angle of descent, it became a crazy airborne transport for its passengers. But it slipped the tracers, and down into the fray rushed three Hurricanes, the flying-boat's first-stage escort.

An air battle commenced. The *Messerschmitts* were the faster fighters, the Hurricanes the more manoeuvrable, the more agile. The flying-boat slipped away, leaving its escort to frustrate and down the enemy. One *Messerschmitt*, its tail blazing after ten minutes of combat, cartwheeled out of the sky. The other turned east and fled for its base near Tripoli.

The flying-boat's passengers straightened themselves out. A crew member helped them. The Very Important Persons were bruised, shaken, but intact. One wounded officer felt his healing process had suffered a nasty setback, and Tim had to put up with all kinds of pained protests from his afflicted sternum.

The flying-boat landed in Southampton Water off Portsmouth the following morning. Cars awaited the Government men and their aides, and two ambulances were summoned up to take care of the officers.

On the outskirts of Lys in the south of France that afternoon, Bobby and Helene were approaching the main road by a roundabout way. Their walk was an unhurried stroll, and they were arm in arm, like lovers, Helene with a hatbox in one hand. Houses thinned out and ceased to be when they reached the main road. It was two o'clock as they turned into it. Away to their left were the serried slopes of vineyards, the grapes long since harvested, and the air laden with the mild scents of benign winter. Ahead were dusty verges, dry hedges and, in the distance, a bend, a sharp bend that preceded the straight stretch leading to the concentration camp.

Not many people of Lys, lovers or otherwise, took a stroll that brought them within close reach of the camp. Keeping themselves at a distance from it was all part of the process of ignoring it. Indeed, if one never saw it or mentioned it, one could even begin to believe it wasn't there. Not that it was a place of the kind said to exist in Germany, Austria and Poland. There were no killings, no deaths by starvation or disease. It was a camp where French Jews were detained under strict surveillance while awaiting resettlement, which meant, of course, deportation to Germany or Poland and into the hideous confines of ss-run concentration camps.

These French Jews were rounded up by Vichy's French authorities, transported by French policemen to Lys and subsequently herded into the deportation trains by the camp's French guards.

Helene was in a perpetual rage about it. She felt all the disparaging words she had given to Bobby about the British were flying back at her like burning arrows.

She said now, 'We are early enough, Bobby.'

'Maurice,' said Bobby.

'Oh, shut up.'

'Keep calm,' said Bobby.

'How can I? I'm on fire with shame. Isn't France supposed to be the most civilized nation in the world?'

'The French say so,' said Bobby, 'but they chopped up Marie Antoinette and lynched a few hundred aristocrats.'

'That was in order to establish a civilized way of life,' said Helene, 'and it did.' The bend in the road was sixty yards away, and Bobby was looking for a break in the hedge. 'Ah, you English, you are still uncultured and cannot even cook.'

'Is that so?' said Bobby.

'You have no music,' said Helene, 'no artists, no finesse, no subtlety, no true theatre, no Sarah Bernhardt and only mediocre poetry.'

'Sorry about that,' said Bobby. 'I thought you were beginning to like us. And I had no idea that a farmer's daughter was a follower of poets and painters. Are you sure our own poets don't rate much of a mention?'

'They are inferior to French,' said Helene, her mood ragged. 'Look, if we walk round the bend we'll be seen from the camp.'

'We both know that,' said Bobby, and took a look over his shoulder. There was no-one behind them, and no traffic. 'And we both know we've got to go to ground just before the bend. I'm looking for a gap in this hedge. Don't be awkward, there's a good girl.'

'Can I help it if I'm angry about that concentration camp?' said Helene. 'Ah, you may be made of wood, I am not.'

'Look, there we are,' said Bobby. There was a narrow gap some twenty yards from the bend. 'Watch your skirt, don't leave it hanging in the gap.'

'Your jokes are still terrible,' said Helene.

They were quite alone as Bobby watched her push her way through the gap, hatbox held in front of her. He followed, and they sank down on their knees. Helene opened up the hatbox. Inside was a straw creation with a deep crown. It was upside-down, and in the crown nestled four round bakelite objects topped with little metal knobs.

'Well, there's a nice set of quads,' said Bobby, and they went down on their stomachs to await the arrival of the truck that always appeared at about three o'clock on Monday afternoons. 'By the way, Lynette, now that I know you still don't like my island or its people, I promise to deliver you safely back to your parents as soon as the war's over. I owe them that.'

'Good,' said Helene.

'I'll be sad, of course,' said Bobby.

'Good,' said Helene.

'I've heard of Sarah Bernhardt,' said Bobby.

'Everyone in the world has,' said Helene.

'Didn't she have a wooden leg?' said Bobby.

'Oh, shut up,' said Helene.

Bobby smiled. His young French lady was not at her best.

They lay there, waiting while minutes crept by like crippled snails. It was a long ten minutes before Helene broke the silence.

'Bobby?'

'Maurice.'

'No, I wish to speak to you as yourself. That was a joke, wasn't it?'

'What was?'

'About getting rid of me when the war is over.'

'I didn't say that.'

'It was what you meant.'

'No, it wasn't.'

'But was it a joke?'

'No, a promise to take you back to your parents.'

'You would do that?'

'Yes, if it would make you happy.' Bobby was keeping his eyes and ears wide open. By a shift of his body he could seen a stretch of the road through the gap. What was important was to ensure that neither himself nor Helene became visible to the driver of the lorry and the two guards who were always in the cabin with him. 'That counts, making you happy.'

'Oh, you pig, you think getting rid of me would make me happy?' breathed Helene.

'Let's talk about it later,' said Bobby, 'let's concentrate on the truck and its arrival, and let's hope that when it does arrive there'll be nothing behind it.'

Helene lay brooding, simmering and waiting.

Inside the camp, the guards were also waiting. For the arrival of a new intake of Jews, the enemies of the New Order embraced by Vichy France. A group of inmates stood in conversation outside a hut not far from the gates. One might have thought their exchanges forced because they sounded cheerful. Any kind of cheerfulness, however, was acceptable to the camp staff whenever a new truckload of Jews was expected. It made the arrivals feel the camp was a place of happy families, and accordingly they gave no trouble. Trouble was a nuisance.

A Jewish scientist, Professor Victor Leischler, was among the talkative group. A tall lean man who combined a scholarly appearance with an athletic look, his own contributions to a discussion on hares and hounds were of an amusing kind. Hares, he said, could always escape the hounds if the hounds were confused.

'How does one confuse them?' asked a woman.

'By throwing them a fish.'

'A fish confuses them?'

'Yes, as long as it's a red herring.'

The woman laughed, then cast a glance at the gates and the guards. The guards were watching the road.

It was a few minutes to three when Helene whispered that a vehicle was coming, that she could hear it. Only two other vehicles had passed by during the time she and Bobby had been waiting, both cars of ancient vintage.

'If it's the truck, be ready,' said Bobby.

'Be ready?' breathed Helene. 'I am.'

Bobby craned his head. He saw it, the large truck that always arrived with its rear doors securely barred. It was coming at a steady pace, and would slow down to take the sharp bend in low gear.

Bobby held one of the round bakelite spheres, and so did Helene. The remaining two were in her open hatbox.

'Yes, it's the truck,' whispered Bobby, and drew his head out of sight.

They heard the noise of its engine. Nerves galloped and adrenalin flowed. Flat on their stomachs behind the hedge, they came up on their knees as they glimpsed the bonnet of the truck. It passed the gap, and the driver changed down to take the bend. Bobby and Helene came fast to their feet. Bobby burst through the gap and Helene followed, and they rushed at speed to place themselves behind the truck. They were close to it as it began to slowly take the bend. The guards at the gates of the camp saw it as it appeared. Behind it, Bobby and Helene were hidden. Bobby pulled the metal cap free of his sphere and rolled it fast under the truck. Helene, carrying the hatbox, gave him the second as the first ran free of the front of the truck. He pulled the pin of the second, and whipped it under the truck as the driver changed up. The first bakelite ball exploded then with a crack and a flash, and the next moment it belched rising tongues of black smoke. The second, another smoke bomb, ran spinning ahead of the truck and also exploded. The road filled with black fumes. The driver, visibility suddenly nil, trod hard on his brakes, the engine stalled and the truck stopped.

The guards at the camp gates watched stunned at what appeared to be exploding bombs, one, two, three, four in quick succession, and all in the path of the truck, completely enveloping it in clouds of back smoke. Bobby and Helene turned and retreated at high speed, their going covered by the smoke and the truck. In the cabin the driver and his escort of two policemen were coughing and spluttering as smoke filtered in.

The gates of the camp opened and panicking guards, rifles unslung, came running out, all intent on dealing with bomb-throwing saboteurs. The alarm was sounding in the camp as the group of inmates nearest the gates took note of the rushing, scrambling exodus of guards. Immediately, they made a concerted rush of their own, risking being fired on by other guards at a farther point in the camp. Out through the gates they sped, but when clear of them they turned left towards the centre of Lys and away from the incident. They ran fast, the athletic professor in the van. They were the only people who had not been surprised by the sudden alarm. They were supporters of the scientist, Professor Victor Leischler, and by a message smuggled in they had been waiting for something dramatic to occur this afternoon and to take advantage of it. Their primary objective was to ensure the escape of Leischler, even if they themselves were recaptured. A number of the remaining guards, recovering their wits, rushed through the compound and out through the gates, turning left in pursuit of the escapees. Others stayed where they were to prevent any dashes for freedom by the rest of the inmates.

The black smoke, billowing in front of and around the truck hindered examination of exactly what was happening. Nor did it allow sight of any saboteurs. The driver and the two policemen emerged from the man-made fog, coughing and with eyes streaming. The charging arrival of the camp guards was marked by an immediate rush through thinning smoke to the rear of the truck, where the doors were checked. The locked bar still held them shut tight. There had been no attempt, apparently, to rescue the consignment of Jewish people. The smoke, confusing and confounding guards, policemen and driver alike, not only made it impossible for them to detect the presence of the person or persons responsible for stopping the truck, but it also now shut them off from any view of the camp.

Nothing was happening there except the herding of inmates into huts and locking them in. But elsewhere, certain Jewish men and women were helping to secure the escape of Professor Leischler, and then to look after their own interests.

Leischler had an appointment in Carbonne, with the man Bobby and Helene knew only as Paul.

'What do we do now?' asked Helene. They were far down the road, but not on it. They were walking on the other side of the hedge, keeping out of sight. There was a sense of elation at having stopped the truck and set up the required smokescreen. The tension of the preceding period, the waiting time, had drained away, although they still had to get back safely to the shop.

'In a few minutes, we'd better go to ground and take our clothes off,' said Bobby, and Helene thought him much calmer than she was herself. That was typically English, of course, the wearing of what was called a stiff upper lip. He was amusing, crazy and dear to her, but always in control of himself.

'Take our clothes off?' she said.

'And beat them against the hedge,' said Bobby. 'They smell of smoke. They're bound to. It's up my nose, so I'm certain it's all over our clothes. We can't go back into town just as we are. The police will be stopping people and sniffing them.'

'Yes, you are right,' said Helene, 'they'll point their long noses at us. I hope all that smoke did what it was supposed to do, help the scientist to escape.'

'Paul will let us know through Marcelle,' said Bobby. 'By the way, my French nightingale, thanks for being so quick and efficient.'

'Oh, my admiration for what you did is total, *cheri*,' said Helene, casting a tentative glance at him. He gave her a smile and she hoped he had forgiven her for her bad temper.

They were treading rough ground, but making steady progress, and Bobby supposed that if an escape of certain inmates from the camp had been made, then the guards would have their work cut out to round them up, while any search for Helene and himself would be largely guesswork, since he and she were an unknown quantity. It would be on their way back to the shop that they would almost certainly have to run the gauntlet of suspicious eyes and awkward questions. Lys would not be quite as peaceful as it usually was.

In the mild warmth of the afternoon sun, he and Helene stopped. At that moment, they heard the sound of a slow-moving car. They dropped at once to the ground, staying silent. They heard the car pass. The hedge hid it from them, but it contained four uniformed policemen, and they would not have been surprised to know that.

After it was well beyond them, Helene said, 'If that was looking for us, it will be travelling the road for the rest of the day.'

'I'd share your belief if I didn't suspect it will turn back for a fresh look around here,' said Bobby. 'Right, clothes off.'

'I am to undress in front of you?' said Helene.

'What's your lingerie like?' asked Bobby, taking his jacket and hat off.

'French,' said Helene.

'I've heard some very complimentary remarks about French lingerie,' said Bobby.

'You have only heard?' said Helene. 'But you have seen much of mine.'

'Only briefly on certain occasions,' said Bobby, and stripped down to his singlet and short pants.

Helene took off her costume, blouse and hat. Her while satin slip, lace-hemmed, covered the rest of her underwear. Before going to Britain with Bobby, she had, as a farmer's busy daughter, worn plain and practical underwear. Bobby's family, associated with the garments trade, had supplied her with much more delicate items. And since arriving in Lys, she had purchased some more. SOE in London had sent her and Bobby off with a very generous amount of French francs, and there was no reason to revert to the plain and practical. There was every reason to elect for lace and silk.

They began to beat their outer garments against the hedge. Dust flew.

'Bobby—'

'Listen, keep to—'

'Oh, Maurice, then. You wouldn't ever be really serious about getting rid of me, would you?'

'I'd be sad, not serious, I told you that,' said Bobby, beating his jacket.

'You're mistaken if you think I'd ever let you cast me off,' said Helene.

'I don't recall talking about getting rid of you or casting you off,' said Bobby, shaking the dust from his jacket. 'If you remember, you—'

'You are not to mention that,' said Helene, beating her own jacket. 'I didn't mean any of it, you know I didn't. I was simply very angry about what is happening to French Jews. It horrifies me that it's being done to them by Frenchmen. Ah, that old man, Pétain, he should fall down and die as a puppet of Hitler.'

'He's already as good as dead, Lynette,' said Bobby, giving his trousers a thrashing. 'From senility.'

'*Cheri?*' Helene was wheedling.

'It's safe to talk,' said Bobby. The road was deserted.

'You have very good legs and thighs,' said Helene, threshing her skirt.

'Anything else?' asked Bobby.

'Yes, you do have excellent poets,' said Helene, 'and your Shakespeare, of course, is supreme.'

'This is a funny conversation,' said Bobby. 'I'm stuck on thoughts of getting back to the shop without being asked questions we can't answer. I can't cope with what my legs look like or how good Shakespeare was. So let's get dressed and go on our way, shall we?'

'Yes, we must,' said Helene, 'and I'm happy you still love me.'

'I'm happy you're no longer taking me to pieces,' said Bobby.

'No, no, I was only expressing my bad temper,' said Helene, putting her blouse on. 'I'm usually very good-natured and pleasant.'

Bobby smiled. His young French lady, in fact, was a proper young madam at times.

Chapter Twenty-One

They returned to the town by the roundabout way. Bobby at once noticed the unusual number of uniformed policemen about, and also that people did not seem as unhurried and unworried as they normally did. Which meant, he hoped, that an escape from the assembly centre had definitely taken place. There was no sign, however, that a hunt was still going on. Not in the town, at least.

The policemen were disposed in pairs on street corners, their attitude watchful. But as Helene and Bobby approached the town square, it was a civilian who crossed the street to detain them. He was casually dressed in a blue shirt, black trousers and a black beret, a man in his thirties and with a lean face that did not match the broad features prevalent among the indigenous people of Haute-Garonne.

'A moment,' he said, holding up his hand.

Bobby and Helene stopped.

'M'sieur?' said Helene, smiling.

'Who are you and where do you live?'

'You're asking to see our papers?' said Bobby.

'I'm asking who you are and where you live.'

'I should like first to know who you are,' said Helene.

'Security Police.'

'The Security Police of our President, Marshal Pétain?' said Helene.

'Yes.' The man glanced at her hatbox. 'I can identify myself.'

But you aren't French, thought Helene, sure she could detect an accent.

Gestapo agent, thought Bobby, collaborating with the Vichy police.

'I accept your assurances,' said Helene. 'I am Claudette Dubois, and this gentleman is my fiancé, Henri Beaumonte, and we live in the apartment above a millinery shop in Avenue du Parc.'

'Why aren't you at work? And what is your work?'

'I own the shop and my fiancé is a journalist specializing in political commentaries for American journals,' said Helene, and Bobby at once fished out his notebook and pencil.

'Is it possible to have your observations, officer, on what you think of the present situation in Europe?' he asked. 'Do you consider it promising for the New Order on a long-term basis, bearing in mind that the two most important European nations, France and Germany, are at peace with each other?'

'Answer your own questions, m'sieur. Let me see that notebook.'

Bobby handed it over. It was unhurriedly scrutinized. It contained quite coherent versions of interviews Bobby had had with various citizens of Lys.

'I'd like to include an interview with you,' he said.

The man leafed through the notebook with deliberation.

'Why do you ask that of me?' The notebook was handed back. 'You should be interviewing the kind of people who are known to the Americans, such as Marshal Pétain himself and his ministers. At the same time, you should take into consideration the fact that the Americans are now at war with the New Order. What is in that box?' The question was put suddenly, but quite pleasantly.

'A hat,' said Helene.

'A hat?'

'Yes, this is a hatbox,' said Helene.

'Open it.'

'If you wish,' said Helene. She opened it, disclosing the hat, now crown upwards.

'Take it out.'

'Ah, you like it?' said Helene, smiling again.

'Take it out.'

Helene lifted it from the box, and hat and box were both inspected, the man deliberate again in his survey.

'You are thinking of a hat for your wife?' said Helene. 'This one has been made to order and requires a little alteration, but—'

'I am not thinking of my wife, but of an incident that took place this afternoon.'

'An incident?' said Bobby. 'Would it be of interest to a journalist?'

'Enquiries from any journalist are forbidden.' The man came closer, and despite her taut nerves, Helene could have laughed, for she was sure he was sniffing at them. 'Where were you two an hour ago?'

'With Madame Raison, who lives in the Rue du Lys at number four,' said Helene. 'She's a client, and the one who ordered this hat. My fiancé came with me. M'sieur, we heard nothing about any incident. It could not have taken place near Madame Raison's house.'

'What kind of an incident was it?' asked Bobby.

'A Government vehicle was held up, attacked with explosives, and the driver and guards killed.'

That's a try-on, thought Bobby, it's an attempt to provoke an automatic protest in the guilty.

It's a deliberate lie, thought Helene.

'It happened here, in Lys?' said Bobby, simulating a nice line in disbelief.

'There are assassins like that in this lovely town?' said Helene.

'Yes.' The man still had the hat in his hand. 'Tell me, Ma'moiselle Dubois, why did your fiancé go with you to your client?'

'Oh, he's always doing things like that,' said Helene. 'It's to interview my clients. He has an idea that Americans are interested in the political opinions of ordinary people, not the important ones you mentioned. Madame Raison will tell you he interviewed her. It interfered with the happy conversation she and I were enjoying about the hat, but she was flattered, of course.'

'It's in my notebook,' said Bobby.

'Your papers, m'sieur. And yours, ma'moiselle.'

'Ah, you now want to see them?' said Helene.

'As a formality, and because of the incident, you understand.'

'Yes, understood, officer,' said Bobby, and he and Helene produced their identity documents, issued, it seemed, by the Vichy Government. Each was examined with interest. Questions of a mild nature were asked and answered, and the documents were then returned.

'This hat.' The man regarded it with a pleasant smile. 'Yes, I think my wife would like it, after all.'

'But it's the one ordered by Madame Raison,' said Helene.

'Make her another instead of altering this one.'

'Am I to receive payment, m'sieur?' asked Helene.

'Make it a gift, and I should also like the box.'

'I don't think that very fair,' said Helene.

'It's taking advantage,' said Bobby.

'The Security Police appreciate gifts, although not bribes, and I'm sure you have other boxes, Ma'moiselle Duvais.'

'Dubois,' said Helene.

'Ah, yes. Your pardon. I should like to carry the hat home in the box.'

'I thought you might.' Bobby shrugged. 'Give it to him, Claudette.'

Helene handed it over. The man placed the hat inside it.

'Many thanks. Good day to you, ma'moiselle, m'sieur.'

'I feel you've made idiots of my fiancée and myself,' said Bobby.

'Come along, Henri,' said Helene, and walked away, Bobby beside her. They entered the square and crossed to Avenue du Parc. Bobby stopped, put a hand on Helene's arm and she stopped too. They let a car go by before going on.

'He's following,' said Bobby.

'To check we've given him the right address?' said Helene.

'I'd say so.' Bobby was frowning.

'You think he's suspicious?' said Helene.

'It's probably just a germ in his mind at the moment,' said Bobby. 'You know why he's robbed you of that hat and box, don't you?'

'Why?'

'I made a mistake,' said Bobby. 'I should have let the hat and the box see the light and the fresh air while we were beating our clothes, to make sure neither smelled of smoke. We know we did, and we also know the hatbox was open during the time we spent at the rear of the truck. The police will do a forensic job on it, and the hat.'

'The pigs,' said Helene.

The late afternoon sun was going down as they stopped at the shop. Bobby opened the door. Helene entered and Bobby followed. There were two customers. The shop sold accessories as well as hats. Bobby and Helene, giving Madame Clair a smile, went through the shop and up to their apartment.

'Did you see him?' asked Bobby.

'Yes, a glimpse,' said Helene. 'He was there, at the entrance to the street, watching us.'

'Gestapo agent, bound to be,' said Bobby, 'and he'll follow any lead, however slight. We've been taught that.'

'Could we make our story stick if we were interrogated?' asked Helene.

'My French treasure, I've a feeling their kind of interrogation will find a few holes,' said Bobby.

'If the pig had suspicions, why didn't he arrest us?' asked Helene.

'Some of them like playing cat-and-mouse,' said Bobby. 'We've been taught that too.'

'Yes, it fits,' said Helene. 'He was much too pleasant at times.'

'Lynette, we've now got to think about leaving Lys,' said Bobby.

'Ah, Lynette,' said Helene. 'Do you realize how confusing it is being Lynette and Maurice to ourselves and to people like Paul and Marcelle, and Claudette and Henri to the police?'

'I've thought about that,' said Bobby.

'So?' said Helene.

'It's confusing,' said Bobby.

'Idiot.' Helene threw a cushion at him.

'But it serves a purpose,' said Bobby. 'Suppose Paul's real name was George Brugnon. And suppose we were asked one day to tell all we knew about George Brugnon. We wouldn't know a thing, because we wouldn't know the name. We only know a man called Paul. And he only knows us as Lynette and Maurice, not as Claudette Dubois and Henri Beaumonte.'

'I know all that,' said Helene.

'So?' smiled Bobby.

'It's still confusing,' said Helene.

'This evening it'll be time to go,' said Bobby, 'and to make contact with Marcelle in Carbonne.'

Marcelle was always to be found drinking coffee and cognac at a certain cafe in Carbonne between eight and nine in the evening.

'Ah, yes, she will find us a new address,' said

Helene. 'We simply can't risk being arrested and interrogated.'

'It'll happen late tonight, an arrest, if it happens at all,' said Bobby. 'I've a feeling about that, and they'll have toothcombed the hat and box by then. On our way out of Lys after dark, we'll call on Madame Raison and tell her to put herself in the clear by denying whatever part of our story she chooses to. And we'll have a word with Madame Clair before she closes the shop.'

'Yes, she must not be implicated,' said Helene. 'Let us get ready now for our departure later. Let us pack.'

'Include your French lingerie,' said Bobby.

December darkness fell early. By eight o'clock, they were ready to leave. They came down the stairs, their belongings packed in valises, the shop closed.

The doorbell rang stridently.

'Christ,' hissed Bobby, 'they're early, they're here.'

Helene pulled at him, and brought him behind the counter. In the darkness, they dropped together to the floor.

The bell rang again, more stridently and for a longer period. Then a fist hammered the door.

'Open up!'

I'm not stupid, thought Bobby, and I know Helene isn't.

Outside, two uniformed policemen broke the door down, while the man in the clothes of a farm-hand stood by. The shop was in darkness, and the beam of a torch sprang light. It revealed the inner door leading to the apartment stairs. It was open. The policemen rushed through, the man followed in leisurely fashion. The policemen took the stairs two at a time. Their Gestapo collaborator ascended with slow deliberation. Bobby and Helene heard one policeman shout.

'Gone! Flown!'

They heard another voice, a quieter one.

'Search the place. Be thorough. Something incriminating will be found. There's always something.'

Silently, Bobby and Helene departed.

They were young, adventurous and versatile. They made their call on Madam Raison.

After which, they vanished from Lys.

Chapter Twenty-Two

The phone rang in the Farnham convalescent hospital that same evening. Clara, off duty, was with Felicity in the recreation room when she was called to the phone by an orderly. She took the call. Back to the recreation room she came at a rush.

'Felicity! Come with me, quickly.' She drew Felicity up from her chair.

'Who's on fire?' asked Felicity.

'Nobody. Come on, best foot forward. Tim's on the line.'

'What?'

'Yes. Tim. He's back.'

'Oh, my God. Where's the door? Is this the door? Where's the corridor? Where's my left foot? Clara, don't let go, get me there. How do I look? Is my hair all right?'

'Tim's on the phone, not here in person, and you look fine, love. Here we are.'

Clara brought her to an extension in a consultant's office, and left her there. She waited outside.

Felicity, picking up the phone, swallowed, drew a deep breath, and spoke.

'I'm here, are you there, Tim?'

'Hello, Felicity, you darling, yes, I'm here.'

'Where's here?'

'Military hospital, Maidstone.'

'Oh, my God.'

'My lovely old grandma believes a lot in God,' said Tim.

'Tim, you're in Maidstone? Maidstone in Kent?'

'Yes, bloody marvellous, don't you think?'

'I can't believe it. You're in hospital in Maidstone and not a prisoner of war camp?'

'It's a long story,' said Tim. 'I'll write telling you all about it, and Clara can read it to you. The short of it, though, is that I slipped Jerry and have just been flown home to have my sternum X-rayed and nursed.'

'Your what?'

'Breastbone,' said Tim. 'It's cracked or something and bones take a long time to knit in hot climates. What with that and my cousin-in-law Jonathan with a ruined patella, I think carelessness is running wild in the family. Still, better my chest than yours.'

'I can't get hold of myself,' said Felicity, 'I'm still fighting disbelief. Is it true, I don't have to wait until the end of the war to see you again?' That came out naturally.

'Believe me,' said Tim.

'Oh, my God, if you only knew what this is doing to me,' said Felicity.

'Nothing injurious, I hope,' said Tim.

'No, you clever old escapist, it's turning me scatty, and if I could get my legs to work, I'd jump over the moon singing Hallelujah.'

'Don't worry about your legs,' said Tim, 'I'll

267

see to them as soon as we get together.'

'I don't think I'm going to struggle,' said dizzy Felicity.

'It'll be my treat,' said Tim. 'Look, would you know if Colonel Lucas, my sister Eloise's fiancé, is OK? Only he and I were in the same dust-up that put me on my back, and I'm wondering if he made it back to base.'

'More than that, Tim, he must have made it all the way to Alexandria, since he married your sister there at about the time those sneaky Jap bounders bombed Pearl Harbor,' said Felicity, happy to be able to pass this news to Tim. 'Your father mentioned the marriage to me on the phone. He frequently rings for a chat. What a lovely man he is.'

'I'll let that pass,' said Tim. 'I don't want to fall out with me dear old respected dad. Still, I'm delighted about Colonel Lucas and Eloise. Listen, Cleopatra, I don't know how you're fixed with your phone, but there's a demand for this one. The staff need the line. Could you possibly make two phone calls for me, one to my parents and one to my grandparents? My grandparents will let the rest of the family know I'm home.'

'Oh, I'll phone for you, old chum,' said Felicity, head happily spinning, 'I'd love to be the one to let your parents and grandparents know.'

'There's a lovely girl,' said Tim. 'Must ring off now, but I'll phone again tomorrow. Love you, want to see you, sleep tight, keep your beauties in good shape, and put your best stockings on when we do get together.'

'Stop making me feel madly sexy,' said Felicity. 'Tim—'

''Bye now,' said Tim and rang off.

It took Felicity a while to get her head to stop spinning. Clara offered her an aspirin.

'I don't need an aspirin, woman,' said Felicity, 'just a few pinches to help me feel I'm not dreaming and to use the phone.'

'Something's got to be done,' said Polly, standing between the twins' cots. The infants, fed, were asleep. Boots, just home after one more long day at headquarters, gazed down at the cherubs like a man who, having been given so much by life, was still in wonder at this gift of twins.

'Can't help these long hours at the moment, Polly,' he said. 'London's making demands. We're losing our top armoured division to active service overseas.'

'Oh, I understand that, old bean,' said Polly, 'and it's not your long hours I'm complaining about. It's me. Look at me.'

Boots looked at her and thought, as he always did, how well she stood up to the offensive of Father Time. Forty-five and now a mother, she still had the sprightly air of a woman able to hold off the advances of all his agents. There were no lines, no eye wrinkles, no mouth droop.

'I can't see anything I'd complain about myself,' he said.

'How sweet,' said Polly, 'but you need glasses, old darling, if you can't see I'm turning into a lump.'

'Are you?' smiled Boots.

'My bosom, for God's sake,' said Polly, and offered him a look at the pronounced curve of her bodice. 'It's taking me over. My bras don't fit. If I end up with a pair of lumps instead of something nicely reasonable and a pleasure to both of us, watch out for ructions. Well, you're responsible and so are your twins. So what's to be done, sport?'

'Unfortunately, Polly, I know absolutely nothing about bosoms,' said Boots.

'You know about mine,' said Polly, 'and I'm pleased to say so. Your devotions have contributed to their happiness, and I don't want you going off them. You do care for them, don't you?'

'Constantly,' said Boots. 'But I'm still ignorant about how to cure the problem of – um – expansion. It wasn't until I reached the ripe old age of twelve that I realized bosoms existed and that they were different from chests. I think I found the discovery embarrassing.'

'I don't want to hear about what you did with saucy schoolgirls,' said Polly. 'I want you to know that I'm thinking of Glaxo and feeding bottles.'

'You'll put the twins on bottles?' said Boots.

'Not until they're a little older,' said Polly, 'and then only for the sake of self-preservation.'

'What if they don't take to a bottle?' asked Boots.

'I'll talk to them like their own mother,' said Polly.

'You are their own mother,' said Boots.

'Yes, old love, so they'll listen to me,' said Polly. 'You don't want me to turn into a top-heavy lump, do you?'

'The largest lump I ever knew was Ma Earnshaw,' said Boots. 'She ran a fruit and veg stall next to Sammy's glass and china, and had an unfortunate habit of falling over frontwards into her choice tomatoes. Gave her the pip, poor lady.'

Polly laughed in low key to avoid waking the twins, put her arms around him and said, 'Lover, you've just made that up, haven't you?'

'Ask Sammy,' said Boots.

The phone rang downstairs. Kate answered it and called up moments later.

'Uncle Boots, it's your daughter-in-law Felicity. She wants to talk to you.'

Boots grimaced, suspecting bad news about Tim. Down he went to pick up the phone. Polly hurried after him.

'Felicity?'

'Greetings, father-in-law,' said Felicity, 'and don't mind if I sound off my chump. Happy wives do have scatty moments. I'm rapturous to be able to tell you Tim gave the Germans the slip and has just been flown home. He's in hospital in Maidstone to have his wounded chest repaired – oh, something like that. Isn't it wonderful? No, not his wounded chest, his homecoming.'

'This is a fact?' said Boots.

'I've just had a giddy phone conversation with him,' said Felicity. 'Now I'm having one with you.'

'Felicity, I can't tell you how grateful I am for your call,' said Boots. 'My dear girl, thank you.'

'Oh, well, you know,' said Felicity. 'Isn't it true that in the words of wedding speeches, you haven't lost a son, you've gained another daughter? Tell me if you like that.'

'Love it,' said Boots. 'There's always room for one more like you, Felicity.'

'I'm touched,' said Felicity. 'Please give my love to your wife. How are the twins?'

'Fat and lumpy,' said Boots, 'and angelic.'

'Lovely,' said Felicity. 'Now I have to phone Tim's grandmother, Mrs Finch. I promised him I would.'

'She'll let everyone else know,' said Boots, 'but tell her I'll talk to Rosie. Yes, it is wonderful, Felicity, and I can't tell you how glad I am for you.'

'Be like me, be happy,' said Felicity.

Boots, putting the phone down, thought about her blindness. He could not remember finding it easy to be happy during the years when he was sightless himself.

Tim had acquired a treasure. So had the family.

Polly was delighted by the news. So was Rosie on hearing from Boots. Kate was very impressed, so much so that she thought about writing another story. The headline sprang to her facile mind.

'*How I helped the Escape of a War Hero from the Germans* by Kate Trimble, Special Secret Agent.'

Well, it would be close to a real life story.

Chinese Lady blinked, struggled with a lump in her throat and held the phone at arm's length.

'Edwin,' she called huskily, 'come and hold this phone for me. It's saying things I can't believe.'

Mr Finch came to the rescue and he too heard things difficult to believe. However, he reacted in calmer fashion and enjoyed a very coherent conversation with Felicity, his words touched with affection for this blind young woman, to whom Tim was exceptionally devoted.

Afterwards he asked Chinese Lady if she would like him to phone the family, and save her any further contact with an instrument that she regarded as new-fangled and electrically suspect.

'Oh, that's kind of you, Edwin,' she said, 'but I'm not going to let the blessed thing get the better of me. You go up and tell Sammy and Susie, and I'll tell the others.' She could not, in fact, resist the pleasure of passing on such good news herself, even if the phone did try to give her electric shocks, which she was sure was what it always had in mind for her.

The family celebrated. Boots and Polly, Rosie and Matthew, Sammy and Susie, Lizzie and Ned, Vi and Tommy, Aunt Victoria and Uncle Tom, all opened a bottle, even if Polly, a nursing mother, had only the merest sip of what she fancied, and Aunt Victoria, on speaking terms with the local vicar, had only a small glass of sherry.

Letters were written the following day to Eloise, now the wife of Colonel Lucas in the Middle East, to Emma and Jonathan in Somerset, to Annabelle in Wiltshire, and to the Adams and Somers boys and girls living as evacuees in the West Country.

The good news, however, hadn't registered with little Phoebe, who had woken up wet again that morning.

In America, Mr Churchill was invited to address a joint session of the US Senate and House of Representatives. He was given a tremendous ovation and his address was a powerful one. Towards the end of his speech, he emphasized the importance of Britain and the USA being together once more in defending the free world against tyranny, and he confidently predicted that in the days to come their united endeavours would surely open the way to victory and peace.

That earned a standing ovation.

New Year's Day came and went, and 1942 arrived.

The British and Empire troops in Libya were still pushing on, stretching their lines of communication.

In Russia, Stalin's massive Red armies had been dealing Hitler's armoured might heavy blows, and only the central German force aimed at Moscow was standing firm. Its flanking armies were in full retreat. Stalin was now asking his generals to destroy the German centre, and to remove all threat to Moscow.

In the Far East, the initiative still lay with the swarming Japanese.

From the occupied Low Countries and from Northern France, *Luftwaffe* bombing squadrons were still launching assaults on Britain: London and provincial cities frequently targeted. The people of the East End, bombed and battered, endured. The people of the suburbs, emerged from their shelters at the end of each raid, surveyed their shattered semi-detached homes, and found help from friends and neighbours. If the people of London and the provincial cities mourned their dead, they did not petition Churchill to sue for peace.

Churchill and his Cabinet still pursued a policy of hanging on while hitting the enemy with massive bombing raids by day and night.

On the other side of the Atlantic, the Americans were preparing to despatch planes, troops and armour to the United Kingdom, and to join the RAF in the air war against Germany.

'The Yanks are comin', Bert.'
'Bloody 'ell, lock up yer daughters, Alf.'

A letter arrived for Sammy and Susie.

Dear Mr and Mrs Adams,

I daresay it's been a bit of a headache to you me not writing to you again till now. I'm thanking you for replying to my first letter, it was kind of you to let me hear from you and to let me know you'd be taking care of my niece Phoebe until I could come and sort things out with you. Well, I'm pleased to tell you I'm getting my first week's leave on February the 6th, which I'd say I've earned along with my first stripe, which makes me Lance-Corporal Willis, and if it's OK with you I'll make it my business to call on you on the afternoon of February the 7th, which I hope will be convenient. As you'll see, we're stationed at the Middlesex Barracks, not all that far from my old family home in Bow, and I know my way to your place.

I hope young Phoebe is bearing up, which I'm sure she is seeing how you're caring for her. Tell her her Uncle Herbert is coming to see her in just about four weeks or so.

Yours sincerely,
Herbert Willis.

Susie's reaction was to tell Sammy that caring for Phoebe for further weeks wasn't going to be easy.

'It's putting a bit of a strain on you, Susie?' said Sammy.

'What do you think?' said Susie. 'It'll make it even harder for us to let her go, won't it?'

'She's had two dry nights this last week,' said Sammy, 'and each time there's been a smile for me when I went in. I tell you, Susie, that little smile of hers, it fair knocks me off balance. We've got four lovely kids, Susie, so why don't we feel comfortable about letting Phoebe go? If we had no kids at all, well, wanting to keep her would make sense.'

'Lonely little girls like Phoebe make sense fly up the chimney, Sammy dear,' said Susie. 'Paula simply loves her, but we have to do what we're always saying we should, go along with what's best for her, a life with her uncle and aunt in Canada. Herbert Willis is her father's brother, and that's as close a family tie as you and me could wish for her.'

'He's in the Canadian Army now, Susie,' said Sammy, 'and he'll be in action one day. That's not too healthy, action against the Jerries. They're buggers at making war and, as Boots'll tell you, they fight like the devil himself. Herbert Willis will be up against killers, and he might never get back to Canada and his wife.'

'What are you trying to do, Sammy, find an excuse for not letting Phoebe go?' asked Susie. She smiled wryly. 'I suppose I'd like a good excuse myself. I'm sure Phoebe sort of instinctively knows she's not going to be permanent with us, and I don't think that's helping her.'

'It gets me, the fact that that's just how Rosie was all those years ago, a lonely little girl aching to have a mum and dad and a home,' said Sammy. 'It gets me that all of this is a repeat of everything that happened then. Oh, well, let's see what Phoebe's Uncle Herbert comes up with.'

'A boat to Canada, Sammy,' said Susie.

'Um, a ship, Susie.'

'Same thing,' said Susie, a feminine female and accordingly not given to splitting hairs in the way men did.

'By the way,' said Sammy, 'talking of young girls, I'm informed by Rachel that Leah, her younger daughter, is hitting it off with Lizzy and Ned's son, Edward.'

'I like Edward, he's so straightforward and with a happy sense of humour,' said Susie. 'Do I like Leah? I don't know, I've never met her.'

'She's a young beauty,' said Sammy.

'Sammy, you know a lot more about Rachel and her daughters than is good for you,' said Susie. 'And for me.'

'That's it, have your little joke, Susie.'

'Listen, Sammy,' said Susie, 'the whole of the male branch of the Adams family is a jokes department.'

'Now, Susie—'

'Never mind, I like it,' said Susie. 'I feel I'm married to all of it.'

'It, Susie?'

'The Adams jokes department,' said Susie. 'There's a horrible war on, Sammy, and the bombs keep falling, but you're still funny ha-ha, and so are Boots and Tommy and Ned. When you see Rachel tomorrow, tell her from me that if Leah would like a life with a lot more laughs than tears, to hang on to Edward for all she's worth.'

'There's religion to consider,' said Sammy, speaking for Rachel, not himself.

'What's that got to do with becoming an Adams?' asked Susie.

'A Somers in this case, Susie.'

'Good as the same thing,' said Susie, 'seeing Lizzy's an out-and-out Adams and Ned's a leading member of the jokes department.'

Sammy smiled.

'I'm a lucky bloke to have you, Susie,' he said.

'Yes, I know,' said Susie, 'and I'm glad you know too, Sammy.'

'Don't mention it,' said Sammy.

'Rachel,' said Sammy the following morning, 'a message from Susie.'

'From Susie?' said Rachel, burdened at the moment by more horror stories of Germany's concentration camps, stories that were going the rounds of London's Jewish community. Representations had been made to the Government, whose spokesman pointed out that so far no country, including the United Kingdom, was in possession of factual evidence or unchallengeable proof. 'Am I going to like it, Sammy?'

'I don't think you'll dislike it,' said Sammy. 'She asked me to tell you to tell Leah that if she fancies a life that's a laugh a minute, she's to hang on to Edward.'

'Sammy?'

'Susie reckons the best part of the Adams family is a jokes department,' said Sammy, 'that she's married to all of it and recommends Leah follows suit, as you might say.'

'Sammy, Susie said that?'

'All of it,' said Sammy.

'That Edward and Leah should marry if they fall in love?'

'Good idea, would you say?' suggested Sammy.

Emotion welled in Rachel. Leah marry a Gentile, the son of an Adams mother? She would be safe for ever as a member of that family. They would close ranks around her if ever there was trouble, they would defend her heart and soul as one of their own. Rachel desperately wished Mr Churchill and his ministers would interest themselves more positively in the horror stories by commissioning an examination of and an investigation into the sources. Successful findings would enable them to broadcast the fact that the Nazis truly were monsters. Such was the reputation of Mr Churchill internationally, that the whole world would take serious notice if he spoke up.

'Sammy.' She swallowed. 'If the Germans had invaded in 1940 and occupied our country, and Hitler had sent in his *Einsatzgruppen* to round up—'

'His what?' said Sammy. 'Could you say that again, Rachel?'

'The *Einsatzgruppen* are Hitler's ss killer squads, Sammy. If Hitler had sent them to round up British Jews, would you and your family and most other people have stood aside in the same way the German people have?'

'Here, steady on the rudder, Rachel,' said Sammy, taken aback, 'you're landing me on the rocks.'

'If Benjamin and myself and our daughters had been taken, Sammy, would you and Boots and Tommy have turned your backs?' asked Rachel.

'Flaming Holy Joe,' said Sammy, 'is that a fair question?'

'I think so, Sammy,' said Rachel.

In all the years he had known her, Sammy had never seen her looking so serious and so emotional. He groped for an answer, and found the only one he could express with belief.

'Well, I'll tell you what Boots would've done,' he said. 'He'd have rounded up his old West Kents and East Surreys, and gone after you, with Tommy and me treading on his heels. And the same kind of people that hammered Mosley's Blackshirts would've joined in.'

'At the risk of being machine-gunned, Sammy?'

Sammy looked as if the dialogue was getting at him.

'I don't know how many times Boots and his old comrades went over the top, Rachel,' he said, 'but I know it wasn't just once, so yes, I'm going to say they'd have taken the risk.'

'Are you sure, Sammy?'

'Ask Boots,' said Sammy, and Rachel saw that for the first time in their long-standing friendship, he was angry with her. She had put him into a corner, she knew that.

'Sammy, are you angry because it was an uncomfortable question to answer?' she asked gently.

'Don't you have faith, Rachel?'

'In the Adams family? Yes, Sammy, I do, but terrible things are happening in Germany and Poland, and no-one outside of my people in London wants to believe it.'

'Rachel, you've got to credit people for not knowing what's rumour and what's fact,' said Sammy. 'Aren't there any photographs being smuggled out of Germany as well as messages? They'd help everyone to believe, photographs.'

'I've not heard of any photographs, Sammy,' said Rachel, and sighed. She changed tack. 'Sammy, would you and Susie like to see Leah married to Edward?'

'If that's what the young lovers came to want, Susie and me would give 'em a tea party, and Chinese Lady would go out of her way to supply shrimps and winkles,' said Sammy. 'That's the only kind of tea party that means anything to my dear old Ma, one with shrimps and winkles, Rachel.'

'Sammy, they're not lovers yet,' said Rachel, 'they're good friends.'

'That's a promising start,' said Sammy.

'You'd be happy about new relatives being Jewish?'

'Now listen,' said Sammy, 'what's up with you? People are people, and either they're nice to know or they're not, Jewish, Catholic, Protestant, Quakers or whatever. What they call mixed marriages don't happen to be a problem to me, nor to Susie, and might I say Boots and Polly wouldn't raise half an eyebrow between them? Rachel, stop looking for ways to give me headaches. Now suppose we do some work. That might make both of us feel a bit better.'

Rachel smiled faintly.

'Yes, Sammy,' she said, and wished there was the freedom to tell him she loved him.

Chapter Twenty-Three

An Islington gent name of Russell phoned Sammy later that morning. Sammy had received from Mr Greenberg details concerning owners of some of the bombed properties at the Elephant and Castle, and had gone to work on them. These included the gent name of Russell.

'Pleasured to have you call, Mr Russell,' said Sammy.

'Knock it off,' said Mr Russell who, although he wheezed a bit on account of being seventy, could still deliver the kind of lingo with which Sammy was intimately acquainted. 'I ain't on this blower to invite you to tea. Now, about your final offer for my bombed freehold at the Elephant and Castle.'

'Satisfactory to you?' said Sammy.

'Stuff it,' wheezed Mr Russell, and rang off.

Just lately, thought Sammy, I'm not having too many good days. I hope Hitler's suffering as well.

Little Phoebe certainly was. Still, it was her birthday tomorrow, there'd be presents for her at breakfast, and Susie and Chinese Lady were going to give her and Paula a little tea party in the afternoon.

God, said Sammy to himself, I hope she wakes up dry in the morning.

Russell's playing hard to get. Well, some ancient Islington landlords are like that. I'll dangle a sweeter carrot in front of his dentures and make a donkey of him. Anyway, I've got acceptances from other owners, and I'll write to Rosie telling her I'm putting her investment to good work. Wish she wasn't so far away. I'm missing our Rosie. And my evacuated kids.

War's never been a good idea. If Hitler had been put in charge of a Chinese laundry, and Fatty Goering a fish and chip shop, they might have found doing a bit of peaceful business more to their liking than clanking about in armour and turning Europe into a blood-and-thunder nightmare. Except, of course, the bleeders were natural Huns.

'Bugger it,' said Major Clarice Robbins.

'Ma'am?' said Captain Rosie Chapman.

'Sorry about my Bulgarian,' said Major Robbins, 'but your discharge has come through. End of the week. Here's the documentation. Looks like more bloody bumph to me. I ask you, Rosie, how the hell could Henry of Agincourt have scorched the arses off the French if he'd been loaded with bumph?'

'I suppose he could have set fire to it and hotted up the scorching,' said Rosie.

'Well, this latest lot means I'll be losing you in a few days,' said Major Robbins. 'Not good, y'know, Rosie. Bad show, in fact. The Army can't afford to lose officers like you. Pity I never had the chance of talking to your husband before he forgot himself.

Tell you what, as soon as you've dropped your little colt or filly, hire a nanny and apply for re-admission.'

'I don't think my husband—'

'Hire a nanny for him too,' said Major Robbins, 'that and pottering about in the garden shed'll keep him happy.'

'Can't be done,' said Rosie, adopting her commanding officer's brisk and practical approach. 'In the Army himself, y'know, knocking the kinks out of tank engines. Splendid feller, damn' fine officer and first-class mechanical engineer. Damn' fine physique too.'

'Eh?' said Major Robbins.

'Couldn't shove him into the garden shed, ma'am,' said Rosie, 'he'd blow it up. Wouldn't be surprised if he didn't blow the nanny up too.'

'Damn me, Rosie, haven't you trained him yet?' asked Major Robbins, growling a bit.

'Not yet, ma'am, but I'll have a go, damn me if I won't,' said Rosie, face perfectly straight.

'They've got to be trained, Rosie, or they get under our feet,' said Major Robbins. 'Can't let 'em think for themselves. Gives 'em ideas. Be tough. Don't take any back answers. D'you keep a stable and a string of nags?'

'Afraid not,' said Rosie, 'just a dogcart.'

'Pity. There's always useful work for a man to do in a stable-yard, without letting him get too near the nags. Bucket, spade and broom, and a sluice down under the tap, that's all he'll need.'

'Can't think my old man would take to that,' said Rosie. 'Not without kicking holes in the bucket. Bit of an awkward chap at times, y'know.'

'Stopped mine cluttering the place up years ago,' said Major Robbins. 'Started to train him as soon as we came out of the church. Well, it's damned disappointing, having to hand you your discharge papers, but we'll have a drink in the mess the day you go.'

'Good of you, ma'am,' said Rosie. 'Mine'll have to be just a tonic water. No gin. My condition and all that, y'know.'

'Well, get it over with, Rosie, and apply for re-admission,' said Major Robbins.

Rosie smiled, saluted and left, taking her discharge documents with her.

It was seven-fifteen the following morning when Sammy slipped out of bed and went to Phoebe's room. There she was, curled up and asleep. But she woke up as he leaned over her, her eyes dreamy. Seeing him, a little smile came. It touched Sammy to the quick, especially as he knew what it meant. She was dry, bless her. It happened once in a while.

'Hello, me pet.'

'I'm woke up,' she said.

'So I see,' smiled Sammy. 'Happy birthday, little girl. You're five.'

'Is Paula five?' she asked.

'She was,' said Sammy, 'she's six now.'

'She goes to school.'

'And so will you when – well, you will one day,' said Sammy.

'Will it be Paula's school?' asked Phoebe shyly.

'We'll see what your Uncle Herbert says, eh?' said Sammy.

A little shadow seemed to fall, and she said

quietly, 'Yes, a'right'. Then, 'I don't fink I 'member an uncle.'

'Well, he was away when you were born, me pet.'

Phoebe thought about that, then asked a question.

'Did 'e go away wiv my mummy and daddy?'

'I don't know, Phoebe,' said Sammy, 'but I daresay we could ask him when we see him. Listen, there'll be presents for you at breakfast.'

'Oh, for me birfday?'

'That's it,' said Sammy.

'Oh, fanks.'

She was happy with her presents. Chinese Lady and Mr Finch, Lizzy and Ned, Vi and Tommy, Sammy and Susie, and Paula, had all given her something. Paula shared Phoebe's happiness, and showed excitement and delight at the unwrapping of each.

'Crikey, look, Phoebe, a painting book.'

'Oh, crikey, yes,' said Phoebe, given to copying Paula.

'No train set?' smiled Mr Finch.

'Grandad, girls don't have train sets,' said Paula, 'they're for noisy boys.'

'Pity,' said Mr Finch, 'your dad and I could have helped Phoebe put it together.'

'Like noisy boys,' said Susie.

'I never heard you speak more true, Susie,' said Chinese Lady, and Phoebe cast a glance at Mr Finch and then at Sammy. Susie, noting this, experienced heartache for the girl. The glances, although brief, held the wistfulness of a child who had no family. Yet she did, thought Susie. An uncle, aunt and grandfather in Canada. It was where she belonged. Canada.

Felicity was feeling her way through a novel in Braille when Clara arrived and interrupted her.

'Rise up, Mrs Adams, there's another phone call from Tim.'

'What a sweetie,' said Felicity, putting the book down and coming to her feet. She had received a letter from Tim giving her the promised details of how he slipped the Germans, and a further phone call. 'Why don't you get one like him?'

'I'm working on Dr Railton,' said Clara. 'Or should I say he's working on me? I'll fall from grace any night now. This way, love.'

Felicity arrived at the phone.

'Tim?'

'Watcher, me beauty,' said Tim.

'Watcher, mate,' said Felicity, 'taking off your cockney relatives, are we?'

'I'm proud of all of 'em,' said Tim. 'How's your sexy self?'

'How's yours?' countered Felicity.

'I don't think I'll go into details over the phone,' said Tim. 'How's your other self?'

'Still groping about,' said Felicity, 'but I can mix a cake and fill a kettle. How's your own other self?'

'Improving daily,' said Tim, 'I'm in the hands of medical experts who've read my x-rays and know what's good for my sternum and ribs. I'm not to go in for lifting sacks of coal, just for reasonable exercises. Listen, lovely lady, you're going home next Monday, aren't you?'

'To my parents? Yes,' said Felicity.

'How would you like to go down to Dorset with me the following Sunday and stay at my sister Rosie's cottage for a fortnight?' asked Tim.

'Tim? You and me, you mean?'

'I hope you haven't got some other bloke in mind,' said Tim. 'Rosie's coming out of the ATS and moving on Saturday week to Bovington to be near her husband, and they've offered us use of their cottage. Myself, I'm being offered two weeks convalescent leave. I'm told I'll be fit enough to begin the leave on the Sunday, and my uncle Tommy and his wife Vi will drive us there, and pick us up and drive us back Sunday fortnight, when they'll be on their own way back from seeing their evacuated sons and daughter in Devon. Petrol coupons no problem. My Uncle Sammy looks after those kind of things. Felicity, you there?'

'Yes, but breathless,' said Felicity. 'Tim, I'd love two weeks with you in Dorset, you know I would. We'd manage, wouldn't we?'

'Well, as the cottage will be strange to both of us,' said Tim, 'we'll be groping about together. Any comments?'

'Yes, sounds a yell,' said Felicity.

'We'll take some cake mixture with us, as I daresay there's an oven in the kitchen,' said Tim. 'And d'you know anything about chickens?'

'Roasting them?' said Felicity.

'No, looking after them,' said Tim. 'Rosie keeps chickens, she inherited them from her sister-in-law. She's going to leave us instructions on how to feed them so that we can harvest the eggs for the time we're there. Then her sister-in-law will transfer the obliging little darlings and the cocky old rooster to her own place. I had a long chat with Rosie on the phone about all this.'

'Two weeks in Dorset, no bombs, no doctors, no therapists, just a cottage and chickens and us, that's what I'm being offered?' said Felicity.

'Hope you like the prospect,' said Tim.

'Oh God,' said Felicity, 'how I wish—' She checked.

'I know,' said Tim, 'I know, Felicity.'

'I still have bloody awful moments, Tim.'

'Share them with me for a fortnight and we'll knock 'em on the head,' said Tim. 'By the way, Rosie asked me to give you her love.'

Felicity took hold of herself and said, 'D'you realize I've never met her?'

'Makes no difference,' said Tim, 'you're an Adams now.'

Felicity found the resilience to laugh.

Bobby and Helene were now in a safe house in Marseilles, waiting for local members of the French Resistance to let them know when and where they could keep a rendezvous with a British submarine that would take them back to England. SOE would then arrange a new mission for them. So Marcelle, the radio operator, had said. She had also said the incident concerning the truck had successfully effected the escape of Professor Leischler and four other Jewish people. That, she said, was the first feather in their caps, and that they'd be able to spend some time at home before being sent to France again.

In the public library, Leah sat at a table poring over books about the Civil War fought by the Royalists of Charles I and the Roundheads of Cromwell. Leah was an earnest scholar, if not as gifted as her sister Rebecca, who was quite brilliant.

Leah, who had had lunch with Edward as usual, kept interrupting her studies to glance at him as he collected returned books and replaced them. Her glances were compulsive. She thought him very pleasing to look at, but wasn't so gauche as to let his looks alone govern her feelings. What she liked best about him was his frank and friendly nature, and his moments of sensible seriousness, when he spoke of the war and how it made people uncertain of the future. She never experienced awkward pauses with him, when neither knew what to say next. Edward was very grown up. Kate Trimble could have told her that his cousin, David Adams, was just the same. Leah didn't know Edward's family, nor did she know the other families, those for whom her mother had a deep liking and even admiration. The only Adams she did know was the one who had always shown a kind and affectionate interest in her and Rebecca. That was Sammy Adams, who had always been a sort of uncle to her and Rebecca. Although she had met Edward's cousin Rosie on her wedding day, she didn't really know her.

Her susceptible heart seemed to do a little somersault as Edward, catching a glance from her, gave her a smile. Oh, my goodness, she thought, I'm getting a crush. There's an awful war going on, but I'm nearly always thinking about Edward when I ought to be praying for our country and all our soldiers, sailors and airmen. Rebecca's getting cross with me. She keeps reminding me that our duty to our grandfather and our late father is to marry into our faith. Well, of course, I know that, but I'm living in the present at the moment, not the future, and if I have got a crush on Edward, I don't feel I want to fight it.

Miss Murchison is being very tolerant, but she's watching me, she calls me to her study every Saturday when I come back from Salisbury and questions me about the progress I'm making on the history of the Civil War. I think she feels my good name is very much her responsibility. What's a Jewish girl's good name? One, I suppose, that doesn't mean I'm getting too intimate with a Christian boy. I daren't let her know that Edward has kissed me, which I suppose is very intimate, or she'll think it's her duty, on behalf of my mother, to make sure I never see him again.

Leah dug back into history to take her mind off her enjoyable problem, but began to make little faces. Oh, that Oliver Cromwell and his suppressive policies. Religious fanatics were a menace.

'You look cross about something.' The whisper reached her ear. She looked up and there was Edward, leaning over the table and smiling again.

'Well, it's Oliver Cromwell,' she whispered, 'he was an awful puritan.'

'You're not, you're sweet,' whispered Edward, and sidled adroitly back to his books, leaving Leah pink with pleasure.

She left, as usual, at three, giving Edward a little

goodbye wave. Outside, she met Pauline and Cecily, and they walked to the bus stop together, all three warmly wrapped in their winter coats.

'Anything exciting to tell us?' asked Pauline.

'Well,' said Leah, 'it was exciting reading about how King Charles hid in the oak tree to escape the Roundheads—'

'Yuk,' said Pauline, 'that's exciting, reading about it?'

'But if you use your imagination—'

'She's going potty,' said Cecily.

'Leah, you haven't got a crush, have you?' said Pauline.

'Mavis Godwin told me that can send a girl potty,' said Cecily.

'Do I look potty?' asked Leah.

'No, you don't actually look it,' said Pauline, 'but how'd you feel, sort of freaky?'

'What's sort of freaky?' asked Leah.

'Jolly strange, I should think,' said Cecily. 'I get strange funny feelings myself when I dream about being on a desert island with Errol Flynn.'

'You can't be on a desert island with Errol Flynn when you're only fifteen, you booby,' said Pauline. 'Listen, Leah, you're not supposed to go with Christian boys, are you?'

'Well, I'm blessed,' said Leah, 'there's not an Act of Parliament forbidding it, is there?'

'Golly, we don't know, do we?' said Cecily.

'But what does your mother think, Leah?' asked Pauline.

'Mama thinks all kinds of things about everything,' said Leah, as they reached the bus stop, 'and they're all sensible thoughts.'

'Daddy says my mum only has flights of fancy,' said Cecily.

'Like you, you poor thing,' said Pauline.

Leah, called to Miss Murchison's study a little while after getting back to the Academy for Young Ladies, was greeted kindly and asked about her studies at the library.

'Oh, I've made a hundred notes, ma'am,' said Leah.

'Excellent,' said Miss Murchison. 'I think you can now confine yourself to the relevant textbooks that are available here.'

'Oh,' said Leah.

'There's no further need for you to use the resources of a public library, Leah,' said Miss Murchison.

'But I don't mind spending some of my free time there, really I don't,' said Leah.

'Confine your studies to your evening homework times,' said Miss Murchison, 'and take your Saturday lunches here.'

Oh, some rotten girl's been talking, thought Leah. It couldn't be Pauline or Cecily. They were her best friends and had sworn a school oath never to tell on her about her lunches with Edward. Could it be Rebecca?

'Yes, Miss Murchison.'

'That's all, Leah,' said Miss Murchison.

Leah went looking for her sister, found her and demanded to know if she'd been talking to Miss Murchison.

'About you?' said Rebecca.

'About me and Edward,' said Leah.

'Of course not,' said Rebecca. 'Why d'you ask?'

'She's stopped my Saturday outings to that Salisbury library,' said Leah.

'Not because of anything I've said to her.' Rebecca looked hurt. 'Leah, I should tell tales about my own sister? No, Miss Murchison has obviously put two and two together, and decided you're a little too enthusiastic about the library Edward works in. In any case, she wouldn't have looked at your visits as permanent.'

'Oh, bother,' said Leah.

'Buck up, it's not the end of the world,' said Rebecca.

'My life, I should think not,' said Leah, 'I'm too young to go into a decline.'

She wrote to Edward.

Dear Edward,

I shan't be able to meet you any more in Salisbury, not in the way I have been, although I think that whenever I'm allowed to visit the town I could pop into the library for a few minutes just to whisper hello to you.

Miss Murchison has put a stop to my studies there, and perhaps she thinks I'm consorting with you. That's a word that headmistresses and parents sort of dread to hear, but of course headmistresses and parents dread to hear all kinds of things that most of the girls here only giggle about.

I'm fortunate that my mother is broadminded. Did you know she was born an East End cockney? She says you have to be broadminded in the East End or you'd have to wear ear muffs. It wasn't until the family had moved to South London that her

*father, my grandfather, decided to make a young
lady of her, and she spent two years here from 1917
to 1919. It's always accepted Jewish girls, it was
founded by an English lady who had a Jewish
husband.*

*I hope not seeing a lot of each other won't affect
our friendship, that it won't mean it'll sort of die a
death as I like you very much and hope you like me
just as much. I'm not able to visit Salisbury this
Saturday, as there's a lecture being given by some
lady professor, but I'll be there Saturday week, only
not to do any more studying. Still, we can always
write regularly to each other, can't we?*

*Yours sincerely,
Leah*

Edward replied by return.

*Dear Leah,
I like it that we like each other, it's what I'd call a
nice state of affairs. Regarding your mum, I do know
a lot about her because she's always been a friend of
our families, and when she was an East End
cockney, which was before I was born, my mother and
uncles were all Walworth cockneys, although my
Uncle Boots used to be called Lord Muck by the street
kids because when he was at grammar school he
started to talk posh. The families have come up a bit
in the world since then, mostly because my Uncle
Sammy founded a successful business.*

*I understand about you and me not being able
to meet like we have been, but I daresay I can suffer
it as long as you don't take up with some other
bloke. Stick to consorting with me whenever you're*

*able to pop into the library on one of your free time
visits to Salisbury, and even if we only have to
whisper, well, we can still do a bit of it. Consorting,
I mean.*

What exactly is your idea of consorting?

Signed with best wishes and a kiss,

Edward.

*PS An English lady with a Jewish husband
founded your school? That's interesting.*

Dear Edward,

*Thanks ever so much for writing so quickly, and
I don't know what my idea of consorting is as I've
never done any. Would it be a sort of forbidden tryst
in the moonlight? Miss Murchison would certainly
forbid it for me. Anyway, I'm sure meeting you in the
library couldn't be called consorting.*

*Yes I like it too that we like each other, and of
course I won't take up with any other bloke. My life,
there's not much chance of that, anyway, when the
headmistress and the teachers set the dog on hopeful
boys, well, they would if there was a dog and it
had teeth.*

*I'll be in Salisbury in my free time next Saturday.
Did I tell you we're always allowed to visit the town
on the grounds that it's a sort of respectable and
cultural place, and not like Soho on a Saturday
night? No, I haven't been there on a Saturday night
myself, I've just heard about it. I'll pop into the
library and see you just for a minute or so, I'll look
for a book, and if you helped me that would sort of
be in your line of duty, wouldn't it?*

I do agree it was interesting to know that the lady

who founded this school had a Jewish husband, it just shows religion needn't keep people apart, doesn't it?

I do like your letters. Always your friend,
Leah.

Chapter Twenty-Four

In Libya, the British Eighth Army was striving to consolidate its gains and to bring up supplies and reinforcements that would enable its armoured divisions to renew the offensive and strike out for Tripoli, the main German and Italian base. The Long Range Desert Group of SAS men and Commandos, with whom Colonel Lucas was now operating, was at its destructive work behind German lines, while at British headquarters in Cairo, Lieutenant Eloise Lucas, when not working, was mesmerizing sister ATS officers with her stated conviction that her extraordinary husband was destined to hang Hitler.

'Good Lord, Eloise, is he as extraordinary as that?'

'Of course. Do you think my outstanding English father would accept a son-in-law who was less than extraordinary?'

In the Far East, Japan was still on the offensive, the British and American forces fighting desperate rearguard actions.

In Russia, the Germans were at last finding themselves up against armies mightier than their own, and Hitler was beginning to lay blame on his generals for the failure to take Moscow. Conditions were frightful, the snow a thick white blanket, the cold intense, tank engines freezing up, dead Germans and Russians turning into iced corpses.

In the Atlantic, Allied convoys, heavily protected, were fighting the constant menace of attacks by U-boats hunting in packs.

In the United Kingdom, the people were still suffering air raids, but so now were an increasing number of people in Germany as the RAF bombing squadrons ranged deeper and deeper into the Third Reich that Hitler had boasted would last a thousand years. Dr Goebbels called the RAF raids barbaric which, of course, was a case of the bitten biter losing his marbles.

Sammy and Susie were waiting for Lance-Corporal Willis of the Canadian Army to call, while doing all they could to create for little Phoebe an atmosphere happy enough to cure her of her bedwetting. Sometimes she woke up dry, more often she did not, and on the latter occasions she was a forlorn little girl who only Sammy seemed able to comfort.

Winter was laying its cold hand on Dorset, but Corporal Higgins, Boots's batman, having recovered from breaking his leg, was back on duty and had reclaimed the kitchen as his own. Kate put up a fight.

'I've got to tell yer, girlie, it's me natural 'abitation,' said Higgins, 'and also me prime place of duty.'

'There's all sorts of other jobs you can do,' said Kate, 'and don't call me girlie. I 'appen to be Miss Trimble.'

'Well, I 'appen to be official batman to Colonel Adams, which firstly puts me in charge of this 'ere kitchen,' said Higgins. 'Tell yer what, Miss Trimble, you can peel spuds and wash the carrots, if yer like. Under me supervision, of course.'

''Ere, I'm not a skivvy,' said Kate, 'I'm a fam'ly friend and guest.'

'Which I hope is an 'appy state of affairs,' said Higgins amiably, 'and I want yer to know I've got respect for all the Colonel's friends, only would yer mind if I took me kitchen back into me line of duty?'

'Oh, all right,' said Kate. 'Well, I've got to admit you look pretty in that apron.'

'Eh?' said Higgins.

'Ever so pretty,' said Kate, and left it at that.

But she had a word with Boots, who dished out some very complimentary remarks on how invaluable she'd been in the kitchen, and how helpful and decorative around the house.

'Can't thank you enough, Kate,' he said.

'Oh, complimented, I'm sure,' said Kate.

'Glad to have you around,' smiled Boots.

'Oh, you're always so nice to me, Uncle Boots,' said Kate, 'and I don't want to be a burden to you. I liked doing the cookin' and everything.'

'Kate, we simply like having you with us,' said Boots, 'you're a delightful girl. Don't worry about Corporal Higgins and his eccentric ideas about whose kitchen it is. You're still invaluable – very much so – a companion to my wife and a great help with the twins.'

'Oh, aren't they lovely babies?' enthused Kate. 'I'd like two like that.'

'Speak to David about it,' said Boots, 'he'll be here tomorrow for the weekend.'

'Speak to – oh, Uncle Boots, I didn't know you could be as downright shockin' as that!'

'We live and learn,' said Boots.

When she was helping Polly to bath the twins that evening, Kate said, 'D'you know what your husband said to me this morning before he went off to his duties?'

'No, I don't know, Kate,' said Polly, cooing over infant James like a Victorian nanny, 'but I don't think you're going to surprise me. What did he say?'

'Well,' said Kate, holding baby Gemma whose pink bottom was immersed in warm water, 'when I said I'd like two babies like yours, he told me to speak to David when he comes tomorrow. Oops, Gemma, upsadaisy. Can you believe that?'

'About my husband?' said Polly. 'All too easily.'

'I told 'im he was downright shockin',' said Kate.

'He is,' said Polly.

'But he must've known I only meant when I was married,' said Kate.

'Oh, he knew,' smiled Polly, 'but as you say, Kate, he's a shocker.'

'Has he always been like that?' asked Kate.

'Always,' said Polly, 'it was one of the reasons why I married him.'

'Crikey, d'you like shockers, then?' asked Kate, lifting Gemma out and placing the infant on the warm towel over her lap.

'I like mine,' said Polly, gently drying baby James.

The following day, Saturday, after Boots's nephew David had arrived, Kate was walking with him in the countryside beyond the village of Corfe Castle. Damp winter had turned crisp and bright, and the contact with frosty air made their faces tingle.

'Don't you think Aunt Polly's twins are gorgeous?' said Kate.

'Not half,' said David, 'and so's Aunt Polly. She still sparkles and she's still got pretty good legs.'

'Oh really?' said Kate. 'What about mine, then?'

'Yes, I know you've got two,' said David, 'and I admire both of them. Did you know Aunt Polly was a giddy flapper in the Twenties? Well, she was according to my mum and flashed a pair of frilly garters when she was doing the Charleston, which my mum thought pretty saucy. Pretty and saucy, I'd say. It wasn't something Mum would have done herself, she always paid due regard to the way she'd been brought up by my grandma.'

'She always paid what?' said Kate. 'D'you know what you sound like, you dummy? Like a toffee-nosed bank clerk in a stiff collar. I don't know how many times I've told you you're gettin' more middle class all the time, but you don't take a bit of notice.'

'Wait a minute,' said David, 'you told me once you could live with my middle class faults.'

'I didn't know they were goin' to get worse, did I?' said Kate.

'Well, when I tried to make myself more to your

liking by talking like my Walworth ancestors—'

'Crikey, like a Walworth barrow boy with adenoids, you mean,' said Kate. 'Anyway, you know what me late dad thought of the middle classes.'

'I'd like to have met your dad,' said David, 'we could have had a chat about what to do with bank clerks. Send 'em down a mine, I suppose.'

'Best place for most of them,' said Kate. 'Listen, was your Aunt Polly in love with your Uncle Boots while he was married to your Aunt Emily?'

'Eh?' said David.

'Well, was she?' asked Kate, naturally curious.

'I never asked her, and she never said,' replied David, 'but even if she was, nothing would have happened.'

'How'd you know?' asked Kate, face glowing.

'My grandma wouldn't have allowed it,' said David.

'But she wouldn't 'ave known,' said Kate.

'She knows everything about everyone in the family,' said David.

'How could she?' said Kate. 'That's barmy.'

'She's got second sight,' said David. 'She probably knows I'm out with you right now. Anyway, Uncle Boots has got too much respect for her to ever do something she seriously wouldn't approve of.'

'What was your Aunt Emily like?' asked Kate.

'A bit like my Uncle Sammy, a live wire,' said David. 'She hardly ever stood still. There was a lot of grief, believe me, when she was killed by a bomb. It racked Uncle Boots. Well, he and Aunt

Emily grew up next door to each other when their families lived in Walworth.'

'Was your family shocked when he married again?' asked Kate.

'Shocked?' said David. 'No, I don't think so, not by the time the actual wedding day arrived. By then, everyone thought Uncle Boots needed someone to take Aunt Emily's place, and that he and Aunt Polly would be good for each other.'

'Well, they are,' said Kate.

'Why're you asking me all these questions?'

'I like to know, don't I?' said Kate. 'Yours is the only fam'ly I've got. I'm sort of borrowing it.'

'You're very welcome, Kate,' said David.

'It's funny, though,' she mused, 'that Aunt Polly's upper class and your Aunt Emily was working class.'

'Oh, there's all sorts in our family,' said David, 'but we put up with each other. Well, we have to, it's against the rules to chuck bricks at each other.'

'You've got rules in your family?' said Kate.

'Yes, my grandma's,' said David.

'Who thinks them up, your grandad?' asked Kate.

'No, my grandma,' said David.

Kate laughed.

She put out her hand, David took it and they continued their walk, while in a Salisbury library the younger son of Lizzy and Ned Somers wondered if he'd have the pleasure that afternoon of seeing the entrancing younger daughter of Mrs Rachel Goodman.

Chinese Lady would have been pleased to know two of her younger grandsons weren't letting life pass them by.

* * *

'Oh, excuse me, young man, but I'm looking for a book.'

Edward turned and fell into the melting brown eyes of Leah. Well, melting was how they looked to him.

'Oh, good afternoon, madam,' he said for the benefit of eavesdroppers. 'Exactly which book, madam?'

'Madam? What d'you mean?' whispered Leah. 'Do I look like a madam?'

'My mistake,' whispered Edward, ' I meant young madam.'

'Oh, thanks, I don't think,' whispered Leah. 'Listen, I can only stay a minute, I'm sort of on my honour not to dally. Edward, you look ever so busy, your hair's ruffled.'

'Washed it last night, can't do anything with it today,' whispered Edward. 'You look a peach. Is it against your honour to tell you that?'

'Blessed angels, what's my honour got to do with it when I like it?'

'Here's a good book, madam,' said Edward.

'What is it?' asked Leah.

'*Three Men in a Boat*, by Jerome K. Jerome,' said Edward.

'I've read it,' said Leah.

'Well, what about *Fires of Love*, by Priscilla Dearing?' suggested Edward.

'My life,' breathed Leah, 'd'you want me to be expelled?'

'What for?' whispered Edward.

'Taking *Fires of Love* back to school with me,' whispered Leah. 'The teachers would faint. I mean,

I suppose it's all about fiery passion, is it?'

'I haven't read it myself, madam,' said Edward, and rummaging borrowers glanced at the young man and the schoolgirl. At the counter, Miss Williams smiled. 'What about *Portrait of a Lady*, by Henry James.'

'Oh, I'll take that one, thank you,' said Leah, then whispered, 'It's your turn to write.'

'Pleasure,' said Edward.

'I must go now.'

'Glad you popped in,' whispered Edward. 'Well, good afternoon, madam,' he said politely.

'Good afternoon,' said Leah, and added in a whisper, 'Fathead.' She took the book to the counter, where Miss Williams stamped it for her. Leah had a student's ticket.

'There we are, Miss Goodman,' smiled Miss Williams.

'Thanks ever so much,' said Leah.

'Come again,' said Miss Williams, and watched the girl as she left. What an extraordinarily lovely girl. No wonder Edward did all that whispering with her behind the shelving. For the sake of such young people, the war had to be fought.

And it had to be won.

When Leah got back to school, she went up to her dorm to put the book in her locker. Books left about were pounced on by teachers in a censorship mood or picked up by students out of interest or nosiness, and ended up anywhere.

Having safely stowed the library book, Leah thought her bed didn't look quite as neat as she'd left it. Girls did lark about with beds sometimes.

You could discover a dead beetle between the sheets.

Leah turned down the top sheet and blanket, then stared in disgust at a little heap of damp grass around a dead frog. She knew at once that it wasn't meant as a joke, it was meant as a spiteful reminder that she was Jewish, and that Jews weren't popular with everyone. Miss Murchison came down hard and heavy on that kind of attitude, but it still existed among some of the girls.

Leah winced.

Carefully, she removed the offending heap. Fortunately, it couldn't have been there long because the bottom sheet was only a little damp and not yet stained. She threw the grass and the frog out of a window, first making sure no-one was below. She left the top sheet and blanket turned down to let the air get at the damp patch on the bottom sheet.

She went down to rejoin Pauline and Cecily. She said nothing to them, or to anyone else, and she hid her upset.

Later, when she was going in to tea, she was detained by Miss Miles, the history teacher.

'A moment, Leah. I've just discovered your bed isn't made. Why?'

'Oh I spilt a little water, Miss Miles,' said Leah, which was perfectly true. Everyone spilt water sometimes.

'Careless, careless, dear me, yes,' said Miss Miles. 'I should give you lines for an unmade bed, but very well, make it as soon as you've had your tea.'

'Yes, Miss Miles, thank you,' said Leah.

Going into the hall noisy with girls seating themselves for tea, she passed behind Mavis Watkins, sitting beside a crony. She stopped and lightly tapped Mavis's shoulder. Mavis turned, looked up at her and could not keep dislike out of her eyes.

'Oh, it's you,' she said.

'Yes,' said Leah, 'and I want to say I'm sorry you're still not very well.'

It was a shot in the dark, but Leah didn't stay to see if it had found a target. She went on to join Pauline and Cecily, firm and loyal friends.

Mavis made spiteful faces.

On Monday, Felicity received her discharge from the hospital, and Clara accompanied her on her journey home in an ambulance. There, the most emotional moment of her departure occurred. It had been a wrench saying goodbye to staff and other patients. Saying goodbye to Clara, her devoted nurse and caring friend, was painful.

'No, Felicity dear, it isn't goodbye,' said Clara, 'I'll come running whenever you invite me to stay on one of my free weekends.'

'Which I will as soon as Tim and I have a home of our own, even if it's only a tent,' said Felicity.

'I'll bring my own,' said Clara, 'and camp next door.'

'Clara,' said Felicity, 'you know how much I owe you, how much all your care and support have meant to me. That includes reading and writing letters for me. If it hadn't been for you, I'd have sunk without trace.'

'Don't leave Tim out,' said Clara.

'Could I ever?' said Felicity. 'He's been my lifeline, my lifeboat, you've been my nurse, doctor and friend, and never were two people more encouraging and so necessary to me.'

'I'll stay in touch with letters,' said Clara, eyes moist as they engaged in a hug. Behind her dark glasses, Felicity's scarred eyes were wet.

'I'll have Tim or my mother read them to me,' she said huskily.

'Goodbye, sweetie, take care,' said Clara, and got back into the ambulance. It drove away, and Felicity heard it go, her mother beside her.

She was home, but it was a hard day for her, one of flat reactive depression, her mother too attentive, her father trying too hard. No, that was unkind. Since the day she lost her sight she had known close attentiveness or forced heartiness from everyone with whom she came into contact. Professional attentiveness from nurses and doctors experienced in their treatment of blinded casualties, and sympathetic jocularity from fellow patients who tried to cheer her up. Her parents were no different. All the same, only Clara and Tim gave her a true release from depression. It was only their kind of approach that induced response in her.

Tim came to her rescue during the evening by phoning her, and at a moment when she was at her lowest. At once, his lack of fuss, his reassurance and optimism lightened her reactive depression. He made her feel, as he always did, that her disability wasn't something they needed to talk about all day, even if it was on their minds so much. He then spoke of their coming time in Dorset, a whole two weeks by themselves apart from the company of

Rosie and Matthew's egg-laying chickens and the crowing rooster.

'Crowing at dawn?' said Felicity.

'I believe it's usual,' said Tim.

'Well, if it wakes me up at dawn every morning, I'll chop its head off,' said Felicity.

'You'll find that on a par with playing blindman's-buff,' said Tim, 'so make sure you get hold of the right neck or some lovable egg-layer might get victimized.'

Felicity liked that. It was typical of Tim's attitude towards her blindness, to go along with it, not to make a despairing thing of it, or to pretend it didn't exist.

'You find the right neck for me, Tim,' she said, 'and I'll make a guess with the chopper.'

'I'll pass on that one,' said Tim, 'or I might get victimized myself. Are you glad to be home?'

'The day's been flat,' said Felicity, 'but I'm glad to be talking to you. Tim, when will you be returning to duty?'

'I'm coming back here for a week after our fortnight in Dorset, and then I'll be advised on my new posting,' said Tim.

'I'm frankly hoping it won't be overseas for a while,' said Felicity. 'How's your sternum?'

'Slightly bent,' said Tim.

'Poor old darling, how awkward for you,' said Felicity, 'and for both of us, I suppose.'

'I think you're confused,' said Tim. 'If you are, let me tell you the condition of my chest won't interfere with anything personal.'

'Is that a promise?' asked Felicity.

'It's a promise,' said Tim. 'I don't know what you're

feeling like up there in Streatham, but down here in Maidstone I'm feeling I've got some catching-up to do.'

'Hang on to it, then, don't let it go away,' said Felicity, and she heard him laugh.

They enjoyed an extended conversation about Dorset, including how to cope with two weeks in the cottage without Felicity coming into damaging collision with the furniture too often. Felicity said she was fairly used to receiving knocks, dents and bruises from furniture that was always lying in wait for her. Tim said he could readily believe that that kind of thing was a daily hazard for her, but hoped the dents weren't changing her shape, since her shape had always had his sincerest admiration.

'I'll let you find that out when we get to Dorset,' said Felicity.

'If there are any dents,' said Tim, 'we'll look for a way of ironing them out.'

'You look, I'll think of England,' said Felicity, and she heard Tim laugh again.

Chapter Twenty-Five

The days of January, 1942, were running out.

The first contingent of American troops, tall, rangy and masculine men, had arrived in the UK, landing in Northern Ireland, much to the excitement of young ladies, either Catholic or Protestant. Northern Ireland, as part of the United Kingdom, was accommodating thousands of young men from the British Army, Navy or Air Force, and large numbers of young women in the ATS, Wrens or Waafs. The sudden influx of GI's went to the heads of girls not yet old enough to volunteer for the Services, and Catholic mothers began to panic.

'Father Donnelly, will you be so good as to speak to my Kathleen?'

'Ah, so I will, Mrs O'Brien, if I might know why I should.'

'She's taken to using lipstick, Father.'

'Don't I remember your doing so as a young lady, Mrs O'Brien?'

'But, Father, Kathy's only fourteen.'

'God's mercy, is that a fact, Mrs O'Brien? And is she sinning?'

'I'm mighty sure she will be with one of those

American soldiers, saving you don't speak to her or I don't tie her up.'

'I'll speak to her, Mrs O'Brien, so I will, for I won't have you coming to confession to tell me you've tied Kathleen to her bedpost.'

However, this first contingent of GI's was quickly denied any chance of getting among the Catholic or Protestant lambs. Their commander, modelling himself on John Wayne, and accordingly set on winning the war in Europe by himself, led his General Grant tanks and his infantry into immediate daily battle manoeuvres over rough and tough countryside in co-operation with British artillery.

For these Americans the war in Europe was on, even if only in mock battle for the moment, and the Northern Irish girls had to wait for fully-fashioned stockings and candy bars. However, they waited optimistically, for they knew what that rough, tough countryside was like, and that General 'John Wayne' would fall off his horse sooner or later.

Stalin's armoured hordes had finally smashed all Hitler's hopes of taking Moscow by recapturing a town called Mojaisk, a German-occupied stronghold containing the last of the Fuehrer's armies threatening the capital of the Soviet Union.

Stalin, a jealous man, grudgingly congratulated his victorious generals.

Hitler, an unforgiving man, dismissed several of his defeated generals as incompetent cowards.

In the Far East, the Americans had lost Manila to the Japanese, who had also landed on Borneo, were deep into Malaya and invading Burma.

Sammy spent part of one morning at Islington in the cobwebby office of Mr Oliver Russell, a rusty old dogsbody known to many as 'Appy Olly on account of never being happy at all. Islington, hideously scarred by bomb damage, didn't raise a smile in him, either. A property-owner, he was also known for being an awkward and cantankerous landlord.

Concerning the bombed property at the Elephant and Castle, Sammy dangled the carrot of an extra five per cent in front of the old goat's sniffy nose.

'Sod off,' said the old goat.

'Don't be like that,' said Sammy, 'I've enough trouble helping Mr Churchill to win this war.'

'We're bleedin' losing it,' said the old goat.

'You and me had better emigrate, then,' said Sammy. 'Where'd you fancy?'

'Eh?'

'Germany, say?' suggested Sammy, who knew the value of getting an awkward geezer confused. 'Well, if they're going to win, we'd do better business there than in the Isle of Wight.'

'Where the 'ell's that?'

'You're right, Germany's the best bet,' said Sammy, 'and I daresay a couple of smart blokes like you and me could get to like Hitler.'

'Eh?'

'Bit of a pain in the elbow just now, I grant you,' said Sammy, 'but if you consider the kind of business he could put in our way, we could get to love him.'

'Sonny,' said the old goat, 'you're bleedin' drivelling, and I ain't emigratin' nowhere.'

'Well, back to business, then—'

'Pee off,' said the old goat, and did some destructive work on a cobweb.

'Kindly note I'm offering payment on exchange of contracts,' said Sammy.

'Stuff it.'

'I'm always in favour of a friendly discussion like this one,' said Sammy. 'Now, if I was friendly enough to offer ten per cent extra—'

'Eh?' The old goat's sniffy nose sharpened.

'Seven per cent's very friendly,' said Sammy.

'I 'eard ten.'

'Something went wrong with me arithmetic,' said Sammy, 'but not having had the same kind of education as me brother Boots, I do slip up occasional.'

'I ain't bleedin' daft,' said the old goat.

'Well, I don't do business with that kind,' said Sammy, 'they can't read or write. Now, regarding ten per cent extra—'

'I 'eard that definite,' said the old goat. 'Ten per cent.'

'I'm willing to consider it,' said Sammy.

'That's my privilege, considering it,' said the old goat.

'Give it a go, then,' said Sammy.

'Done,' said the old goat, and shoved some written matter across his worm-riddled desk. 'Sign that.'

Sammy grinned.

'Ready for me, were you, old cock?' he said.

'I wasn't born yesterday, sonny.'

Nor was I, thought Sammy, to whom the concession of ten per cent extra related to a modest raid on the petty cash.

* * *

Boots left headquarters a little after seven the following day, Saturday. There were no short hours for the Corps on any Saturday. He felt drained. The pressures were mounting, the war in the Far East doing considerable damage to the morale of the CIGS and his staff in London. The Japanese were eating up British colonial possessions, and the War Office and the Admiralty too, for that matter, were off balance. The Empire needed thousands of troops and a new fleet of battleships to appear in the Far East overnight if the Japanese were to be stopped. High Command's sense of urgency was being transmitted to every divisional and corps commander in the country.

Churchill was opting for a practical long-term solution, to take back in due time everything the Japanese gained. Nevertheless, the Empire could not sit passively on its bottom. Even Australia was under threat. Something must be done in an attempt to stem the tide. But what kind of combined Army and Navy force could reach the Far East in time? Can't be done, said General Sir Henry Simms to his staff. Boots shared his headaches and worries.

On arriving at his wartime home, he met Polly in the hall.

'Late again, old scout?' she said with an understanding smile.

'It's a filthy night and I think I'm feeling my age,' said Boots, delivering a kiss.

'Will a Scotch help?' asked Polly.

'Very much,' said Boots, removing his trench coat and hanging it, with his cap, on the elegant rosewood hallstand. 'Are the twins down for the evening?'

'Down and out,' said Polly, 'and won't wake until ten. Any earlier and they'll be unlucky.' Polly believed in regular and reasonable feeding times, not on demand. She led the way into the living-room, prettily furnished, poured two fingers of Scotch and handed the glass to Boots. He took a reviving swig. 'Tell me,' she said, as they sat down, 'what's going on between you and a Mrs Beatrice Freeman?'

'Beatrice Freeman?' Boots cast his mind back. 'Rosie's aunt?'

'That's the lady,' said Polly. 'She called this after-noon, informed me of her family connections as the widowed sister of Rosie's natural father, and was disappointed at not seeing you. She left an invi-tation for you to join a hunt and to stay the weekend at what she termed her pile of bricks.'

'Did you tell her I fall off horses?' said Boots.

'I told her you were otherwise engaged, perma-nently engaged, as a husband and father,' said Polly. 'You old devil, she fancies you.'

'I've only met her once, at Rosie's a few months ago,' said Boots.

'One meeting and smack, she wants you in her bed for weekends,' said Polly.

'I'll have to duck out,' said Boots, 'and is there any hunting in wartime?'

'Yes, Rosie's Aunt Beatrice is hunting you,' said Polly.

'No point in that,' said Boots. 'Even if she caught me, I'd fail her in my present state of health.'

A voice from the kitchen intruded.

'That you back from 'eadquarters, Colonel?'

'Yes, it's me, Corporal,' called Boots.

'Permission to serve me onion soup in twenty minutes, sir?' called Higgins.

'Onion soup?'

'It'll be steaming hot, sir, and 'ighly nourishing.'

'What a splendid bloke you are, Higgins.'

'Yessir. Same to you, sir. There's fish to follow.'

'What kind of fish?'

'Well, all I know is that it used to swim about in the sea, sir. It's this perishin' war, yer know.'

'I do know,' said Boots, and drank some more Scotch. Kate came down from her room and entered the living-room. Polly noted the gleam of dark auburn hair burnished by a brush, and the luminous green of the girl's eyes. Shades again of Emily, thought Polly.

'Oh, 'ello, Uncle Boots, you're home,' smiled Kate.

'Just about,' said Boots.

The phone rang. Kate answered it, then turned to Boots.

'It's for you, Uncle Boots, a lady,' she said.

Polly, suspecting it was Beatrice Freeman, gave Boots a warning look as he came to his feet.

Taking the phone from Kate, he said, 'Hello, who's that?'

'Colonel Adams?' said a lady's voice.

'Yes.'

'Colonel Adams, I'm Dr Margaret Pitt of the Park Infirmary, Winchester. Do you remember me?'

'Your name's familiar, yes,' said Boots.

'We've met several times,' said Dr Pitt, 'but not since before the war. You made periodic visits to a patient of ours, a Mrs Elsie Lansberg, who was transferred here from the Maudesley Hospital of South-East London in 1927.'

'I'm with you now,' said Boots. Mrs Elsie Lansberg, yes. English widow of a German, formerly Elsie Chivers, a neighbour of the Adams' in their Walworth days and tried for the murder of her mother at the Old Bailey in 1914. Found not guilty and acquitted. He himself had been a defence witness. She disappeared with Mr Finch in 1916, both suspected by Naval Intelligence of working for Germany. She reappeared in England from Germany in 1926, and was committed to an institution for the deranged after an incident at her old home. Elsie Chivers. His first love. A woman with soft myopic eyes that always seemed to reflect gentle sweetness. He and Emily had visited her several times after her transfer from the Maudesley Hospital. Dr Margaret Pitt, he now remembered, was one of the neurologists on the staff of the Park Infirmary. 'Dr Pitt,' he said, 'you're going to tell me something about Miss Chivers?'

'Miss Chivers? Ah, yes, she's always preferred us to call her that,' said Dr Pitt. 'I phoned your home a little while ago, and your mother kindly gave me this number. I'm so sorry to bother you. I understand your Army responsibilities keep you extremely busy. But I thought I should let you know Miss Chivers is a very frail lady, very frail, and isn't expected to last more than a few days. Colonel Adams, she has been asking to see you, she's been asking again and again. She's a woman who has no family, and no friends, apparently, except for you and your wife. Is it possible you could come and see her? She's in mental distress, and I think she feels you could ease her worries.'

Boots gave the request some thought, although he knew it would be difficult to refuse. Elsie Chivers was a woman whose life had been tragic, who had known little of happiness and whose very soul must still be burdened. Did she want to ease that burden by turning his visit into an opportunity for a confessional? Did he want that to happen, did he want to see her in the last days of her life? He thought of her as she had been, gentle, smiling and, to his eyes, quite lovely, a woman who had never offered one word of complaint about her impossible mother. Older than he was, yes, but still his first love.

'I'll drive up to Winchester tomorrow, Dr Pitt,' he said. 'I'll try to arrive by about eleven.'

'Well, thank you, Colonel Adams,' said Dr Pitt, 'and I do apologize if your visit takes up valuable time, but I promised Miss Chivers I would try to get hold of you.'

'I understand,' said Boots, 'I'll be there.'

'I'll tell her,' said Dr Pitt.

Polly knew a great deal about the Adams family, and many of its crises, but she knew next to nothing about Miss Chivers, and Kate, of course, was totally ignorant of the woman. Over the nourishing onion soup, Boots referred to her as an old neighbour and treasured friend always remembered with affection by the family. She had suffered a breakdown years ago. Would Polly mind if he went to see her?

'She's close to dying?' said Polly.

'It seems so,' said Boots.

320

'And she's asking to see you?' said Polly.

'Dr Pitt says so,' said Boots.

'Oh, you 'ave to go, doesn't he, Aunt Polly?' said Kate.

'I think Lizzy mentioned her once to me,' said Polly, 'as a neighbour who used to join you regularly for Sunday teas.'

'Right,' said Boots.

'Is she an old flame?' asked Polly.

'An old friend,' said Boots. Polly looked at him. She thought him serious, reflective. As much now as ever, she wanted to believe she meant more to him than any other women he had known, even Emily. His serious look changed as his smile surfaced. A reassuring smile.

'Yes, go and see her, old sport,' she said lightly.

Higgins called from the kitchen.

'Onion soup to everyone's likin', might I ask?'

'First-class,' called Boots.

'A tiny bit too salty,' said Kate.

'It's what?' called Higgins.

'Passable,' said Kate.

'Young females should be seen and not 'eard,' growled Higgins.

Chapter Twenty-Six

'Is Dr Pitt available?'

The young receptionist at the Park Infirmary, doubling as the switchboard operator, looked up and went swoony. The Army officer in his peaked cap and trenchcoat was just about as sexy as any man could be.

'Pardon, sir?' she gulped.

'Dr Pitt, is she around?' asked Boots. The time was ten-fifty.

'Dr Pitt?' The girl blinked.

'Are you having an off-day, young lady?' smiled Boots.

'Me sir? Oh, no, it's just that – oh, did you say Dr Pitt? Just a moment, sir.' She rang through. 'Dr Pitt, there's an Army gentleman asking for you.'

'I'll be there immediately,' said Dr Pitt.

'She's coming rightaway, sir,' said the slightly flushed receptionist.

'Thank you,' said Boots. He took his trenchcoat off and placed it over his arm.

Oh, help, thought the girl, I've just gone off Cary Grant, my favourite dreamboat.

Dr Pitt appeared, a woman in her forties, her

white coat flapping to her brisk walk, her horn-rimmed spectacles enlarging her eyes.

'Colonel Adams, thank you for coming,' she said.

'It's a few years since I last saw you,' said Boots. He removed his cap and shook hands with her.

'I recognize you, even if you are in uniform,' smiled Dr Pitt. 'This way,' she said.

The receptionist sighed as her new dreamboat disappeared with Dr Pitt.

'How is Miss Chivers?' asked Boots, turning with Dr Pitt into a long corridor with its tiled walls typical of the building's Victorian origins.

'Fading,' said Dr Pitt. 'Yes, I think that's the word. Our senior medical officer assures me he can't treat her for a specific illness, only prescribe vitamins for her physical weakness. She's a very tired woman and is simply slipping away. We know her history, of course, and you and I once talked about that.'

'Miss Chivers has lived a sad, tragic life,' said Boots, 'and if she's slipping away, without pain or suffering, that perhaps will be the one kindness life has offered her.'

Dr Pitt stopped at a door and turned to face Boots.

'I think there's suffering, Colonel Adams,' she said, 'in her mind.'

'Let her go, then,' said Boots.

'Ethics won't allow us to stand aside,' said Dr Pitt with a wry smile. 'Give me a moment.' She opened the door and went in. Boots waited until she reappeared. 'Yes, you can see her now, and you may have as long as you like with her.'

Boots entered and Dr Pitt pulled the door to.

The room was quite bright in the light of a high window. Elsie Chivers lay in the bed, head and shoulders resting on heaped pillows. Her eyes were closed, her breathing even. Boots placed his hat and coat on a chair and advanced quietly to the bedside. He looked down at the woman who had fascinated him not only in his early teens, but during his time as a young man. How old was she? He was forty-five himself, and he knew she must be well past fifty. But, astonishingly, her light brown hair, so well remembered for its touch of soft gold in the sunshine of summer, showed not a single trace of grey. Her forehead was smooth and unlined, her face thin and pale, the paleness almost translucent, a sign, he supposed, of a woman wasting away. Her arms were outside the covers, and her hands, as pale as her face, lay on the blanket, fingers plucking at it. How often he had stood beside the family piano to watch her long graceful fingers moving over the keyboard. Once a month she had come to tea on a Sunday and always to play the piano afterwards. He had thought her a lady, a lovely lady, the uncomplaining daughter of the frightful woman the street kids called the Witch. She was a figure of enchantment in his compulsive examination of life and people in those days. What had he learnt from studying her, knowing her? Perhaps, as much as anything, a certainty that women were a more civilizing influence than men, although not all men were aggressive, and not all women were temperate.

Here was his first love, Elsie Chivers. He would always acknowledge that.

'Elsie?' he spoke gently.

Her eyes opened, eyes softly myopic, her spectacles on the bedside table. Wearing them, she had always looked studious. Without them, lovely.

She gazed wonderingly up at him, her lashes wide open, her translucent skin shining. Recognition arrived, and with it the faintest of smiles.

'Boots, dear dear Boots,' she said softly. 'So tall, so fine. I've so wanted to see you.'

'We're old friends, Elsie,' he said. He reached and took her left hand. Her fingers closed around his, her clasp gentle.

'Will you sit with me for a little while?' Her voice, always soft, lacked some of its musical timbre now.

'Gladly,' said Boots, and seated himself. 'Will you forgive me for not having been to see you since before the war?'

Elsie Chivers sighed.

'Yes, there is a war, Boots, isn't there? Another one. How sad. And I am so old, my dear, and so tired.'

'Old?' Boots smiled. 'Not yet. Let's say you and I are both getting on a bit.'

He felt another light pressure of her hand.

'I think, Boots, you were always the kindest and most tactful of friends,' she said. She was conversing with surprising lucidity. 'We travelled to work together sometimes, didn't we?'

'On the occasions when I was lucky enough to meet up with you,' said Boots.

'You thought that lucky?' Another faint smile.

'Uplifting,' said Boots. 'It made my day.'

'Dear Boots, that was a lifetime ago,' she said.

'A few years,' said Boots, 'a few gallons of water under the bridge.'

A little shadow of pain darkened her eyes.

'If only – if only—'

'If only is something that bedevils all of us,' said Boots, 'and I keep mine under lock and key. Much the best place for all our "if only" moments.'

'But they won't always stay there, will they?' she said. 'Oh, so many mistakes, Boots, so many.' She sighed at the advent of unwelcome memories. 'My marriage, how absurd that was.'

That was the first time, in his presence, she had voluntarily mentioned her marriage to a German landowner.

'Was it absurd at the time, Elsie?'

'I thought I needed protection, Boots.'

Yes, according to Mr Finch, she had been alone in Germany then.

'Many women have found themselves in that position,' he said.

'But to choose only half a man, Boots, one already coughing himself to death, so silly, so very absurd,' she said, and looked anguished.

'What happened, Elsie?' asked Boots.

She reflected, became vague and a little remote, then reflected again and rejoined him.

'I was never a wife, only a nurse,' she said.

'Then you were alone again?'

'So many mistakes,' she said again, 'so many.' Her eyes closed, a little sigh came, and she journeyed away. Boots kept hold of her hand, watching her, feeling for her, remembering the day when her dreadful mother had been discovered stiff and dead, her throat slashed. Then Elsie's arrest and trial, with Mr Finch one of her defence witnesses, calm, composed and unequivocating.

And he himself, the last witness on her behalf, giving evidence that put him into the forefront of newspaper reports. The jury had returned a unanimous Not Guilty verdict. For years, Boots had never been sure about that, never been sure who actually committed the crime, Elsie herself or Mr Finch. They were lovers at the time. There had been a day in 1926, however, after she had been arrested for creating a disturbance in her old home while carrying a knife, when he thought he was sure about her guilt. But, thinking it over, he decided the incident still did not amount to proof positive.

Mistakes, she had just said. What did she see as mistakes? Her submissive role as her wretched mother's daughter? Turning down every opportunity to live apart from her? Throwing in her lot with Mr Finch while he was still a German agent? Marriage to a man that was no marriage? The murder of her mother in a moment when all her years of being tormented caused a flashpoint of rage?

Which of these was her greatest mistake? He would suggest her inability to leave her mother and to live apart from her. All the other mistakes stemmed from that one.

Her fingers stirred around his hand. Her eyes opened. Her lashes fluttered, and he wondered if she would reach for her spectacles. She hadn't seemed to want them so far. Her initial recognition of him had been almost immediate.

'What were your mistakes, Elsie?' he asked, and wished at once that he hadn't put the question.

'Boots?'

'I'm still here.'

327

'I'm so glad to see you.' Her voice was a little stronger, carrying a hint of warmth. 'I loved you when you were young, did you know? And Emily too. How is dear Emily?'

'Emily always thought the world of you,' he said.

'I loved all of you. Your dear mother, sweet Lizzy, all of you. Boots, I wanted to see you, I have so much I must tell you, and you are the only one I can tell.'

That he didn't want. Not for the sake of his peace of mind, but for the sake of her distress, particularly if it meant confessing to the worst. What did it matter now if she herself had cut the throat of the Witch? It mattered to her, yes, of course it did, and it was that which gave her so much distress, he was sure. But he was also sure she would not ease that distress by confessing. To tell him and then to realize he and his family would have to live with the certain knowledge that she had committed the unforgivable sin of matricide, what could that possibly do for her if not make her last days mentally unendurable? He knew how she had always regarded his family, his mother, his sister and his brothers. With emotional affection. What could he say to her that would comfort her, that would help her to take her worst secret with her? First, he could refer, as she did, only to mistakes, not deeds.

'Elsie you need tell me nothing. Everyone makes mistakes, and most of us make secrets of our worst mistakes. Does that matter so much, does it matter to others if others see us for our better side? Not every skeleton needs to be brought into the light.'

'Boots, my dear, some cry out,' she whispered, and her hand trembled around his.

'Let me tell you something,' he said gently. 'Let me tell you that all my family, whom you knew so well, have never forgotten you. My mother, my sister Lizzy, my brothers Tommy and Sammy, and Emily and myself, have always held you in love and affection. For myself, you were my first love, the first woman I cherished, and all the water under all the bridges have never carried that away. Elsie, live in peace with yourself, and next time I come to see you we'll talk about the times we travelled to work together on a tram.'

Doubt cast its shadow, and she said, 'Can that be true, Boots? That you all have affection for me? Your dear mother? Lizzy? Sammy? Tommy? All of you? But I left without a word for any of you.'

He was fairly sure she was thinking of the day she disappeared with Edwin Finch, when Edwin had known Naval Intelligence men were after them. She supposed, of course, that the latter had informed Chinese Lady and the family that she and Edwin were suspected of spying for Germany. That was the word used in the Great War. Spying.

'Yes, all of us, Elsie,' he said. 'I know of no reason why that affection should have changed.'

A long sigh escaped her pale lips. He thought she might have asked why those who still held her in affection had not come to see her, apart from himself and Emily, but that was probably not within the range of her failing comprehension.

'Boots, the only truly happy hours I have known were those spent with you and your family at Sunday tea. And Edwin too.'

Edwin. Mr Finch, the family's lodger and an unsuspected German agent in those days. One thing he was not going to tell her was that Edwin Finch was now his mother's second husband. Only he himself of the family knew his stepfather's full history.

'Edwin Finch, Elsie?' he said. 'An understanding man, and an entertaining one at those Sunday teas.'

Another sigh, another wondering look.

'Dear Boots, if I could only undo so much, so much,' she whispered, voice in her throat. He thought she was close to weeping, but she had always had an inner strength, and it did not fail her now. 'Thank you for coming, thank you for your love and understanding. Boots, oh, I'm so old, so tired.'

Lightly, he said, 'Whenever I feel like that, Elsie, I have a whisky. Next time I come, I'll bring a small bottle and we'll have a nip together.'

She looked perplexed at that, then the faint smile came again.

'You were always so humorous, weren't you?' she said. Her lashes drooped and her eyes closed once more. He stayed there, holding her hand, watching her, caring for her.

If she had done that deed, she was no murderess, only the involuntary executioner of a woman who owned neither love nor pity, neither gratitude nor virtue, and who forced on her daughter a life of misery and repression.

He sat silently, his own being full of pity. In her dreamlike state she was almost ethereal. He remembered words the vicar had spoken at Emily's burial.

'Receive her, Lord, into the peace of your Kingdom.'

That would be as fitting for Elsie Chivers as for Emily.

A light knock on the door preceded the entry of Dr Pitt.

'How is she, Colonel Adams, sleeping?' she asked quietly.

'Resting,' said Boots.

'We shall try to make her eat a little lunch in fifteen minutes.'

'Somehow, doctor, I think lunches are no longer important to her,' said Boots.

'Trying to make her eat is important to us. We have a duty to try to sustain her.'

'I hope very much that all you can do for her is what she would wish.'

'You'll stay a little longer, Colonel Adams?'

'At least until her lunch arrives.'

'I have known no woman so sad,' said Dr Pitt, and quietly left. She could have told Boots that the one thing that never failed to disturb this patient was the sight of a knife, any knife. Food that needed cutting was cut before it was brought to her.

The hand loosely linked with Boots's fingers stirred again. Her eyes opened, their softness misty.

'Boots, you're here again?' she murmured.

'I did promise,' said Boots, going along with her illusion.

'Oh, so kind, my dear, so kind.'

'Remember only that we love you, Elsie.'

'Yes. Thank you, Boots, thank you.'

She went away again. From somewhere came the sound of a woman shouting, then screaming. A door slammed and the screams faded. Boots doubted if Elsie Chivers had ever shouted or screamed in all the years of her unhappy life. She was like Vi, gentle and equable.

But perhaps there had been one moment, one scream of utter hatred for a monster of a woman. Then the flash of the carving knife.

Perhaps.

He realized, that the thought had lain there for years, that he did not want to be burdened with absolute certainty.

He stayed until he heard the sound of trolleys and the opening and closing of doors. Lunch was being served. Soon something would arrive for Elsie. He looked at his watch. Twelve-fifteen.

He was still holding her hand as he came to his feet. She lay restfully, head depressing the top pillow, light brown hair soft and tidy. She looked fragile, yes, but not as if life was yet ready to leave her.

'Elsie?'

They opened at once, those expressive eyes, and there was actually the distinct light of a smile. His deepest emotions surfaced.

'Boots? I'm so glad you're here.'

That moved him the more, her quick recognition again, and it caused him a moment of bitter self-dislike for not having visited her for so long. He had made do with one or two letters.

'Elsie, I want you to know you're not forgotten, not by any of us,' he said.

'I have dreams, Boots, many unhappy dreams,' she said, 'but I also have memories that are dear to me.'

'Then live with them, Elsie, and in peace with yourself,' he said very gently. 'Do that for us, for the family, won't you?'

'Yes. Yes, my dear.'

'Then goodbye until next time, sweet woman,' he said, and bent and kissed her pale lips, and her lips came to life, to warm life, for a fleeting moment. Then the long sigh.

'I'm so tired, Boots, so tired.' Her hand slipped from his, and her lashes fell. He looked down at her for long seconds, then gathered up his hat and coat and left. He found Dr Pitt and asked her if she knew how many days remained to Miss Chivers. Dr Pitt said four or five perhaps, according to the chief medical officer, but who could ever be certain?

Boots drove back to Dorset, mouth set, mind on the sadness of a woman who had deserved some kindness from life and received none. He thought of Emily, as he often did, despite his devotion to Polly. Emily was always an echo of his life in Walworth, of Walworth itself and its resilient people. She had been the girl next door, a young hussy, a torment and, finally, a godsend. She had known Elsie Chivers, watched her, observed her, remarked how ladylike she was, and, in the end, striven to be ladylike herself. Well, as much as she could.

Elsie, Emily, Polly. Could a man genuinely love three women one after the other? Genuinely? He only knew each had a cherished place in his life.

A horn blasted his ears. A large black Daimler, its driver aghast, was coming straight at his nearside front wheel. God, he himself was right over the centre line of the road. He swung his steering-wheel in an instantaneous reflex action and missed a collision only by a whisker. The Daimler's horn blasted again, cursing him.

How precious life suddenly became when the threat of death was a mere few inches away.

Where was he going?

Home, of course, to Polly and the twins.

But his sadness for Elsie Chivers went all the way with him.

That evening, the twins having been bathed and fed, Polly and Boots were tucking the sleepy infants into their cots. Down in the kitchen, Kate was preparing a light Sunday supper, Corporal Higgins being off for the day.

Polly had received from Boots details of his visit to the ailing Elsie Chivers. That is, the details he chose to give her. Not to Emily, or to Chinese Lady or any of the family, had he ever disclosed all he knew about Elsie Chivers and Mr Finch. And so with Polly. Polly, however, intelligent and sophisticated, looked him in the eye and said, 'There's something else.'

'Is there?' said Boots.

'Look here, old darling, I'm not a sweet and innocent Girl Guide who thinks helping grannies to cross the road is the height of dangerous living, I'm a grown-up woman with a fair helping of the old grey matter. There is something else about this woman Elsie Chivers, widow of a German. What is it?'

'Nothing that makes any difference to the fact that she's a dying friend of the family,' said Boots, 'and nothing that comes between you and me.'

'She's not an old flame, like Rachel is of Sammy's?' said Polly.

'Positively not,' said Boots.

'Well, if there's something crooked lurking about in the bushes,' said Polly, 'I'll find out.'

'Leave it,' said Boots.

'What?'

'Leave it, Polly.'

'Am I to infer there's a skeleton in the unfortunate woman's cupboard?'

'Yes,' said Boots. 'Favour me, and don't ask me to open the cupboard.'

'You're serious?' said Polly.

'Yes.'

'I want to know, would it affect my relationship with you if I knew what it was?'

'No,' said Boots.

'That's a true no?'

'Absolutely,' said Boots.

'Well, all right, old thing,' said Polly. 'It's just that I hate being left out of any part of your life.'

'That part was before we met,' said Boots.

'Touché,' said Polly, who had never been terribly keen on letting him know the extent of her affairs on the Western Front in the Great War. During the years she had wanted him as her lover, she had thrown in a few careless remarks here and there, sometimes to provoke him, but Boots had never asked her for details, not then nor since their marriage. He was like that, a man who preferred to let sleeping dogs lie. 'Sorry about being nosey. Subject dropped.'

'There's a sweet girl.'

'Think nothing of it, old sport.'

Two days later, in the evening, Boots took another phone call from Dr Pitt.

'I'm so sorry, Colonel Adams,' she said, 'but I have to tell you that your friend, Elsie Chivers, died two hours ago.'

Boots sighed. Elsie, perhaps, had been glad to go as a woman who had nothing to live for.

'That was sooner than you expected,' he said.

'She slipped away from us, very quietly, very peacefully,' said Dr Pitt. 'For several days before your visit, she suffered periods of extreme distress. She was better from the moment I informed her you were coming to see her, and after your visit, she was quiet and relaxed. Yes, she did slip away peacefully. I assure you of that.'

Peacefully. Had he helped her, then, in telling her that her mistakes could never matter to himself and his family, to everyone who had known her during the years when she had experienced the only happy hours of her life? Had it helped to tell her he loved her? He hoped so, with all his heart he hoped so.

'Thank you for letting me know, Dr Pitt,' he said, 'and I'm sure I also have to thank you and other members of your staff for all you did for her over the many years she was a patient. The war, I'm afraid, checked my visits.'

'Colonel Adams,' said Dr Pitt, 'I know you as her only friend. Would you have any thoughts about her burial, perhaps where you think she would like to rest?'

Not next to her mother, thought Boots, not that of all places. As for her long-dead father, he had no idea where he was buried. But there was one cemetery he thought suitable for Elsie. Southwark Cemetery, where Emily lay.

'That's a very compassionate thought of yours, Dr Pitt,' he said. 'I'm sure I know just the place. Southwark Cemetery in South-East London. She lived many years in that area. I'll write and give you all the details, which perhaps you'll pass on to the undertakers, together with my promise to pay all expenses. Will you do that for me?'

'Willingly, and with pleasure,' said Dr Pitt.

'Thank you,' said Boots.

'We shall miss her, you know, and remember her.'

'I'm glad to hear you say that,' said Boots, 'she was a woman with a history, yes, but she doesn't deserve to be forgotten.'

'No, indeed. Goodbye, Colonel Adams, it's been a pleasure to know you.'

'Thank you. Goodbye, doctor.'

He wondered, as he put the phone down, would Elsie like that, a plot close to Emily's?

Yes, I think she would.

They were women worth remembering, Emily for giving so much to life and her family, Elsie for her gentleness and the tragedy of her mistakes.

He wrote brief but telling letters that evening to Chinese Lady, Lizzy, Tommy and Sammy.

Twenty-Seven

'Where are we?' asked Felicity.

'God knows,' said Tim, 'we happen to be going where this amiable old gee-gee is taking us.'

They had been at Rosie and Matthew's cottage four days, and the February weather was sharp, bright and invigorating. Matthew's sister Maisie had called, given them her address in case they needed help, and introduced them to Matthew's horse and dogcart, stabled in a nearby field.

Rosie herself had called, meeting Felicity for the first time. Rosie being Rosie, entirely natural and infectiously engaging, it did not take Felicity long to realize she had a sister-in-law as fascinating as her parents-in-law.

Next Sunday, Boots and Polly were going to call, bringing the twins and Kate with them. Over the phone, Tim said Felicity would put on a Sunday tea for everyone.

'What?' shrieked Felicity from the background.

'Sunday tea for seven,' said Tim.

'For five,' said Polly, who was making the call. 'I'll see to the twins.'

338

'For five,' said Tim over his shoulder to Felicity.

'I'm married to a sadist,' yelled Felicity.

'I heard that,' said Polly, 'so tell Felicity from me that Kate will be a tower of strength to her.'

Felicity made up her mind that she'd have everything ready by the time the guests arrived, even if she bumped blindly into everything in the kitchen. Tim said he'd slice the bread and boil the home made eggs. The chickens were laying daily.

On this, their fourth day, they were out in the dogcart, Tim at the reins, his ribs and sternum healed, the nag ambling, the countryside sharp with the greens and browns of winter.

'Tim,' said Felicity, warm coat hugging her bouyant body, 'I can't see a bloody thing, which is a curse, take it from me, but I can smell Dorset and I like the smell. It's clean, it's fresh, it's lovely.'

'It's winter,' said Tim.

'Well, yes, it may be, but I love the clear feel of it,' said Felicity. 'When the Huns chucked that lousy bomb at me, it was like a death blow. Then you came along, and that and this tell me there really is life after death.'

'That's how you feel?' said Tim, letting the nag amble lazily.

'That's how I feel, Tim chummy,' said Felicity, and Tim wondered if Rosie and Matthew would let him rent their cottage for her, providing he could fix her up with a companion. She couldn't manage by herself.

Was there someone? It was worth thinking about.

                    *   *   *

Letter from Edward to Leah.

> Dear Leah,
>   I don't want to complain, not much, but this busi-
> ness of you popping into the library every Saturday
> afternoon to spend ten seconds whispering to me and
> then popping off, it's not doing me a lot of good. So
> how about if next Sunday afternoon I ride over to
> your school on a borrowed bike and crash off it just
> outside your gates? Say about three. You be at a
> window, you see the accident and get one of your
> friends to find Miss Murchison and tell her there's a
> bloke off his bike with a broken leg. Don't give the sad
> news to Miss Murchison yourself or she might smell
> a rat. She'll naturally hurry out to inspect my
> damage, I'll tell her my leg's OK but that I'm uncon-
> scious with shock and bruises and could she get me
> into the school where I can recover. That way, she'll
> probably let me stay to tea, when I can sit next to you
> for a couple of hours.
>   Let me know what you think.
>   Love, Edward.

Leah to Edward by return.

> Dear Edward,
>   What an imagination you've got, I've never read
> anything more brilliant, except I don't pop in on you
> for only ten seconds. That's a fib, it's more like ten
> minutes. Still, I do feel flattered that you'd like to
> sit next to me for two hours, only I don't think
> Miss Murchison would fall for your idea, and
> anyway how could you talk to her about getting

340

*you into the school to recover if you were uncon-
scious?*

*My life, could anyone unconscious sit up and
start talking? That bit sort of knocked holes in your
theory of how to get into the school. Think of something else and when I pop into the library on
Saturday you can whisper to me about it and I'll see
if it's workable as well as brilliant.*

Love, Leah.

Quirky fate being what it was, it probably made a
capricious note of the fact that for the first time
each letter was signed with love.

Mrs Lizzy Somers, in her forty-fourth year,
regarded with disgust two minute lamb chops she
had just unwrapped. Her morning's shopping had
been downright pestiferous in that the grocer, the
butcher and the greengrocer had all got on her
nerves with their references to the fact that short-
ages came about because there was a war on. As if
she didn't know, as if anyone didn't know.

'How can I give my hard-workin' husband one of
them?' she demanded of the butcher and his tiny
lamb chops. 'I just don't know how you can call
them chops. They look more like shrimps.'

'Now, Mrs Somers, you know I don't sell
shrimps.'

'You're trying to sell me two,' said Lizzy.

'Missus, I put it to you, what I'm offering is all I
can offer against the coupons you're giving me. It's
the war, y'know—'

'I do know, don't I, Mr Bristow?' said Lizzy. 'I
ought to, seeing me and my fam'ly's been in it from

the start. What's upsetting me is what kind of lamb did those chops come from? It must've been a little dwarf, poor thing.'

'You will 'ave your little joke, Mrs Somers.'

And so on.

Inspecting the chops now, Lizzy sighed, placed them on a plate and put them in her walk-in larder. A tin of corned beef caught her eye. It was the kind of thing wartime housewives kept for a rainy day. I'll cook both chops for Ned, and have some corned beef myself, she thought. I'll do lots of nice mashed potatoes and leeks from the garden, and I'll think up how I can make a creamy sauce for the leeks. Creamy sauce, that's another little joke. Oh, this rotten war, I'd ask Mr Churchill to give in if we were fighting against Bulgaria. Well, Boots once said Bulgarians were very kind to their mothers, so we could get along a lot more easily with them than with Hitler and his Nazis. No, wait a minute, Lizzy Somers, you ought to know by now you have to think twice about what Boots actually means when he says something like that.

She took the rest of her purchases out of her shopping bag and put them on the kitchen table. Everything related to minimum, and even the two eggs from Mr Reynolds the grocer looked as if they'd been laid by undersized pullets. Still, he'd supplied some powdered egg from America, and that was a bit of a boon.

I'll have a cup of tea in a minute to cheer myself up. Lor' this house, there's only me and Ned now, and he's only here in the evenings when he's not on duty down at the ARP post. Where's my family? Bobby, Annabelle, Emma and Edward? Well, I know where Annabelle, Emma and Edward are, in the country away from the bombs. But where's Bobby and his lady friend, Helene? We haven't heard from him for ages. Sammy and Susie are so lucky still having Paula at home with them, and they've got that sweet little girl Phoebe as well. They're going to be upset when they have to give her up, so I hope they're being sensible about it.

I mustn't forget to go to the funeral of Elsie Chivers on Monday, poor woman, what a sad life she had. Boots wants Tommy, Sammy and Chinese Lady to go too, all of us.

She put the kettle on, then switched on the kitchen wireless set to catch the eleven o'clock news. She heard that the British were retreating in Burma, evacuating Malaya and trying to resume their offensive in the Middle East. The Americans were still having a hard time of it in the Pacific. But so were Hitler's Germans in Russia, where some of them were freezing to death. Well, thought Lizzy, with the war going on everywhere, the next thing my butcher will tell me is that there aren't any lamb chops at all, and Ned does like a nice lamb chop.

Rat-a-tat-tat, said the front door knocker.

'Who can that be?' Lizzy asked of the kettle that had just begun to steam. The kettle couldn't say, so she went to find out for herself. She opened the door.

'What-ho, Mum,' said Bobby, 'couldn't find my doorkey. Must be a hole in my pocket. A treat to see you. Say hello to Mum, Helene.'

'Ah, he is still crazy, your son, Mrs Somers,' said Helene.

They were both in uniform, both vigorous with health, and each carried a valise.

Lizzy came to.

'Bobby – Helene – oh, my goodness, I was just thinking about you two, and here you are, like a conjuring trick.'

'Like a couple of rabbits out of a hat?' said Bobby. He put his valise down, swept his arms around his mum and gave her a loving smacker on each cheek. 'Hope you can find some lettuce for us, we're home for a fortnight.'

'Bobby, I've hardly got anything in the house,' said flustered but delighted Lizzy. 'Why didn't you phone and let me know you were comin'?'

'I did phone but you were out,' said Bobby.

'Oh, yes, I was doing my shopping,' said Lizzy, thinking what a good-looking couple they were and how attached to each other.

'Don't worry about an empty larder,' said Bobby, 'we've got ration coupons galore.'

'Yes, we will do some shopping quickly,' said Helene. 'Mrs Somers, it is so nice to see you again.' And she too kissed Lizzy on both cheeks.

'Oh, havin' you both home again is lovely,' said Lizzy.

Someone else was home again. Rachel's father, the distinguished Isaac Moses, had at last travelled back from a fruitless stay in Palestine. The international deputation of Jews that had tried to persuade the Pope to intercede with Germany on behalf of their persecuted brethren, had received a qualified re-assurance that the Vatican would use its influence to protect the Jews of Italy.

*   *   *

General Sir Henry Simms, falling ill from the strain of overwork, was hospitalized, and Lieutenant-General Montrose had taken over his command. Sir Henry took the blow philosophically. Well, he was sixty-seven and knew that only the incidence of war had allowed him to be given a command instead of compulsory retirement. From London had come a message of sympathy and an invitation, when he had fully recovered, to chair a new board overseeing conscription and recruitment, or to opt for a well-deserved retirement. Either way, remarked Sir Henry to his wife, I'll be put out to grass.

Boots went to see him in Dorchester Hospital on Friday, three days after the death of Elsie Chivers. Lady Simms was there, at her husband's bedside in a room exclusive to very important patients. Her eyes brightened when Boots arrived. Her liking for him was no secret, and she was delighted to have him as a son-in-law, particularly as he had played his own part in giving her what she had never thought to have, grandchildren. The fact that they were step-grandchildren was merely incidental.

Boots leaned, kissed her and said, 'How's the patient today?'

'Quite the same as yesterday,' said Lady Simms. 'Grumpy.'

'I challenge that remark,' said Sir Henry, who looked comfortable, if a little wan. 'Further, I consider it impertinent. Confine her to barracks for a week, Boots. Tell me about the twins, my amazing grandchildren.'

'They're fat,' said Boots.

345

'Splendid,' said Sir Henry. 'Um – should they be?'

'Of course,' said Lady Simms.

'Can't remember ever being fat myself,' said Sir Henry. 'Can't remember Boots ever looking over-weight, either.'

'Your grandchildren, Sir Henry, are in fine shape,' said Boots, 'and Polly sends her love. She can't leave the infants for the time being. Feeding times and all that. She asked me to tell you not to kick over the traces but to go home to Dulwich and grow cucumbers and tomatoes.'

'Damned if I could nurse cucumbers while that blasted scoundrel Hitler is still creating havoc and misery for millions,' said Sir Henry. 'The man's a genius in his way, but a damned destructive bugger as well.'

'Henry my dear,' said Lady Simms, 'I've a request from Matron for you not to swear when a nurse is present.'

'No idea what she's talking about,' said Sir Henry. 'Never swear in front of a lady, it's a principle of mine.'

'That's news to me, and probably to Boots too,' said Lady Simms.

'Boots will vouch for my conduct in mixed company,' said Sir Henry.

'Blameless as my own,' said Boots.

'Then I apologize to my sex for the pair of you,' said Lady Simms, 'although I fear Polly's language frequently lets us down.'

'Boots,' said Sir Henry, 'how are you getting on with Lieutenant-General Montrose?'

'So-so,' said Boots.

'H'm,' said Sir Henry, who knew the new commander of the Corps favoured a staff shake-up.

'I'll stand my ground,' said Boots, disinclined to accept a possible transfer that would take him away from Polly and the twins.

'He'll make Colonel Lewis his adjutant if you give him half a chance,' said Sir Henry.

'As Corps commander he doesn't need half a chance,' said Boots, 'but I'll still stand my ground.'

'I'll back your wish to stay with the Corps,' said Sir Henry, 'I'm not bedridden yet.'

Lady Simms smiled. Her husband and her son-in-law had long been her favourite men. Neither was aggressive or overbearing, but together they made a formidable pair of old soldiers.

Chapter Twenty-Eight

That afternoon Sammy was home from his work in order to be with Susie when Herbert Willis, Phoebe's uncle, arrived. He left Rachel in charge of the offices where, despite the limitations that clothes rationing put on the sales of his shops, Services contracts kept the place humming with phone calls and paperwork, and in constant touch with the firm's factory at Belsize Park. Rachel, a natural businesswoman, would handle everything as if she had been born a director of the Adams ventures.

Home at two o'clock, the waiting time from then on became a strain for Sammy, and for Susie too.

Not until it was a little past three did the front door knocker send its message into the house. Phoebe for the moment was with Chinese Lady in the kitchen. Sammy made quick strides to the front door, Susie compulsively following.

A sturdy, broad-shouldered man in a greatcoat and forage cap of the Canadian Army stood on the doorstep.

'Afternoon, folks,' he said, 'might you be Mr and Mrs Adams?'

Sammy and Susie, detecting a cockney accent slightly overlaid by the transatlantic tones of Canadians, took a good look at their caller. He had homely features, a healthy colour and a friendly if enquiring smile.

'Could you be Mr Herbert Willis?' asked Susie.

'Lance-Corporal Willis this here moment,' he said. Sammy judged him to be about thirty. 'And I guess I'll make corporal come Easter.'

'I'm Mrs Adams, Mrs Susie Adams, and this is Sammy, my husband.'

'Pleased to know you both, pleased to meet you, sure thing,' said Herbert Willis.

'Step inside,' said Sammy, hiding the onset of tension. Little Phoebe had been a forlorn child again on waking. Her bed was wet once more. Sammy, going in to see to her, had responded to her tearful admission by being his usual comforting self, telling her not to worry, and that her little problem would go away when she had a mummy and daddy. Which you will have in time, he said, so don't worry, pet. He thought now that Herbert Willis looked very capable of being a comforting and homely father to her. A daddy.

He and Susie took the visitor into the parlour. Invited to sit, he requested the pleasure of removing his cap and greatcoat, and that done he made himself at home in an armchair by the fireside and referred to the house as handsome, Mr Adams, handsome. Regarding Susie, he looked frankly approving. Susie dressed well, carried herself with the self-assurance common to most members of the family, and with her fair hair, blue eyes and attractive features, looked as photogenic as any woman of thirty-seven possibly could.

It was a fact that Susie considered life had treated her with great kindness. It had not given her the worries that aged a woman in advance of her years. There had been worries, yes, but they had been the worries of long ago, when her dad had endured years of unemployment after the Great War, and her mum sometimes hadn't had even a penny for the gas meter. However, from the day Susie met Sammy, just before she was sixteen, fortune favoured her and her dad. Sammy became her good luck charm and her shield against any of those spiteful arrows that life aims at women.

Phoebe's Uncle Herbert had come, of course, to make his claim on the girl. Susie knew she was going to be sad when the time came for Phoebe to leave, and she knew Sammy was going to feel wrenched, but they'd agreed a new life with her aunt and uncle in Canada was all for Phoebe's good. Sammy at this moment seemed to be carefully weighing up Herbert Willis, and Susie knew it would help if they both came to like the man.

Sammy said, 'It's a relief to know we can sort things out with you, Mr Willis.'

'Well, it was up to me to show meself as soon as I could, Mr Adams,' said Herbert Willis, 'and now I've got seven days to meself, well, 'ere I am. I've hoofed it down from our base at the barracks near Hendon. I 'ad the cops in touch with me a while ago, but couldn't make it here till I got some leave. Today's OK with you for a parley-vous?'

'Well, we did think the sooner the better,' said Susie. 'Would you like a cup of tea?'

'Tea out of a china pot, eh?' Herbert Willis

looked happy at the offer. 'I guess I downed more'n few hundred cups during me time in Bow, and I won't say no to one now, no, I won't. And might I see young Phoebe? Bad luck that was, losing her Aunt Lily in the way she did. Poor old Lily. I tell you, Mr Adams, back there in Canada we suffered 'orrible over the murder of me brother and sister-in-law, and never thought on top of that to hear Lily 'ad committed suicide.'

'I call everything brutal bad luck for Phoebe,' said Sammy.

'I've never known such tragedy,' said Susie, 'and it's had its effect on Phoebe. Excuse me, and I'll make tea for all of us.' She did so, while telling Chinese Lady about the visitor. Chinese Lady said she'd come and stand with Susie and Sammy. Susie carried the tea in on a tray, and Chinese Lady followed with Phoebe, letting the girl know she was going to meet her Uncle Herbert.

'Please, who's 'e?' asked Phoebe.

'Your uncle, love,' said Chinese Lady, and held the girl's hand as they followed Susie into the parlour, where Sammy was giving Herbert Willis exact details of how he and Susie came to be looking after his orphaned niece.

Phoebe's uncle came to his feet on the entrance of Chinese Lady and Phoebe. Susie introduced him to her mother-in-law, Mrs Finch. He declared himself pleasured to meet the lady, who gave him a polite measuring-up look, and professed the pleasure was mutual, which it would be, she thought, if the outcome made a happy girl of Phoebe. Susie then introduced him to Phoebe, the little niece he'd never seen. He and his wife had emigrated just before the child was born, and he hadn't been able to come over to attend the murder trial. He hadn't wanted to. He'd have done murder himself, he told his wife.

He turned a friendly smile on the slightly nervous child.

'So you're Frank's little girl, eh?' Frank was the name of his murdered brother. 'Well, you're pretty, that you are, just like your mum, and I'm thankin' these here people for takin' good care of you and dressing you pretty. Like it 'ere, do you, Phoebe, with Mr and Mrs Adams?'

Phoebe didn't answer that. Looking up at him, she said, 'Mummy and Daddy went away and didn't come back.'

'No, they didn't, did they?' he said, and glanced wonderingly at Susie, and Susie thought that, like herself and Sammy, he couldn't understand how a girl only just five could remember the disappearance of her parents well over two years ago. 'It's been hard luck on you all the way, Phoebe, and I could say that ten times over easy enough, but there's got to be a silver lining hanging about somewhere, eh?' He glanced at Sammy. 'Well, if I could talk to you and Mrs Adams? In private, say?'

Sammy thought the man visibly touched by his meeting with his dead brother's child, and now all too ready to get down to discussing arrangements for her future.

'Come along, Phoebe,' said Chinese Lady, accepting the man's wishes as reasonable, 'you can help me make some rockcakes if we can find just a bit of dried fruit.'

'Oh, fanks,' said Phoebe, who didn't seem upset

at leaving her new-found uncle in favour of helping to mix rockcakes. But she did cast her familiar hesitant glances at Sammy and Susie before going back to the kitchen with the elderly lady who was always kind to her.

Herbert Willis sat down again, and Susie poured the tea, handing cups to Sammy and their visitor.

'Much obliged, Mrs Adams,' said Herbert Willis, and took pleasure in gulping the hot tea. Susie and Sammy sat down opposite him. Sammy, she thought, was very sober. She was tense. 'Well now, Mrs Adams, Mr Adams.' Gulp. 'It's like this.' Gulp. 'A couple of coppers got me CO's permission to talk to me, and put me wise about everything.' Gulp. 'Great stuff, English tea, can't beat it.' Gulp.

Oh, please get on with it, thought Susie, then chided herself for her impatience. At least he was here, Phoebe's uncle, and it hardly mattered if he took a little time to outline arrangements.

'We're rationed, of course, because of the war,' she said. 'Lord, I hate having to say because of the war so much.'

'Mrs Adams, old England's up against it again, so don't apologize for it,' said Herbert Willis. 'I'm here, like a lot of other English Canadians, to do me bit for the country I was born in.' Gulp. 'I only left because me wife Connie saw some pictures of the Rockies in a magazine and couldn't wait to sample all them gallons of fresh air and wide open spaces. Well, being born next to Hackney gasworks like she was, you couldn't blame 'er, I guess. Mind, she's had ants in 'er frilly pants for years. Me old man, a widower, followed us a bit later. I tell you, it was a hell of a shock to all of us when we got the news back in '39 about me brother Frank and 'is wife Amy. Salt of the earth, both of 'em, and livin' happy with Phoebe accordin' to their letters until some bleedin' crazy maniac—'

'I don't think we want to talk too much about that,' said Sammy.

'It's very painful, Mr Willis, so can we leave it?' begged Susie.

'Right you are, Mrs Adams,' said Herbert Willis, battledress a good fit on his sturdy body. He placed his empty cup back in its saucer. Susie quickly refilled it for him. He thanked her. Get moving, man, thought Sammy.

'You know everything that concerns Phoebe,' said Susie.

'Everything that's affected her,' said Sammy.

'So you know just how much she needs a home and a family,' said Susie, pushing the man towards the starting line.

'You're right, she needs that all right,' said Herbert Willis, and gulped at his second cup. 'Well, it's like this. I'm signed up for the duration, and me wife Connie ain't around any more. Left me three months ago, and all I got from her was a note.' Gulp.

'What?' gasped Susie.

'Fact. Just a note.'

'Your wife's left you?' said Sammy.

'You got it, Mr Adams.' Herbert Willis's homely amiability had taken a walk somewhere. His voice was rough. 'There was this American guy from Colorado in a Stetson and with a bleedin' Buick six yards long suddenly livin' next door to us. I'd got a foreman's job by then, earning decent oof, and me

354

old man was also earning as a mechanic, and we were livin' in Cardigan Road, in a place called Etobicoke, which was what you'd say was a suburb of Toronto. Nice pile of bricks and mortar, central 'eating, the lot. Well, when this American git in a Stetson started calling, Connie went bleedin' gaga. Started tarting 'erself up like some fancy New York dame.'

'Oh, Lord.' Susie was listening in a kind of horrified fascination.

'Next thing she wasn't where she was supposed to be,' ground Herbert Willis. 'She was in the bloody Buick, heading over the border to Colorado, and 'er note just told me she was sorry and to get a divorce.' Gulp. 'Can you credit that, Mrs Adams?'

'It's unbelievable,' said Susie in a husky whisper. Wasn't that what Rosie's mother had done, gone off with a man and left a note? Wasn't that what Sammy had mentioned more than once?

Sammy, reading her thoughts, said, 'I've heard about coincidences, I don't recall hearing one like this.'

'Coincidences?' said Herbert Willis.

'It's a long story,' said Sammy, 'and we needn't bother with it. What we do need is to know how this affects Phoebe.'

'It's what you might call unfortunate, Mr Adams,' said Herbert Willis, 'but what with this and that, my side of the fam'ly don't happen to be in a position to take care of her.' Gulp, gulp. 'I'm sold up, and her grandpa's makin' do in a small downtown apartment, and workin' in an Army equipment factory. There's no way he could look after Phoebe.'

'Mr Willis, this is awful,' said Susie.

'Don't I know it,' said Herbert Willis. 'Pa cabled me to suggest you and Mr Adams might care to foster the girl till such time as he could take 'er, which probably means he's got hopes of earning enough to hire a help.' Gulp, finish. 'Now I'm havin' to ask you two people, could you do that, foster Phoebe for a bit? I'd 'elp with an allowance.'

Susie and Sammy looked at each other in shock.

'We didn't have that in mind,' said Sammy firmly.

'Mr Willis,' said Susie, 'I don't think me and my husband would want to do that, especially if it was for months and months, or even a year. We'd get too fond of Phoebe to let her go.'

'I 'ope that wouldn't happen,' said Herbert Willis. 'Being the only family she's got, me and her grandpa wouldn't take too kind to you refusing to let us have her.'

'Hold on,' said Sammy, 'you're in your Army for the duration, as you mentioned, and there'd only be your father, her grandad. And a hired help? You can't be happy with that, and would Phoebe benefit? It's parents she needs, not any hired help.'

'Well, that's straight from the shoulder from both of you,' said Herbert Willis, 'which I appreciate, even if it upsets me a bit. You got a point, I can't say you 'aven't. Are you fond of Phoebe already?'

'Yes,' said Susie, 'and we really need to let her go now before everything gets too difficult, not just for us but for her as well. I've got to agree with my husband, I know we wouldn't like to let her go to a hired help.'

'Would you 'ave any suggestions to make?' asked Herbert Willis.

'If you'll excuse us, I think my husband and me would like to talk to each other in another room,' said Susie.

'Go right ahead, Mrs Adams.'

'Won't be a tick,' said Sammy, and he and Susie took themselves off to Mr Finch's study.

'It's not good, Sammy,' said Susie.

'It's not good for Phoebe,' said Sammy.

'What d'you think of the man?'

'Bit of a rough diamond, but honest, except I'm not partial to the noisy way he drinks his tea,' said Sammy.

'I suppose we could foster her,' said Susie, 'I suppose we could look at fostering as our Christian duty.'

Sammy showed a faint smile.

'Well, you've got through a fair amount of Christian duties in your time, Susie,' he said, 'but I don't know, fostering the girl for how long? That might be convenient for her Uncle Herbert, I'm not sold on it myself. I agree with what you said, we'd get a lot too fond of her to let her go. As Sergeant Burrows pointed out, there'd be ructions, and things would get messy. The real point is, Phoebe wants parents, not minders.'

'She can't go to Canada as things are,' said Susie.

'I'm getting a foggy brainbox,' said Sammy, 'I'm groping on Phoebe's behalf and getting nowhere. Did you ever know me mental deficient before, Susie?'

'Something's got to be decided,' said Susie, and jumped as the phone rang. She picked up the extension.

'Hello, who's that?'

'That was quick, Susie.'

'Boots!'

'None other,' said Boots. 'I've been trying to get hold of Sammy at his office, but he's out. He sent me a long letter concerning the purchase of bombed properties at the Elephant and Castle. To save me time, Susie, would you tell him that buying now and selling for development, or retaining for development, either has my approval, but I favour the first option. It shortens the time factor. There's got to be a rebuilding programme there, sponsored by the Government, and that's bound to mean profit for Adams Properties one way or the other.'

'Boots, Sammy's here, you can have a word with him,' said Susie. 'But could I talk to you first if you're not in too much of a hurry?'

'I've always got time for you, Susie.'

'Well, you're a love,' said Susie, and went quickly into details about Phoebe. Boots only knew she and Sammy had taken the child in to look after her on a temporary basis. He listened now to a lot more than that.

'There's one thing that's certain, Susie,' he said at the end, 'the child can't go to Canada. I think what you now want to say to her uncle is that you and Sammy will only consider adoption.'

'What?' said Susie.

'Am I right?' asked Boots.

'I've just come to,' said Susie, with Sammy trying to listen. 'Yes, of course, that is what we want now that the answer's not in Canada, only I think we're afraid to say so.'

'There's one thing that might persuade her

uncle to make an immediate decision in your favour,' said Boots.

'What's that, Boots, what's that?'

'Tell him of Phoebe's weakness,' said Boots, 'tell him she wets the bed, that it's the obvious consequence of losing her parents in a way she can't understand, that they went away and never came back. Impress on him her need for acceptable substitutes. All that should make it impossible for him not to face up to the obvious, and the obvious would be to leave her with you and Sammy on your terms.'

'Oh, we thought we might have to mention her weakness,' said Susie, 'but only to let him know he and his wife would have that problem.'

'Tell him only a normal family environment and caring adoptive parents will cure it,' said Boots. 'I doubt if a grandfather who has to leave her in the care of a hired help every day would go halfway towards a solution. If her Uncle Herbert's a bloke with feelings, he'll see what's best for the child.'

'Boots, thanks ever so much, you're always a lovely help,' said Susie. 'Oh, everyone was so happy to hear about Tim, wasn't that wonderful? It must have given Felicity such a lift to know he'd escaped the Germans. And then there's the twins, everyone's tickled pink for you and Polly. Well, I am. Boots, how are they, and how's Polly?'

'They're thirsty, and Polly's blooming,' said Boots. 'Susie, I'll just say hello to Sammy, then I must put this phone down. Good luck with Phoebe.'

'Bless you, Boots,' said Susie, and handed the phone to Sammy, who had a few quick words with

Boots before his elder brother excused himself and hung up. Sammy then received from Susie all the advice Boots had given her concerning Phoebe.

'Susie,' said Sammy, 'what happens that every time I can't see for looking, it's all clear to Boots?'

'Well, this time, Sammy love, it was all too personal for us,' said Susie, 'while Boots was able to look at it like an outsider – oh, a nice one, of course, the darling man.'

'Back to the ranch,' said Sammy, and they rejoined Phoebe's Uncle Herbert.

Sammy took the floor, addressing him like a man who had a worrying problem and needed a good, understanding listener. Herbert Willis was visibly shaken by the revelation that his little niece, obviously because she believed her parents had gone away and left her, had distressing and frequent accidents in bed. Sammy set out the suggestions for a solution, and the circumstances being what they were for both parties, it did not take Phoebe's uncle long to decide that any idea of the girl becoming the responsibility of a hired help was out of the question. However, because she was his late brother's child, it took him longer to consider giving her up for adoption by Sammy and Susie, but he finally came round to saying he'd go and see a solicitor about drawing up an agreement, and then get in touch with them again. By next Monday or Tuesday, say. He wanted, he said, to do what was best for Phoebe in the long run. He shook hands with Susie and Sammy, thanked them for everything, told them he thought they were a nice friendly couple, and left after saying goodbye to the shy and nervous little girl.

'Susie, I'm lost for words,' said Sammy, after seeing Herbert Willis out.

'First time ever, Sammy?'

'You could be right,' said Sammy, 'but it's got its welcome side.'

'Good,' said Susie.

'Yes, it doesn't actually hurt,' said Sammy.

'That's my Sammy,' smiled Susie, 'you're feeling better, aren't you? So am I.'

'But don't let's count our chickens immediate,' said Sammy. 'Uncle Herbert's going to see a solicitor to get a document prepared. Is the solicitor going to advise him to think it over? Solicitors don't always settle for a quick bit of business if there's a chance of making a meal of it, and earning themselves five guineas instead of seven-and-six.'

'Let's look on the bright side, all the same,' said Susie. 'If the adoption goes through, then somehow we've got to try to have Phoebe accept us as her parents. I just hope this strange instinct of hers won't mean she'll always be looking over her shoulder for her real mummy and daddy.'

'If she does do that, Susie, her weakness could be with her for years.'

'Then say a prayer, Sammy, because I dearly hope I won't have to wash sheets every day for years.'

Chapter Twenty-Nine

The funeral service of Elsie Chivers took place on
Monday afternoon in St John's Church, Larcom
Street, Walworth. With pressure of duties
preventing Boots being there himself, his earnest
request for Chinese Lady, Lizzy, Tommy and
Sammy to attend induced complete response.
They were all there, and so were Vi and Mr Finch,
together with a lady representative from the
infirmary. Mr Finch, having taken the afternoon
off, attended in a sombre mood. Mr Finch had his
own memories of Elsie Chivers. Exactly what the
full extent of these were, no-one had ever asked.
Emily had thought his disappearance with Miss
Chivers pointed to an elopement, but that turned
out to be a wrong supposition. Only Boots knew the
full story, and he had always kept it to himself.

The service at St John's brought Chinese Lady
and her sons and daughter back to the church they
knew so well. It had escaped bomb damage so far,
and its familiarity gave them cause to reflect on its
association with their years of struggle. It gave
Chinese Lady cause to remember that finding
pennies for the collection had been a struggle in

itself. It gave Sammy cause to remember how his dear old Ma had made him attend for the good of his soul which, she said, could always do with improving. It gave Lizzy cause to remember how she had attended regularly with Emily, and how Emily always looked a bit of a ragbag, even on Sundays. Poor Emily, robbed of life while she was still such a lively member of the family.

They all went down on their knees to pray in concert with the vicar for the deceased and for her acceptance by God at the end of her life on earth. Chinese Lady kept her thoughts strictly on the virtues of the unhappy daughter of a mother liked by nobody. Tommy, remembering the Sunday teas and the quiet charm of the favourite guest, felt touched and moved by the service, and was glad that Boots's letter had persuaded him to be here.

After leaving the church, they followed the hearse to Southwark Cemetery in Sammy and Tommy's cars. The afternoon was cold, the war a thing apart for the moment, the February sky undisturbed except by restless, rolling clouds, precursors of the wind-blown clouds of March. It was beneath the moving grey masses that the coffin was lowered into the grave, while the vicar intoned the burial lines. They stood around the grave, the men and women who had come to say goodbye to Elsie Chivers. The coffin, coming slowly to rest, settled, and they each took their turn to spill earth. Soft-hearted Vi, of course, was tearful, even if she hadn't known Elsie Chivers as well as the others. Tommy put his arm around her.

'I'm making an exhibition,' she said muffledly.

'Well, she was a nice woman, very fond of the

fam'ly, Vi, so you're not cryin' over someone un-deserving,' said Tommy. 'Boots wouldn't have asked us to come if she had been.'

There were family wreaths, and a lovely floral spray from Boots. The card read, 'With love and cherished memories from Emily and Boots.'

Emily. Not Polly. Well, of course, thought Chinese Lady, Polly hadn't known Elsie. And Vi thought it was like Boots to make it a farewell from Emily as well as himself.

Boots at this moment was standing at his office window, looking out over the moistly dark winter greens of Dorset, remembering the first love of his life.

Chinese Lady, alone with Mr Finch that evening, said, 'It was a nice quiet funeral, Edwin.'

'It was, Maisie.'

'I can't help thinking she had a sad life.'

'She did, Maisie.'

'We were all very fond of her.'

'I know, Maisie.'

'Such a terrible thing, that trial, Edwin.'

'Which I'm sure haunted her for the rest of her life,' said Mr Finch.

'It haunted most of us for years, I should think,' said Chinese Lady. She sighed, then shook herself. 'Still, it's all over for her now, she's gone to her rest, and we've got to get on with our lives and this aggravating war. I've been thinking, it's very odd, Edwin, another adoption in the family.'

'Another happy one, Maisie, if it comes about?' said Mr Finch.

'Well,' said Chinese Lady, 'Rosie was never

happier than on the day Boots and Emily adopted her, so let's hope Phoebe's uncle will give Sammy and Susie the letter they need.'

'And let's hope he doesn't take too long,' said Mr Finch.

'Sammy and Susie need to be on firm ground with the child, and the child needs to be convinced she's loved and secure. I agree with Susie, only that will cure her of her weakness.'

'Well, Susie did say Mr Willis promised he'd see a solicitor and get things settled,' said Chinese Lady, then bit her lip as she glimpsed the creeping silver in her husband's hair. 'Edwin, don't you think it's time you retired?' she asked.

'I do,' smiled Mr Finch.

'Can't you tell the Government?'

'I can, Maisie, yes,' said Mr Finch, 'and I will as soon as I'm certain the Allies are on the way to total victory. It has to be total, or Germany will rise again in belligerence, as it did after the last war.'

'Well, I hope it'll come about before Christmas,' said Chinese Lady.

Not for a week did Susie and Sammy hear from Herbert Willis. Then they received a letter.

Dear Mr and Mrs Adams,

I've got to thank you for welcoming me like you did, and for letting me meet Phoebe my niece. As I said I would I went to see a solicitor and had a long talk with him, and he advised me to give myself time to make a decision. Well, it's a fact that I'm Phoebe's nearest next of kin, and I can't forget she's my own brother's little girl. Now it so happens I've

*met a nice woman that lives in my old neighbour-
hood in Bow, I met her before I came to see you and
she struck me as being more of a caring woman
than that ungrateful wife of mine that I'm getting
a divorce from. My old dad is acting for me back
in Canada, he's seeing to all the divorce papers,
and when it happens I'll be thinking of marrying
Doris Little, my new lady friend if she'll be consent-
ing. If that happens I know she'll have Phoebe
and be very caring of her, and then after the war
we'll take her back to Canada with us. I appreciate
young Phoebe's suffering that weakness you mentioned, but I know Doris would be very caring of
that as well, she being that kind of woman. I'm not
saying any of this is what you might call definite,
but the solicitor said it's a consideration I ought
to keep in mind and not give Phoebe up for adoption just yet. I hope this won't be upsetting to you,
I hope you'll feel it's natural for me to make a
claim when there's a chance of me marrying again
as soon as my divorce comes through. Like you said
Phoebe needs a new mum and dad, which could
be you two or me and Doris and I hope this can be
settled soon or late. Would you give my love to
Phoebe?*

Yours sincerely, Herbert Willis.

*PS I might be out of touch for a bit as my regiment's
leaving the Middlesex Barracks in five days for
special training in Scotland.*

Sammy and Susie, having read all this, looked at
each other, Sammy tight of mouth, Susie dismayed.
They were in the parlour. Everyone else was at
breakfast. The letter had arrived by first post.

'It's not the kind of letter I wanted to read,' said Sammy.

'It's a blow, Sammy,' said Susie, 'it's a shock.'

'It's a twenty guineas contribution from the perishing solicitor, not five,' said Sammy.

'The depressing thing about it is that it sounds reasonable,' said Susie. 'How could we fight it, Sammy?'

'Well, first off,' said Sammy, 'nothing's been said about what happens to Phoebe while Willis waits for his divorce and then for the day he's allowed to marry again. It'll be months.'

'I don't know much about divorce,' said Susie, 'and I hope no-one in the family ever does.'

'I'll take the letter to the office,' said Sammy, 'and answer it immediately, or sooner if I can manage it. I'm going to ask if he expects us to care for Phoebe for – let's see – yes, for what they call an unspecified amount of time. That's not reasonable, Susie, anything unspecified. I'll do my best to push Herbert Willis into a hurtful corner.'

'Do it before he goes up to Scotland, Sammy,' said Susie.

'Right,' said Sammy, 'anything unspecified isn't going to help Phoebe. Or you, Susie. Or me.'

'She was dry this morning for a change, wasn't she?' said Susie.

'Gave me a smile when I went in,' said Sammy, 'and I knew that meant good news. What do the smiles of little girls first thing in the morning do for you, Susie?'

'The same as the smiles of little boys,' said Susie, 'make me feel that first thing in the morning has a lot going for it.'

*   *   *

Sammy roughed out his letter at the office, and Rebecca did a private, confidential job for him by typing it. He made it clear to Herbert Willis that before he and Susie could come to terms with Willis's hopes and plans, they wanted to know what was proposed for Phoebe. Was she to be handed over to Doris Little? (Sammy doubted that, since Willis hadn't mentioned it as a possibility.) Further, Phoebe's welfare was under the official supervision of the Walworth police, and they would want a lot more information regarding time and so on. Was it proposed that he and Susie should foster the child until Willis and Doris were married? Sammy pointed out he and Susie had already said no to that. He asked for a quick answer.

He didn't get one. He and Susie didn't hear from Willis again until April, by which time Phoebe, although more settled, still wondered in forlorn fashion where her mummy and daddy were, and still wet her bed most nights.

Dear Mr and Mrs Adams,

I've just got time to drop a few lines to you, we're up against the kind of training up here that's nearly killing us, but I've got my second stripe. About Phoebe and my solicitor's advice, I'll do what I can to get a move on as I can see things are a bit of a problem to you right now, and if you can take care of my niece just for a bit longer I'll be grateful. I'm in touch with Doris, the lady I've got attached to, and I'm expecting to hear from my Pa about the

*divorce any day. Got to go now, my platoon officer
is shouting his bonce off.*

Yours sincerely, Herbert Willis, Corporal.

'That's a gorblimey nothing,' said Sammy after he
and Susie had read the letter.

'Sammy, he's using us,' said Susie.

'So he is,' said Sammy, 'but I won't say he meant
to, I'd say his solicitor is telling him not to let us
rush him. I honestly don't dislike the bloke. Well,
let's face it, Susie, he's got feelings for Phoebe,
family feelings, and we know what family feelings
are. All the same, we're being mucked about, and
I'll have to write to him again, and on a piece of stiff
cardboard.'

'Sammy, we simply can't go along as we are,' said
Susie. 'Make him realize that until Phoebe is in the
care of two people she can see as loving parents,
she'll always be an unsettled little girl with the weakness we told him about.'

'I'll do that, Susie,' said Sammy.

The further letter from Sammy, however, only
produced a blank silence. He was not to know it,
but Herbert Willis, along with other picked
Canadian Army troops and Free Polish soldiers
were being trained for an ambitious raid on Dieppe
and its formidable German garrison. The training
was arduous, exhausting and dangerous in itself.

The Americans were being driven out of their
strongholds in the Pacific by the Japanese hordes,
and Hitler, having lost the chance to capture
Moscow, was initiating new German offensives

aimed southwards at the Crimea and Russia's oilfields. Battles were titanic affairs, and neither Hitler nor Stalin concerned themselves with the appalling death rate suffered by their soldiers and airmen.

Rommel, having stopped the British advance in Libya, was preparing to take the offensive. Hitler had promised reinforcements of men, armour and planes, and given orders for the conquest of Egypt as far as the Suez Canal, a lifeline of the Royal Navy.

President Roosevelt, at one with Churchill, was providing American Navy warships to assist the British in the protection of merchant shipping.

The excitement and romantic expectations of girls in Northern Ireland were now occupying the minds of Welsh, Scottish and English girls. The landings of American GI's in Northern Ireland were now being followed by landings in Britain. Newspapers were producing headlines such as, THE YANKS FROM OVER THERE ARE OVER HERE. The first of the men of the American Air Force's mighty bomber and fighter squadrons had arrived. With them were members of the Women's American Army Corps, the Waacs, most of whom were hoping to do some rubbernecking around Buckingham Palace and Piccadilly Circus. The men of General de Gaulle's Free French troops were waiting for them while polishing up their Gallic charm. Cockney spivs were getting ready to sell them souvenirs. Highly dubious characters were looking forward to introducing vitamin-packed GI's to the delights of Soho establishments run by Madame Belle, Madame Olga or any old madame.

Generally, Churchill's people considered the

arrival of the American Air Force meant Hitler was going to get more than he bargained for.

Alas, so were some of the United Kingdom's more naïve girls.

Leah received a letter from her grandfather, the estimable Isaac Moses, in which he advised her that he knew of her friendship with Edward Somers. He wished her to know that, like her mother, he had no objection to this friendship, especially as Edward was a member of a family with whom he had long been acquainted. Perhaps, however, she would remember that the strength and endurance of her race came from loyalty and devotion to it. Nevertheless, that did not mean he would fail to understand if she developed feelings that in time required her to make difficult decisions. He would, in that case, be happy to help her make those decisions, and he hoped, accordingly, that she would accept his help.

Leah wrote an affectionate reply to the effect that he and her mother were both so dear to her that she would always be happy to go to them for help and advice on anything that had an important bearing on her life.

She did not, however, say that at the present moment she was struggling with feelings that suggested she was falling in love with Edward. Sensibly, Leah was telling herself that at only fifteen she could be mistaking a crush for the real thing.

All the same, little nerves jumped about whenever she saw Edward, and she disliked intensely the thought of him in a serious relationship with any other girl.

*   *   *

By late April, Sammy and Susie had heard nothing more from Herbert Willis, although Sammy had written twice more, and they were having difficulty in keeping a restraint on their feelings for Phoebe. The little girl obviously could not quite understand how she fitted in. Were they waiting, she hesitantly asked once, for her mummy and daddy to come back and collect her? Sammy said not to worry, pet, you'll have a mummy and daddy one day.

Her weakness continued.

Felicity was spending a month with Boots, Polly, Kate and the twins, and discovering the sounds and scents of Dorset in these first days of spring. She went walking daily with Kate who, having met her on the occasion of the Sunday afternoon in Rosie and Matthew's cottage, thought her wonderfully resolute in the way she fought her blindness. She admired her for being able to make wryly amusing remarks about her disability.

'Kate, I sometimes don't know if it's midnight or noon. I'm like a parrot with the hood down over its cage. What a curse. There'll come a time when I'll go out shopping in the middle of the day and find when I get to the shops I'll be bumping into closed doors, that they're shut because it's the middle of the night.'

That kind of thing.

They liked each other, Felicity and Kate, and Kate could see that Felicity had a growing affection for Boots and Polly, who gave her just the right kind of kindness and understanding. They never fussed her or overdid their attentions.

Tim, posted back to Troon in an instructional

capacity until he was physically A1 again, kept in close touch with phone calls. When Boots advised him that Felicity and Kate were the best of friends, Tim began to think about asking his good old dad if Kate might consider being a companion to Felicity and live with her in Rosie and Matthew's cottage, which Felicity liked so much.

As for Rosie, she was now in her seventh month of pregnancy, and receiving letters of grand-motherly interest from Chinese Lady. Interest, yes, not concern. Chinese Lady had faith in Rosie to do everything a sensible mother-to-be should do at this stage.

A cold night of bright moon, the sea untrouble-some except for a slight swell, the several landing craft full of men rehearsing a Channel crossing. There were to be many such rehearsals. This was the first. They were silent, eyes straining over the running sea, the craft gently pitching. Away to the starboard was their Royal Navy escort, a frigate, assigned to protect their going and to cover their retreat when they turned for home before actually reaching the French coast. It was a test of timing, conditioning and endurance. There would be similar tests, and not always in such benevolent conditions.

There was a sudden blare of warning from the frigate as its radar picked up the approach of a stranger travelling at speed. Just as suddenly the straining eyes of helmsmen and picked troops were dazzled by a blinding light from port. A patrolling German E-boat had discovered them. Its mounted machine-guns opened up almost at once, and the portside landing craft were raked by storms of bullets. The frigate made a sea-churning dash, the E-boat, lights off, turned, cutting an arc through the swell as it powered away. The action had lasted only a minute, but two landing-craft wallowed, their helmsmen wounded, and there were dead men among the trained assault troops, Canadians for the most part.

They were men who in the main had volunteered for military service, service that had taken them into the war against Germany in Britain's days of need.

Chapter Thirty

Chinese Lady had come to a decision that evening.

'You'll have to stand your ground,' she said to Sammy and Susie prior to retiring to bed.

'About what?' asked Sammy.

'About Phoebe,' said Chinese Lady. 'It's my firm belief she needs parents. Uncles or aunts or grandparents won't do. So you two should definitely adopt her, which I know is what you want. You've got to get hold of a good solicitor and fight, never mind what her uncle, Herbert Willis, thinks is best for her. Are you listening, Sammy?'

'We're both listening, Mum,' said Susie.

'That's good,' said Chinese Lady. 'Listening can always be a help. So can a good solicitor, even if he does charge you a bit more than seven-and-six. Well, I'm going to bed now. Good night.'

That night. It was April, yes, but the weather was crisply cold, German bombers absent from London, and a full moon flooding the capital and its suburbs with light.

Phoebe opened her eyes and sat straight up, all in one movement. She slipped from the bed, put her bare feet into her shoes and took up her woollen dressing-gown from a chair. The garment, inspired by Tommy at the beginning of Phoebe's stay with Sammy and Susie, had been run up from a blue blanket by Gertie Roper, his faithful charge-hand at the firm's factory. It came to Phoebe from Tommy as a warm and cosy present.

With the dressing-gown wrapped around her, out of the bedroom and down the stairs went the little girl, much as if the darkness of the house was of little account. She walked through the hall to the front door, but couldn't quite reach the doorknob. She went into the parlour, came out with a footstool, stood on it and turned the knob. The door opened and the moonlight beckoned. She pushed the stool aside, opened the door wide and pulled it to as she stepped out. It closed with a slight rattle.

Upstairs, Sammy was sleeping lightly. Close to the surface of his consciousness was an ever-present uncertainty concerning the future of a lonely child heartbreakingly lamenting the disappearance of her parents. If he and Susie took their place, would she understand what it meant, or would she still pine for the parents she thought had gone away?

Sammy turned in his sleep and came awake.

Into the crisp outdoors went little Phoebe, walking in venturesome exploration of the night, her footsteps quite steady. Frost glittered, covering the pavement with myriads of moonlit pearls. Her clad feet trod them. She looked straight ahead, eyes wide open and searching. She stopped, her head lifted and she listened.

'Mummy?' The light-flooded night received her appeal silently. 'Daddy?' That too brought nothing.

With a little sigh, she resumed her strange, steady walk, her eyes searching the emptiness of the way ahead.

Again she stopped, again she made her appeal, this time with her face turned towards a house, its blankness outlined by the light from the radiant moon.

'Mummy? Daddy? Mummy?'

There was no response. No-one appeared and no sounds arrived. She stood still for a few moments, as if waiting in hope, then sighed and went on, oblivious, it seemed, of the coldness of the night.

'Susie, wake up! Susie!' It was an urgent whisper from Sammy, accompanied by a touch on Susie's shoulder. She opened her eyes. The bedside light was on and Sammy was leaning over her, a man in alarm. 'It's Phoebe – she's gone, she's not in her bed, not in the house, and her shoes and dressing-gown are missing.'

'Oh, Lord,' breathed Susie, and came rapidly out of the bed. Sammy disappeared, descending the stairs in his bare feet to run into the kitchen and look for the torch they used whenever they had to repair to the air raid shelter. He did not want to fill the house with light and bring his mother and stepdad awake, and especially not Paula. Finding the torch, he ran back into the hall as Susie, dressing-gown on, came down the stairs.

'Jesus,' breathed Sammy. The beam of the torch, illuminating the hall, revealed the footstool to one side of the front door. He knew what that meant and what had woken him, the rattle of the door closing. 'Susie, I'm right, she's out of the house.'

'Oh, my God, she'll freeze,' gasped Susie.

Sammy dashed back up the stairs, Susie following. Sammy put his overcoat on over his pyjamas, and pulled on his shoes. Susie, winding her nightdress up around her thighs and fixing it, rushed herself into skirt, jumper and jacket. Despite alarm and panic, they were as quiet as possible, not wanting to disturb the sleepers. But on their frantic way down to the hall again, the landing light came on, and Mr Finch, from the top of the stairs, issued an urgent whisper.

'Sammy, what's wrong?'

'Phoebe's left the house! Look after Paula if she wakes up!'

Out they ran, Sammy and Susie, and down the drive to the pavement. The white night sparkled with frost.

'Sammy, which way, which way?' begged Susie.

'It can only be one of two ways, left or right, down the hill or up the hill. Susie, go down the hill, I'll go up. Oh, wait, she hasn't been long gone, her bed was still warm. Go, Susie, go.'

Susie ran, thankful for one mercy, that the moon was giving light. Sammy ran, silently praying. He was not averse to believing in the Almighty.

Phoebe was walking on, looking, searching and stopping.

'Mummy? Daddy?'

There was no answer, no response, only silence, and each time she sighed and walked on again. But there was always another stop, another appeal.

'Mummy? Mummy? Daddy?'

The listening, the silence and the little sigh were repetitive.

Susie had never known such panic, her speed down the hill reckless, her loose hair flying, the sharp frost attacking her flushed face.

Phoebe, Phoebe, where are you, where, where?

On she went, the downward slope giving impetus to her flying feet.

She glimpsed the child.

There she was, there, thirty yards or so ahead, walking steadily, the hem of her nightie trailing below her little dressing-gown, her head bare. Susie rushed.

'Phoebe?' It was a husky gasp.

Phoebe stopped. Her head turned and she looked to her left. Something made Susie pull up. Wait, be careful. If the child was sleepwalking, and she had to be, surely, was it true that she should not be startled into a wakeful state?

The child spoke.

'Mummy? Daddy?' Phoebe made her recurring appeal, and then listened. 'Mummy?'

Susie had never known emotion take the kind of hold as it did now. It choked her.

Again the heartbreaking appeal.

'Mummy? Daddy? Mummy?'

Susie knew there was only one thing she could say, whatever new problems it brought about.

'Phoebe, I'm here, see?'

Phoebe slowly turned. Her eyes opened wide as she saw Susie, and a little quiver attacked her.

'Mummy?' It was a final appeal.

Susie opened her arms.

'Yes, I'll be your mummy from now on, Phoebe love.'

379

Phoebe, eyes bright with reflected moonlight, lost all hesitation and ran at Susie. Susie, stooping, received her and hugged her, and if the little dressing-gown felt touched by the frost, the child herself felt warm.

Phoebe said with amazing naturalness, 'Oh, dear, I've been looking for you and a daddy for ever such a long time.'

Whether she'd been sleepwalking or not, the child, thought Susie, was now wide awake.

'Oh, I'm sorry, darling, but everything's going to be all right now, you'll see. You're going to have a new family.'

'With you and my new daddy?'

'Yes, with us, my sweet.' The lump in Susie's throat was painful. Herbert Willis had to make a decision in favour of herself and Sammy, he had to. If not, she and Sammy would fight, they must, for in saying what she had to Phoebe, she had burned her boats, and there was no way the child would ever understand a reversal. She would ask questions in the years to come, yes, but then it would be easier to talk to her. Lifting her and holding her securely, Susie straightened up. 'Let's go home now, shall we, darling?'

Phoebe, clinging, said, 'Will my new daddy be there?'

'I think we might bump into him on our way.'

'Is he somewhere near?'

'Yes, very near,' said Susie, beginning the uphill walk back.

'He found me first, didn't he?' said Phoebe, arms around Susie's neck. 'But now I'm not lost any more, am I?'

'No, Phoebe love, you're not lost any more.'

Sammy was pounding back, running down the hill, sure that the child could not have gone as far upwards as he had. So she must have gone down the hill. He passed the family house at speed, hoping to God that Susie had found her.

Susie, carrying the little girl, saw him coming.

'Here he is, Phoebe, here's Daddy.'

Out in the Channel, the dead soldiers were being brought back with the living.

Among the dead was an English-Canadian, Corporal Herbert Willis. His endeavours to do his bit for his old country had come to a sadly premature end, but there was a letter in the hands of his solicitor to the effect that if anything happened to him, he would like his niece Phoebe to be adopted by the people presently caring for her, Mr and Mrs Sammy Adams.

THE END

CHURCHILL'S PEOPLE
by Mary Jane Staples

In 1941, the United Kingdom was in desperate straits, standing alone with its troops against the might of Nazi Germany. There was always Prime Minister Winston Churchill, however, who growled his defiance to Hitler and induced in his people a determination to endure.

The Adams family shared that determination and their own kind of optimism. Emma went happily into her marriage with Jonathan, while Boots's son Tim, in between his hazardous exploits as a Commando, helped his fiancée Felicity in her courageous fight against blindness, the result of a terrible injury in the bombing. Rosie Adams was due to marry Matthew Chapman from Dorset, but Chinese Lady was unsure about it. He seemed a fine enough man, but what with a lame leg that prevented him from doing his bit for his country, and the uncertainty of his garage business, she felt that he was hardly the ideal choice for such an eligible young woman as Rosie. As for Boots and his new wife Polly, they came up with some very unexpected news for the family . . .

Here again is the Adams family from *Down Lambeth Way, Our Emily, King of Camberwell, On Mother Brown's Doorstep, A Family Affair, Missing Person, Pride of Walworth, Echoes of Yesterday, The Camberwell Raid, The Last Summer, The Family at War* and *Fire Over London.*

0 552 14657 9

BRIGHT DAY, DARK NIGHT
by Mary Jane Staples

It is summer, 1941, and the country is still at war. In the Devon village of Ashleigh, however, evacuees from the bombs in London are living in an atmosphere of rural peacefulness, although Daisy Ricketts of Bermondsey isn't sure if she'll ever get on with carping Mrs Mumford, the subject of whispers because of her husband's mysterious disappearance.

David, the elder son of Tommy and Vi Adams, meets Kate Trimble, a cockney girl from Camberwell who has just arrived in Ashleigh with her aunt. Kate is imaginative and precocious, while David is happy-go-lucky, and as the war is directly affecting the lives of so many other members of the Adams family, Kate and David establish a friendship in the summer sunshine of Devon. But as they become closer, an incident occurs which brings home to them the darker intrigues of wartime and provides a devastating shock to everyone.

Here again is the Adams family from *Down Lambeth Way*, *Our Emily*, *King of Camberwell*, *On Mother Brown's Doorstep*, *A Family Affair*, *Missing Person*, *Pride of Walworth*, *Echoes of Yesterday*, *The Camberwell Raid*, *The Last Summer*, *The Family at War*, *Fire Over London* and *Churchill's People*.

0 552 14708 7

A SELECTED LIST OF FINE NOVELS
AVAILABLE FROM CORGI BOOKS

THE PRICES SHOWN BELOW WERE CORRECT AT THE TIME OF GOING TO PRESS.
HOWEVER TRANSWORLD PUBLISHERS RESERVE THE RIGHT TO SHOW NEW
RETAIL PRICES ON COVERS WHICH MAY DIFFER FROM THOSE PREVIOUSLY
ADVERTISED IN THE TEXT OR ELSEWHERE.

14447 9	FIREBIRD	*Iris Gower*	£5.99
14537 8	APPLE BLOSSOM TIME	*Kathryn Haig*	£5.99
14567 X	THE CORNER HOUSE	*Ruth Hamilton*	£5.99
14692 7	THE PARADISE GARDEN	*Joan Hessayon*	£5.99
14599 8	FOOTPRINTS ON THE SAND	*Judith Lennox*	£5.99
14693 5	THE LITTLE SHIP	*Margaret Mayhew*	£5.99
14658 7	THE MEN IN HER LIFE	*Imogen Parker*	£5.99
10375 6	CSARDAS	*Diane Pearson*	£5.99
14577 7	PORTRAIT OF CHLOE	*Elvi Rhodes*	£5.99
14636 6	COME RAIN OR SHINE	*Susan Sallis*	£5.99
13951 3	SERGEANT JOE	*Mary Jane Staples*	£3.99
13845 2	RISING SUMMER	*Mary Jane Staples*	£3.99
13299 3	DOWN LAMBETH WAY	*Mary Jane Staples*	£5.99
13444 9	OUR EMILY	*Mary Jane Staples*	£5.99
13856 8	THE PEARLY QUEEN	*Mary Jane Staples*	£3.99
13975 0	ON MOTHER BROWN'S DOORSTEP		
		Mary Jane Staples	£3.99
14106 2	THE TRAP	*Mary Jane Staples*	£4.99
14154 2	A FAMILY AFFAIR	*Mary Jane Staples*	£4.99
14230 1	MISSING PERSON	*Mary Jane Staples*	£4.99
14291 3	PRIDE OF WALWORTH	*Mary Jane Staples*	£4.99
14375 8	ECHOES OF YESTERDAY	*Mary Jane Staples*	£4.99
14418 5	THE YOUNG ONES	*Mary Jane Staples*	£4.99
14469 X	THE CAMBERWELL RAID	*Mary Jane Staples*	£4.99
14513 0	THE LAST SUMMER	*Mary Jane Staples*	£4.99
14548 3	THE GHOST OF WHITECHAPEL	*Mary Jane Staples*	£5.99
14554 8	THE FAMILY AT WAR	*Mary Jane Staples*	£5.99
14606 4	FIRE OVER LONDON	*Mary Jane Staples*	£5.99
14657 9	CHURCHILL'S PEOPLE	*Mary Jane Staples*	£5.99
14708 7	BRIGHT DAY, DARK NIGHT	*Mary Jane Staples*	£5.99
14640 4	THE ROMANY GIRL	*Valerie Wood*	£5.99

Transworld titles are available by post from:

Book Service By Post, PO Box 29, Douglas, Isle of Man, IM99 1BQ

Credit cards accepted. Please telephone 01624 675137
fax 01624 670923, Internet http://www.bookpost.co.uk
or e-mail: bookshop@enterprise.net for details

Free postage and packing in the UK. Overseas customers: allow £1 per book
(paperbacks) and £3 per book (hardbacks).